W9-AMB-839

*I Love You
Like a Tomato*

I Love You Like a Tomato

Marie Giordano

A Tom Doherty Associates Book
New York

for my mother

This is a work of fiction. All the characters and events portrayed
in this novel are either fictitious or are used fictitiously.

I LOVE YOU LIKE A TOMATO

Copyright © 2003 by Marie Giordano

All rights reserved, including the right to reproduce this book,
or portions thereof, in any form.

This book is printed on acid-free paper.

Edited by Anna Genoese

Book design by Michael Collica

A Forge Book
Published by Tom Doherty Associates, LLC
175 Fifth Avenue
New York, NY 10010

www.tor.com

Forge® is a registered trademark of Tom Doherty Associates, LLC.

Library of Congress Cataloging-in-Publication Data

Giordano, Marie.
    I love you like a tomato / Marie Giordano.—1st ed.
        p.   cm.
    "A Tom Doherty Associates Book."
    ISBN 0-765-30668-9 (U.S. Edition) (alk. paper)
    ISBN 0-765-30927-0 (Canadian Edition)
    1. Italian American families—Fiction.   2. Italian American
Women—Fiction.   3. Minneapolis (Minn.)—Fiction.
4. Young women—Fiction.   I. Title.

PS3607.146113 2003
813'.6—dc21

                                                        2002045454

First Edition: July 2003

Printed in the United States of America

0   9   8   7   6   5   4   3   2   1

ACKNOWLEDGMENTS

I'm grateful for winning a college short story contest with a somewhat autobiographical story about two Italian immigrant children growing up in Minneapolis. I was so encouraged by the prize, I continued writing about ChiChi and Marco and haven't been able to stop yet.

Bacci e abracci to my Italian friends and family in the U.S. and Italy for all the loving encouragement and help while writing this book.

Grazie mille to Joe Russo for the loaned books; to my Italian teachers and friends at the Italian Community Center in San Diego, Maria, Rosella, Chiara; to Antonio and Assunta in Positano, Italy, for the dinners, the love, the apartment, and the stories; to Margherita and Peppino of Margherita Albergo in Praiano for historical advice and loving care; to Enzo Espinoza of Positano for much help and information on *il Mal Occhio*, and for the friendship and the great food; to Tim's computers in Praiano; to Tito Mazzi of Meta, Italy, for music research; to Father Kenney of Our Lady of Mount Carmel Church in Minneapolis; to Genny Zak Kieley and her excellent book on northeast Minneapolis; to Mary Ann Rush of northeast Minneapolis; to the Vermont Studio Center, the Milton Center, and the AAUW for grants and scholarships while writing this book; to the San Diego Book Awards for granting *I Love You Like a Tomato* winner of "Best Unpublished Novel of 2000"; to George of Delmonico's in northeast Minneapolis for the stories, peppers, and incredible mozzarella; to the wonderful people in Sicily and southern Italy who opened locked churches, fed me, allowed me into their private lives; to the loved ones in Minneapolis who birthed and nurtured the Maggiordino story; and finally, for invaluable scrutiny and feedback of the manuscript in its various stages:

Dorothy Nordstrom, Liza Lou, Alison Harding, Sydney Lea, Peggy Lang, and Chiara Camelos-Johnson. *Grazie mille* to my writing mentors, Kate Braverman, Sydney Lea, Richard Jackson, and Larry Woiwode. *Tante grazie* to my agent, Jill Grosjean, my editor, Anna Genoese, and to Mario Lombardo, who never stopped believing in me—*con il mio cuore, grazie tutti.*

Part One

I was asleep when the world began.

On an early morning in August when I was no bigger than our goat, Tuzza, I slept while the world was busy getting itself born. Mist from the sea drifting through the parted shutters of our kitchen, the wet tile smell of the kitchen floor, coffee boiling below the loft where I lay coiled in sleep on the corn husk mattress with my cousins, Rosa and Sofia, and two chickens—I can tell you now that nothing existed before this morning. No, everything began with *him*. The raucous rustle of bodies, excited voices growing louder, my grandmother's shouts. Women chattering, sighing, shuffling their feet, shifting, stirring in their bodies.

I followed Rosa and Sofia down the loft ladder to the kitchen. Chickens murmured in their wings and flew to the table to the chair to the cupboard. I walked on the sides of my feet to the room where the aunts stood and sat in awe before my mother lying in the bed.

I waited by the door, worrying and chewing the end of a braid. Smells of disinfectant and stale smoke. A sour, sweaty smell. Aunts and neighbor women gawked at the messy bundle on my mother's stomach—gawked, with reverence reserved for saints' days.

A new day inched its way through mist and shutters toward my mamma lying propped with pillows beneath the crucifix. Her face turned to the wall. Mamma shapeless, like chunked stone, something chopped at, unformed. I crossed the room and stood by the bed. She held the bundle for me to see.

Moments earlier, as the village snored in their beds, my mother, Giuseppina Sapponata Maggiordino, had produced a boy.

—*Cosa?* Such fuss over a plucked chicken?

Give thanks to God, *Carina,* Nonna ordered. Heaven has given you a brother.

I'd seen prettier sardines.

Mamma looked at me as if I were a bit of dust floating just beyond her reach. She always looked at me that way, her Don't Bother Me look. The baby wrapped like a prosciutto lay across her stomach, its face no bigger than a chicken egg.

Take him, Leticcia, Mamma said.

Again, in a louder voice: Leticcia, I said *take him.*

The creature was in my arms.

Smooth, easy like wind.

Like hair.

Nonna crossed herself. *Grazie a Dio!*

Poverino. Poor thing, from the chorus of aunts, and they clicked their tongues, folded their arms.

Mamma scowled. Leave me in peace, she told the aunts. Her hands fluid, like water. Face squeezed shut. The crunch of Nonna's corn husk mattress.

Sunlight on the baby's face, his eyes fluttering. Pale sequin of a mouth, spongy skin like sea anemone. *Mah,* is it possible the creature could be beautiful? I stared at the face. Something kissed by agates and starfish.

I lifted my head. *Questo bimbo è il mio fratellino, il mio fratellino,* I announced in my bravest two-and-a-half-year-old voice.

The aunts laughed. *Mah, guarda che dice la sorellina!* Look what the little sister is babbling! Ha ha! they laughed.

But it would never be disputed, I can tell you this moment, the baby DID belong to me.

Nonna's cheeks chafed from wiping with the coarse sleeve of the sweater she wore under her dress and apron. What joyous tears my grandmother cried! The first male child to be brought forth in the Sapponata family since she buried her Nino, her Francesco, her Tomasio, the babies she was certain died from eating dirt while she dug for roots to cook. She would light candles for this new grandchild, this miracle of a boy baby, her mourning for her own sons would end, she would fall to her knees.

But!

Ah, then. Then!

The priest arrives.

See how hard this baby takes in breath! The blue hue to his skin—tch. Tch.

God's will be done.

Like Nonna's three lost baby boys. The priest arrives. They baptize my brother so he won't go to hell. But he is not dead yet. Blue and gagging on life, he is not dead. I tell Nonna he won't die. I know this for a fact because the world had begun and I am his angel. Marco lives through the day. And the night.

And the next day and night.

Nonna boiled water and camphor, emptied sulfur in the air, choking the rest of us. A week passed. Two. And Marco did not die.

In late summer the terraced gardens along the mountainside of Praiano brought forth figs, grapes, melons, persimmon, pomegranate, broccoli, cucumbers, *melanzane,* beans, *broccoletti,* cabbage, tomatoes, peppers. Every spoonful of dirt

had a seed planted in it. I helped pick the tomatoes to be dried
for the winter. I picked peppers and beans and carried them in
the basket to the kitchen, where Nonna and the aunts pickled,
stewed, baked, and boiled. During the day in late summer the
air in Nonna's house was thick with the smell of sauces froth-
ing on the stove, simmering onions, garlic and rosemary, peppers and *basilico,* the sound of chopping, peeling, coring,
endless clatter, gossip. My mother silent, brooding.

Mamma?

Si.

Are you crying?

No. *Vai via.* Go away.

Bougainvillea and geraniums bloomed around the windows
and rooftops of the village, blooms of pink, crimson, and
yellow. Red peppers with their long damp faces hung from
fishing line as they dried in the sun at the side of the house.
Every day I climbed to our roof to gaze across the rooftops
of the village to the sea. The colors like pretty dresses.

Leticcia, you *pazza,* said the cousins. Like you mamma.

If you were me in that house you wouldn't want to think
about *pazza.* Was *crazy* bad like war? You'd sit in the sun
listening to the aunts chattering as they sewed in the shade
of the chestnut tree, and you'd look up at the sky and it
would remind you of an embroidered coat only rich Romans wore in stories. You'd play in the dust with your feet
and sing the songs you believed were the only songs anybody
anywhere sang. You would know nothing of craziness and
war, but it would be all around you. In your hair, in your
hands, between your toes.

You'd hold your brother, and your nonna would take you
by your arms and say careful, careful, you'll smother him—

There'd be neighbors who brought prosciutto cured with their own hands and kept hidden from *the Naziste,* olives in jars stashed under the floor by the woodstove.

Then the gossip.

Always the gossip.

They eased their fear with gossip.

Did you hear how Antonio's nephew caught the influenza and gave it to the pig?

A grasp of the shoulder, the hand, the thigh.

Allora, you'll take an *orzo,* yes?

Sighs, exclamations, murmurs, sipping. He's an old profligate, that Antonio. I heard he has a mistress in Sorrento.

Oooo.

Vecchio degenerato. And, ah, the signora will have just one cup, dear, ah, a little more, that's it, of Nonna's toasted oat coffee. *Grazie.*

If you were me, you'd be loved by a grandmother, a loving Nonna, who favored you over the other girl-children and who called you her beloved ChiChi, and you'd be sister to a brother who everyone expected, if he didn't die tomorrow or the next day, God-preserve-us, to one day work in *questura, come commissario o capopolizzia,* as judge or police chief, sit-down jobs.

Maybe a priest, like Padre Scizzo, Nonna's brother, a Benedictine contemplative at the monastery at Cassino which was blown up by the Allies. He was one of the six priests who stayed in the monastery's dark underground to pray while the bombs struck. The monastery was completely destroyed along with the town of Cassino, but the priests survived unharmed. One priest in the family was enough, said Nonna.

The war. Always the war. The people of our village ate carob and tree bark to survive. There wasn't a bird left in

the sky to shoot. Vipers, those German S.S., *vipers,* said
Nonna. They occupy every shoot of grass from Amalfi to
Naples. They take our grapes, our olive oil, beans. They rob
us of our rabbits and hens, our donkeys. They take all.

Where are they now?

Who?

The vipers.

Not you worry, ChiChi. The war is over. We dry our
tears.

But I know the war is with us. The war makes Mamma
cry. War lives in her teeth, her hands, her eyes.

The baby Marco is wrinkled, and grey, like an old sock. A
path of black furry hair travels down his shoulders and spine,
like the hair on my arms and legs. The hair on his head runs
across his forehead in little ovals. Soft fuzz below his ears,
down his jaw, the same fuzz on his thighs and ankles. Thin
wisps of hands, skin so transparent I can count the veins.
But he has stopped crying so much. His eyes focus. See how
he coos and hums in his cradle. In less than a year he sprouts
teeth in his drooling mouth like raindrops. He mumbles
words I understand.

Mornings before breakfast while Marco sleeps, Nonna
bakes bread. I am beside her, between her elbows, under the
flesh of her breasts, hanging on to her apron, stepping on
her feet. Nonna, my Nonna, NonnaNonnaNonna.

Cara Mia! she says, you are like moss on stones!

Nonna baking. Kneading the dough, punching it down,
rolling it out, cutting it into mounds, rolling, folding over,
rolling, pinching the ends, patting into little hills, rising, slip-
ping into the brick oven, baked brown and stiff, and then,
fripp, into the straw basket hanging from the beam in the

ceiling. Nonna gives me the end of a loaf to chew on. Marco playing on the floor or sleeping in his wood cradle, and me, Leticcia ChiChi Maggiordino, his angel.

Here Marco, this is for you, my brother.

Muffffnf.

Nonna, Marco says he's thirsty.

A shadow leaned across this picture as Marco and I ate our bread in Nonna's kitchen, a shadow within a shadow. Unhappy, silent, a shadowy woman working in the garden, a woman carrying a basket of fruit on her head, picking grapes, chopping onions. Sometimes she held Marco in her arms and rubbed her chin along the top of his head. But always her face like stone.

Mamma's refusal to smile was defiant, angry, like a curse, as if the act of smiling were brutal; an act that could tear the skin, break a tooth, pop out an eye. Mamma was trapped in the stone house against the mountain, her life over and finished at eighteen. The weight of her unhappiness bent her back, cracked her knees, dried her milk. I followed her and the aunts as they carried the buckets of water from Monte Pertuso each day.

Go away, Leticcia. Go away!

Yes, Mamma.

$\mathcal{T}$he war was over in Europe on April 25, 1945, when Adolfo Hitler shot a hole in his head. Everybody was happy when Adolfo Hitler shot a hole in his head. Nonna said the angels kept me on Jesus' lap in heaven long enough so I wouldn't be born during the worst of the war. War meant the vipers. Vipers shaped our lives.

Now 1946 and the village full of what the war had done. Nonna holding me by the shoulders, the creases under her eyes wet. *Carina*, I tell you a truth, we fight those Germans, *tedeschi animali*, animals with sticks, with mud cakes, they come with *tanki*, machine guns, they take our food, our houses, our churches, they bomb and blow up towns, cities, villages, kill us, but they no take our strong will. They can never take that. Always remember, *Carina* . . . Never bow you neck, never put you nose in dirt for anyone. Fight, *Carina*, fight for what you love.

Years later she would tell me the same thing, *Fight for what you love*. In the war Nonna fed her family weeds, roots, anything she could hide from the viper Nazi soldiers. The viper *Naziste* leered at the coastline villages from their headquarters in Positano, only seven kilometers from Praiano. Under the nose of *diavolo* every minute!

When food became available again Nonna read coffee grounds, saved the hearts of chickens to bury in the tomato plants, practiced *Mal Occhio,* the Evil Eye, like a scientific skill.

Nonna had buried three infant sons and then laid her husband in the ground after a viper Nazi S.S. stabbed him in the throat. *Naziste* no trust Sicilian people, *Carina.* Nonna began telling the story of how he was caught and murdered for helping a Jewish family from Rome to escape—

No! Mamma yelled. Mamma by the door, face bubbly with sweat. No! she yelled again.

Not to tell that story! *Per l'amor di Dio!*

All right, all right. But Nonna would tell her ChiChi how before war her husband, ChiChi's grandfather, had been a quiet man who drank too much, and when *Naziste* come, he change. He find courage in himself. He discover a brave man lived inside his pathetic skin, he became *Partigiano,* and he fight for what he love. Your Nonno, he tell us, *never bow you knee to fear.*

Mamma made a sound like *Ooooooo.*

I copied the sound. *Uuuuuuuu.*

Here was Nonna, a widow with four nasty tempered daughters, two of them widows themselves, the youngest being my teenage mother, and now the new bambino to bring her joy, *il maschio,* Marco Guglielmo Francesco Sapponata Maggiordino. Our Boy Blessed From The Sacred Gracious Heart of Jesus.

Which Marco was. Because another summer passed and he was still alive. Cheeks plumped up, eyes shining like polished eggs. But Mamma a stranger to us. Mamma digging in the garden alone. Washing clothes alone. Sewing alone. The aunts ignored her. Neighbor women avoided her and lowered their voices to a whisper when she was nearby, as though afraid of her. Sometimes Mamma would look at me with such a vicious look on her face, it would make me cry. Ah, my little girl, she would snap, and walk away.

She became an object like a cup or a wooden spoon.

The aunts talked behind Mamma's back, talked loud enough so she could hear. Look at Giuseppina! Look how she wait for postman to bring her letter from the American soldier. Haho. The American soldier with one leg!

What's that? Nonna, explain me please! Mamma's American soldier had only one leg because the doctors cut off the other one, says Nonna. With a saw. Like pruning a bad branch from the fig tree. Screech screech, and off it plopped. Mamma was there when they sawed off his leg. At the hospital in Maiori where she was a volunteer with five other young girls from Praiano. The leg was thrown in the garbage. Thrown in the garbage to smell and rot without anyone to love it.

Scema s'ta' donna, foolish woman! A one-legged man is like chair with no seat.

You never cared for him, Giuseppina. Admit it, frowns an aunt. You just wanted to marry an American! Admit it.

The aunt was a widow of a *Partigiano,* and she bragged at least *her* husband was Italian!

Do you know what they call you in the village, Giuseppina?

Please! Nonna interrupted. The children have ears!

Beh! Children! What do I care? Giuseppina is *puttana!* She is whore.

And Mamma sank into a quiet sadness so dark and bottomless she seemed not to breathe.

I forget how to sleep.

Rosa and Sofia toss on either side of me in our loft bed, the chickens muttering, Tuzza the goat snoring in the kitchen below. I climb down the ladder, walk on the sides of my feet to Mamma's bed, where she sleeps with Nonna. I pull myself under the blanket, curl my body around hers. She stirs, reaches her hand behind her and takes hold of mine.

Your mamma is dying, little girl, she whispers.

I learned things. I listened. I sat by the chestnut tree near the aunts and they said Mamma had once loved two American soldiers, not just one. Mamma folded bandages in the hospital and loved two men. One got his leg hurt bad in an invasion of Maiori. The doctors sawed the leg off and it would never grow back. He was the one Mamma married. That would be my pappa. But the other one made her a *svergogata,* shame of the village.

All she ever wanted was love.

She waited for the postman. Someday there would be a letter. Someday she would spit in their eyes. That's what she believed.

In Italy, in our village, when a sin was committed and made public, although God, Jesus, Mother Mary, and all the saints forgave and forgot through penance and contrition, the villagers never forgot. The sin followed the penitent to the grave. And even after the grave. How many times did we hear the story of Giacomo and Filippe, young sons of Anna and Benito Tintorra, who had been caught stealing an icon from the church! How the carabiniere snatched them up from their hiding place under the nets of Carlo Matta's fishing boat and held them in jail, where they tried to escape and were caught and beaten with a broom. It happened over fifty years ago.

Mamma didn't care if her story followed her to the grave. One day many years later she would give me permission to tell it. She'd say, Leticcia, write it down. She was sorry for nothing.

The letter did arrive. The postman climbed the steps to the stone house and handed Mamma what she had been waiting for.

Have you a drink of water? said the postman.

Sì, sì. Anything you want. Take the bucket. Take the goat if you like! A letter!

Sign here, said the postman. Her American husband, U.S. Army, Intelligence Division, had written her a letter. Special Delivery.

Nonna sat the postman down at the table, served him a coffee, two biscotti. Then a glass of *nocino digestivo,* her walnut liqueur.

Look at that stamp. That postmark. From Germany!

Read it, Giuseppina, read!

The letter was short, no words of love like Mamma expected. No, *ti amo amore mio, non posso vivere senza di te.* Nothing about how he couldn't live without her, loved her madly, etc., etc., but instead a short note in his adequate Italian explaining to her that he had arranged for her passage to the United States.

The United States.

He would join her within a few months upon his discharge from the army, and in the meantime she was to wait for him at the home of his parents in Saint Paul, Minnesota.

What is Minnesota?

Paradiso.

Nonna sank to a chair, poured a *digestivo* for herself. One hand across her forehead, eyes blinking.

Emigration had been processed through the American Army Headquarters in Heidelberg for Giuseppina, the little girl, and *Nonna*—if God willing, Nonna would please assist and chaperon Giuseppina and the child . . .

Dio mio.

O Gesù.

Read it again, Giuseppina! Once more *per favore.*

How Mamma changed. She read the letter over and over, out loud, to anyone who would listen, read the letter from the soldier who got his leg sawed off. She had only to take the bus to the *Ministero Dello Stato* in Naples with the *carte d'identita,* then to the Consulate for visas and the bank for the £300,000 deposited in her name. Oh! Oh! The Blessed Virgin had heard her prayers. *La Merica. La Merica.*

Mamma's spine straightened. Her movements became quick, like foot dancing, she washed her face, she shone, unrecognizable.

Blustering on in an ear-numbing voice about the Promised Land of America. Radios everywhere! Electric lights in every room! Hot water from spigots!

Protests from Nonna. *Mah.* Tulio, the tailor and his sons, they go to *La Merica,* they live like rats in filthy crowded *Nuova York,* practically starving and treated like *criminali.* I hear plenty bad stories about *La Merica.* No *Paradiso* that place. Italian women are put to work in filthy factories like prisons in *La Merica.* They slave twelve to fourteen hours a day for starvation wages. Italian men made to labor like *animali.* Is better to die of hunger at home on our own soil.

Mamma would not be discouraged. My husband is rich American! she cried. Think of it! Floors with carpets. Telephones. Beds soft like cream.

I fed the chickens and rabbits. What you refuse to hear makes no sound, no matter how near or frightening. I climbed to the roof and watched the sky make faces at me, I played with Marco by the chestnut tree, chewed bites of *salsicce* and fed it to him. (He wrinkled his nose at the first taste of the spicy sausage, but always opened his mouth for more.) We napped together under the tangled branches of the chestnut tree, me counting his noisy breaths, choosing what I wished to hear, the whistle of his throat when he inhaled and exhaled, and his chuckle like rain falling on metal.

When the heat of summer arrived to burn up the whole world and the aunts sat in the shade, languid and sweating, sucking on fig seeds, and the cousins played catch with a lemon, Nonna's cool hand caressed my cheek.

ChiChi *mia*, where are your shoes?

On Rosa's feet, I said.

They are too small for Rosa. They are yours now.

She laced Rosa's shoes on my feet and tied my shopping basket around my back and shoulder.

Something was not right. Her teeth biting her lip. Nose runny. I took her hand and she led me down the mountain to the open market in the center of the village below, away from the narrowed eyes of the aunts and their mouths like legs of crabs.

We passed the gypsy trader from farther south selling herbal medicines, roots, and potions in bottles; the long displays of tapestry and brocade; threads and lace; the glass merchant from Vietri sul Mare selling bowls, plates, and pitchers; a Napolitano selling fresh made marzipan and candies from

Tunisia; fish stands of *vongole verace, calamari, polipo,* and *triglia;* oiled and salted hams, fruits and vegetables, villagers bargaining, cajoling, children running and playing, rabbits in cages, chickens, pigeons, wooden carts and bicycles, the aroma of animal waste and leather. Nonna stopped at the display of *dolci* in a stall run by an old Siciliana. She selected a handful of sugared citrus rinds from the open tin platters and the woman weighed them, gave her a price. Nonna said no, weigh again. Nonna knew how to buy, she was *furba,* smart.

I remember these things, Nonna. I remember how we sat on the stone bench along the old wall, how you squeezed my cheeks, pulled me close while above our heads the mosaic of the Virgin and Baby Jesus stared with eyes of blue stone out at the blue sea. I remember you handed me the sack of citrus rinds and said, ChiChi, *amore mio, dai. Prendi un dolce,* and the yellow one stuck to my tongue. So bitter it was, it brought tears to my eyes. Then you tried to explain a mysterious something to me: *Cara mia,* you said at least ten times, *Cara mia.* So mysterious. Like all your stories, Nonna. So funny you are, my Nonna. I remember how your eyes congealed into mine when you said the words you thought might leave a permanent stain on the air: Mamma is going to *La Merica . . .*

She blurted the words out fast and in a hoarse whisper, like the way she spoke in church or when she said her rosary—*La Merica!*

—To live with your pappa. Okay?

It had something to do with the letter. I knew about the letter. The whole world knew about the letter.

Please I have another sweet, please, Nonnina? A green one?

Pay attention, ChiChi. Your mamma, she is go to *La Merica*. She make up her mind. You will go and I will go too.

A fly sniffed at her hair. She shook her head. Took my hand in hers. The three of us, she said. We go to *La Merica* . . .

And Marco, too! I said, a mouthful of citrus.

No, *Cara mia*, Marco—Marco, he stay here. He will not go to *La Merica* with us.

Silly Nonna. I put my arms around her body, warmer than a heavy sweater and smelling of bread dough and basil. Didn't she know Marco and me together were one person? Maybe this was a prelude to one of her stories. Tell me another one, Nonna. Tell the one about your brother, the priest at Cassino, his hands folded in prayer while six hundred tons of bombs fell on his head. A pillar of smoke, remember? Five hundred feet high shooting up into the blue sky, flames everywhere, the abbey demolished, and *madonna*. Padre Scizzo comes out with not one drop of blood on his coat. I like that story, Nonna, that one.

On a morning when the *melanzane* were sliced and packed in jars with garlic and onions and peppers, there came a letter from Germany for my mamma. And Mamma became another mamma.

She carried the letter from Pappa in the pocket of her underskirt next to her skin. This stranger called Mamma. She carried it there while slicing the tiny cuts in the olives and preparing the salt for preserving. Her sisters turned on her, their indignant faces hot. You boast too much, Giuseppina. You will bring bad luck on yourself. Watch and see!

Hah! snapped Mamma. I go where *melanzane* roll like
jewels in the streets! Milk flows in rivers, beefsteak on every
plate! She walked away from the bench where she worked,
left the olives in the bowls, their red pimiento eyes staring
up at the ceiling like a jury.

An aunt screeched after her, waving a knife: And the boy,
Giuseppina? What will you do about the boy? Don't imagine
you can leave him here with us like a cut-off finger! Don't
expect us to care for him, feed him, sick as he is, he's your
bastardo and no concern of ours. Are you listening, Giuseppina? Do you have ears to hear?

We went to church. Mamma wore the new shawl she
knitted for *La Merica*. I wore a pinafore of navy blue, my
torrents of hair braided and giving me a headache. Mamma
strutted before her sisters and the rest of the village. She
boasted how she would leave this village where a woman's
doom is her appetite for affection, where poverty and disgrace are her food, babies and wretched labor her curse.
She'd leave this village which was like a thousand others
strewn through the cracks and steep ridges of the Apennines
and the sea below—where crops were planted in patches and
on rocky ledges of the mountain, where the drinking water
was three kilometers away and in her opinion, the *festas* colorless.

Dai. Giuseppina, how you exaggerate, said Nonna. Why
you not keep you mouth quiet. Everybody talk now.

Puh! Let their tongues clatter, said Mamma. Let them cast
stones, call her bad woman, she had proof, proof in the
letter, see? Her husband was a rich American.

—I will live in big house with electric refrigerator and a
stove for heat in every room. Eh? In Minnesota! And a radio!
Two pairs of leather shoes!

When she talked like this she had to pause to wipe tears

from her eyes with the hem of her sleeve. No more washing dishes in sand and cinders. Machines for everything. Sheets washed in machines. Think of it.

I must tell her Marco and I are one. I, being his angel, can never leave him. *Marco è mio.* Marco is mine. I can't go to *Paradiso* without my Marco.

Per l'amor di Dio, shut up, Leticcia.

She took the bus to the *Ministero Dello Stato,* the American Consulate, the Cunard Lines. She wrote letters, filled out papers, and in the shifting of seasons, she finally announced, resigned, in a rage, that Marco would go to *La Merica* with us. It was better he die with us than with those snakes, those daughters of *diavolo,* her sisters. And would Leticcia now please shut up?

The photographer in Positano snapped our passport pictures. Nonna, Mamma, Marco, and me, our black eyes glaring into the lens, hair pressed down, collars up, unmistakably what we were in the thump of the camera's white light.

Nonna's house was smaller with the aunts and *cugine,* girl-cousins, cowering in chairs against the walls watching Mamma sorting and packing for the journey.

Neighbors came the night before we were to leave. They stood in the doorway, staring, smiling, fidgeting with their hands. Signora Botticco had a *cugina* in New Jersey, could Mamma take a jar of *pepperoncini?* A bottle of *Limoncello?* And the niece, the nephew, the brother, or father in New York, Cleveland, Dallas—could Mamma take this shirt, this fine tooled belt?

Now they ask me for favors, scowled Mamma. When their noses smell success, their tongues wag. I say to hell with them all, to hell with them, damn their eyes.

Nonna swept me up in her arms, pushing Marco's head into her skirts, Giuseppina, take the *Limoncello*.

Provolone, olives, figs, and bread wrapped in paper and tied with string. Our clothing washed and folded. Hammer and small nails to repair shoes, what else? Yellow soap, the picture of the Madonna, crucifix, anchovies in jars. Blankets, tin boxes of medicines and herbs, shawls, everything Mamma said we needed. She stood before the large wicker hamper tying the leather straps around it while the aunts watched on in silence. They had called her bad names. Now they blinked back tears.

On the morning of our departure we ate our breakfast of bread and roasted peppers. I remember the silence. The aunts' faces stern, somber, the cousins frowning. Mamma nervous, dropping her spoon, spilling her coffee. Nonna stood at the window with her hands knotted at her chin. Tuzza's hoof pushed against the door.

Then Nonna said, Here comes Memmo.

Memmo, Signora Botticco's nephew, coming up the hill in his delivery truck to drive us to the bus stop. Memmo at the door, carrying our possessions out to the truck. Cheerful Memmo. Then an explosion of arms and cheeks and breasts. Aprons, skirts, feet, wet faces, sobs, wails. The aunts clawing at us, crying as if we were going to our doom. Loud, very loud. Screaming loud. Many deaths loud. A consolidated keening, awful. I will be back soon, Nonna choked into the neck of *Zia* Lola. Some months, maybe two, three, and she'd be back.

Marco cried. The whole world cried.

We boarded the bus for Naples, heads leaning out the window for a last look at our village, our house, and the aunts sobbing in the dust. I'd never see Sofia and Rosa again. The bus wound its way down the mountain and bumped along the steep twisting Amalfi coast to Napoli.

Nonna adjusted the cotton bag slung from her shoulder carrying our salami, cheeses that smelled like feet, and the corked bottles of lemon liqueur. Marco was wrapped in wool blankets and bundled in a wicker basket in Mamma's arms and I sat holding my breath in the stockings Nonna knitted for the journey and shoes once belonging to Cousin Sofia, our hamper of clothing and cooking utensils under me. Nobody spoke.

When we entered the city the sun was rising up over the bay. Santa Lucia! Look, Nonna, Santa Lucia! Naples was on fire with light.

Is a good omen, said Nonna. Is sign from God.

The ship waiting in the silver bay of Naples was called the *Vulcania,* and it had once been a hospital for the Allies during the war (another good omen, said Nonna). Hundreds of emigrants like us were praying for a better life—or, as was said among the peasants of Campania, Calabria, and Puglia, we were Following The Bread.

We boarded the ship to the new country, strained our eyes for a last look toward our fishing villages along the coast. We didn't know that this quiet stretch of sea and land would one day become an international tourist vacation attraction, with fine beaches and hotels. The memories of our village life would become vague, shadowy, like paintings with in-visible ink.

The *Vulcania,* a city of sickness.

Crying, crying sick. Unable to sleep, whining I wanted to go home—pleaded for steady ground, my bed, my goat. Mamma giving a slap, Stop that! In America you can have ten goats.

I don't want ten goats. I want Tuzza. Aaaahhhhhhhh.

Everybody sick. I watched from the bunk I shared with Marco in our cabin deep down in the boat. Men, women, and children sick and retching their bread and cheese, groaning, holding their knees. If only we could see the sky. On the second day the storm hit. Icy ocean water lashed over the *Vulcania*'s deck, Nonna screamed her prayers out loud. Mamma held her face in her hands and moaned like a cow.

Water can blow up the world. The storm of hundred-mile winds that hit us sent water exploding like bombs everywhere. The *Vulcania* was under forty-five-foot ocean swells. Someone ordered us to hang on to the edges of our bunks and pray. Some of the women threw their Saint Christopher medals into the ocean, praying on their hands and knees as they were tossed around the cold, slippery deck.

Holy Mother, have mercy.

I hung on to Marco and Marco hung on to me. We hung on and hung on. Save us, we prayed. Bring us safe to the foreign shore, and thanks be to God, Jesus our Lord, all the saints and Santa Maria forever, amen, the Holy Mother heard and did.

We knew we had finally arrived safe in the United States when voices on the deck shouted, *Statua della liberta! Statua della liberta!*

At 9:30 A.M. September 30, 1948, we floated on our knees up to Paradise.

We were like dazed chickens, weak and foul-smelling. We were taken to a pier warehouse to have our luggage sorted and inspected and then chucked onto a barge to Ellis Island. Bedlam! We were caught in a swirl of frightened, confused people who screamed in languages we didn't understand. Children, men, women, inspectors, stevedores, sailors, detectives, watchmen, and vendors—all pushing and yelling at once. Marco began coughing into Mamma's shoulder, his face turning a pale grey.

Customs inspection. Swarming wool coats, leather boots, leggings, bundles, packages, bags, boxes, trunks. Millions of trunks. Black skirts with greyed lace trim. Tattered petticoats. Lost was the scent of our sun-kissed village on our little ribbon of sea; we now reeked of sour garlic and human waste.

Then the physical inspections. Ears, eyes, and heads examined with picks and wire probes. A fat man with noodle nose poked in my mouth. (Marco smiled when I say Noodle Nose.) Mamma stiff like wood. She wiped our faces with the back of her hand and her spit. She warned us that children with runny eyes are refused entry. Warned us if we cry the men in the uniforms would throw us in the ocean and sharks would eat us. Grown-ups were thrown in the ocean all the time, she said. If a big *T* was tagged to our clothes, it means Trachoma. An *F* was for Favus, a fungus skin disease. These were very bad. We saw a mother with the *T* on her sweater being separated from her children. Everybody screaming. Mahmi! Mahmi! A boy my age with a wool cap over his ears cried great honking, howling tears, his dripping nose splashing down his chin and onto his collar. A guard held him back so he wouldn't run after his mother. The distraught boy would get thrown into the ocean if he didn't shut up.

Any person with an illness or a physical deformity, even if they had a suitcase full of money, was refused entry to Paradise.

A man in a uniform points to Nonna. Nonna's bones harden. She halts. The man speaks to her, motions her forward.

Nonna doesn't move. He pushes her and Nonna stumbles. The man watches her fall, but doesn't help her. I yell *Nonnina! Nonnina!* I hurl myself after her. Mamma grabs my hair. *Stai zitta!* she warns with a yank. Shut up and mind your business!

The man looks Nonna over like he's buying a goat. He draws a big white chalk mark on the back of her coat and shoves her into a crowd of others being taken away.

Mamma, hauling our hamper and bags, carries her health ticket in her teeth. She digs her fingers into my shoulder, *Zitta!* Quiet! The panic is bigger than me. Mamma slaps my head.

We are moved to a big noisy room with long tables. People eat sandwiches that look like small cakes, they drink milk from snubby bottles. Mamma hits the side of my head again. Stop crying, Leticcia. I'll throw you in the ocean myself.

Bad girl. I'm a bad girl to cry and make noise. The man in the uniform will think I'm sick, he'll shoot me with his gun. I hold Marco so tight he chokes, he coughs. Mamma cries out in horror. No! He must not cough! No!

Marco e mio, I tell her. He is mine.

Managgia! I could kill you right here, she tells me.

I refuse to let Mamma take Marco from me. I don't eat the cakey sandwiches the Americans give us. I'm shaking and clinging to Marco, who is also shaking and clinging to me. Would they throw our nonna in the ocean? Nonna wasn't sick, she just walked a little crooked in her dead husband's shoes.

Long columns of people crowd into the big room. Some sit on the floor with their sandwiches. Dark faces, heads lowered, every one with eyes like Nonna. We are not real people like we had been just a few days ago in Italy when we had names and our faces were recognized. If you are not a real

person you could be anything, an old hat worn by the don-
key or a piece of wood. You could be a book without pages,
a lemon with spots. You could be a coat with a number
pinned to it.

Nonna finally materializes in the maze and the world tips
right-side up again. Mamma rushes to her, doesn't stop hug-
ging her. I hold her leg through the thick wool skirt and
leggings. She has passed all what they call The Tests.

Even they test you for crazy in the head, she explains. Did
I know which hand is right hand? Left hand? How many
fingers on my hands? Why I come to *La Merica*? Did I want
to change the world? Was I *Communista*? Did Jesus speak to
me personally? *Managgia*.

We wait without our real selves on a bench in a big room
with high ceilings where every sound echoes, rises up, and
then falls with a thud. We watch as families are reunited,
becoming people again. We hear names called out and the
rush of joyous reunions. But Pappa's family does not come
for us. At the end of the day we are thirsty and hungry and
a man in a uniform tags our jackets with placards reading
RAILROAD, which means we aren't going to *Nuova York*
and nobody is meeting us. We take the stairs to the right
and board a ferry boat. I sit on the wood bench of the ferry
boat looking out at water which reminds me of lettuce wilt-
ing. We're bound for the Hoboken train terminal.

Mamma said the Hoboken Terminal was like king's palace,
like cathedral. A man cleaning the floor with a machine
heard us speaking and told us he, too, was Italian, from Calabria. Big smiles. He said we better get used to being *grig-
noni,* greenhorns.

Nonna asked, what means this, Green Horns? The man

gave a snort and said, You'll see. Nonna's face shone with pride. We were blessed, we were on top of things, we were Green Horns.

That night we slept on the train, rocking and rocking. The train was better than the ship. Nobody was sick and messing up the floor. Nobody cried and screamed about dying. At a place called Chicago we got off the train and got onto another train for Saint Paul, the city where our beautiful new life waited for us.

The other passengers slept, ate, talked; people with pale skin wearing patterned clothes in bright colors, women with hair clipped around their ears and sheer stockings exposing their legs. A girl Marco's age with unbraided hair wore trousers! Voices made sounds that made no sense. Nonna held Marco and me close to her. We were four proud Green Horns.

In Saint Paul a man driving the taxi read the address Mamma handed him and we rode in awe, shocked silly. Even Napoli wasn't this big, this clean. Buildings stripped to straight edges, flat surfaces and tops, streets that met a horizon of other streets long and big enough for ten horse carts to travel at once. Cars bigger than henhouses, lights on in every store.

Houses like castles, trees of a thousand colors. Land so flat you could get dizzy standing up, you could tip over. And the air had a peculiar rabbity smell to it. Thick and fuzzy, a tickling smell, fishless, saltwaterless. Where's the sea, Mamma? Where's the water?

Is here somewhere.

I pressed my hands to my face and breathed in. The sea was still in my hands.

We arrived at Pappa's parents' house on Summit Avenue breathless and giddy.

Exhausted and sick.

One coughing boy, one feverish girl, two haggard, black-shrouded women. Mamma knocked and knocked. A lady with hair like an orange answered the door.

Good Lord, what's this?

Her mouth points down, her chin puckers, and her neck stretches back in her collar. (She does not like us.) She looks at each of our faces like she's deciding on the price of veal knuckle. It takes a long time for the lady to allow us to enter the *palacio*.

Why on earth don't you just ring the bell? Where are you coming from? Who *are* you people?

She smells of mimosa.

Our bags and boxes fan out around us on the nice clean floor of the lady's hallway. I have to make ka-ka. Mamma doesn't understand what the lady says.

Ka-ka, I whine.

I try to open the door to go outside to the grass. Nonna says, Wait, *Carina*, in *La Merica* they ka-ka inside. The woman suddenly understands and I do ka-ka in a toilet like a wreath that you sit on top of.

The lady with hair like oranges speaks a little Italian; she says it is beautiful in Milano this time of year. She met her husband in Milano.

Mamma sighs, radiant with good manners. Ah. *Che bello.* How very nice!

The lady leads us upstairs to a room with a bathtub and water faucets and another toilet with a wreath seat. Hot water falls out of the faucet without heating it over a fire. We take off our clothes and sit in the tub. First Marco and me. Then Nonna's turn, and then Mamma. We all use the same water, like at home.

After we dress in the clean clothes smelling of stale cheese from our hamper, we sit at a table in an American kitchen as big as our house in Praiano. We eat soup with meat and store-bought bread. We eat in silence while the man and woman sit across from us staring at our faces in disbelief.

So. You say you're *who?*

That night we sleep in a room with two beds. Both beds are covered with blankets made in factories, sheets, pillow covers. We climb into one bed together. We think somebody else must be coming to sleep in the other bed.

I inch very close to Nonna, curl around her back, listen to her prayers, and I worry how Jesus will ever be able to find us in such a place.

We don't remain in the *palacio* with the orange-haired lady for long. Though she is nice to me and gives me chocolate, something is wrong.

Bad words. Anger.

A man with white hair: Exactly who *are* you people? What do you want?

When he talks he makes puffs in the air. His teeth are small and brownish, like nuts. No son of theirs could possibly have married a southern Italian peasant girl—would his son marry a child? How old are you anyhow, Giuseppina? And the nerve to come here with two kids! How is this possible that our son could have two children? The little girl about three years old, right? And what's the boy? Two? Oof-tah! Our son's been stationed in *Germany* since the war ended! He couldn't be the father of these children.

Cosa?

Puff. Grunt. They're from the *mezzogiorno,* these people! Look at them. Who knows what kinds of diseases they could be carrying. (I am sick with dysentery. On the toilet every five minutes.)

The orange-head lady yells at Mamma. Her advice, young lady, if Mamma could be called a young lady, is to go back to Italy and marry the *real* father of her children. What did she want with them, decent American citizens that they were?

All Mamma can say is, Bruno, he my husband. Bruno, he my husband. Her voice strained, like a rib ready to break. They scratch their chins, shake their heads.

Mamma is called an impostor, *impostora*.

Nonna tries to correct them and explain we are Green Horns. Nobody listens.

Unhappiness gives you eyes of wood, and such eyes transform the most resplendent of visions into the dreary, the lamentable, the unbearable. All the pretty pictures and figures made of glass and carpets and chairs with cushions and a useless small, hairy dog became ugly to us. Nonna asked the lady with the orange head how, if Americans were so smart, could they waste food on an animal that didn't provide protection or sustenance?

Nonna looked with wonder out the window at a tree raucous with jabbering birds. These *Americani,* she muttered, these *Americani* are so rich they give their food to the dogs who don't lay eggs, give milk, or provide meat. And look, the trees are bursting with food they don't shoot.

Where was the *melanzane* rolling in the streets that Mamma had sung praises for? Where were the rivers of milk? The ten goats like my Tuzza?

Mice would not find peace in that house on Summit Avenue. Nonna tried to comfort us. What did we care about such *Americani,* puh! We'd be back home in Italy soon, oh yes, *carissime miei,* soon!

She called out my mother's name in a tearful voice. Giuseppina, my daughter, Let us go home where the soil beneath our feet welcomes us! Let us go back home to our own country and our own people. Puh! Puh on such family you husband he born into. *Dico io fasciamo il Mal Occhio.* I say we give them the Evil Eye.

The Evil Eye!

Yes, let us leave Paradiso, return home to Italy! The war, she over. The *Cassa per il Mezzogiorno* rebuilds roads in the south, they are putting in plumbing, drainage for sewers, telephone wires. There is assistance for agricultural development, more jobs. Young women like you, Giuseppina, like you, they are getting work, going to school.

Mai! Never! screamed Mamma. *Io non saró una disgraziata!* She wouldn't disgrace herself. She would never return to Praiano. No, never. Like a dog to its vomit. Never.

Nonna argued it was no disgrace what happened to Mamma, God had forgiven her and what is done is done. We must put the cover on the kettle. Mamma growled and hit her thighs with her fists, and Nonna held her shoulders tight.

The lady with the orange hair and the man with walnuts for teeth sent us to a place they said where we'd be with our own kind until we went back to Italy where we belonged. A taxi arrived for us.

So you're right off the boat, said the driver. Jesus!

Gesù, Maria, said Nonna. Crossed herself.

We got lots of aliens in the Twin Cities, getting more all the time, the driver said. Too many if you ask me. Yup, they come from all over. For the welfare money, no offense.

We're being taxed up the kazoo to give aliens like you free money. But real lucky for you folks you got somebody's willing to help you out. Where I'm taking you ain't nothing fancy, but it's probably better'n what you come from in your own country. You here for the welfare, right?

Nonna grinned and nodded her head up and down.

The man drove us to the lower flats of the Mississippi, where shacks and clapboard houses clung above and along the river. He parked his taxi in front of a fresh-painted white shack surrounded by dusty geraniums and a battered wood fence. A sign above the door read MANAGER.

Wait here, said the driver.

Such a nice fellow, said Nonna. Saint Christopher sent him to us.

A man with white lardy skin eyed us from the door, then signaled us to get out of the taxi and come inside.

You folks is plain lucky we happen to have a availability, he said.

He handed Nonna a key and pointed down the hill.

Your rent's paid for two months, he said. Swell family you got.

Man, I seen it all, muttered the taxi driver. I guess a fella's got to look at it this way: Suffering is just part of the great tapestry of life.

The tapestry of life, honked Manager. That there's a good one.

We moved into our first home in America, a one-room clapboard house by the river in an area populated entirely by Polish and German immigrants. We got on our knees on the cold, damp floor and Nonna thanked The Blessed Virgin Mary and Saint Christopher. We were alive and not dead in

La Merica and for these favors we thanked the Lord and all the saints, amen.

And poor ChiChi, our sick little rabbit, making ka-ka like Vesuvius—here, open you mouth, sulfur with sugar, ahhhh. There there, *amore,* no more shitting for today.

*O*ur new home. We met the winter sleeping in one bed and kept warm during the day huddled close to the stove. The Minnesota ice and snow closed in on us like frozen covers of a book. We were pressed down in cold, we were flattened like paper, dazed into silence. We wore our blankets from home all day, afraid to go too far from the stove.

Nonna held Marco and me on her lap, rocking, humming, staring out the window at the wall of ominous white while Mamma sat with her knees up to her chin on the bed, her face clouded and dark. Immigrants' lives are like flies on wall—we not like human.

So? said Nonna. If we are flies, we do like flies—we use our wings.

Mamma gave a snort. It's brains we need, she said. I'm think of plan. I'm use my brain.

In the new country the flat clipped consonants of English confused us, the peculiar chopping sound made by the tongue. We couldn't understand the Polish and German languages of our neighbors. At first Mamma and Nonna were afraid of the Germans, worried there might be a Nazi among them. Marco cried constantly. I tried daily to quiet him, make him laugh.

Mamma didn't respond to the friendly gestures of the other women who lived along the flats. She was retreating

into the same Mamma she was back in Praiano. She offered
Marco the nipple of her breast and then withdrew it absently,
as though she forgot she had no milk, so he wailed until
Nonna fed him water heated with honey from a teaspoon.
We ate only pasta and polenta in order to stretch Nonna's
savings while Mamma figured out her plan of the brain.

Nonna said if it weren't for our living in that place by
the river and practically freezing to death, Marco might not
have gotten worse with the lung disease. Mamma splurged
and bought chicken backs for soup and sometimes a beef
bone, but Marco stayed sick. When the snow began to melt,
I was free of sickness, but not Marco. Listless. Fever. Crying,
crying. It was as if he was damaged, broken somehow, like
a plate that the edges never quite fit right once glued back
together. He grew thinner and his skin took on the bluish
tint he was born with and Nonna wrapped him in his blanket, tucked him into her coat, and carried him down the
winding dirt road to the Polish priest at the Catholic church.

Signora, the child needs a doctor, not a priest, he told her.
Nonna cocked her head, *scusi?*

Hospital! Hospital! shouted the priest.

I cried as though mortally wounded. We didn't understand the English-speaking doctors and nurses at the hospital,
didn't know what was happening to Marco when they took
him from us.

A doctor with thin grey hair and hands like flowers said
Marco had little chance of living beyond the year, maybe
less.

What he say, Leticcia? Do you understand?

The doctor went on, said the situation was grave. He
spoke while looking over our shoulders at the hallway behind us. I see these cases all too often, he said.

Che cosa?

He went on. You must know, he said, if he survives this, his life expectancy is, well, let me just say, cases like this don't usually see adolescence.

What is he saying? *What?*

A nurse led an old man toward us. A patient in a long bib with the back side open and his *culo* showing. He tapped his stomach, *Il fegato,* he groaned to Mamma.

Oohhh ah, *il fegato,* the liver, Mamma repeated. She tried to tell the nurse when an Italian had a bodily pain, any pain in the body, it was usually blamed on *il fegato.* No to worry yourself. It would probably pass.

If you please, interrupted the doctor, and he addressed the sick liver man. Tell this woman, he said, if her boy lives to see ten years of age it will be a miracle.

The man sick with his liver did as he was told, then shuffled back down the hall. The doctor shrugged, uneasy in his skin, and left us, too.

Three times that winter Marco received Last Rites for his final heavenly journey by the Polish priest who spoke no Italian.

The Little Sisters of Saint Agnes of the Poor gave us clothes and food. Mamma said she would repay them every one. She was not one to take anything for free. Not her. She did not bow her back to the wall, no. She would not go to the welfare office. She wrote letters every day to Pappa in the army, but an answer didn't come.

I prayed for sick Marco, I was his angel after all. It was up to me to keep him alive.

*S*pring and melting snow, the shock when nature met humanity in a foaming rush of floodwater. Marco came home from the hospital and was carried by ambulance attendants who scaled old boards and pieces of wood over the mud surrounding the house. You guys ought to get out of here, they told us. Floods happen awful fast, you know. One minute you got mud, next minute you're floating downstream on your back with your house on top of you.

Tank you verry mootch, said Mamma, wondering what the men were upset about.

Marco and I ate bowls of polenta until we could barely lift ourselves from our chairs. He was home. He was well. Everything was going to be just fine.

But we couldn't plant a garden, like Nonna hoped. The river swarmed up the banks of the Mississippi rumbling over the land, burying trees and shrubbery, sending animals and rodents rushing into houses for shelter. Nonna bought us rubber boots and rain coats at the Salvation Army store on Washington Avenue. She also bought rattraps and Coca-Colas. And fava beans and *pepperoncini,* which the Little Sisters of Saint Agnes hadn't heard of.

Nonna said when the rains stopped we would plant our garden, *basilico,* tomatoes, and peppers. We'd hang our laundry in the sun.

Can we get a goat? Can we, Nonna, a goat like Tuzza?

One day a lady called a social worker from the city visited us and gave us what she called a Final Warning. We must vacate, which means Get Out. Immediately. Our German and Polish neighbors had packed their belongings and vacated their houses as the neighborhood turned sour with dampness and mud and rising water. The water crept higher and higher and the air took on a smell of manure and burnt rubber. The clothes we wore stayed damp. Our bed smelled like dirty hair.

The Catholic church became a hotel for the families whose houses were overtaken by the rising river, but when the water began to seep into the basement of the church and up through the floorboards of the sanctuary, the Red Cross stepped in and set up an emergency rescue tent station on Hennepin Avenue by the train station.

The people slept on cots in their coats and boots. Their faces were seen in the evening papers and if you looked carefully, you'd see tablecloths and chintz curtains floating downriver, a toy or two, dead rabbits and squirrels lying bloated in the water, and you might sigh at the frightened children sucking on Red Cross bottled orange juice. You'd see women, their good thick hands lying helpless on their laps; men with gelatinous faces, eyes tired, resigned. You'd see displaced human beings aching in their damp clothes from the old country, their feet stinging in their thick stockings and worn shoes; you'd see them in the evening papers, and you'd see how, at the urging of the photographers, they gave their broadest smiles for the camera.

Nonna tried comforting us by singing:

Sul mare luccia, l'astro d'argento!
Placida è l'onda, prospero è il vento . . .
Sa-a-nta Luccia! Santa Lucciiiiia!

Nonna tried to coax Mamma to sing, but Mamma put up her hand. Refused. The heart who is broken cannot sing, she said.

Rain dripped from the ceiling into the cooking pots set along the floor. Rain leaked down the window sashes and sills. Rain fell on the rented furniture. Our bed was fast becoming a pool of floating yarn. The electricity had stopped working so Mamma kept candles and matches wrapped in newspaper in the bed with us.

Moving the bed didn't help. We slept in our jackets and raincoats in the cold wet blankets. One morning we were awakened by a loud thumping against the door. Mamma took her time answering.

A woman wearing a thick coat and high boots stared at us from the doorway as though she were seeing ghosts.

You people are *living* here?

Mamma didn't know what to say or do. Maybe it was the Little Sisters of Saint Agnes, ah that's it, those sneaky nuns, they had turned her in. Called the police on her, blown the whistle, told the officials how her husband's family had rejected her, cast her out. How she had no return tickets to Italy.

But this house is condemned! screamed the woman in the coat and boots. The whole area's condemned! Everyone's evacuated the area! What are you doing for electricity? For heat? My God, look at the water!

Then she saw Nonna, Marco, and me huddled in the soaked bed.

Jesus Christ!

You want to pray, go to church, Mamma said in Italian.

The woman handed Mamma a telegram. Is this your name? Is this you? She held a large heavy package.

Mamma took the telegram. *Guarda!* Look! Her name on

the package! Giuseppina Sapponata Maggiordino.

I'm going to get help for you! the woman yelled, her face startled and pink. She handed Mamma a paper on a clipboard to sign.

You folks can't stay here! Do you understand?

Mamma scribbled on the paper, took the telegram and the package, and closed the door while the woman was still talking.

Tank you verry mootch.

We waited.

A letter! A letter! A package! More than likely toys, cakes for the children, clothes, gifts!

Mamma's husband had written to her. At last a letter and a package from Bruno. The room became quiet except for the steady dripping of water, the creaking of the walls. Whatever was inside the package was sent by the American army and had been wrapped in a long heavy box and covered with paper and string. Mamma and Nonna pulled and cut the string, rolled the box on its side so as to not tear the paper; careful, careful, easy she goes; ah, that's it . . .

Marco and I waited, grinning and nudging each other. My feet didn't feel as cold. My hands weren't as stiff. Marco moved close to me and put his arms around my neck. We could hardly keep from chuckling. The world had turned warm and dry. Mamma, too, was smiling. She wiped her sleeves on the folds of her skirt, took a breath, nodded to Nonna, and then opened the lid of the box.

Still smiling, she looked inside the box, and then staggered back as though struck in the chest. She screamed. Nonna crossed herself, didn't move. Mamma went on screaming.

Mamma pulled at her hair. Has he been killed? *Lui è morto?* The army had sent a wooden leg.

The telegram! The telegram! What does the telegram say?

Is written in English! We could hear the truck grunting back up the hill. Nonna ran in the mud after it.

Wait! Please! Please explain the telegram!

When she returned she fell exhausted on the bed and said the river called Mississippi was ready to eat us up.

Marco sensed something bad, began to cry. He's scared, Mamma, I said, and she slapped me on the face.

Nonna took Mamma into the little kitchen, holding her up by the waist, leaving the box with the leg on the bed near Marco and me. Marco crawled to the box, reached inside, and touched the leg. Pappa, I said.

Pappa, he repeated.

I put my hand in the box next to Marco's and with the tips of my fingers, stroked the knee, the calf, the ankle. Pappa.

*W*e ride in the back of a Red Cross covered truck. We are being taken to a new place to live called Temporary Housing. A Polish family rides in the truck with us, four children with faces like small adults. The baby looks like somebody's old uncle, its frown pushed in place by a scarf wrapped around its head. Two Red Cross ladies climb into the truck smiling at us, talking their peculiar talk. They place Red Cross packages in our hands. Talking, smiling, nodding. Cluttery words. Words that make disorder of the air. They hand out hard candies to us children, candies as big as our mouths called Jaw Breakers.

The truck pulls away and we watch the Mississippi flats fade and disappear behind us. The river has created a simple silver line of what had been a community of shanties, gardens, trees, roads, fences. Real people had lived in a real place, people with voices and smells, people who made the sign of the cross before going to bed at night and when waking up in the morning. Now a silver line of river water. Nonna, what happened to all the people? Where did the trees go?

Don't you worry youself, ChiChi *amore*. People have feet to walk and hands to work. God, He watch over all of us. Trees will return.

Will we return?

Mamma's rigid face next to mine. No, Leticcia. We go

and never return. It is the way with life. Go and do not look
back.

Marco sucks on his jawbreaker with his mouth open. Close
your mouth, says Mamma. I can't, says Marco. The four
Polish children suck their jawbreakers and transparent shades
of orange and red dribble down their chins. Marco drools
purple. One of the Polish boys coughs and a brilliant string
of yellow arcs through the air and lands on the shoe of one
of the Red Cross ladies. We laugh and Mamma says, What's
so funny? Nonna sees the yellow puddle on the Red Cross
lady's shoe and laughs, haHA, and then the Polish parents
are laughing, and soon we're all laughing. It's the first good
laugh we share in the new world. And it's over a wad of
spit.

The truck stopped at a long flat barracks building. No trees,
no hills, land flat like a piece of paper. The barracks looked
like a toy, something that connected to something else and
you'd stand it on one end and make growly sounds. People
lived in the barracks, lots of them. People like us.

Nonna begged Mamma to call her husband's parents.
Didn't she want to know where he was buried? Such the
hard head, Giuseppina. *Testa dura!* Surely the army had informed the parents that Bruno was married to her, no? But
Mamma refused, considering the shame she was suffering at
the parents' hands. She would grieve in silence like a men-
dicant Carmelite, she said, a curse on those two, may they
die of boils.

Summer without trees. Crying babies, tight-lipped
women with bandannas around their heads. Women with

hands like men. Cleaning, sweeping, washing, lifting. Sun turning the ground inside out. Sullen faces of sons and husbands smoking hand-rolled cigarettes and waiting in doorways. Marco's sickness, my fever, the torpid heat swarming our bodies. Ants in our bedding. Mosquito welts on my arms and legs, welts I scratched until bloody. I pulled at the scabs like someone longing for scars.

Leticcia, stop that! You want to kill you leg?

A social worker from Minneapolis came to talk to Mamma. Mamma, eyes narrowed, shawl pulled up to her chin, listened without speaking. The woman said she herself was of Italian extraction, don't tell anyone. Both parents. From Bari, way down there near the heel of the boot, you know.

Viva Italia.

Good thing you folks wound up here in Minneapolis and not somewhere like say New Orleans. My god, they were lynching Italians in New Orleans not that long ago. That's right. *Lynching.* Did we know what *lynching* was? Sicilians especially. They thought all Sicilians were Mafioso. Are you folks of Sicilian extraction? Ah oh. That explains the dark skin. Well!

I sucked a mosquito bite on the inside of my arm.

The woman's chin sank into her neck.

And her uncle who was a miner? In West Virginia? Oh, he was almost killed when the workers went on strike until they got rid of all Italian workers. Talk about discrimination.

Nonna puzzled. Nodded. Folded her hands on her stomach. Smiled.

Was a time, said the woman, when Italian children weren't allowed to attend white schools. We were called the Europe's scum.

Capisce?

We stared at her.

Oh, don't let it bother you too much. Prejudice is human nature. It's not as though you're Negro or anything. But here in Minnesota today, Italians aren't thought of as exactly white. If you get my drift. Haha.

Nice lady, said Mamma. Haha. Laugh. Be polite.

We smiled, nodded.

She went on. The kiddies won't be able to start right off in the regular school. You kiddies speak any English?

She had lipstick on her teeth. Gooey stuff. She looked like she was bleeding from inside her head. She spoke in a strange Italian dialect, one with flattened r's, all in a monotone. A baby talk way of speaking. Everything in the present tense. She told Mamma about a furnished apartment she found for us on the second floor of a house in northeast Minneapolis in a neighborhood called Tar Town.

How-nice-you-to-live-in-ALL-Italian-neighborhood!

A section of Minneapolis nestled along the northeast hem of the city between the river and two sets of railroad tracks, a two-square-mile neighborhood of small neat houses on cramped lots with burgeoning flower and vegetable gardens, spotless walks, rutted streets, and dirt alleys—Tar Town. Here the Italian immigrants of the 1920s and earlier had formed a community of homes, shops, businesses, a settlement house, and Catholic church, all bought and developed by and for Italians, mostly from the south, like us. Our new home was the upper floor of a wood frame house on Taylor Street, a street named after an American president. At a rental price we could pay with Nonna's savings. Three rooms, a bathroom with a toilet and bathtub, a kitchen with an elec-

tric refrigerator, gas stove, hot water in the faucets, and furniture in every room.

In Praiano families slept together in one bed. Marco and
I would have our own beds, beds that didn't crunch with
corn husks. We would sleep in a room of our own with a
door that opened and closed. Mamma and Nonna would
sleep in a room of their own, too. How baffling to have so
much space for so few of us. And no animals to share the
comforts.

From our windows we could watch the railroad tracks
and trains entering and leaving the Northeast Minneapolis
train yard across the street. Surely the Madonna had blessed
us. The river water wouldn't reach us here.

Praise and light candles.

Many of the families in Tar Town had come to the United
States from San Giovanni in Fiore, as well as other villages
in southern Italy and Sicily, and they opened their arms wide
to their *paisani*. Welcoming and friendly, the people considered us all family. They told stories of the grandparents and
great-grandparents who came over at the turn of the century
to work on the railroads. The *progenitori* who had settled
here, raised families, built a community. Nonna at once made
friends and became part of the community, but Mamma kept
her distance. She avoided personal contact with people and
it was rare that she left the apartment. Nonna did the shopping and Mamma sat in her chair by the window and stared
out at the railroad tracks.

The neighborhood had a tipping-over feel to it. Flat,
straight, without hills or rocks or anything steep to climb.
No mountains in the distance. No blue sea below high cliffs.

We walked on flat land with sidewalks like narrow cement roads. The houses were arranged in straight rows with a street set between them. Like Summit Avenue in Saint Paul, there were no donkeys or carts. In their place, loud smelly cars.

The Madeline Brown Settlement House was a depository for children not ready for regular Catholic school with regular Catholic children. Marco and I would begin our special classes to learn English and the American ways here. Father Tuttifucci, the Saint Joseph School principal, explained to Mamma that Marco and I would be given personal attention at the settlement house, and we'd receive good opportunities as we adjusted.

Fine with Mamma.

On our first day of adjusting, Marco and I were separated into our own age groups. I sat with my head down, my hands over my ears. I refused to speak, to open my eyes. In another room Marco shivered and coughed. When we found each other at something called *recessa*, his face had turned a pale blue and he had wet his pants.

Nonna came to school with us the next day. She explained to Father Tuttifucci how it must be that Marco and I be kept together. For Marco's health, she said, a sick boy, and the girl, she not so regular either.

Our teacher was Sister Ursula, a small wrinkled nun from Trapani with eyes black and glittery like crumbs dropped by fairies. She had a slight mustache above a mouth crowded with overlapping teeth, and so gentle and kind she was, her students, including me, would do almost anything to please her, to see her teeth all pushed out in a smile.

Sister Ursula taught us we were the jewels in God's crown when we were good, obedient, attended Mass, went to confession, and learned our English.

Marco next to me, our sweater sleeves touching.

How do you do, Missis Brown? I am well, tank you, Mistir Giones.

(No, not Giones, *Jones*.) Oh. *Scuzi*, Mistir *Giones*. Will you take the tea now? No please, Missis Brown. I am taken.

Tar Town was to be our home for the next seven years, and we lived as though the world outside us was an illusion. If we could just hang on, season by season, hang on to each other, to life, and if I could keep Marco alive.

Mamma found out it was possible for us to stay at the settlement house school through sixth grade. She could save money by keeping us at the settlement house school. I was almost nine, Marco seven. We were learning how not to be Italian. In another part of town Ukrainian kids were learning how not to be Ukrainian. Polish kids were learning how not to be Polish. Germans learning how not to be German.

We began taking a long way home after school through our neighborhood to scale the empty fruit crates in the alley behind Bernardi's Produce and then stop for a smell of the bread at Gino's Bakery and buy *biscotti,* two almond chocolate ones, and then head on our homemade scooter for Spring and Fillmore and roll along East Hennepin all the way to where Tyler and Cemetery Streets crossed. We pitched forward on the scooter, our school jackets winged behind us, grinding around corners and over the cracks in the pavement. Me on the back, him on the front, our cookies stuck in our mouths like pacifiers, bouncing along the sidewalk, pausing at the lip of the curb for a proud, exhilarated moment, then hopscotching the sloping sidewalk to our front steps.

Climbing the stairs to our apartment, Marco moved with

slow, careful steps one at a time, his clothes hanging from him like a frown. Pants blousing around bony legs, shirttail trailing, everything too big. Our mother had bought our school clothes large enough to wear for the next three years. Marco looked like a traveler in somebody else's life.

I was one landing ahead of him. By the time he caught up to me, his skin had the familiar blue tint to it. He held the railing tight, his eyes straight ahead. It would always be this way. My brother was like those orchids Sister Ursula read to us about, the ones that only grew in a certain perfect air. No air was good enough for Marco. He was pale and thin, and the grief of his respiratory problems suffocated us all every day.

Mamma believed God had done Marco's sickness to her alone, like a slap in the eyes, a kick to the backs of the knees. Marco was her shirt of boar hair. Her punishment. She waited for us at the top of the stairs. That's how I see her to this day, outlined in grey by the dim hall light, scowling down at us.

Leticcia, you race you brother up stairs? What you think? She scolded in questions. What I am going to do? Why you no listen to you mamma?

To disagree or argue was an indictment against her, an insult; her face would crumple and cave, she would cross her arms, uncross them, open her palms to us, whine.

Why you hurt you poor mamma? Why you kill me so much?

How many times I tell you slow down!

You *pazza*, Leticcia? *Pazza?*

Si, Mamma, I am *pazza*. Crazy.

In the kitchen Nonna waited for us with glasses of American milk. Without our Tuzza, we had gotten used to the slippery, gluey taste of store milk.

*M*onna bought a radio at Zimo's Electronico and it was placed in a position of honor at the center of the kitchen table. For years we would eat our meals listening to the radio like it was an important guest. We listened to Cedric Adams and the news. We listened to the Lakers defeat the Knicks for the N.B.A. title, we listened when the Yankees won the World Series beating the Brooklyn Dodgers. We listened to Kate Smith (too bad Kate Smith wasn't Italian), we listened to Frank Sinatra, Tony Bennett, Louie Prima. We listened when Rocky Marciano won the heavyweight championship, we listened to Toscanini conduct Verdi, we listened as President Eisenhower was sworn in as thirty-fourth president. We listened to the Texaco Opera. We learned about the world because we listened to the radio.

Marco and I had dreams of owning a bicycle so we could explore the world. We had dreams of stealing our way outside Tar Town and peddling to the city limits where the capital city of Saint Paul shook hands with Minneapolis.

Downtown!

Cement and steel, flying skyways! Smells of office building lobbies and department store perfume counters! The endless arrays of exotic American foods! Wieners in buns, fried hamburger meat and cut up potatoes in paper boats, corn dogs on sticks, runny barbecued things, pretzels!

Cotton candy, Marco. Mayonnaise, popcorn!

Oh, to be a mouse on the street and observe the blond heads, the pale-fleshed faces; how we ached to be one of them. Translucent.

We could be like the Hi Ho Silver guy on the radio who always traveled around stamping out evil. We could pretend to be rich people who traveled to other places for no reason except to be going somewhere else.

The first Wednesday of the month was garbage pickup day. Wednesday, day of sprung gears, worn trappings and fittings, broken appliances, wheels going nowhere, unwanted levers, handspikes and sheaves, dead plants, soiled upholstery, books smelling of cats. Marco was skilled at sorting through trash with his fine slim fingers, an expert at winnowing out, tossing, keeping, cleaning, fixing. He was brilliant. A genius. And I, Leticcia ChiChi Maggiordino, was his angel.

Nonna said, Such a life for children. Drink you milk, every drops! And we should not think so much about garbage, we should learn about the world! Do good in school. Listen to the radio!

At the settlement house school, we were not supposed to speak Italian. Mamma watched with growing indifference as we learned English. Mamma angry, smoldering. I can't think of her face in those days without seeing its shine, as though she were oiled from within with some special incandescent substance that could ignite rain. Who knew what she thought? There, in her starched aprons, wool ankle socks, and chenille slippers, padding about room to room. What did she think as her small dark fingers held the mason jar just so while watering the fern in the window? And when her children were sitting in their classes at the settlement house or out gathering forbidden treasures for their inventions, did she stop existing entirely?

Nonna was different. Nonna talked, laughed, was a bottomless reservoir of stories; I was her ChiChi, her *amore*, and she slapped my behind with a hand like silk. I didn't wonder how she thought because she wore her thoughts in her words, in her actions, in kisses on the face, the arms, legs. *T'amo*, Chichilina, *t'amo*.

Nonna with a story. In Campania the sky so blue you can reach up and slice a big chunk to wear in you hair, is true! And she fell asleep with her mouth open, snoring and chattering in her sleep.

I wanted to remember Italy as she did, turn back the shadows, let my thoughts unwind like long ribbons, let my brain loose to drape itself on the soil of the country where I was born.

When Marco was strong enough to ride our scooter, we went on a treasure hunt and came upon a demolition on East Hennepin and discovered rock and brick treasures among the debris. Bricks! Rocks! Worn and disintegrating in our hands, exhausted, spent. We held them in our hands, talked to them the way you'd talk to an uncle deaf in one ear.

I see *il Mediterraneo* in this rock.

I see the Amalfi cliffs in this one.

No, you don't. That's Napoli.

We sat cross-legged in the dust of the condemned fenced-off lot.

Look ChiChi, here's Maiori.

What Is Maiori
By ChiChi Maggiordino

Mairoi is a place where war is. Our pappa lost his real
leg in the Allied invasion at Maiori. He was American
soldier and when he got wounded they took him to a
hospital that had been a monastery. The pews were
pushed up against the walls in the chapel to make way
for rows of beds for wounded Allied soldiers. Surgery
was done by kerosene lamplight and Pappa's real leg
was sawed off by a doctor without a shirt wearing a
rubber apron over his pants. The reason the doctor
didn't wear a shirt was so he could wash the blood off
himself easier. In the next room Italian carpenters were
hard at work building pine coffins to keep up with the
dying men. And that's what happened to his real leg.
A little later, after the terrible hole where his leg had
been got healed, he got a wooden leg to wear. Mamma
was a volunteer worker and Pappa wasn't the only soldier who fell in love with her. Mamma and Pappa got
married and, and then Pappa got killed.

                        The End.

We kept the wooden leg in the kitchen by the door. Summer afternoons when the apartment was so hot we stuck to
the chairs with our sweat, I was sure the leg spoke to us,
asked to be moved near the window to catch a breeze.

We came to call the leg *Pappa*. When we swept the
kitchen or washed the floor, I asked Mamma, I'd say, should
I move Pappa to the closet?

Marco and I searched the rocks for explanations, defini-
tions, reasons, equations, something we could hold on to
and then sit back telling ourselves, yes, that's it, that's it. That
explains everything, doesn't it?

Mamma's face bent inward, pouting. Please, no bring no more junk in here! This house she look like war zone. You want live in war zone?

I wasn't sure what a war zone was. Maybe Maiori. I carried Pappa to the hall, straightened out the sock, adjusted the shoe so he leaned just right against the wall, and then I gave him the tiniest of kisses right at the point of the off-cutting.

C ame 1954, the year the U.S. Supreme Court declared segregation in public schools unconstitutional. The year the Salk polio vaccine was licensed in the United States and the year the U.S. Senate condemned Joseph McCarthy for abuse and misconduct; it was the year Under God was added to the Pledge of Allegiance.

Nonna planted a garden alongside the house. *Melanzane, basilico,* arugula, tomatoes, peppers. What Italian didn't have a vegetable garden? Dirt is good for one thing only: for planting seeds. So we ate *melanzane, basilico,* arugula, tomatoes, and peppers every day.

Melanzane, melanzane, such a nice sounding word for eggplant, I said.

Eggplant, said Mamma, like you head.

Hey, she said suddenly, using some of her new English words. Marco, he go away for one week. Maybe two.

Marco had won the Our Lady of Mount Carmel Junior Writing Contest. The prize, because he was so-called handicapped, happened to be two weeks at Whispering Valley Camp For God's Special Boys and Girls

You should be president, Nonna told him.

Handicap, said Mamma. Is special. How's about that?

Handicap as a word made me stutter.

I looked past the wooden leg against the wall to the closed window over the sink. I could see a small patch of sky. Sky the color of a brown paper bag. The color of an army jacket.

Signora Constanza, from the church benevolent commit-
tee, brought us the news. She handed Mamma the letter and
wore an expression of sympathy, as though the occasion were
someone's funeral. I realize, she said, it's not easy here for
you, Signora Maggiordino. Yet—(she sighed)—we know all
is in God's hands and suffering is, you know, a part of the
great tapestry of life.

Had we heard that one before? Marco and I laughed out
loud.

But! Marco going away! I felt my face drop off my head.
Bravo, Marcuccio! tolled Nonna.

He looked like someone told him his ears were linked to
explosives. He thought the winner of that contest was suppose to get a set of Minnesota wildlife books.

Mamma got the old suitcase from the closet, the bag that
had carried the cheese, salami, and *limone liquore* to Ellis Island and the Promised Land five years ago. She packed the
new clothes she bought with the checks she now received
each month, clothes placed in the bag like pieces of a soft
puzzle.

Mamma believed in warm clothes because a person could
always take clothes off. But a heavy sweater or a wool coat,
she not live in trees.

Maybe I'll just stay home with ChiChi. Okay?

Never! screamed Mamma, who was grateful to everyone
in the Holy Catholic Church, the nuns, the priests, the laity,
the pope, for such an honor as this, giving her son an opportunity to learn about the Great Out-of-Doors.

When Marco left for Whispering Valley, I walked around
the apartment in circles, trailing from the sofa to the chair,
to the kitchen sink to the bathroom towel rack, to my bed,
to the window, to Mamma's bedroom, her dresser. I played

with the objects on the dresser top, a brush, comb, hair clips, an empty rosewater bottle, until she burst at me, threw her arms into the air, Leticcia! Stop! You bring me crazy!

I'm worried is all, Mamma. Who's taking care of him?

A slap on the side of the head. Saint Christopher, the Virgin, *e Gesù Cristo!*

Another slap. Selfish Leticcia! Why you not happy for you brother?

But I *was* happy. See how happy I was?

Marco, listen. My wires are pulled and I'm plugged into nothing. I'm disconnected, unhinged. It's nice that the disabled kids with their secret diseases and damaged bodies get to go to camp and I don't. Am I a terrible person? Me with my healthy lungs, my good body? Am I? Please answer.

In this state of mind I swept our bedroom so clean you could kiss the floor with your mouth open.

I left the apartment to go for a walk. The landlady's granddaughter Natalie, who had just moved in, bounced a ball by the porch steps. She was a year older than me, twice as big. High whining voice, she smelled like bad fruit. She glared at me like she had pencils stuck up her nose.

So how come your brother gets to go to camp and you have to stay home? She sniffed and talked at the same time.

She stood in front of me, crossed her arms. Catholics are going to burn in hell, she said, because you worship the pope who is only a man. Did I, Leticcia Maggiordino, worship the pope?

Natalie was American and spoke good American. She went to Pierce Elementary with the kids who lived on the other side of Central Avenue. Her grandfather, our landlord, was named Franco and he hung around the house all day and didn't work. We'd see him occasionally at Our Lady of Mount Carmel Church hunched in a pew muttering his rosary.

Talk to your grandparents about the pope, I said.

They aren't real Catholics. They believe in *Jesus,* not *Mary,* she snarled, jamming her face up close to mine.

You know what, Natalie?

What.

I cranked my elbow at her. *Va fa n'culu,* Natalie.

I walked to 17th and Washington to watch the construction of the new senior high-rise apartment building. It was the first time I told anyone *up your ass.* Marco would love it. I stood with my fingers curled around the wire fence and watched the men haul and guide lumber and steel girders from the forklifts and cranes. I watched the steel beams make geometric patterns on the sky like thick crayon lines. Marco and I could ride on the end of one of those steel beams, us, human paintbrushes and part of a cosmic linear design, the sun bouncing off our backs and making reflections of ourselves on the world below. I could feel my body soaring through the air, high above the city, the heat, the dust, the Natalies and the peculiar Protestants. Marco and I floating and gliding on solid steel, painting the sky with ourselves. I was no longer disconnected. I was attached. I was flying sure and steady on steel.

Mamma sat on the sofa studying a newspaper, its pages cast around her lap like cabbage leaves. She glanced up, looked at me, and then returned her attention to the newspaper.

Hunh. So it's you.

Mamma, what if Marco doesn't take his medicine on

time? What if he gets cold out there in the wilderness? Suppose he plays too hard, has a relapse?

She smacked the newspaper shut. *Basta!* Enough! You nose going to fall off you worry so much! Why you no give you mamma some peace?

But what if he falls in the lake? Drowns?

Gesù, Maria!

I was starting to panic. I had my hand in my mouth.

Vattene, Leticcia. Go away! And stop how you eat you fingers.

When you're nine, almost ten, and an experienced steel girder flyer, when you can brush tops of skyscrapers with your shadow, you can fork your pasta onto a Melmac plate and sit on the chair in the kitchen without turning on the light. You wonder what they're feeding your brother and you smear tomato sauce around on the Formica tabletop with your finger. You pour a glass of milk and you hold it in your hand. You sit there for a long time. You drop your pasta shells in your milk, dump it in the garbage, and go to your room. At nine years old you think you're born to sit on steel, fly the skies, leap stairs six at a time with your healthy self, you're Nonna's Chichilina, a lover of stories, but you're stuck, disconnected on earth with all your wires sprung. You entered that essay contest, too.

*E*very disease has its first symptom. The cold that starts with the first cough, sniffle, the torn nose membrane. Marco's asthma happened with his first scream for air. Nonna said his lung affliction began on the Mississippi flats in *La Merica*. Would he grow up to be big and strong like Joe DiMaggio? No. Not possible said the doctor. Disease, at a juncture, meets with words where war happens. Now his lungs were scarred. *Fibrosis,* a terrible word. Like burnt lilacs, the word had a smell to it. Rotted newsprint, pig drool.

I started writing things down in a notebook.

Marco came home on Saturday. The orange-and-yellow school bus grunted up our street, rocking back and forth like a loose rolling apple. It read SPECIAL across its front. At the corner, it came to a swaying stop and an enormous Negro nurse wearing white stockings and white shoes eased herself down the three steps. She held Marco's suitcase with one hand and a bulging shopping bag in the other. Sideways she came. One foot, other foot, feet together. One foot, other foot, feet together. Ahh.

Marco hopped along behind her. He wore sunglasses with magenta rims and a green cap emblazoned with ALWAYS A WINNER in bright yellow. The rows of other children on the bus wore the same caps. They waved at him from the windows, jerky, happy arms, high little kid voices, Good-bye! Good-bye!

Marco jumped from the bus step to the pavement, thin hair flipping up as he made the final landing.

This is my sister, he explained to the nurse.

Me-oh-my, child, you think you can carry these heavy things all by yourself? she said to me, all breath and sugar. I said, no problem, I was not one of God's special boys and girls, I could DO stuff.

How sparkly the street became. A planet of happiness had dropped right down on Taylor and Summer Streets. You sure made a TON of artwork, I said, limping with his bags. He hopped at my side, touched my arms, my face. Oh ChiChi, ChiChi. He had so much to tell me.

A breeze like honey, Marco and me, skipping cracks and turning circles around each other, him promising he would never go to camp again without me and us laughing and talking for two days straight, even during Mass, me especially flabbergasted at the works of art he created. Drawings of suns pushing against hills and tops of trees, assemblages made of fish bones, clam shells, twigs, and pinecones. Collages of leaves and bird feathers, casein paintings of roads lined with wortweed, sunflowers, and trailing bluebells, each named and labeled. He had fashioned tiny vests and necklaces of braided dandelion stems, created ribboned wreaths dipped in the plumes of dried hyacinth (labeled *hia*sinth.)

At the bottom of the shopping bag was a notebook of crayon drawings of children playing, tossing balls, swimming, eating, praying. In the lower half of each page something that made my stomach quiver, my neck go wobbly. An ominous epigraph. On every single page, real small so you could hardly make out what it was, Marco had drawn a row of wheelchairs, each one empty.

Were there lots of kids in wheelchairs? I asked him.

Enough, he said.

The cold begins with that first cough and sniffle. Autumn was happening like a lapse of memory. Sweater weather, knee socks, smells of burning leaves, mosquitoes gone back to their swamps. Frost whiskers on the storm windows. Us blowing in our hands, pulling up our collars. Camphor and winter.

Mamma sat in silence by the window, the carpet worn where her feet rubbed at it, she sat and she waited and she said, what will be will be. I wouldn't be like Mamma, no. She wasn't making a plan with her brain at all. She said she would make a plan with her brain. If I let myself be like her, my face would become her face, blank and staring out the window as she counted passing freight cars. I'd be empty like her, empty, as, as, as, a kid's empty wheelchair.

Nonna listened to Perry Como on the radio. She said if we sang along with Perry Como we'd learn to speak English perfect.

I began going through things in the apartment. Drawers and cupboards, I opened anything with a lid or a handle. I snooped under the sofa cushions, behind chairs, inside containers, jars. I wasn't looking for anything special, I was just checking on what was there or not there. Checking. Making sure. Taking account. I wrote things down in my notebook. Three candles of a peanutty color, a Number 2 pencil without an eraser, a bank deposit slip . . .

Keep looking. I said short incantations and blessed Mamma's pillow and then Nonna's pillow in the name of the Father, the Son, and *Spirito Santo*. They needed me. Oh how they needed me.

I shouldn't have poked around the closet Mamma shared with Nonna, but Nonna had left for Our Lady of Mount Carmel Church with Signora Lucca to play *Briscola* and Mamma was in the basement putting a load of darks in the washing machine. What was I supposed to do with myself? I had to keep control, guarantee our safety, had to take charge. I ran my hands over Nonna's clothes, smelled the hems and folds, and came upon a small tin box, the sort a store-bought *pasticcino* came in.

What are you doing? Marco in the doorway.

Praying.

Call that praying?

I'm making sure everything's okay, I said. The tin box was still in my hands.

Mamma will kill you dead.

He returned to our room to draw with his Whispering Pines pens.

I opened the box. Inside was a leather folder held together by a frayed black ribbon. I slid the ribbon off and pulled apart the folder.

Photographs of sleeping babies!

Each baby wore the same ruffled and lacy night dress like it was some grand occasion, say a wedding or baptism.

ChiChi! (Marco's warning.)

I replaced the box and hurried out of the room just as Mamma entered the back door with her laundry basket.

Mamma stood at the front door as we left for school the next Friday. She grabbed my arm as I passed her and handed me an embroidered handkerchief from her drawer.

You like this so much, Signorina Leticcia, you take it.

I looked at the floor, guilty.

She took hold of my chin like she might give me a kiss and then slapped me hard. Next time you touch my things, she growled, I'm break you face. You keep your *culu* out of my room! I'm break you face good!

Marco watched from the hallway, mouth jacked downward, face a sticky shade of grey. ChiChi, he whispered, *non ti preoccupare,* don't worry yourself, just don't let her worry yourself.

I'm not worried, I said.

He pushed his hands in his pockets. ChiChi, I don't like it when she says those things.

Puh, I said. It's just part of the great tapestry of life.

That always got a laugh out of him.

Snow flurries in October. Mamma wouldn't let us ride our scooter to school. (You break you legs! You smash you head! You kill you face!) So we walked to school kicking at the dead weeds in the cracks of the sidewalk.

I once saw someone's mamma laugh, Marco said.

Naw. Mammas don't laugh. They're not supposed to. Only Nonnas laugh, I said.

Marco gave a chuckle when I said that. And I laughed. HAHAHEE.

I felt like singing. Let's sing a song, Marco.

Sul mare lucica—

Hey, Marco, don't you want to sing with me?

Naw.

The bread wrappers we wore over our shoes to keep them dry in the snow crinkled on the pavement.

How come you won't sing?

All right, all right, ChiChi. How about we sing "Home on the Range"!

That's a stupid song.

It's a *American* song.

But it doesn't make sense, I said. Where the dear Anne Auntie Lou play—

Marco gave a crackly stomp with his foot. He talked in his muffler. You know what this kid called me at camp? This kid at camp called me a F.O.B.! Ever hear of that?

F.O.B.? No. What's that?

Fresh-Off-The-Boat! Do I look like I'm Fresh Off The Boat?

Madonn'a, no!

You know why he called me that?

Why?

Because I didn't know the words to "Home on the Range."

The air smelled of wood smoke and frost on leaves.

What'd you do for revenge?

I stole his medicine.

Santissimo! The guy's medicine.

There it was again. You try to fit in. Pretend you're right at home on the range, and what is range anyhow? A stove? The world was not a Hot Diggity Dog Ziggity Boom What You Do To Me sort of place like Perry Como sang.

Insulin, said Marco. I stole his insulin.

How could you do that? What if something terrible happened to the kid?

I shivered, suddenly cold.

Shoot, Cheech. I put it back. I just did it to scare him.

The sky was grey and spitting out trees. We were quiet, then Marco said, How come you're walking on the sides of your feet like that? Something wrong with your leg?

I'm pretending it's lopped off above the knee, I said.

Marco took my hand, turned his toes out, and limped along beside me on the sides of his feet.

Nonna managing her life in Tar Town as she had her life in Campania. Nonna, friend of store clerks, strangers, priests, the volunteer ladies and nuns at the Madeline Brown Settlement House, men and women, young and old. She made it her business to know the business of as many of the neighbors as she could. She sought out old *paisani* to share conversation and gossip, *una tazza di caffè*, slices of cake. They shared thimbles of *Limoncello* saved in cupboards from back home. Summers Nonna sat outside in the shade at the side of the house slapping mosquitoes with the women trading stories and complaints. *Sta' senti.*

Yes, yes, we're listening, said the ladies.

When the weather turned cold, the women sat in each other's kitchens. With their approving and disapproving dark eyes, their bodies smelling of bread dough and sour milk, their hair tied up in kerchiefs, these women were our dispassionate aunts, women who regarded children as household necessities, like salt or oregano.

The women asked about Mamma's strange ways and Nonna dismissed the questions with a shrug, a lift of one shoulder, a *tsk*, a flutter of a hand, *La vita è dura, non vi scordate*, don't forget the life she hard, she said. Mamma was a closed subject. The life she hard, and for some of us, *troppo* hard.

The women sighed, drank their coffee. *Mah*, she is cold fish, that one, they said into their sleeves. They turned their backs when Mamma approached on the street or in church, gave a crisp *buon giorno*, and didn't look her in the face.

Nonna was proud of Marco and me. *Venite, ragazzi miei,*

she called when fanning herself on a lawn chair in the summer or sitting by the stove in the winter.

See how beautiful are my children? (She always called us *her* children.) How smart! How clever! Sing once more, my children, *i miei amori!* And Marco and I took each others' hands and bellowed out in our smartest, cleverest voices the ribald lyrics of "Lazy Mary, Will You Get Up" to the delighted clapping hands of the women.

Nonna and her women friends sat at the kitchen table, their voices drifting down the hall to our room. Nonna stirred a pot of boiling fruit for *pastice* while Signora Lucca talked about the future. We should think of the future, she said, and forget the past. The past, she is finished, but the future—the future we can bow down to.

What you say? Nonna's voice an octave higher than usual. The past is everything! How many sons you bury? Your husband, does he still walk above this earth? Eh? How many daughters you have without men? How many evils you got to pay back?

Evils to pay back?

Sì! How many debts you got to collect? Eh?

Debts . . . Ooh. *La vendetta!* A curse returned.

They stirred the sugar in their coffee.

N'a vendetta. Capimmo.

Vendetta they understood.

And I began to understand, too. I turned to look at my mother who sat at the window alone, the darkness we lived in had something to do with *la vendetta.*

Fiction is imagination and imagination is fiction. Marco and I sang "Fratelli Di Italia," the Italian National Anthem, and the women wept in their handkerchiefs. Nonna fed us al-

mond cake and black coffee and now I try to remember
what can't be deciphered, I labor with codes in alien con-
figurations, and the images popping up here and there, images that are as real and true as the skin on my hands, but
without classification and too far away to hold on to. Marco
and I would have cut out our tongues for our Nonna, would
have gladly left a toe or a kneecap on the altar in the church
in exchange for her health and long life. When we learned
the word *love* the picture we drew up was the darling creased,
brown face of Nonna.

And what would she say if she knew I sneaked into her
closet almost every day to look at the baby photographs? I
had chosen one photo as my favorite, the one of the child
with hair like ivy. Where was he now? Who were these
children?

During the day Mamma sat in the chair by the window
staring out, her face set as in sleep. Pappa's wooden leg
leaned against the kitchen door as part of the family and was
moved only when Nonna's lady friends visited. Nonna entertained her friends in the kitchen rolling out pastry dough
on the tabletop, her hands thick with flour (she had a *love
relationship* with flour), apron tied around her waist, stockings
leveled at the ankles, her feet settled in slippers worn to the
shape of her crooked toes and bunions. *Figli miei!* she
shouted when she heard us coming in the door. Come greet
to Signora Musetti, or Signora Luppo, or Signora Ciccione—
Signora this, Signora that. Come here you two and show
Signora Fuetti how smart you are. Sing for us "Oh Beautiful
for Lotsa Skies," okay? Okay? No more "Lazy Mary."

She enjoyed gossip as much as cooking or eating. It was
an important element of living. She told how a young man
from Firenze wanted to marry our aunt, Filomina. But
Nonno, our grandfather, he say he too big the head. Those

men of the north, he said they were foolish and proud.
Noses in their armpits he say, and not a callus on their hands.
Now poor Filomina is an old maid at the age of twenty-
five. No man will have her.

Mamma's face became a corruption of primary colors
when Nonna spoke of the sisters. *Puh! Puh!* Filomina should
have *Mamma's* sorrows!

Now now, *Amore,* hush. The children will hear—
Puh!

Nonna found me with the baby photographs.

She let out a scream. *Mah! Che fai?*

I'm sorry—I'm only—

Mah! Tu! Che fai?

Doing? *Niente. Niente.*

She puffed out her cheeks. How you can say *nothing?* You
have in you hands my *sons.* And she slapped my ear.

She looked more sad than angry, picked up one of the
photographs. Her face went spongy, completely vulnerable,
as if at that moment an armed person had burst in and
shouted, Your life or the photos! She would have willingly
taken a bullet in the neck. My Nino, she said.

A little boy with full round cheeks, spidery eyelashes, a
mass of black hair like a lake of purple grapes. So pretty
asleep.

Asleep? *Si.* ChiChi, Nino is asleep in the arms of angels.
(What's that?)

Dead! The babies are *dead?*

Three dead babies, their heads on satin pillows and dressed
like small princes in the same white baptism dress, babies
never photographed when alive.

The expression on my face gave her a grunt. Poor ChiChi,

always thinking and worrying. She tapped my head with her thumb and said she knew a girl in Italy who did so much thinking, all her hair fell out. She became bald. No man would have her.

She stared at her lap and then said how every year she gave birth to a son, but by the next year she was laying a son in the ground.

I find Nino with dirt in his mouth, on his face, she said. I say, No eat dirt! But what can you do when babies, they hungry? *Gesù, Maria, e Giuseppe*, mother's children eat dirt for their meat!

My grandfather's watch ticked on the dresser. Nonna stood, said, Each of my babies, they look like Marco.

It was quiet and then she said, Your mamma must not know about this. Listen, babies make good saints, no? Because they suffer worst sorrow. They not get chance to grow up. So God, He make the little babies saints. You uncle Nino, he a saint. Now *andiamo!* Let's get out of here before your mamma finds us looking at these pictures and it make her cry.

She replaced the box in the closet and gave me a look I understood. ChiChi had stolen some of her suffering. ChiChi must pay sorrow with sorrow.

$\mathcal{S}$ ister Ursula tells us we can be anything we want to be. When she says this, the room becomes very quiet. The city outside our windows stops breathing.

I can feel all my body parts. I can feel my kneecaps, my lower teeth, the pores of my nose, the dome where my thighs meet, the webs of hair on the back of my neck.

Be anything?

Did that mean Mamma had the same permission to be whatever she wanted? And Marco? And everyone I ever knew or would know? *Santissimo, Gesù, Maria!*

Sister Ursula's mustache bristles above a plump lip and uneven teeth. Her fingers tremble in blessing.

Joey Minichilli stands in the corner of the room beneath the American flag. He jams his finger into the pencil sharpener on the wall. He grinds the handle and makes horrible faces. Carlina Ricci giggles into her *Weekly Reader.*

I feel my mother's shame. I press my eyes shut, the shame of being looked at, examined. Mamma won't allow someone to look too long into her eyes. Her hands move to her mouth, her face collapses all sour and damaged. She doesn't know her soul can't be taken from her by a simple gaze.

Sister Ursula goes right on telling us how we are the future generation, the hope of tomorrow.

Us! Twelve children with runny noses and ragged elbows. We look around at each other, surprised, dopey. Carlo Umbria throws a spitball at Carlina Ricci. I try to think of objects to define this idea of tomorrow: a brace and bit, tape measure, shovel, string, faucet, trowel, paintbrush, plaster, bricks, the entire *Child's First Book of Mechanics,* Marco's inhalator. I don't remember the future. I know right *now.* Me, sitting at my desk in Sister Ursula's classroom at the settlement house pulling on my sock and chewing my braid.

Joey Minichilli gets his name written on the blackboard for sticking his finger in the pencil sharpener again. So does Louisa Genoese. When you get your name written on the blackboard it means God has to turn his face. This is no way to prepare for First Communion.

Boys and girls, you are born into this world to contribute to this world, says Sister Ursula without getting up from her desk. Born. A shiver flies up the insides of my arms. My brother born. My brother dying.

Antony DeSantis, the new boy in the desk next to mine, pipes up, I'm going to be a soldier, he shouts, Fight in war! I'll kill those *Naziste* bastards!

The *Naziste* had burned down his town and killed his family. He shakes his fist. How-you-say, contribution, Sister Ursula? I do contribution. I kill the bastards.

Twelve 5th graders cheer. *Mazza le bastardi!*

The war is over, Sister Ursula tells us in her calm, toothy voice. There will be others, you can be sure of that, but the war you speak of is over, Antony. Our Savior has told us to love our enemies. Which is not easy, I understand. That is why He died to send you the Holy Spirit—so you can love and be loving. Trust Him.

Antony lets out a snort. His eyes burn with so much heat, his tears are like little matches that could set all our hair on fire.

Marco is coughing again. I can hear the scattered chunks of his breathing. Here comes the future.

That night I slip out of bed and walk on the outside edges of my feet to the living room. Mamma sits in her chair by the window wearing her brown worn bathrobe, her hair pulled into a thick long braid. She embroiders cross stitches on a dish towel.

Mamma?

She seems small in her nightclothes, reduced to soft flannel and undone hair. The night is large and autumn rushes up the stairs at us, chilling the floorboards and smelling like gunsmoke.

Figlia . . . Why you not sleeping?

Mamma, guess what.

Uh?

Today was my birthday.

She doesn't look up. Ah. *Buon Compleanno, Cara.*

Thank you, Mamma.

Go to bed.

She raises her eyes without moving her head. *Buona notte—amore.*

Back in our room, Marco snores like an old man. I lower myself to my knees at my bed.

I remove the rosary from my pocket where Nonna had put it so I wouldn't forget to pray. Yes, pray. *Buon Compleanno, Cara.* Happy birthday to me. . . .

I'll wear a white dress for First Communion, white, the color of purity and innocence. Purified in preparation for the sacrament, purified in body, my sins confessed as purification of the conscience. Leticcia ChiChi Maggiordino comes to Jesus prepared to partake of the body and blood of Holy Communion, this I will do in remembrance of

Him. In the name of the Father and of the Son, and of the Holy Spirito. Amen. I believe in God the Father Almighty, Creator of heaven and stinky old shitty earth. . . .

Once a month a dreaded volunteer nurse came to our school to do routine checkups. I wanted to hide Marco from her clutches. She was a large woman whose nylon stockings made a sound like snoring when she walked or crossed her legs. She sat on a folding chair in a room used as the ladies' sewing room and we lined up at the door for her to poke at us. We felt like Ellis Island.

Did we eat breakfast regularly? (Poke, poke.)

Scusi? Speak a little slower please.

I *said*—do—you—eat—breakfast—regularly?

Nurse Nimm was her name, a woman with the raucous, noisy legs. Did we sleep eight to nine hours at night? Did we eat at least one piece of fruit a day? Did we brush our teeth? We answered yes to everything even if we hadn't slept, eaten, or brushed. We wanted to appear healthy, vigorous, smart, and happy, worthy of being American. We would never admit to weakness, even though sometimes when she poked our stomachs and tapped our chests we felt like falling down. Carla DiGidio came to school with a toothache that grew worse until her cheek swelled like a melon, but when Nurse Nimm questioned her, Carla said she was fine, no problems whatsoever. No, *mamma mia* no, this was her normal face, she took after her father whose face was also an eggplant.

We knew what Nurse Nimm thought of us. Her hesitant hands like mice touching our wrists for the pulse of our blood, the disdain in those hands when she thumped our backs for echoes of illness, when she inoculated our downy

arms, examined our eyes and ears, and always avoided looking directly into our faces which were so dark they hoarded
light and reflected back to her mere blank stares. She inter-
preted these stares as expressions of ignorance.

Marco stood before her, his scrawny arms crossed on his
chest. Nurse Nimm read from the sheet on her clipboard.
How often do you get colds?

Never.

Never?

Never.

What about that cough?

I don't cough. I clear my throat.

We had our pride. All our mothers were GOOD
COOKS, our bellies were ALWAYS full, our bathwater always HOT and SOAPY. When Nurse Nimm picked
through our hair with her pencil and examined our ears and
waists for worms and bugs, we readied ourselves for the
fight.

That's not a bite. I bumped myself is all.

Uh. Huh. Really. Well, tell me, Salvatore, when is the last
time you took a bath?

Uh. Huh. Tell me, Nursie, when is the last time you took
a biscotto up the *culu*?

Sometimes we were punished.

Sister Ursula wants us to write a paper about what we want
to be one day. Can it be that Sister Ursula is connected to
mysterious voices behind doors and inside books that speak
in a language only she hears and understands? She tries to
pass these messages on to us, and it's transmitted as a jumble
of sound. Was it Sister's prayers that helped us survive Nurse
Nimm?

Wires are sprung left and right. Okay, this is America. I sit with one ankle twisted around the other. I am not wearing clean socks.

What did Sister Ursula hear in her head? Did Sister Ursula hear the voice of God speaking directly to her? Did He hold her hand by day and by night blow kisses from heaven to her dear hooded ears? (Marry me, honey bunch!)

Could God love a girl with dirty feet? A girl with socks gone grey rolled down in her shoes like an old person's eyelids? The other children, with parents from Napoli and Salerno, Catania and Palermo, wore socks like mine. By our feet you can tell we lived in Tar Town and we learned English at a settlement house—where we struggled with more than the tangled spellings and boring pronunciation of English words.

Nurse Nimm makes us realize we must never let our guard down, we must always be on the lookout. We must watch out for the enemy, for those who might hurt us or our families. And now we're supposed to write a paper about what we want to BE one day? Oh, that's a good one, Sister Ursula.

Sister Ursula says people are born to be what they will become.

Hunh? You mean great people like Giuseppe Verdi, Leonardo DaVinci, Gugliermo Marconi, Brunelleschi, Garibaldi?

Yes, Marco, says Sister Ursula.

Not a girl's name among them.

We must climb into the Great Mind of God, my children, and know His loving thoughts toward us. Then we will fulfill His desire for us.

Okay. We are born to be what we are. My white Communion dress and veil, Marco's white shirt and black tie, our first gulps of God in a wafer and sip of red table wine, our Blessed First Communion and all the prayers in the world can't change things, can't make Marco well. He coughed through the mass, and was so exhausted when it was over, he fell asleep in his new shirt and tie over his soup at dinner.

How would it happen? It might be July or February and Nurse Nimm would call me for a little private chitchat. I'll tell her she was wrong, whatever news she had for me is the wrong news, there is a place of Perfect Safety for Marco and me. Couldn't the world wait to eat up his air? We're smart, we're clever, art lovers, singers, collaborators of inventions. We are God's little lambs, like Sister Ursula said. We're good, *good* little lambs.

November. Snow falls like teeth.

The wind is an angry mouth. By December it will chew us senseless.

Winter with camphor and potions, closed windows, medicines, steam.

Marco's cough.

The Future.

Marco, I remember you wrapped in the red and black plaid blanket, wool scarf around your neck—you're sitting by the gas stove in the living room where it's warm. A pan of water sits on top of the stove in an effort to spread moisture in the stale air. You're reading a book about trains. You reek of Vicks. I had scraped my knee and Nonna bandaged it with the skin of an onion. I reek of onion. Remember?

Nonna tells us stories to cheer us up. How would a young boy named Giorgio get revenge on a cunning farmer who sold him a sick goat? Marco and I slap our hips and harumph at Giorgio's ignorance. Giorgio must do something to keep his pride! *Vendetta!* But how? says Nonna. He is only a little boy. This is a serious matter, you see.

Giorgio should kick the bastard in the *coglione,* Marco yells.

Scuzi? says Nonna. You can't end every dispute with a kick.

Which reminds Nonna of another story. There was once a man who fought for Mussolini in the war and in a big battle he lose his trousers . . . The trousers, they go flying through the air to a little hut where sits a young girl sewing. The trousers fall in her lap and nine months later she give birth to a baby boy!

She laughs so hard, she wipes tears from her chin.

Marco was still thinking of Giorgio's revenge.

Mamma listens, her mouth closed tight like a hyphen. She cleans around us, brushing lint from the sofa, shaking the embroidered and tatted coverlets, wiping the coffee table surface with the edge of her apron. When Nonna leans back on the sofa cushion and snores, the stories finished for the day, Mamma sits in her chair by the window, back erect. She watches the train yard across the street and speaks to the window glass.

La vendetta, says Mamma in a loud voice. Giorgio will get revenge with *Il Mal Occhio,* the Evil Eye.

My ankles go soft.

Mamma looks directly at me. Ask you Nonna to tell you about *Il Mal Occhio*. It is big powers. Ask her. Evil Eye not only is charm for luck. Not is superstition! *Il Mal Occhio* work like magic from God if used right. Ask you Nonna.

A cold breeze blows across the floor and Marco cheers *Brava!* before erupting in a shattering chorus of coughs.

What did Mamma know of *Il Mal Occhio*? What stories did she and Nonna share at night as Marco and I slept in our beds? Sometimes when I awoke in the mornings I thought I had heard her voice, low and smooth, telling her story, but then I shook the thought away. Maybe it was a dream. Did I dream her whispering to Nonna that she should not have walked to the piazza to the dance that night so long ago? She should not have talked to him, the handsome American airman in beige, should not have blushed at his touch, lost her knowledge of breath when he spoke her name, *Giuseppina*.

There was the story I must have dreamed and only now am remembering, the story she told about her wedding day, and about the witch. About the old man who lived in our village called a *stregone,* witch. Mamma said she was terrified of him. He wore tattered rags on his twisted, crippled body, and his face was always streaked with sand and dirt. But worst of all, Mamma said, was his smile. His perpetual smile was so horrible, it frightened children half to death. Mamma would run and hide when she saw him on the street as if he were *il diavolo* himself. The *stregone*'s smile was ferocious, contaminating. It sent poison to the brain, she said. It was a venom that seeped into a girl's heart and lungs; it could lay a girl out dead on a slab of white wood with only a spring of dried sage to keep her company. Yes, that horrible.

She wore the wedding dress that had been her sister Felicia's. (The dress was too small for her and the top part had to be pinned together in the back with a wool scrap used for mending winter jackets. This was Nonna's job.) The day of the wedding—I can hear Mamma tell it even now, but I am still not sure I dreamed it. She was alone in the house of her mother staring out the window at the cliffs of the mountain, and beyond the blue of the sea, so blue it was red, filled with blood, she said. She turned to the door and who do you think was standing there! Like an evil omen not two feet from her was the *stregone!* Smiling! His eyes stung her. She became paralyzed with the burning weight of his eyes. He kept smiling at her, and Mamma said she went deaf. She could hear no music in the courtyard, no sound of voices in the street, no laughter, no clatter of dishes in the kitchen. There was only the thunder of that smile and then the thud.

Mamma got married with a bloodied right eye and a headache the size of Pompeii, and Aunt Felicia said she fainted on purpose just so she could tear the dress.

Poor Mamma couldn't remember a thing about the wedding. Couldn't remember the sleeve of her groom touching hers as they knelt at the altar, nor the brush of his lips as they were pronounced married, nor his hand on her waist leading her in the first dance. She remembered only the heinous smile of the *stregone.*

In the weeks that followed, Mamma practiced the secret powers of *Il Mal Occhio,* which Nonna taught her. Then something strange happened. On a deserted path of weeds and tares along the road to Amalfi, the dead body of the *stregone* was found. He had been dead for almost three weeks, but his face had the gentle expression of a child asleep.

And Mamma was pregnant.

*M*arco shuffles the cards on his bed for a game of *Scopa* and I decide to check out Nonna's closet once more. Marco hates it when I leave in the middle of a game, complains it's just because he's winning. I grope around in the darkness of Nonna's closet amid the smells of lime sachet, old sweat, and pine. I find the tin box of photographs and it gives me a queasy, throw-up sensation. These babies weren't just any dead babies, let us face facts, these were my uncles, *famiglia*. And Nonna said Baby Nino was a *saint*. Isn't that what Nonna had said? God rewards babies for dying so early and makes them saints. Isn't that exactly what Nonna had said? Didn't I need another saint on my side what with winter on our backs? What with Marco's sickness and Mamma's troubles? It was up to me to act, wasn't it? I tuck Baby Nino's photo inside the flap of my red wool cap. I cross myself and push the cap tight over my head and ears. Who needs *Il Mal Occhio?* I have a *saint* in my hat. Marco wins at *Scopa* again.

What to clean next? What could Mamma scrub, wipe, dust, polish? What to sweep? What to rid of dirt, of its past? The wallpaper with its tired blue and yellow poppies? The one thing she was proud of was the carpet remnant she bought at a restaurant going-out-of-business sale on East Hennepin.

She liked to sweep it, bend down and pick flecks of dust with her fingernails, liked to stand back and admire. The carpet had once warmed the floor of the restaurant's ladies' rest room and had a faint bathroomy smell to it. I thought the flowery pattern was as dull as dandruff and without stories. I imagined the ladies who relieved themselves and then powdered their noses standing on this carpet. Their shoes ate the roses.

Temperature: 9° below zero Fahrenheit, windchill 15° below zero, a bit of a nippy winter afternoon in our beautiful Twin Cities. Nonna and I walked against the wind to D'Amico's grocery, Nonna in her heavy black coat and shawl, me in my jacket big enough for a fat boy. I wore my red wool cap with the photograph of Saint Baby Nino tucked inside. Nonna wanted to explain something to me. She wanted to be alone with me.

The wind hit us hard as we turned the corner on Summer Street. Nonna stopped short, pulled herself up, sucked in her breath, and struck a pose as in preparation to blow her human breath back at the storm. I thought she was making a joke and I started to laugh until she raised her arm and with an angry thrust, then shot it out in front of her chest while forming the Evil Eye with her fingers.

The gesture startled me. Nonna!

Her body was rigid in its intent, her face fierce, like when she spoke of the *Naziste*.

Nonna! What are you doing? Are you trying to stop the wind?

Not me, she said through her teeth. *Il Mal Occhio!*

Il Mal Occhio can stop the wind? Is it possible?

She gave a snigger. ChiChi, what you think, she said.

How you think *Gesù Cristo* stopped storm on Sea of Galilee?

Our Lord Jesus used the Evil Eye to do miracles? I said this in amazement. Sister Ursula had hidden this information from us. Father Tuttifucci never said!

Certo! What you think?

She spoke with her free hand circling in front of her as though beating back the forces of darkness.

How you suppose they finally stop Mussolini? *Il Mal Occhio!* Evil Eye to them all!

The war again. She'd never forget the war. War was in her body, her bones.

I pulled my cap down over my forehead, jumped on one foot.

Listen to me—*Le Naziste* blow up railroad tracks, they bomb everything. They make Napoli like dust. Smoke, fire—I tell you, young children fight those German *porcocanne,* those pigdogs—babies your age, think of it, children with guns, sticks, stones! Until—until Evil Eye! *Cara Mia,* the Madonna she answer our prayers, she send rain! She send mud slides! She defeat the *figli d'uncanne,* the sonsofbitches.

Nonna was angry. Thoughts of the war heated her up.

Listen to me, ChiChi—the Holy Mother, she squeeze the nose of sleeping Vesuvius because she hear our prayers, because we hold up in front of those pigdogs *Il Mal Occhio!* Is true! The Holy Mother send fire and lava from the volcano flying across bay of Napoli! We are saved from the Nazis! We're saved! Those *Nazisti,* they run like rats, they die fast, like flies.

I hopped on the other foot.

—American G.I.'s come to Italy and win war—first they fight us, then they love us—because we never wanted war in first place. Your Mamma she work in hospital to help Allied army—*Guarda,* ChiChi, why you jump like that?

Stop to jump like that! You feet cold? (No, yes. Nonna, my feet are cold.) Stop! Where I was? Ah. G.I.s come, build again bridges, stop booby traps, clear harbors. That was 1944, God had not thought of you yet. You ask me—STOP THAT JUMPING!—you ask me, is *Mal Occhio* real? Eh! I tell you, yes!

Tell me more about Mamma working in the army hospital, Nonna. The place where our Pappa left his leg, where they gave him the wooden one.

Nonna held my shoulder, speeded up. Such a weather is this. Who ever heard such a weather? Is like North Pole in this Minnesota! Polar bears catch pneumonia in this Minnesota!

She ignored my questions about Mamma. ChiChi, she said, when we come here to *La Merica* a big storm, she press down on our ship. We almost all of us drown. We throw our saints' medals in the angry ocean, we pray on our faces. I call on *Il Mal Occhio* to beg the Madonna. What happen? Eh? (crossing herself) God the Father, God the Son, and God *Il Spirito Santo,* they come to our aid. The Holy Mother, she hear our prayers. She hear *Il Mal Occhio.*

I burrowed my head under Nonna's arm. Her body beneath her coat and shawl felt warm, felt strong. She hugged my shoulder and we walked in silence. But then something happened that made my teeth wrinkle up. The street felt as if we'd been sucked into a hole. It had become quiet. Quiet like inside the snow. My nonna had stopped the wind.

Carina, you eyes are as big as buckets, she said. Such a small face for such the big eyes. Poor ChiChi.

Poor ChiChi? Why you say Poor ChiChi?

Simple. When *bambini* born, eyes are black like coal. No? What was she getting at?

ChiChi, no you worry. Is good that God make our ChiChi little bit different.

Different?

He give you green eyes, of course!

(Saint Nino, are you up there?)

I started jumping on one foot again. Nonna pinched my chin with two fingers. God make you different, just like my Nino.

(Is that BAD? Am I BAD?)

You inherited your green eyes from my Nino.

Dio mio! The green of dead Nino's eyes was dripping down into mine from under my cap. His eyes were leaking all over my own.

Nonna gave my chin another pinch. Why you make such ugly face? You look like you just swallowed dog ka-ka. ChiChi, STOP that!

Nonna's step quickened as we neared D'Amico's grocery. I hurried behind her with a mitten over my eyes. She had stopped the wind, but my eyes had gone all wrong.

Luigi D' Amico owned the grocery with his brother, Leo. From Bari in the south of Italy, Luigi had lost his wife of twenty-five years to cancer last year. Her picture hung over the cash register with a gold cross pinned to it. The D'Amico brothers knew all their customers by name and ran the best Italian grocery and delicatessen in Minneapolis. Their mozzarella was fresh. Luigi called Nonna by her first name.

We entered the store shivering, me holding on to the back of Nonna's coat and keeping the greens of my eyes hidden.

Angelina! crowed Luigi D'Amico. Where have you been, my sweet beauty?

Ptuh. Sweet beauty, sighed Nonna.

He swayed, he swaggered. Nonna's smile was pulpy, quivery. She swayed, too.

Was that man flirting with my nonna? At forty-five years old she was attractive to a man? Could it be? She moved along the narrow aisle to examine the porcini mushrooms. I thought I heard her hum.

Luigi peered at me over the counter. This girl is too skinny, Angelina.

My shoulders went up, elbows jerked out. He was looking at my eyes. He thought he saw death in my eyes. Death like Saint Nino's permanently shut eyes. I covered my eyes with my mitten.

Luigi D'Amico slid from behind the counter and approached Nonna.

Angelina, he said in a low voice, is something wrong with your granddaughter? Nonna glared at me.

Maybe you should feed her more, said Luigi.

Nonna humphed, then whispered in Luigi's eager ear. Don't give her attention, Luigi, she's a little—well, you know.

Oh.

Try feeding her more, he said.

Then he did something so amazing I could have swooned in the tomatoes. He reached over and stroked Nonna's cheek.

I watched him between the thumb and forefinger of my mitten as he returned to his place behind the counter. (Stroked Nonna's cheek!) He reached to a shelf behind him and removed a spice cake wrapped in waxed paper and tied with a bow.

Here, is for you, Angelina, he said. And your family, of course.

Nonna's body turned soft, porridgelike. All of her bones collapsed in her coat at once and she became a hill of mush. Sigh. Sigh.

Luigi D'Amico pulled out a bottle of Italian wine from under the counter. He blinked at it, then handed it to Nonna.

And this is for you, also, Angelina.

What for this is?

It's gift. We need a good wine, Angelina. At our age, we need a good wine. The best for the last.

Nonna beamed, then composed herself.

How much?

No how much. Is free. Is gift.

No, Luigi . . . She pushed the wine away, blushing.

You can't refuse a gift. Is bad luck, said Luigi D'Amico.

He was right. It was bad luck and bad manners to refuse a gift. And we didn't want any more bad luck. Nonna took the cake from Luigi, *Grazie*, took the wine, *Grazie*. She'd sew a bedspread for him, but please he was too kind, why he was so kind? I swore she was flirting. On the way home she said how she would pay him with gifts of her own; she'd bake him a bread, bring him jars of her own peppers; no, he had enough food, she'd sew for him, sew and sew and sew. She was respectable Italian woman. She slapped me across the shoulder. Why you so skinny, eh! Why you not eat more! *Che vergogna!* Shame on you!

Nonna bought herself a new shawl. Pink. Mamma laughed like a dog barking. What respectable old woman wore pink? Widows wore black, period. That's how it has always been. Pink? May the saints turn their faces. Besides, since when does an old woman buy a shawl made with someone else's needle? *Dizgracia.*

Everything was a disgrace. The whole tapestry of life was a disgrace.

One evening Luigi D'Amico showed up on our steps. He wore a suit and tie and he carried a bag of groceries. *Buona sera,* Letticia, he sang out to me, sounding like one of the priests at church. *Buona sera, Signore D'Amico,* I answered in the jerky voice I reserved for priests.

I watched him climb the stairs to our apartment and knock on the door. Nonna appeared, all teeth and smiles, and they spoke at once, the delicious flood and flow of the Italian language rushing upon the walls, down the steps, across the landscape, into my face, my arms. I felt trembly, shivery. There stood my nonna chattering like a schoolgirl with a blushing man whose eyes were so happy, they couldn't help but weep.

I couldn't stop thinking about what Nonna said about the color of my eyes. I had faded eyes, eyes the color of swamp spume, mossy eyes nobody else in the entire world would care to look out from. My eyes were not regular eyes, not chestnut like Mamma's and Nonna's and not, *Madre Sacra,* black like my brother's.

Nonna, please teach me power of the Evil Eye.

I knew you'd ask me, *Carissima Figlia.*

Will you? Please? Teach me?

How To Work The Evil Eye (Il Mal Occhio)
Hold the fist down and point at your victim with the little finger and fore finger, like horns, see? Like this. In that way you work magic and bad things will happen to your enemies. However, I, Letticia ChiChi Maggiordino, will put to GOOD use the power of the Evil Eye.

The End.

ChiChi, you have much to learn about *Il Mal Occhio,* said Nonna.

In the winter weeks that followed Nonna sang more songs, laughed harder at her own jokes, cooked more, and sewed like she'd run out of thread. Luigi D'Amico stopped by for afternoon cups of coffee and chunks of Nonna's *panettone;* he arrived in his suit and tie to eat dinner in our kitchen two times, and more than once he took Nonna away in the snow to see the movies at the Hollywood Theatre on Johnson Street. She came home singing and twittering under her breath as if it were spring.

But then she began to sleep later in the mornings, like Mamma. Marco and I boiled our own coffee, ate hunks of cheese, and worried maybe Nonna was sick.

Are you, Nonna? Are you sick?

No, no. Your nonna is just a little tired.

Mamma moved about in the shadows, her black dress and dark presence gliding from room to room, but never attaching to anything, never settling on anything like a tabletop or a corner of the rug or the edge of one of our shoulders. I didn't mind Mamma's gloom because I had my Nonna whose light outshone even the brightest brightness. Nonna who was acting peculiar and who was sleeping too much. I became afraid to kiss her, to draw too near. Nonna? Nonna? Do you have pain? Are you sick?

She slept later in the mornings, her breathing loud with spurts of annoyance, and when we came home from school, we often found her asleep in the kitchen by the radio. She sat alone talking to herself, sighing, dozing. Luigi D'Amico arrived at the door one evening in his suit and tie, all smiles, cheeks flushed. He carried a small bunch of flowers. Blue, they were blue flowers. I said *buona sera.* He said *buona sera.* Mamma said *buona sera.* Marco said *buona sera.* But Nonna was in bed asleep.

Was she expecting you? Marco asked.

Certo, of course. *Sì, sì.* We are going to the Knights of Columbus dance.

Dance! Was he talking about our Nonna?

She didn't go to the dance with him that night and she didn't go to the movies with him the following week. Mamma said I should call the doctor. I should make an appointment for Nonna, but Nonna said, no. She was fine, just a little tired, nobody should worry themselves.

Mamma said she felt an omen. Something terrible was going to happen. I knew different. Nothing bad could happen to us. We had *Il Mal Occhio*.

*M*onna in the bed, her fingers tracing the pattern of the shadows on the wall. The room cold, the heat from the gas heater in the living room not sufficient to heat the whole apartment. She wanted the radio near her bed so she could hear Julius LaRosa *(bel' cantante!)*. She listened to Bill Hailey and the Comets and Elvis Presley while waiting for Frankie Laine, Perry Como, Ezio Pinza. She sighed with delight at Mario Lanza, and every Saturday she played Milton Cross and the Texaco Opera program so loud you could hear our radio in Winona.

Now she looked dreamy, calm and odd.

Mamma brought in a tray with cups of steaming espresso and a cereal bowl of sugar. She set the tray on the bed.

Nonna spooned heaping spoons of sugar into the tiny cup. Her voice, humid and damp. She patted my hand. I sleep now, *Cara,* she said, the smooth rain in her voice now a whisper. A drizzle. She was falling asleep with one eye open. One eye staring at my head.

ChiChi, why you not take off you cap?

My hair is cold.

You not need wool cap inside house. Take him off.

I whispered in Nonna's ear so Mamma wouldn't hear. Nonna, if I take off this cap, we might lose the blessing of our guardian angel Saint Nino. That's a fact.

Saint? puzzled Mamma. There's a saint in you hat?

Saint Nino, I said, surprised at her power of hearing.

Pazzarella, Leticcia, *pazzarella.* Our Leticcia is crazy.

I watched how Mamma massaged Nonna's feet and hands, rubbed her back, and combed her hair. She lathered Corn Huskers lotion on her skin and didn't speak in words as she worked, but she touched Nonna with tenderness like a language.

Grazie, Nonna whispered, taking Mamma's hand and holding it against her heart. Watching them together I recognized with stunned wonder the love they had for each other. I lifted the basin of soapy water to empty in the bathroom sink and out of the corner of my eye saw Mamma smooth Nonna's forehead with the palm of her hand. Their faces were close together, little smiles on their faces like twin melon rinds. Their smiles, the same smile. I emptied Nonna's bathwater and wiped the basin clean with the washcloth hanging from the faucet. A hot, uneasy feeling came over me like being inside the belly of an enormous moth. It was clear to me that Mamma had always been Nonna's favorite child, not Baby Nino, not the others. Mamma.

I had been praying to the wrong saint.

On Sunday Nonna was too sick to go to Mass. Mamma paced the floor, then ordered me to go downstairs and use the landlady's telephone to call the doctor. You speak the good English, she said, wiping her eyes with the heel of her hand. You tell doctor how Nonna she sick bad, what we are going to do?

I hurried downstairs. Mrs. Pazzoli dialed Doctor Spano, the Italian doctor Nonna had visited once for pains in her feet. *Dai,* Mrs. Pazzoli slapped her hand to her forehead, she just remembered. Doctor Spano is out of town for the weekend.

Mamma became frantic. The hospital! Call hospital, ChiChi. Use you good English!

The lady on the other end of the telephone wanted to know my name, my age, and where were my parents? The telephone receiver turned to ice. She told me to call back on Monday during office hours.

We need a doctor now! I yelled. Please locate Doctor Spano for us, wherever he is. Tell him Angelina Sapponata is sick!

I needed to call back on Monday to make an appointment, she said, and she hung up.

I called for a taxi to take us to the emergency room at the hospital downtown Minneapolis, but a taxi never showed up. We waited an hour and then had no choice but to bundle Nonna in extra sweaters, her coat and new pink shawl and walk her to the bus stop. We arrived at the hospital with our faces burned white from the cold, and Nonna limp and shaking. In another hour we had a doctor examining her. Mamma hovered over Nonna's bed working her rosary and wiping at her eyes with the palm of her hand. She asked me to repeat again and again what the doctor said.

Translate for me, Leticcia. Say me again.

She's got pneumonia. *Cia la polmonite.*

Cia la polmonite!

She will get well with the medicine.

She get well with medicine.

But there's something else. The doctor says her heart—

Heart!

Sì. Cuore.

She has to stay here a couple of days.

Zio Nino was a bad saint. He should have been paying attention. He should have watched out for his mother.

On the ride home I sat in the taxi with my hands pressed
between my knees and my eyes closed so I wouldn't be
distracted from my duty to take over where *Zio* Nino had
failed. I didn't look out the taxi window at the city I longed
to see, office buildings, stores, streets, houses, people on their
way somewhere. I was making plans. I'd petition the Holy
Mother on my own. I'd go to Mass and I'd concentrate. I'd
do this right.

The Lord be with you.

And also with you.

A reading from the Holy Gospel according to Luke.

Glory to you, Lord.

The apostles said to the Lord, Increase our faith and he
answered: If you had faith the size of a mustard seed, you
could say to this sycamore, Be uprooted and transplanted
into the sea, and it would obey you . . .

The gospel of the Lord.

Praise to you, Lord Jesus Christ.

Figli miei, always remember God hears your prayers! Sister
Ursula raised the burden of her arms. Mario Cavello jerked
his knee against the back of my chair. I felt the skin of my
ankles. I had changed my socks. They were blue, blue knee
socks. I could feel the color blue on my skin. I was aware
of the sound of his knee on my chair. The troubled thud
of bone against wood.

I slapped my hand to my forehead. I felt blood in my
veins, like small boats on their way to Capri. It was bumpy
sailing in my veins. *Zio* Baby Saint Nino and the Evil Eye
were with me. *Live, Nonna,* I cried in a collapsed voice.
Come Home.

Nonna came home the following Wednesday.

I want I be buried in Campania, she told Mamma, and
Mamma said, no talk of burying, *tsk tsk*.

Remembering, I try to see Mamma in Nonna's last days on
earth, and I am able to recall only smudged images of a
mother, as though she were a photographic error. The
woman in the corner of the bedroom sobbing into a sweater
sleeve, and there again, sitting in the chair by the window
staring down at the railroad tracks. She's alone in a darkened
kitchen, slumped over her rosary, or then a blur of a memory, she's lying in bed refusing to get up because her mother
is gone and she doesn't know what she am going to do.

When Nonna lay in the bed growing silent and thinner,
a mere bump under the quilt, Mamma asked for a priest.
Father O'Toole, the new priest from Our Lady of Mount
Carmel, came up the stairs, knocked on our door, entered,
and performed Nonna's Last Rites. Nonna crooked her fin-
ger at him, drawing him close. How you think the Holy
Mother hear you when you no speak Italian? The Savior
Himself, and she crossed herself, He speak perfect Italian!
And then she asked me to pray the Lord's Prayer in Italian,
the language Latin came from, *Grazie a Dio*.

Irlandese! she murmured when he had gone. Hands at the
mouth in wonder. An Irish priest in an Italian church. Did
we offer hospitality? Make him welcome? Some bread, cake,
a glass of wine, coffee? Did he eat? What did the priest eat?

Cake.

Ah. Her head fell back on the pillow. Is good.

Mamma, Marco, and I climbed in bed with Nonna and
stayed there until morning when the Northern Pacific freight

train, its muddy box cars emptied of their corn and wheat,
rattled and clamored along the tracks into the train yard
across the street and settled.

We slept in her bed with her every night for a week,
praying, singing, trusting the medicine and the saints. Nonna,
I pleaded, how do I use *Il Mal Occhio* to make you well?

On Thursday Marco and I arrived home from the settlement
house to a strange stillness in the apartment. Mamma wasn't
home. The sun was the color of a watery egg. There was a
peculiarity to the silence, it hummed like a celestial heart-
burn, like twirling of wings. I went to Nonna's bed. Her
bowl of breakfast polenta had spilled and splattered on the
wall. She stared at me as I entered the room, asked me what
was the mess on the wall. Spots, I told her.

She smiled at me and a long, slow breath fell from her
lips. *Amore mio.*

I took off my shoes and climbed into the bed. I cleaned
her face with the corner of the bedspread, smoothed her
nightgown, and lay close to her. I saw the book of Psalms
on her bedside table. Want me to recite to you, Nonna?

Sì, Cara, recite me.

I will say to the LORD, "My refuge and my fortress,
My God, in whom I trust!"

Yes, yes, she said. *N'atra vuota.* Again. Recite me again.

He who dwells in the shelter of the Most High
Will abide in the shadow of the Almighty . . .

More!

He will cover you with His pinions,
And under His wings you may seek refuge;
His faithfulness is a shield and bulwark.

Marco stood by the bed and waited for me to open the quilt for him to climb in with us. We hadn't taken off our winter jackets.

You will not be afraid of the terror by night,
Or of the arrow that flies by day . . .

Nonna tapped my head. Is good, she said. And *Cara*, please to take that THING off your head. Nino is suffocating in all that hair.

You knew about the photo? You knew?

Is all right. You good girl. But is not smart for you to carry the dead around in you hair.

Her face was misshapen, eyes open crooked, cheeks pinched inward, mouth sagging.

Amore . . .

Nonna, WHAT'S WRONG?

The sun had set and the apartment was dark when Mamma arrived home. She had walked to the S&L Department Store on 4th Street and Central to buy Nonna a hot water bottle and long underwear she heard advertised on the radio. When she turned on the light she thought it odd to see Marco and me asleep in the bed with Nonna, our arms around her, our heads pressed to her ears. We held on to her as if by holding her, we'd enter her, become her, and she'd take us with her to where she was going. My eyes were closed, but I was jolted upright when Mamma threw herself across the bed, the cold outside air rising from her skin and her clothes.

Mammina! she shouted, struggling to lift Nonna into her arms.

It was then that Marco and I screamed forth our tears and we cried all night, our voices splintering and bloody like the horrible midflight plummet of a failed and useless saint.

The polenta was scrubbed from the wall, the breakfast bowl washed, Nonna's hair combed, and her nightclothes washed and ironed. I helped Mamma dress Nonna in her best black church dress. I rouged her cheeks with mamma's lipstick and I kissed her cold face. A mass was said and the neighbors came, everyone who Nonna had ever spoken to, they came in a steady gathering of bodies and quiet voices. Luigi D'Amico came and looked at Nonna for a long time, then bent and kissed her cheek and her hands. His red face dripped with tears and he blew his nose in a large white handkerchief. The kitchen table was weighted with food. Flowers filled the living room. Marco and I watched the guests, strangers who loved Nonna, as they wailed loud and horrible, wiped tears from their eyes, and then bent to kiss her. They knelt, crossed themselves, wept, prayed, moaned. They paused to pat Mamma's hand, kiss her cheeks, nod to us. Sit.

Angelina, *una angela*. She die of *il cuore*. Too big was her heart for this earth.

Sì. Sì. Too big the heart. Too good. Tch. Tch.

Marco and I sat on chairs at the side of the room as if waiting for an assignment. We looked out the window. We sipped *limoncello*. We dozed, awoke, sat some more. With Nonna gone from us our childhood was over.

*W*inter ate us up. Mamma stayed in bed during the day, getting up only to boil water, stare out the window at the railroad tracks, the spindly naked trees, and the low metal buildings in the train yard. She stopped crying but sat in the chair with the handkerchief at her mouth, whimpering in a low, growly voice. Laments about Nonna lying in the icy Minnesota earth. Buried in a cemetery where Catholics and Lutherans lay side by side beneath a heath of roiling snow. The only way we could get there was by bus and Mamma wouldn't leave the apartment. Wouldn't dress herself, comb her hair, wouldn't speak.

Mamma? Marco and I are hungry.

Go away.

We rubbed our stomachs, chewed the cuffs of our sweaters, and read the *Children's Illustrated Science and Invention Encyclopedias, Volumes 1–10* at the library.

Grief wore us out.

Mamma, we're hungry.

We read in the library where it was warm. We could take off our jackets. We didn't have to sit on our hands to keep them warm. Happy pictures lined the walls, pictures of Tom Thumb, Pinocchio, Davey Crockett. Mothers wearing matching sweater sets held small children on their laps and read out loud about brave kittens, a princess who needed a prince, a lady who hung her long hair out a window. Marco and I watched them from our table by the window and wondered what they were having for dinner.

The librarian, a woman with a perpetual smile on her face, a sticky smile, wet and questioning, helped us find books she thought we'd like. I enjoy seeing children, she said, like you, not wasting your brains.

If you pried up the squares of tile on the floor of the library you'd find miles of writhing, wormy wet brains twisting and flopping around. Wasted. I told Marco this and he laughed.

You're so funny, ChiChi.

We read about magnetic sound. The telegraphone was made of piano wire and passed an electromagnet, coiled and connected in series with a battery and carbon microphone from a telephone. What do you say, Marco? The piano wire becomes magnetized by speaking into the microphone and by substituting a telephone receiver speech is replayed. How about some day let's make us a tape recorder?

Record loneliness.

Hunger.

Luigi D'Amico gave us food on credit. You children got any money to pay for that cheese?

Sure. (Fumble in the shoe, the pocket, the mitten.) Oh, sorry. We forgot the money. Lost it.

Got stolen.

Nonna told us to walk with our heads high, to be proud, never to bow the face in shame.

I could feel her fingers playing with my braids, smoothing the tangles around my ears.

Fear and weakness are our enemies, she had said.

Be brave and do hard things.

Sì, Nonnina.

And stop you worry so much. You wear out you brain.

The librarian gave us her closing time smile. Ya, okay. We're leaving. Marco asleep with his head on his book, *Yi He Yuan, Beijing's Summer Palace.*

Last ones out. We pulled the wool socks back over our shoes, buckled our rubber boots, tied our mufflers over our faces, slipped our hands into two pairs of mittens, and tried not to think about home.

The way the cold strikes at you, the way it closes its fists and punches you. Listen to the squeak of your boots on the snow, the chatter of tire chains on the street, the wind rattling tree branches, metal signs, and birds off course. Listen to your lips cracking and flaking to the ground. Ask Luigi for a can of soup. Tell him you dropped the money down the sewer. Are you freezing, Marco? Pull up your collar. Think about Chinese children in the Summer Palace like in the book. Think of playing beside the quiet lotus ponds and climbing in marble caves. Think of gentle arched bridges, glistening teak, bowls of hot ginger tea, perfumed canopied paths.

Luigi gave us the soup. And a slice of mortadella, two provolone balls. *Va bene,* he said, and he handed us chunks of *capacollo.*

We swallowed without chewing.

Dio mio. Have some more.

Shank you, we said with full mouths.

Take this home for your mother, and he handed us a loaf of olive bread.

Finally spring happened.

The Silver Maple, the Boxelder, and Ash opened to blooms and new leaves like baby hands. The toothed leaves of the Elders and the Nannyberry trees, their flat-topped

clusters flowering, scented the air and the streets; the Red
Oak, Black Oak, and Slippery Elm sprang forth with green
like laughter. Our stripped streets where old American Elm
trees had been desecrated and felled by Dutch Elm Disease
now sprouted chicory, joe-pye weed, and wild grass.

Tar Town welcomed spring like money. In the warmer
weather of spring the people became hopeful, energetic, full
of goodwill. Window curtains were drawn apart, shades
flipped up, plastic sheeting pulled from nails around door
and window frames. Patio furniture was brought out of
basements and sheds, walkways were swept and hosed. Bulbs
and seedlings were brought out for planting.

Mamma woke up. Stood in our doorway. She wanted to
take a bath. Turn on a light.

It was time, she said; she had made a plan with her brain.

She'd shampoo her hair.

Can we eat, Mamma?

I accompanied her to D'Amico's. For the first time since
Nonna's death Mamma lifted her head, looked at the sky.
She uncovered her face.

Is good day, no? I could hear the longing in her voice,
worse than sadness, like a sliver in your finger.

E u' vero, Mammina. E na'bella iurnata. Napolitano dialect.
That's right, Mamma, it's a good day. She made her shopping
list known to Luigi at D'Amico, who was surprised to see
her. His face went sorrowful.

Signora, he said, we all miss her.

Che ditte?

I miss her especial, he said.

Mamma stared at him. Ah. A nod of her head. Her tears
were all used up. She'd have the tortellini, the shells, the
pancetta, the *abruzzi* sausage, olive oil, how fresh is the ricotta?

She'd have brown eggs, cow milk, she'd have almond nougats, the Minneapolis newspaper. No, she didn't want to sample the gorgonzola. How much did she owe him for what her children had been charging?

At home she hunched over the *Minneapolis Tribune*, struggling with the words. The pages flowered out around her like petticoats. What this is? ChiChi, what this is?

The word is *negotiate*, Mamma. It means people talk over a thing. You talk it over and come up with something to agree on.

(She called me ChiChi!)

Marco and I gorged ourselves on ricotta-stuffed tortellini and sausage. We held our faces close to our plates. Our cheeks swelled, our faces pinked, our eyes rolled back.

Are you pigs? Mamma said.

We ate until we hurt. Ate until our toes hurt, our fingers hurt, the skin behind our ears hurt. And then we threw up.

Maiali! Pigs!

Mamma searched through the newspapers under the hanging bulb in the kitchen trying with desperation to learn and understand the language of the new country she both wanted and rejected. Outside, the thin layers of remaining snow stippled grey and black with dead leaves, twigs, and soot. The waters of the Mississippi that had flooded us churned green and gummy beneath melting shelves of ice. Nonna's garden alongside the house surrendered to weeds, mud, and insects. There'd be no more Nonna's fresh tomatoes, *basilico,* and *melanzane.* Spring mourned our Nonna, too.

On a Sunday evening in May, Mamma said she had something to tell us. We weren't listening. We were eating lentil soup.

I'm think with my brain, she repeated.

I dipped a last chunk of bread in the soup, swallowed it.

I got big a plan. My brain she make a plan, she said.

Little did we suspect, did we guess, did we even imagine.

I'm take in a boarder, she said.

Marco said, What's a boarder?

I had stomach cramps.

A boarder she rent a room in our home, she said.

She said *home* as if we lived somewhere real, like the families in the Make And Do Childcraft books. Houses whose families owned things like Scotch tape, all-purpose glue, and typing paper, who ate dry cereal from boxes.

Harry Belafonte sang "Hold 'Em Joe" on the radio and the edges of the scarlet and jasmine flowers of Mamma's rug spread out like open mouths begging an offering. Mamma must have lost her mind.

She was serious about taking in a boarder.

She moved her clothes to the hall closet next to the cleaning supplies. She became flushed and smiley, motivated with a nervous energy. Marco and I tried to steer clear of her because when she was nervous she could change in a second, explode in an emotional storm, arms flying, everything about her igniting. She would hit me hard on the head or the back, *Malvagio!* And when she saw me as a bad seed, she groaned, hit me again.

When I asked if we could please go to the cemetery to visit Nonna, she called me a devil and hit me on the shoulders with the rolled up newspaper. Was it her fault Nonna died on American soil? Was it her fault Nonna's heart was too big for this world and she left her bereft and alone? Why did I torture her so?

She was convinced a boarder would solve her problems. The check she received in the mail each month didn't quite cover all her needs. We didn't ask where the checks came from because we didn't want the emotional eruption that would result if we used the word *Welfare*. She readied herself to meet perspective boarders. She pulled her hair back behind her ears and twisted it into a loop at the base of her neck. She ironed her dress. She boiled coffee, set anise mints on a plate. Twenty-eight years old, how could she endure this life without her mamma? Courage, Giuseppina, *In chisto munno ci vo' coraggio.*

On a warm day late in May when storm windows were traded for screens and the sun shone in miniature flashes across the gas stove to Pappa's leg, there came a knock on the door. A tall yellow-haired lady with skin practically the same shade as her hair stood catching her breath. Is this the place with the room for rent?

She panted (like a horse, Marco pointed out) when she talked. We giggled, poked each other, and rolled our bodies along the wall of our room. We held our stomachs and laughed, Marco honking and coughing like a bus.

I'll need privacy, said the woman. For occasional entertaining, you know.

Mamma smiling, nodding.

The room suddenly seemed like someone else's, the furniture covered in plastic, the polished woodwork, new chintz curtains Mamma bought on Central Avenue. Mamma offered the woman a seat on the sofa. A woman with spongy eyelids and skin the color of tapioca.

Mamma sat erect in her chair at the window, hands folded on her lap as if she were the one being interviewed. She stammered, twisted her ankles together, fidgeted with the fabric of her skirt. I wanted to perform some ritual to help her out, a ritual if performed right could snap her right into being a normal mother.

I stood on one foot, named holy days. I recited the Lord's Prayer twice.

But Mamma was beyond rituals. She looked as though she'd been tossed from a ship in a storm, flung headlong into the sea, and then blown naked and shorn to land belly-up in her very own brown stuffed chair. Who *was* this sticky-smelling lady with no-color eyes wearing nylon stockings and high heels sitting on her sofa? Her words sounded like she had small stones under her tongue. Twenty-five dollars a week. Is too okay?

I'll go eighteen, said the lady, looking around at our walls, the wallpaper with the bluebell motif, the school photos of Marco and me above the sofa, and the picture of the army pals on the shelf by the radiator.

Mamma hesitated, wiped at the side of her nose with a knuckle. We *negotiate*, she said.

What was that? Huh? said the lady.

Meals included, said Mamma.

And a telephone?

I get telephone for you. No you worry, said Mamma.

It's a deal. Just be sure those kids stay out of my way, said the lady.

The lady left and Mamma stood staring and blinking at the door. She made the sign of the cross, smoothed her skirt, turned to her bedroom, and didn't come out until the next morning.

$\mathcal{G}$ renadine Fletcher moved in on Tuesday before dinner. She told us her real name was Gallina but she found out it meant chicken so she changed it to Grenadine, a name which she got from a bottle in the liquor cabinet of a gentleman friend. When she was accepted at the Promenade School of Beauty, she felt inspired to not only change her name, but to take herself downtown to the Three Sisters and buy a new wardrobe, including sling-back high heel shoes. Well, it was a fine day in Hannibal, for here she was, attending beauty school and out on her damn own, pardon her French, living on the bus line ten minutes from the beauty school and her job, a dandy smart move on her part if she didn't say so herself.

She arrived at dinnertime and the landlord, Natalie's grandpa, Franco, must have been waiting on the porch because he sprang up like a rooster when he saw her tripping up the walk. She gave him a greasy smile and he pushed the door open and jumped down the stairs from the porch to haul her luggage upstairs. It took him three trips to carry three round pink hat cases up one flight of stairs.

She didn't talk, she drizzled. Natalie's grandpa leaned against our door with a grin on his face, his neck as red as his socks. My name's Frank, he said. (It wasn't. It was *Franco*.)

Grenadine settled her weight on one hip. Mmm, she said.

Franco sighed, clucked to himself, and with what was

almost a curtsy, told her, You can call on me. Anytime.

I can't thank you enough, said Grenadine. What was your name again?

Franco blushed, gave another little bow.

He said Frank! I yelled. Pay attention!

She shot me a frown, smiled back at Franco, who seemed tangled, like an excited ball of twine. His face spread apart like a cartoon character. His words unwound around him about what lovely weather we're having and how nice to have a guest in the house as though she was the queen bee come to take over the hive. The rug was beginning to smell bad.

After he left, we watched Grenadine unpack her boxes and model cases, which she piled on Mamma's former bed in Mamma and Nonna's former room. Mamma looked on with her hand at her mouth, eyes weathered. I wondered if she was thinking what I was thinking. No Italian woman we knew would dream of piling things on a clean bedspread.

Grenadine Fletcher moved in and became the master of us all. She barely tolerated Marco and me, but we made her our main preoccupation. Franco Pazzoli, Natalie's grandpop, fluttered around Grenadine like he was a bluejacket fly and she was made entirely of sugar. Mamma began getting out of her bed in the hallway before any of us, combed her hair early in the day, hummed along with the radio as she cooked. She prepared strange dishes like waffles and syrup and scalloped potatoes and au gratin from a Betty Crocker cookbook she ordered through the mail.

Mamma, that's very good—you sent for a book in the mail.

Did somebody they ask you?

She hung new curtains in the room Nonna had once shared with her, curtains of Hawaiian greens and yellows, a design of swirling palm trees and pineapples. She bought lime green sheets at the S&L Department store for Grenadine's bed, and bright lemon yellow towels. The dresser that once was Nonna's became a collage of Grenadine's bottles and jars and a collection of distorted stuffed animals that looked like they'd been sewn by the blind.

Grenadine became the star of the universe.

Mamma had a telephone installed for her and we were ordered to leave the room when she received or made calls. Grenadine needed privacy. Giggles fell from her throat, arms, legs. She didn't speak, she splashed. We couldn't escape her nightly love affair on the telephone. It dripped onto the floor, seeped under the floorboards. We stepped in it on our way to the bathroom.

She hung her hand-laundered underwear from the shower pole in the bathroom every night. I brushed my teeth, washed under my arms, and stared at the damp silent stockings, panties, and brassieres. My heart pounded faster as I ran my fingers over their silkiness. I liked the peculiar feeling it gave me to touch a woman's underwear. Marco and I both felt it. We closed the bathroom door and locked it after us. I put the brassiere around my chest and Marco pressed his hands against me, wiggling, imitating what we'd seen in pictures passed around at school. Then the panties, first on me, then on him, we squirmed in her underwear, the stockings draped across our faces. If I imagined Grenadine's body parts fitting into the stockings and panties I would lose my breath and my balance. It was dizzying to consider what throbbed inside women's underwear.

Leticcia! Do you mind? Madame Queen! A voice outside the bathroom door.

Be right out.

(Hear that, Marco? Madame Queen.)

Hey! Is your brother in there with you?

No.

I hear two of you.

That's because you're nutso.

(Nutso, get it?)

Touching, smelling, wearing her underwear, and we were rolling in sexiness. Our hormones flew wild around the bathroom. Guess what I smell, ChiChi.

What?

S-e-x.

And we fell against the toilet laughing. We stuck out our tongues and licked each other on the face. *Hahaheee.*

When Grenadine was home, Marco and I stayed out of her way, but we watched her from doorways, from the edges of rooms, from lying down places on Mamma's carpet. We listened to her talk on the telephone, to her voice pouring from her like boiled soap. She made love on the telephone with her voice and Marco and I pressed our ears to the wall, swooning and touching ourselves and gasping for air. Her voice and words reached our bodies, oozed its way to our sweating palms, and we were on fire. We sloshed in fire.

Mamma waited on Grenadine like a servant to royalty. When Grenadine stayed out late, Mamma waited up for her. When Grenadine asked for something special to eat, Mamma cooked it. If Grenadine needed some article of clothing pressed, Mamma hauled out the ironing board and went to work. Grenadine had a sniffle and Mamma heated up the camphor.

Mamma sat rapt at each meal as Grenadine relayed the details of her day on the Pillsbury assembly line. It was much better pay, she said, than when she worked at Mandie's Candies as a file clerk in training. Three nights a week she attended the Promenade School of Beauty learning how to do the Marcel Wave. Such an interesting life! Grenadine's words were violet-tinted, they worked on us like a deep cleansing shampoo, a carotene henna, a hair straightener (which I could use). Every room smelled of hair spray, cookie dough, and s-e-x.

Grenadine didn't look at us directly when she talked, her eyes bobbed like nervous cats, aimless, bob-bob-bobbing here and there, sniffing for something better than what was before her. Mamma didn't mind that Grenadine didn't look her in the eye. She stretched forward in her chair, laughed too loud when Grenadine said something mildly amusing, exclaimed, No! and, I no believe! again and again at inappropriate pauses. It was the first time I had seen Mamma lean forward with interest when anyone spoke to her.

No amount of hot oil treatments could remove the burnt bread smell from Grenadine. When she wasn't in the apartment her smell stayed with us, stupefying and magical.

Mamma took Pappa's wooden leg away from me. I wanted to rock him in my arms, smooth the slipper on the foot, talk to him.

Per l'amor d' Cristo, Leticcia!

Mamma hid him inside the kitchen cupboard, slammed the door shut. I stood at the cupboard and stroked the door, gave it a hug.

Grenadine had been with us a month and it was evident Mamma was someone else's mother and Marco and I were accidents, transients. She cooked mashed potatoes, corn dogs, food that one would have to go to confession and ask forgiveness for so much as looking at it.

She bought peanut butter, white packaged bread. Sweet pickle relish. Packaged cookies. She resembled the housewives on TV who wore high heels to mop the floor.

Franco Pazzoli loved to come upstairs and sit at our table at mealtimes. He sat and watched Grenadine eat. She ate two and three servings of everything Mamma cooked. Franco sipped his espresso and tried to make conversation.

Let's hope the weather doesn't get too hot; are you comfortable enough up here? That is, at night? At night do you maybe think you'll be needing an electric fan?

The apartment smelled odd, a leftover bacon smell.

Meals were not eaten, they were *performed*. Grenadine Fletcher sighed and chomped in an orgy of delight and we watched.

One hot evening in July at supper, Mamma, all smiles, said something that gave me a real jolt, and I popped up from the table and slapped my knee when she said it.

Grenadine, I tell you something, said Mamma. I, too, am business woman.

That so, Josie! said Grenadine. (She couldn't pronounce *Giuseppina*.)

I no do now, *certo,* Mamma demurred on, I am mother. I have children, but one day I go back to my business.

(That's when I jumped up and slapped my knee.)

What business is that, Josie? Grenadine asked, her fingers strumming her coffee cup. Marco and I dug our knives into our breast of chicken.

I explain you, Mamma said. Leticcia, she remember. Remember, Leticcia? She grinned at me. I stared, opened mouthed, my breast of chicken at the end of the knife.

Music business! said Mamma.

Mother of God. Music.

Tell Grenadine how you mamma she play concertina and sing!

My vocal cords froze shut. I couldn't speak.

Music is how I meet my husband, Mamma raved on. I sing for soldiers in hospital—my husband, he like very much my voice. She laughed.

Our mother laughed.

She brushed her cheek with the back of her hand. Soldiers, *Americani,* some from Texas, very brave these men, my husband, he—she paused, shrugged her shoulders, *Mah.* I sing for soldiers. Some day I'm make plan in my brain, some day I'm be singer in United States.

Marco's mouth sprayed chicken gravy. In all our natural days we had never heard her sing one song, not one.

Grenadine pushed her belly against the rim of the table.

Well, what say you give us a little number for us now, Josie? Is there a concertina around here somewhere?

A string of white gathered on Mamma's lip. Her hands went up to her face, she bit a cuticle, pulled at her chin. Another day, she said in a voice from Mars.

Oh come on, Josie, do us the honor.

No.

Don't be shy, belt us out a good one!

The expression of alarm in Mamma's eyes was more than I could bear.

I hopped up from the chair, the familiar urge taking over to save Mamma from herself.

Marco and I got a song! I said.

I took Marco's hand and we shuffled our feet to a clear space on the linoleum and sang our own arrangement of "Sentimental Journey" without one mistake. It didn't bother us when both Mamma and Grenadine left the table before we finished, Mamma to the sink and Grenadine to the living room and the telephone.

*M*arco and I found two stereo speakers on the curb by a garbage can overflowing with wires, and it wasn't Wednesday, garbage pickup day. Our throats swelled at the sight. We bit our wrists. It had to have been the Virgin Mary Her Blessed Self who sent us such good luck.

Take that junk out of here! Grenadine no like junk. Have respect!

What junk? I don't see any junk.

Leticcia, *chiudi la bocca!* Shut your mouth! *Stai zitta!* Take junk out or I skin you like frog!

The radio played "Ain't Nobody's Business," bluesy and slow, and Grenadine was busy teaching Mamma how to dance American.

Can I dance, too?

The yellows sloshed upward under Grenadine's lids. Tell the kid to get lost, she said.

I want to dance, I said, wiggling my hips like Mamma.

Little girls in braids should mind their own beeswax, Madame Queen, said Grenadine.

(My braids! Mamma had stopped combing my hair, and the braids had become two barbed rows of knuckles springing from my head.)

We waited for dinner and Grenadine's electrifying dinner conversation. Spoken as though silence were an enemy, something to beat up with noise.

It didn't take much to convince Mamma that Grenadine
Fletcher was on the path to success no matter what she set
her mind to do. Mandie's Candies, the Pillsbury assembly
line, the Marcel Wave, she had a career and future that were
promise-kissed. It was like living a fairy tale, a real live fairy
tale where Snow White looked like Mae West and ate like
a truck.

Mangia, mangia, Mamma called out. Eat some more.
(Right, Grenadine, stuff 'er in.) Josie waved two fingers
above her plate, not noticing the shame of my dirty braids.
Eat. Eat. Grenadine's doughy smell and beauty stories inspired and captivated us. She fueled the air with hope; she
generated possibilities, she gyrated the blues.

Really, Josie, Mandie's Candies never knew how lucky
they were to have me. I'll tell you that right here and now.

(Josie was all ears.)

I was in training, Grenadine said, buttering her bread, to
take over the position as front receptionist. The receptionist
at the time just sat and read *True Confessions* all day, thank
you very much. You'd think she'd have more of a mind to
properly represent Mandie's Candies; after all, the receptionist is the first person you encounter when you enter the
place.

She sank her teeth into the bread. Butter erupted between
her teeth.

A pause to chew.

When you walk through that front door, Josie, you see
the receptionist sitting right next to the six-foot plastic fudgy
hazelnut bar, don't you know.

. . . Hazelnut, our mother whispered.

People are so stupid, don't you think, Josie? Just because
I borrowed a few boxes of their stupid candy. I absolutely
planned to pay for them out of my check. Do I look like
the dishonest type?

Dio mio! said Mamma.

You borrowed boxes of candy? said Franco.

Ha, you mean you filched them, said Marco.

I didn't *filch*, Mister Bones, for your information. I *borrowed*. There's a difference.

So how'd they catch you? said Mister Bones.

Well! I was merely loading up a certain truck with a few boxes of candy they'd never miss anyhow. Would Mandie's Candies fold up and hang out the bankrupt sign because I, a poor little receptionist-in-training, borrowed a few measly boxes of vanilla cremes! Jesus Murphy. Well, anyhow, that's all history under the bridge, isn't it?

She wrinkled her nose, stuck out her chin, asked, Is there any dessert?

A letter came from Nurse Nimm. Marco had to have a checkup and X ray before returning to school. Marco had to be vaccinated and tested and checked more often than any other kid in the settlement house school. Not me. Mamma spared herself the trouble of taking me for checkups and vaccinations since I wasn't the sick one. What could a doctor do for me? What could vaccinations do for me?

I slouched on the sofa in the living room, listening to the radio after Mamma and Marco left for the doctor.

Do you mind, Madame Queen?

Mind what?

I need some privacy.

How come? I'm not hurting anyone.

I said, do you MIND?

Can't I listen to the radio?

Get OUT. Just GO. NOW.

Mannaggia.

I took my time. Put on the shoe, take off the shoe, put on the sock, take it off. Scratch the toe, pluck lint from between toes, listen to the commercial on the radio. Colgate makes you desirable.

Hear that, Grenadine? Colgate makes you desirable.

Will you PLEASE.

Back with the shoe. Who's coming over, Grenadine? Your boyfriend I bet.

OUT.

I sat on the front porch steps to watch for the mystery man. Mister Big Secret. I thought about being desirable. I thought about buying that mouthwash, what kind was it again? An hour went by and nobody showed up. Natalie Pazzoli lumped out the door carrying her ball.

Hi, dumb old Leticcia.

Up yours, I said.

She bounced the ball against the wall of the porch, caught it, held it next to her stomach. I could smell her skin, her dirty jeans, a sour smell, like earwax. She had a pushed-out face like her Protestant grandmother. At least Franco had Italian blood. I saw him sitting in a back pew last week at Our Lady of Mount Carmel, his head bowed, his back lifted like a hoop.

I'm not in the mood for your crap, Natalie, I said.

She threw the ball deliberately at my leg. I heard *gumbahs* can't catch, she said.

What did you call me?

Gumbah. Isn't that what you are? A dumb *gumbah?*

I stood up. She was twice as big as me.

They won't even let you in regular school! She leered with her bottom teeth stuck out.

I grabbed her collar, pushed my fingers into her flesh. Her

neck was soft like soot. I stuck my nose close to hers and with a fast jerk of my arm I punched her in the stomach.

Hard.

She gagged and doubled over, then looked up at me with her cheeks sucked in, her eyes like squares of fur.

Before she could speak, I told her next time she called me a name, I'd skin her like a frog.

I crossed Beltrami Park, stopped to watch boys playing soccer, boys I knew from the settlement house school, familiar and safe boys. I knew them by their bodies, the stringy spines, awkward arms, legs too long, too thin, the hard metallic eyes, the broad mouths, the clumsy untamed hair. You couldn't mistake these boys for any others. Natalie and her friends didn't have our look, didn't have our sounds, or movements. The way we chewed with nothing in our mouths, or held our heads while waiting for something to happen, or the way we might wipe a sleeve across a nose, or smile dreamy as though falling in love. The incited rhythm of our movements was different, the storm of energy in our bodies different. No wonder Grenadine didn't like me.

Joey Minichilli waved at me, his hand lost in the sleeve of his too-big shirt. Hey, ChiChi, want to play?

I looked at the sky, kicked at a brown knot of grass, cursed the name *gumbah*.

Is that a yes? hollered Joey.

My body twitched. Marco was getting stuck with needles, probed, and X-rayed. Grenadine wanted me out of the apartment. Toothpaste made us desirable.

Ah come on, we need an extra person, ChiChi. Play with us!

I was desirable.

*M*arco tested negative.

Mamma had been relieved at the news, now she was exhausted.

Is good thing, my son, he not be worse. Fibers not grow.

La–dee–da, said Grenadine.

She brushed her hair and Mamma looked at advertisements for television sets. She gave us a look without actually looking at us. Would Madame Queen and Mister Bones mind if your mammy and I had a little privacy? Hmm?

What's the big deal? Marco said.

Little kettles have big ears, said Grenadine.

We didn't mind being dismissed to our room because it's where we spent most of our time anyway. Marco couldn't play outside for long periods of time, so we stayed where we could read and draw and make things. We cut, pasted, hammered, nailed, sawed, repaired, recreated, fixed, invented, and practiced words in English.

What's so private between them we can't hear? Marco wanted to know.

We cupped our ears to the wall. Grenadine's voice: Josie, listen. You gotta face facts. Those two kids are a heap-load on the strange side. I mean, granted the boy is sick, but what about *her*? Frank told me she beat up the stepgrandkid.

Franco say this?

Sweet little Natalie. Imagine.

He tell you this?

Josie, I don't think your kid is right in the head. Not normal. She uh, does certain things—I hate to tell you.

Things?

Well, okay. She plays with my unders.

Unders? Please explain me.

I caught her playing with my *unders!* She had my *under-mentionables* on her head! Imagine that head of hair in my—well!

No sound.

Are you following what I'm saying? I saw your daughter through the keyhole brushing her teeth with my YOU KNOW WHAT on her YOU KNOW WHAT.

Ohh! Ohhh!

Marco and I walked straight through the living room and out the door. We kept walking.

We stopped, sat down on the curb, and looked at our shoes. Marco took my arm, held on hard, squeezed.

Let's get the bitch, he said.

*Y*ou kids steal this stuff?

No, we found them.

Where? Just where?

On the street.

Mrs. Rizzo tapped one of the speakers with her toe. I'll just bet.

She was Joe Rizzo's Swedish wife and Joe was the caretaker at Our Lady of Mount Carmel.

We don't steal, said Marco.

She worked her mouth the way Father Tuttifucci did when getting ready to try out one of his aphoristic poems on us.

These speakers look new to me, said Mrs. Rizzo. Tony, don't these speakers appear new to you?

Mr. Rizzo was a good Catholic and employed by Jesus, him being the one who kept the pews polished and the grass trimmed around the feet of the Statue of Our Lady.

Inga, the boy said they're not stolen, said Mr. Rizzo.

Fnef.

Marco's face went grey. My sister and I don't steal!

I had seen that look on his face before. It startled me. Mrs. Rizzo whacked a mosquito near her ear. Don't go getting huffy, she said. So sorry, etc. etc. etc.

Then: It's a shame about your grandmother. So young,

too. A crying shame. The dear woman. So friendly and full of life.

Marco's stone face.

A mosquito struck Inga's blood.

I watched her walk back into the house scratching her waist. I could smell the disdain, the preciousness of her whitewashed house, her garden of yellow, cerise, and scarlet-tipped phlox, petunias, and sweet william, her pretty kitchen with pressed tea towels, her bathroom and the fluffy tissue holder, rug, and toilet sweater in sky blue, her spare room for crafts with twigs and dried flowers, tole painting set, Christmas tree ornaments to decorate, her recipes for lutefisk and *lefse*, her lingonberry jams, the blessed and sugary Norman flesh. I scratched my ankle with the toe of my shoe. I wanted her to like me. Hell, I wanted to *be* her.

Mr. Rizzo was telling Marco what we needed was something to rig the speakers up to. He'd show us how to do it. He said he had a Wollensak tape recorder in the work shed. Come on inside, he said, and let's see what we can see.

Joe Rizzo came to the United States from Palermo when he was a young man and worked for two years in a factory in Pennsylvania to pay off his boat passage. He, and many others, took out loans from crooked moneylenders who hung around the Sicilian docks waiting to take advantage of desperate men and their families. He told us how he labored in a boiling cauldron, a factory so filthy you wouldn't want your pig to step foot in it, which was the fate of almost all the men back then who came from Italy for a better life. Brutal working conditions for starvation wages.

I work twelve hours a day to pay back that loan, he said. In one year I hadn't even paid off the interest!

His work shed was an old converted garage on the alley

behind the house. We stepped inside and were stunned dumb. Before us was a wonderland of tools.

We sat on a crate box with our mouths hanging unhinged, our eyes shining with flat-out awe. I held the stereo speakers and Marco held the tangle of wires.

You can put those things down, said Mr. Rizzo. Nobody's going to take them away from you.

We smiled, but didn't move.

I got a good idea, said Mr. Rizzo. How about we make loudspeaker system?

A system! I set the speakers on the floor. Marco dropped the box of wires. We stepped over a pile of old car batteries, boxes of copper and metal wires next to the soldering outfit, and held our breath trying to count the electric parts lined up on shelves: parts of fans, radios, mixers, toasters.

A tape recorder with buttons like thumbs and two spools snarled with papery tape in a shiny new case sat on a shelf.

Does it work? asked Marco.

Let's give her a what for, said Mr. Rizzo.

Rig it up with our speakers, lead the two wires from the receiver in the tape recorder to each speaker, attach and tape with electrical tape. Insert batteries, make her like new, hey-hey.

Mr. Rizzo, why are we called gumbah and wop?

You know where that word gumbah came from? he asked. It comes from the word *compare,* friend or pal. And wop? Means Without Papers. The name began at Ellis Island.

Ellis Island. Where they'd throw you back in the ocean for being sick. I remembered Ellis Island and I remembered the man and woman in the big house on Summit Avenue, the slam of their door shutting us out. Mamma pleading, and then the Mississippi River flooding the world.

Still, said Mr. Rizzo, immigrating to America, it was worth it. I have not regretted one minute of my life in this country. My mamma in Sicily lost seven babies to hunger and sickness, my pappa did the work of three men to farm the land but the landowners took the best of his crops and left him without enough to feed his family.

The factory was a living hell, but we kept working because we couldn't do anything else. We couldn't even speak English. My cousin Tomasio died in that factory. He was sick with the fever but he went to work anyhow. He worked like mule and after ten hours he fainted. He fell under his machine and was crushed. They pulled him out and the boss was angry because he had to stop the machines to pull Tomasio out. They put what was left of him on the factory floor. He was in pieces. Arms, hands, feet. I remember his hands. His left hand lying on the floor without its arm. Still holding the wrench. They swept him up like garbage, put the pieces of Tomasio in a bag. His head was still caught in the machine.

Marco turned pale. I grabbed his hand and we squeezed our fingers together.

So you see, kids, we've been through worse things than being called gumbah or wop.

We carried the tape recorder to the East Minneapolis train yard on Broadway and Johnson. We sat in the dirt by the tracks, the microphone between us. We felt good sitting in the train yard. We felt at home. A generation of Italian men oiled the metal, greased the cranks of the trains. They threw the switches, engineered, roadmastered, and Italian extra gangs shoveled the tracks, repaired the tracks, carried the ties, pounded them in place, shoveled some more, lifted, swung, and labored through every kind of weather. A section foreman could be called at any hour of the day or night to get his crew out to the snowed-under tracks in blizzards and arctic windchill, these men who cleared the tracks, kept the trains running on schedule with their cargo, passengers, and reputation. Our pappa could have been one of these men. What would it be like to be the daughter of a railroad man, a man who saw these tracks as daily bread?

What we wanted to record: terrifying noises to put under Natalie's window while she slept. It's said if you put a bucket under the window of someone who wronged you, they would have to beg you for your forgiveness. But how about the roar of a train under their window? Marco was a genius.

No, ChiChi, you are, he said.

The Lord moves in mysterious ways. Fate runs its own race. The summer could have ended like any other summer, if it had not been for the accident of fate. We connected the wires and the speakers to the tape recorder, that's true. We hooked up the microphone, made our recordings, but how could we have known? It could have been a nice summer. Couldn't it have been a nice summer?

When Mrs. Rizzo wasn't in the house, Mr. Rizzo invited us into their parlor to listen to opera music. Mr. Rizzo leaned back in his big chair with his eyes closed, his hands swaying back and forth conducting. We listened, rapt and overcome. *La Forza Del Destino,* what an opera. *Pace, pace, mio Dio!* Peace, grant me peace! sang Leonora. I hugged my knees, yes. Grant her peace!

We listened to *La Traviata, La Boheme, Tosca, Rigoletto.* Opera was bigger than life, bigger than our reality, than our imagination. Marco drew pictures in his notebook as he listened. I imagined myself on stage. I could die like Butterfly, dance like Violetta, laugh like Musetta, flaunt like Tosca, weep like Leonora. I could, I could.

Mrs. Rizzo threw a fit when she discovered we had been in her house. We heard her from the steps outside by her petunias.

Tony, were those two creatures in my living room? How do you know what kind of germs they're carrying? *My gott in heaven!* Did they put their feet on my furniture? Did they wipe their noses on the upholstery? That boy! What did he touch?

Inga, stop it.

Did that boy cough all over my furniture? Did he? Did he?

Outside Marco and I still reeled from Gigli's lovesick aria,

Nessun Dorma, and the thrill of that final high B. How glorious this world was when there were voices like Gigli, when there were operas like *Turandot.* How magical everything became when there was music to sing along with and swing our bodies to like *Va Pensiero* from *Nabucco.*

O mia patria . . .

I took Marco's hand and we started home. The crusty leafed geraniums along Mrs. Rizzo's walkway turned their faces, their cankered, lying faces.

The act of fate occurred at midnight on a hot Friday night in August when all windows in the neighborhood were left open in hopes of a merciful breeze. The accident occurred, the thing which was not our fault. *Non e la nostra colpa.* Let it be known. It wasn't our fault.

We tiptoed down the stairs in our bare feet and set the Wollensak on the porch floor. We carried the speakers with the long wires outside and hung them from the low branches of the scrub oak outside Natalie's window. Back in the porch we adjusted the volume to its most horrible high decibel and were about to press Play.

However.

Someone came walking up the sidewalk to the porch.

Two someones.

Marco and I had nowhere to hide so we sneaked back up the stairs to our apartment.

Suddenly—a scratchy sound, muffled voices over a loudspeaker! Like the P.A. system at school announcing a fire drill.

FRANK, HONEY—

Marco brought a hand to his mouth, whispered he must have pushed the wrong button.

I'M CRAZY ABOUT YOU, BABY.

OH FRANK, FRANK, FRANK . . .

Muffled crunching, sighs, groans.

So. All those phone calls were from Franco! Lover Boy was Natalie's stepgrandpop, Franco Pazzoli.

DON'T . . . NOT HERE. LET'S GO UP TO YOUR ROOM. Giggles, sighs, grunts. Watery sounds, splashing.

More rustling. DO YOU HEAR SOMETHING? LIKE AN ECHO?

Their voices were loud enough to wake up the neighborhood. On and on they slurped with their promises and grunts.

TELL ME YOU LOVE ME, LET ME HEAR IT . . .

AHHH. OOOHHH . . .

Geez, ChiChi, it's a ninety-minute tape! said Marco.

A light appeared in Mrs. Pazzoli's bedroom window. The lovebirds went on whispering, giggling, making gargling sounds. Grenadine had a laugh like a horse.

Mamma was up now. Someone's radio? she said from the hall.

Mrs. Pazzoli's voice: Quiet out there! People are trying to sleep!

HONEY, DID YOU HEAR THAT?

Grenadine and Frank were amplified loud enough to be heard in Saint Paul.

Now other lights went on in other houses. Other voices. Franco's wife. About fifteen minutes went by and a police car pulled up to the curb.

ChiChi, cops!

We had seen cops hit two older boys from the settlement house with their clubs. A record store owner on Broadway said the boys had stolen records. They tried to get away but two policemen caught them. The boys swung their arms, kicked, yelled in their broken English that they hadn't done anything, and the policemen gave each of them a whack. The boys were handcuffed and crying when they were taken away in a police car. Marco and I were with Nonna when we saw this happen and I hid my head in her skirt.

More screams.

Franco? Is that you out there?

NO.

What's going on?

Voices yelling, neighbors in bathrobes, a deep, Break it up! Break it up!

Scuffling, flesh upon flesh.

We could have created something brainy like a neighborhood watch system, an invention to help eliminate crime. We could have been heros. But no.

This is a decent neighborhood! someone shouted.

Then the click of the Wollensak.

We can kiss those speakers bye-bye, said Marco.

Natalie whining. A wail from Grenadine. Voices talking at once.

Mamma entered our room.

You, she said. *You*, Leticcia. *Disgraziata*.

Me? I'm innocent!

Leticcia, you *Never. In. You. Life. Innocent.*

What went out of me felt like air but it was viscid, like infection, much thicker and porous than air. If it had a color it would be red, a dirty blood red. And I wouldn't get it back.

Mamma pulled me up by one braid and marched me down the stairs to take the speakers out of the tree. I detached the wires from the tape recorder under the porch table and brought the speakers and wire upstairs. I settled them on the floor of our closet. Marco seemed especially satisfied. I caught the look. He had gotten revenge for his sister.

Was it really a mistake that Marco pressed Record instead of Play that night? The contented expression on his face as he fell asleep was enough for me.

Neither Franco nor Grenadine discovered or understood what had happened. The next day Grenadine started packing.

I got no choice, Josie. I'm going back to my husband.

Husband. You married?

Oh sure.

Hey don't act so surprised. Josie, join the twentieth century. Look at you, you live like it's a hundred years ago.

But I can't believe—

Tell you what. Come on down to the beauty school and I'll do your hair for you. For free.

Mamma said nothing, stared, blinked, lowered her eyes.

Grenadine didn't usually come into our room. Not for any reason. Now she walked in without a knock. I'll just say goodbye, Madame Queen, Mister Bones.

The closet door was open.

Not that I'll miss either of you.

So long, we said.

She turned to leave and glanced in the open closet. Hey— are those speakers?

Nah. Yes.

What do you have speakers for?

Her face flushed a dusty orange, the color of her

lipstick. Her eyes filled yellow. She rubbed the undersides of her arms.

You kids did that to me, didn't you?

Did what?

How come? How come you did that to me?

Grenadine moved out, carrying her pink model cases by herself. When she was gone, we sat, the three of us, at our kitchen table, gloomy and silent. Mamma looking at me, her eyes cold as snow.

What? I didn't do anything. What'd I do?

Mamma thought Grenadine and Franco's romance had been broadcast over the radio. She couldn't understand how I had gotten them on the radio.

I'm tell you one thing, she said, If you see Rizzo again, you go to his workshop again, I'm break you legs. I break you legs like I'm squash a bug. I'm break you legs and I'm kill you good. Was Missus Rizzo who did? She hate us. She marry Italian man but she no like his people. Was Missus Rizzo who did?

She sat at the kitchen table hunched over her coffee cup, one tear traveling down her lip to her chin. *Non e giusto.* Is terrible thing, she said. It breaks the heart!

What had happened with Franco and Grenadine was an accident of fate. The unexpected is the plight of innovation, it said so in our book.

I discovered Natalie sitting on the fence in the backyard out of sight of the neighbors. Hunched and watching a bee. (Please, God, don't let me forget that lardy face.) Why had I worried myself about her clubby gang of girls from Pierce Elementary and what they thought about us? Did they make art? Were they inventors like Marco and me? There sat Natalie on the fence in the backyard, sniffing. Wiping her nose on her forearm.

I watched her from the side of the house. I remembered the time when Marco had a fever and Mamma took him to see Doctor Spano. They walked home from the bus stop and Marco was tired; he was worn, flattened, wanting to sleep. Natalie was on the porch steps, I'd remember it long after we were old people. Natalie on the steps with her Pierce Elementary pals. They saw Marco coming up the walk, saw his slow limp. They saw him, they caved on each other and laughed.

Laughed at my brother.

The story of Natalie's grandpop and Grenadine was the gossip of Tar Town. Franco's wife was laughed at, disgraced, and Mamma felt no pity, said she knew what was *disgraziata*.

A FOR RENT sign appeared in the window downstairs and the name Grenadine Fletcher wasn't mentioned again in our apartment. Mamma kept to herself and I moped around our rooms, languid in the late August heat, thinking about what happens between men and women, what the odd connection was that turned them stupid. A juicy romance had erupted right under our noses between certain people we could no longer mention, and what we were left with was its hungry wet sorrow.

Marco and I started thinking up something new to build, something that had never before existed on this earth, something if it weren't for Marco and me wouldn't be at all.

We saw Mr. Rizzo at Mass across the broad oval of pews at church, his gentle face like a saint painted by Botticelli. I wanted to call over to his missus and tell her, Lookie here, we've bathed! I wanted to show her my fingernails, clean knees, the scrubbed gums of my teeth, my sweet polished *culo,* clean enough to spread lunch on. After Grenadine left I spent whole afternoons in the bathtub.

Mamma's anger seemed to invigorate her. She even took a walk with Marco and me one windy afternoon in early September. I pranced alongside her, chattering, sick with happiness at walking with my mamma.

My mother was *talking* to me.

I couldn't identify exactly when the changes began to occur in Mamma, but for one, she left the apartment more often. No reason—for walks, she said. To look in shop windows. She ventured alone to church for Mass, she went out alone at night. She made an appointment at the Promenade School of Beauty and had her first haircut since she was a girl in Praiano. Marco and I danced around her like two rubber balls.

She seemed to be *okay*.

One evening before going out she saw me watching her comb her new bob haircut.

What you think? Come on. Tell me.

(*Talking* to me.)

You look very pretty, Mamma.

She gave a big smile to herself in the mirror, then turned to me. Come here, she said. You too old for braids.

She unraveled my braids, tried brushing my hair. She yanked, tugged, *Gesù!* I inherited my hair from her. Hair heavy as stone. Nonna said such hair could keep the Italian army warm for months.

Is like pulling a plow through rocks, Mamma said, struggling with the brush. We combed and brushed until my hair ballooned out in a tantrum of dark fleece.

What I am going to do with this, she said. A convulsion of hair. Deranged, bloated heaps of it. Crooked ropes with braid marks discharged all over my head and shoulders. A blast of black frenzied stuff towering every which way.

You want I cut it, Leticcia?

What with? The meat cleaver?

She rose and opened the drawer of her dresser for her sewing shears. Don't move.

She cut fast, in a fit of energy. I watched lakes of hair grow and deepen on the floor. When she finished, we sat on the bed staring at each other.

Dio Mio, she said, sweat rolling from her jaw. My daughter is my mirror!

She received telephone calls. Answered in English. She smiled, laughed even. We heard her talking to herself as she washed clothes. I helped her carry the baskets from the basement. We clipped the wet sheets and towels to the clothes-lines, she smiling as she worked. The leaves of trees turned the color of sunset and the wind turned our fingers stiff.

Mamma said autumn was a time to be glad.

I had a new haircut. I was Annette Funicello. I was my mother's mirror. And she said the word *glad*.

Then came the bomb.

She had someone she wanted us to meet.

Say hello to Mr. Metamere.

He held flowers, daisies, the kind you get cheap in Oc-tober at the grocery store because everybody grew them in their backyards. On the floor at his knee was an oversized suitcase bound by two leather straps. Marco and I stared at him with our mouths dropped open and our necks poked up from our collars. We must have looked like the emus in our library bird book, brains smaller than our eyes.

Mr. Metamere grinned a stop-and-go, up-and-down grin and said, Hey there, you two.

We stood riveted in our shoes. Unable to speak. It wasn't just that Mamma was introducing us to a strange man with flowers and a suitcase, he also was a man with the biggest head we had ever seen. It was one huge head! Like a bowling ball, a world globe, an immense watermelon! It was parked on his shoulders with no connecting device and when he moved to give our mother the flowers, his head rolled like a rubber raft on water.

Hey there, he said, wiggling his fingers at us.

Mamma chuckled and lowered her eyes, blushed. You would have thought he had just recited Dante. She was dyed yarn drying in the wind. She swayed, fluttered, became weightless. Whatever words she was saying were swallowed, spit up, dropping into the air like small digestive mistakes.

Something about him moving in. Huh? Another *boarder?*

His smile was filmy. What say, guys? he said, his head toppling.

Marco and I stood growing roots, our toes spreading into the floor and flowering out. Mamma sighed, asked him to wait in the parlor while she spoke privately with her dear children.

Angry. The white line around her mouth.

Voice low and trembling, her face close to mine. Woman need man, she said, my collar in her fist. Mr. Metamere, he love you Mamma. One day maybe you understand, ChiChi. One day you be woman, too.

What I understood was Mamma had lost her mind. Couldn't she see Marco was coughing more? And he was losing weight?

The man looks funny, I said.

A smack on the jaw. My new haircut flipped up.

Marco said, Mamma, ChiChi's right. He does look funny. Is he your boyfriend?

Her answer was a snort through the nose, then a slow crinkle of the eye and a timid smile like a woman offering a full refrigerator.

And maybe something more, she said.

Metameres are what *worms* are made of, I told Marco. Dictionaries didn't lie. We had a human worm in the house.

Call me Uncle Leo, said Mr. Metamere.

We escaped the apartment and outside on the sidewalk we blubbered and whistled and Marco coughed.

Mr. Metamere levitated into our lives. A jittery river of movement, he laid on the sofa most of the day and then slipped through the rooms, from the black lacquer tiger on the coffee table in the living room to the kitchen. He ate. Mostly, he slept. He needed a lot of sleep.

Sometimes they argued. Mamma blew her words out in

sprays where they landed on his blank face like a wind of ink spots.

He slumped, reached for her hand. Giuseppina, I can't really help you with the rent right now. Things will get better though. Trust me. Now about that snack—

Il Mal Occhio. I definitely needed the Evil Eye.

Another birthday come and gone.

Jar Town was struck a fatal blow when city planners decided to build the new freeway, 135W, down the middle of our community. Half of the humble but proud homes, with their flower and vegetable gardens, would soon be torn down and in their place a field of weeds and a freeway. The Fiores, who moved in downstairs, lost their home on Buchanan Street when it was razed to make way for the new freeway. A kind old couple, they immigrated from Salerno in 1928 and had worked hard and long to own the home they were proud of and loved, that was now a gaping patch of dirt.

Signora Fiore brought her religious shrines to put up in our backyard. Most of the houses in Tar Town had shrines in their yards, small grottoes with a saint housed inside. It was important to have *edicole sacre* in the yard as homage to a saint or as a memorial to a dead relative. The Fiore's shrine was a small U-shaped alcove with a pitched roof topped with a wooden cross. Inside was a statue of the Virgin Mary with her arms outstretched.

In Italy shrines rose up everywhere, beside public buildings, curbs, on street corners, embedded in walls. Signora Fiore said along the mountain roads on the Amalfi coast were countless small white chapels looking like little churches, commemorating the dead. I knelt with her before the shrine of the Virgin in the backyard.

I asked Signora Fiore if she had ever been to Praiano, our village in Italy. She was bent in prayer, her mouth moving, the beads clicking between her fingers. Sure, sure, playground for kings, she muttered, and I laughed. Kings with no running water, no toilets, and no shoes! Praiano, the village in the mountains above the sea where Mamma had been a girl and had fallen in love. It was only a few kilometers from Maiori and the battle where our pappa lost his leg. You know, my Mamma, lolling among the camellias, oleander, and trailing bougainvillea, breathless and dreamy, full of war and longing. Then the man who took us for a walk on the beach, no face, but kind hands and a scratchy chest smelling smoky. He held me in his arms. Mamma's laughter, *sì, sì,* laughter. Mamma's convulsion of hair crammed into the small breeze.

Memories of Italy were dim to me, like the sun when it dumps itself into the horizon and the world goes blank. Had he walked with a limp? I couldn't remember a limp. Didn't he take off his clothes, dive into the water?

The water on the skin like a rash. A sore that stung the skin.

Weren't there two legs?

School started. It made me old to walk to the settlement house for our classes. Marco was pale and weak. He talked slower. The spark that kept me from falling into a deep torpor, dumb of spirit and obtuse in the head, were the street fights between a Tar Town teenage gang of boys and the Yellow Shirts from across the tracks. There were threats. Vendettas. Young people were warned not to go out alone at night and the neighborhood became cautious, jittery. I started practicing my Evil Eye powers.

With my new haircut I was Annette Funicello. I was cute.

One afternoon after school Marco and I stood outside the butcher shop on the corner of Broadway and Buchanan near the railroad trestle bridge, chewing on beef and basil jerky, when from across the street came,

HEY, WOPS.

Marco pulled back his shoulders.

OH YA? His hair flipped over an eyebrow.

Dumb wops! came the voice.

Marco blew a scrap of dried beef from his mouth. He jammed a fist to his elbow.

VA FA N'CULU.

The gang leader's name was LaMont. We knew all about him. Tough, and he fought dirty. So he and his boys were going to pick on little kids now? They darted between the cars toward our side of the street.

We took off for the alley, me running ahead of Marco with the beef jerky held between my teeth, my book bag lopping against my leg.

ChiChi, what's wrong with you?

My shoe's untied.

LaMont was gaining on us. We ran through the alley, across lawns and into the Rizzo's front yard. We ducked around the house through Mrs. Rizzo's geraniums to the kitchen door. We banged on it. No answer.

Run!

We ducked behind the garbage cans against the work shed and stayed there until the only sound we heard was our own breath. That is, my breath and Marco's wheezing and gasping into his sleeve.

Listen, ChiChi, he was saying. Brave people don't run from trouble, they *outlast* it.

(Marco. Resilient to threats.)

You're not listening, ChiChi. Are you listening? Let's make a pact. We don't ever let them get to us, eh? Promise. We stick together.

His words came in short spurts. The thin blue veins at his temples stood out and his eyes shone phosphorous. You could kill a Viking with his eyes, with those eyes you could start a revolution. Garibaldi must have had eyes like Marco, the kind of eyes men and women take up the sword to follow, the eyes that see what nobody else sees, like Leonardo or Giotto or Brunelleschi.

I was ashamed to tell Mamma what happened. I was ashamed for myself. For her, because she had wops for children. Two of the boys chased us to the trash cans we squatted behind in hiding. Their feet were only inches from my fallen book bag.

—Where'd the little turds run off to?

—Forget it. We'll get them later. We'll get the dirty little wops all right.

When we sneaked out of our hiding place, I looked over at the Ricci's kitchen window. There was Mrs. Ricci at her kitchen sink with the radio still playing. She'd been there all the time.

I prayed at Signora Fiore's shine that night, prayed for the power of the Evil Eye. Signora Fiore saw me outside in the dark and joined me. She took my hand. Hers were the hands of all older Italian women that had worked digging in the fields, that had picked grapes, hoed, scrubbed, sewn, scoured, cooked, chopped, weeded, kneaded, raked dirty clothes against a washboard, raised children, hands like Nonna's, thick, tough. Hands that now she said were dedicated to prayer. Even though she was like a tire with no air, sad and without her house on Buchanan Avenue, she prayed to the Madonna, giving her praise. Ah, I figured it out: she was *outlasting.* She said she included us in her prayers, Mamma, Marco, and me.

Grazie, I said, embarrassed. I wondered if she prayed for Mr. Metamere, too. She never mentioned Mamma's so-called renter, and neither did any of the other neighbors. They treated Mamma with the same indifference as when Nonna was with us. To Marco and me the women of the neighborhood were warm, huggy, their eyes full of pity.

We hadn't seen the last of LaMont. The following week he and his gang sneaked into the play area at the side of the settlement house during school hours as an act of revenge against Tar Town teenage boys who had beat up one of their guys and wrecked his bike.

Sister Ursula saw them from the window. She stroked her mustache, crossed herself, and pounded on the window. We jumped from our seats to have a look. There were at least seven of them, boys in yellow T-shirts and dirty shoes. They moved as one person—arms, feet, shoulders, in a fractured kind of dance. From where we were, they looked like rest-less goats. Their skin was the color of goats' hooves.

Mascalzoni! Disgraziati! Sister shouted at the glass. Dis-graceful!

Sister's face changed shape as it pooled red from the collar to her eyebrows. Her mouth was two stiff bluish lines. *An-imali!* she yelled. *Cafoni!*

She grabbed my arm, pulling me into her folds of black, and then we are all of us wrapped in the surplus of her habit, twelve children, her flock, her calling, her *bambini,* her lambs. Nonna had said Sister Ursula was God's angel and I believed her, because she was, after all, a Sicilian, from Catania before she married Jesus.

What you learn in school today, *Figlia?*

Who, me?

Mr. Metamere sat cleaning his fingernails with his pocket knife. Mamma poured hot chocolate into our cups and placed a dish of anisette toast on the table.

Nice knife you got there, Marco said to Mr. Metamere.

The man squinted, his huge head tilting off to the side as if too heavy to stay upright. He flicked a fingernail across the floor.

Come here, have a look-see, he said, This baby got everything you need. Scissor, nail clipper, bottle opener, you name it, this knife got it. He handed the knife to Marco who practically caressed it. He held it like a crucifix, turning it over and examining it. Marco looked like someone in prayer.

Tell you what, kid, said Mr. Metamere, his head rolling in the other direction. It's yours. Keep it.

Mamma slapped her thigh. He no need knife! He no Mister tough-a guy!

Aw, Giuseppina, all boys should have a pocket knife, said Mr. Metamere.

Ya! I shouted. I was thinking of the things we could carve, the art we could make, the wonders we could create with a pocket knife.

That night I awoke to a scraping, rasping sound, like wind chasing empty bottles in the alley. I lay very still, hoping it was the ghost of Nonna.

Nonna? I whispered.

ChiChi?

Marco sat on the edge of his bed. His pajamas, which Mamma bought two sizes too big, drooped from his body, and one small bare shoulder poked out like a potato. His face looked smaller in the shadows of our night-light. His cheeks were puckered, his eyes swollen and pulled down at their corners.

ChiChi, we're just like them—LaMont, the big guys, with the sticks—we're all the same—

Marco was cogitating things I didn't want to consider.

It's bad, ChiChi, he said.

What's bad?

Everything.

Marco thought the way I did. It was better to keep such thoughts in our heads. Not speak of them. He held the folded pocket knife on his lap.

Go back to sleep, Marco. *Buona notte,* say your prayers. I pushed my head under my pillow. I didn't understand what he was saying. I didn't get the implication. I should have.

Father Tuttifucci ordered the fifth and sixth graders to walk home with the second graders in pairs. There was trouble brewing. We left the settlement house in pairs and were rounding the corner of Broadway and Johnson when I saw them coming. Marco, who was next to me, saw them first. Three of them, and moving toward us fast. We stopped. It was not possible to run. Behind us were eight smaller children, and another sixth grader, Joey Minichilli.

Joey yelled, They're coming for us! We're gonna die!

Then the yellow shirts were before us. I could see their teeth. I could see the sweat on the insides of their arms.

One of the boys swung his stick in the air and made a fake lunge toward the first grader holding on to Joey Minichilli's sweatshirt.

Marco jumped in front of him with the open pocket knife. YOU WANT BLOOD, IS THAT WHAT YOU WANT, MISTER TOUGH GUY?

LaMont stopped, surprised. The rest of them stood still, momentarily stunned.

Here's blood for you! screamed my brother, and he pulled up his shirt and slashed at his stomach with the blade of the pocket knife. Blood squirted down his fingers.

Blood, is that what you need, what you're hungry for? EH? EH? And he took another swipe with the knife on his chest.

The boys with the sticks didn't move.

The kid's crazy!

Marco shook the bloody knife at them. Blood sprayed on one of the Yellow Shirts' shoes. Marco screamed, YOU WANT MORE?

He had cut deep enough to cause a trickle of blood down his legs. The boys turned together in a huddle like turkeys and sauntered back across the street and into the trees.

A Yellow Shirts yelled back at us, Dagos are crazy!

Joey Minichilli wet his pants and Marco's blood invented new math equations on the sidewalk.

*M*amma hit her fist against the wall.

What you think? she shouted at Marco. You little pip-a squeak, you take on the whole world with you two fists? Bah! You think you change the world by filling the ground with you blood? The ground, she thirsty, she swallow up you blood and then eat you like a flea.

Dr. Spano stitched up Marco's stomach and Mamma made him stay home for three days even though he didn't want to. On the fourth day Marco returned to school and Father Tuttifucci kissed him on both cheeks. Father Tuttifucci said it was *miracolo,* a miracle from God what had happened, and we all agreed. Marco was David in a plethora of Goliaths, he was a hero and a marvel.

Nonna had taught us not to show fear. Be brave and do hard things, she said. She said fear was worse than defeat. Those words I remember. Marco's words I remember, too: *Don't ever let them get to us. Outlast.* There are the things I remember and things I can't remember. Marco, our hero, coughing again. An autumn of pale orange. Autumn in our hair and in our noses, and Marco in his sweat, brushing his eyes with his thumbs. Mr. Metamere snoring in the next room in Mamma's bed. (I imagine terrible things going on between them. Mr. Metamere removing Mamma's long wool stockings, her apron, her slippers. I imagine him un-tying her hair with his fat fingers. Dancing with her like

Mamma danced with Grenadine. Close, swaying, faces and bodies pressed together.)

I climbed on a chair and removed Pappa from the cupboard. I held him, rocked him, stroked him. Pappa, oh Pappa, I said to the wooden leg.

Mamma no longer cooked the American food Grenadine liked to eat. She cooked Italian dishes again because it was Mr. Metamere's favorite, as he said, cuisine. It was as though Grenadine had never lived here, never sat at our kitchen table, never thrilled us with her stories of life at Mandie's Candies, the Pillsbury assembly line, and the Promenade School of Beauty. Mr. Metamere worshiped Mamma's Italian cooking, couldn't get enough pasta, and Mamma spoiled him, turned him into a real *gourmand,* he said, and wasn't she wonderful, beautiful, and frabjous.

She mashed the potato dough for *gnocchi* in a large bowl. A canister of flour and two eggs waited at the edge of the table by the cutting board. Mr. Metamere sat at the table nibbling on a tomato, watching her. Tomato seeds floated on his chin.

Marco made whistling sounds when he breathed like babies crying.

Mamma, Marco needs to see the doctor.

She tapped the edge of the gnocchi bowl with the wooden spoon. She looked at me with eyes so black and pained you could have taken them to India and left them at the edge of the Ganges to be sold as offerings to a hungry goddess. Mr. Metamere sprinkled salt on the tomato, took another bite. A rosy color spread on his neck and shirt.

Marco, he be fine, he no need doctor, Mamma said.

He's not fine, I said.

Mr. Metamere looked at Marco, held out a wet hand with a snail shape of tomato left in it. Let's have a look at you, kid, he said. Marco inched toward him, jerky, like someone about to get a shot in the *culu*.

He's got a fever, Giuseppina. Holy Moly, I can see it from here.

Adults were such a confusion. Mr. Metamere slept on our sofa most of the day. He seemed to be formed of liquid. You never knew what adults were thinking, what they might do. You could never predict. You wonder if they think about adult concerns like bills and dust all day long, but then suddenly they gave you indications that they've seen you, heard you, and you're no longer an impediment, a loss or dead weight, you count for something.

Mr. Metamere wiped his hands on his pants. ChiChi's right. He's not fine. We're taking him to Emergency. Now! He looked directly at me and said, Good for you, ChiChi.

(Good for me, ChiChi.)

I could have told him every minute of what would follow. The gnocchi dough would be stuck in the refrigerator to harden, the milk would go bad on the counter, there'd be a rush of turning off lights, calling the taxi, checking the stove and water faucets, and pulling down shades. Then the stumbling, hurrying down the stairs to the street.

Marco was taken through the double doors of the hospital emergency room in a wheelchair. I ran alongside hanging on to the armrest and then stood in a city of white sheets as men dressed like gym instructors in rumpled green suits pressed the plastic bubble over his face. I pushed my nose against the cold metal railing surrounding him, heard him gag on the surprise of oxygen.

It was here I began my serious dedication to rituals, the rituals to keep our world spinning on its axis, rituals to appease God and all the saints in heaven, rituals to assure us of a future, keep Marco alive on this earth.

How ChiChi Will Keep Marco Alive

ChiChi will hold her breath and stand on one foot. She will remain on tiptoe for an hour. She will repeat the word *heal* for a whole day. She will walk backward for a mile. She will go up and down stairs on her knees.

Good for me, ChiChi.

It was necessary to expand my methodology, to learn names of things and how they worked. I was not smart enough. I needed to read more books and memorize lists of plants, rocks, birds, rivers. I'd name every street in Minneapolis. In this way I'd entertain God, I'd bring Him pleasure. I'd get his attention, make Him smile. Like the nuns who slept on icy stones and stuck thorns in their skulls. I'd learn how to make God happy.

I fly to you, O virgin of virgins, my Mother.
To you I come,
before you I stand, sinful and sorrowful.
O Mother of the Word Incarnate,
despise not my petitions,
but in your mercy, hear and answer me. . . .

It required all my energy and wit, all my powers to assemble my promises, penances, resolutions, and payoffs. Marco's asthma attacks collapsed him from inside. He would appear to be drowning in an invisible sea of himself. His throat closed, his sinuses filled up, and his ears pounded with the beating of two hearts, one for each ear. His cheeks became fiery as his trachea contracted and filled with fluid. His airway tissues swelled to mean proportions. I shouted to him as if to a deaf person, *Blow out, out, easy, Marco, easy* . . .

He knew how to breathe from his diaphragm and I breathed with him. Together we formed a world-class department of sound effects. Sounds I would forever dread and despise.

Like the ugly word *asthma* itself, a choked-on despicable word. Marco had grown around his disease like ivy vines around a sugar pine tree. His sickness engulfed him, preceded him. It could enter a room before the rest of him.

Mr. Metamere sits beside Mamma on the leatherette sofa in the hospital's waiting room. A television program about creating window planters is set on low. Every eye in the room is fixed on the television set like a congregation in prayer.

Mr. Metamere smiles at me, pats the leatherette beside him. I look at Mamma for permission to sit down. She isn't looking at me. Her eyes are lifted upward. She is learning how to brush a cheery redwood stain on a plank of pine.

I must stand on one foot. I must close my eyes and say *breathe* two thousand times. I must do this right.

The doctor with a face like a blank piece of paper told us that three million other children Marco's age suffered with asthma, it's not so unusual. He used words like Touch and Go, Not Responding, We Are Doing All We Can.

Marco was one of the five percent of the population of the world who were cursed with what Mamma called Bodily Limitations. And more children who live in the inner cities had upper respiratory diseases than regular children. This information made Mr. Metamere uncomfortable. He was a man who had never eaten dirt.

Mamma's voice was low, like coming from the bottom of a jar.

My boy. He be all right?

Well, now don't get upset, Ma'am, it's just that he isn't responding to the medication quite the way we'd hoped. He'll have to stay in the hospital a few more days—

After the word *Ma'am* Mamma didn't hear a word the doctor said. An Emergency Room nurse, a large black woman whose white stockings turned her legs silver, told us the big problem in these cases was depression.

What are we worried about? You heard the man. Our boy is merely feeling a little Down At The Mouth, said Mr. Metamere, half talking to himself. He reminded me of the puffy-faced dolls owned by spoiled rich kids, toys limp with the fatigue of being left on shelves.

Our boy. Down At The Mouth.

I promised Saint Christopher lilacs and figs, fresh lemons and oranges, school lunches. I would deny myself coffee, my bed. I would sacrifice one half of every meal, and I would never sit on a comfortable chair again as long as I lived.

You can promise and promise—and still.

The nurse with the silver legs gave Mamma permission to stay with Marco all night, but she were lost at the suggestion. She gave a weak smile as though she were the one who was sick. Mr. Metamere opened his arms and she sat on his lap, burrowed her head in his chest. He stroked her shoulders and back, sat humming and rocking her in his arms, and I thought that could be what a father did if he very much loved his little girl.

Later that night I stretched out on the floor of our room

trying to make the shape of the cross. My forehead hurt against the floor. I rose to my feet and walked on my toes to the kitchen. I could hear Mr. Metamere snoring in Mamma's room. I didn't need light to find Pappa's leg. I wrapped my arms around it and rubbed the knee. Then I sat on the floor holding the leg and rocking.

I fell asleep watching the stars out the window. The night sky looked like a stripped backbone.

In the morning the sky had turned to flannel, like the flannel work shirts worn by the Italian men who worked in the train yard at North Town. The men who left their houses in the first hours of the day with lunch pails tucked under their arms on their way to throw switches and repair rails. If Pappa were one of those men, Mamma would be here in the kitchen now wiping the bread crumbs from the table where she sliced the bread and cheese for his breakfast. We'd be drinking coffee and steamed milk. He'd kiss me on the top of my head like I remember on the beach in Italy. Good girl, ChiChi, he'd say, and my face would press against his shirt.

The garbage wrapped in newspaper lay on the floor by the sink and a circus advertisement caught my eye. Clowns with their mouths turned up.

I stared at the picture. Maybe I could change the future by keeping my mouth turned up like these clowns!

ChiChi? Wha—?

The kitchen light dazed the room. Everything held its breath.

ChiChi, is that you?

I sat upright still holding Pappa in my arms.

Mr. Metamere wore his bathrobe like a pile of laundry. His head twitched. Holy Minerva! What are you doing with that garbage? Izzat a wooden leg? Sheesh!

He shook himself the way dogs do after a bath and sat himself in a chair. The D'Amico's calendar fell to the floor.

What in the name of! Is that a prosthesis? A LEG?

This? Oh this is Pappa.

Big woof of air. Sweet Cousin of God. His voice was between a squeak and a meow.

A long time passed before he said, Well okey dokey, how's about we have us some breakfast?

I placed Pappa back in the cupboard and Mr. Metamere made pancakes sprinkled with sugar. I wanted to talk about clowns. The clowns at our church fairs were somebody's mothers dressed in saggy pants and painted faces. They made zoo animals out of balloons. They pulled wrinkled scarves out of their pockets and brought paper flowers up from their sleeves. When they spoke it was with high screaky voices trying to be funny.

Now take the clowns in the newspaper advertisement: Bongo Bob—Happy Flappy. They were the *real* thing. They knew how to make people happy. At that instant I knew what I had to become. The soul of civilization was the mouth Turned Up.

*H*e gave me an orange to suck on while he put the lentils in a pan to soak. I ate the orange with slow nibbles, rolling the seeds against my teeth. I'd save some as an offering to Saint Julian, patron saint of clowns.

You like the clowns then, ChiChi? He spoke in a muffled voice, like sifted flour. Hey, I'm serious. I'll take you and your brother to the circus some time. How would you like that?

How would I like that. Was he kidding?

Have you seen real clowns in the circus, Mr. Metamere?

Well, sure, sweetheart. Next time the circus is in town, we're going, you can count on that. You and your brother both. Yessir, bet your bottom dollar.

I'd like to be a clown, I said.

Say again?

A clown! I could be a clown, couldn't I? I could be funny, couldn't I?

We left the apartment and walked up Cemetery to Spring, across the park to Fillmore and the bus stop on Broadway. The streets were vacated, like a sentence interrupted, or a wake after the last prayer.

The weather was an omen. Was the weather an omen? Marco lying in a hospital bed with bars up around him like a baby crib, his mind jumbled from too much sickness and medicine, his face turned onto one cheek, eyes open, eyes staring, eyes so deep and black you could sail a ship on them, you could go to Napoli and stay for a week at the shrine of Santa Lucia.

Doesn't that hurt? Mr. Metamere said, shaking his head at my foot. I had been hopping for the last block. I was avoiding the cracks.

No, I don't hurt, I said. My limbs abandoned the rest of me. I had to pee.

We stopped at Walgreen's where Mr. Metamere bought Mamma a bottle of cologne. The sample squirt on my cuff smelled like maybe Tahiti smelled with its orchids and monsoons. You could faint. I spotted a rack of children's books along the wall and one of the books in particular. A heat wave happened in my stomach.

What's the matter, ChiChi? Never seen a book before?

On the cover was a picture of the clown, Bongo Bob.

Mr. Metamere put the book in my hand. *A Child's Greatest Circus,* it was called. You like it? It's yours.

It hit me. I had never opened a store-book. Never smelled its spine or pressed my face to its pages like I did the books on the shelves of the settlement house and the public library. New books with fresh ink and smooth unstained pages! I felt the need to walk on tiptoe, to cover my head. Tourists on their way to the capital should come here first, touch the books.

Follow me, Sweetheart, said Mr. Metamere. You want to be a clown? He led me down an aisle of cosmetics. Here you go. Start practicing. He showed me a set of face paints called Fun Face For Kids, four colors plus white, a brush, sponge, and powder, $2.98 tax not included.

Go ahead. It's a gift from me to you, he said. Now pick a book out for Marco.

The clerk at the cash register was Carla Tomini, who lived two doors from the Rizzos. She graduated from the settlement house and was a freshman at Edison High. Her eyebrows were as big as her eyes. She saw the circus book, the clown makeup.

Isn't it a little late for Halloween, ChiChi? she snickered.

Teenagers were only nice to us if they were coaches or Sunday School teachers. Before leaving, I gave her a flick of the chin.

We stopped at Russo's bakery for pastries to bring to the hospital. I asked Russo if I could use his bathroom. I propped the book with Bongo Bob's picture against the sink faucet and tried to duplicate his face onto mine with my face paint kit. The first thing I did was to draw the mouth turned up. I covered my nose with red lipstick. I drew pomegranates on my cheeks.

On the bus Mr. Metamere held the box of pastries like money. (I lost my appetite using Russo's bathroom, an experience something like maybe catching a priest with his trousers down. You don't want to know what's beneath the holy robes, and you don't want to know the best baker in town relieves himself in a dank airless coffin of a room painted seedy green with a toilet awash with old shit.)

They put Marco in a geriatric ward because there wasn't an available bed in pediatrics. The ward was dark and smelled like boiled potatoes. A television set played at the far end, the only source of light. A figure covered with a thin blanket was hunched in a wheelchair, a figure small enough to evaporate, a sawdust doll with bones soft as saline. In his lap was the familiar albuterol inhaler.

Mr. Metamere left to find Mamma and here's where I lost control, where a string inside was pulled and I turned into a taffy twanged astral body jumping and slapping my hips, tapping my feet, turning circles. I did what I hoped clowns did, and Marco raised his head and watched.

I turned another circle.

I shook my head.

I took his hand, knelt by his wheelchair.

His fingers tightened around mine. He smiled.

Tired, very tired.

A nurse hurried into the room. For pity sake! Shocked. What's that all over the child's *face?*

Uh, Marco—I tried to explain—Marco, Marco, we brought cannoli, your favorite, and brand-new store books, our very own books about clowns and the circus and a book of *Drawings by Minnesota Artists* for you. Marco, I'm going to dedicate my life to making mouths turn up, I won't stop, no not ever, and you'll be well, I am sure of it!

And get lost, Nurse, you're getting on my nerves.

Oh Marco, smile.

Marco, listen. Mr. Metamere is a nice man. We can even start imagining he's our father. What do you think about that? Marco? Mr. Metamere—our father.

The three other beds in the room held men snarled in their sheets. One of them had a left eye open, his right eye pinched closed. Each man was connected to instruments invented by some healthy person. I could hear the rattle of a dry throat, the popping of a hip joint, the hiss of a wrist vein injected with medicine.

The nurse ordered me to be quiet. What did I think this was anyhow? *Really!*

I wanted to know why dying required quiet. You would think the dying would prefer a band, music, clowns, maybe a monkey.

Don't agitate your brother, snapped the nurse. He

shouldn't get excited. It could bring on another episode.

That's what they called the thing that happened to Marco—episode. He didn't have attacks, he had *episodes*.

Has your mother seen that stuff all over your face? said the nurse. Your brother, well, your brother is like a vegetable now, but this will more than likely pass in time . . .

Later the doctor came, said Marco was out of the woods and could go home. I wanted to kiss his hands.

This is your sister, Marco?

Uh huh.

Does she always do unusual things like this?

Yup.

What Marco suffered was post-episode letdown. The most common medication for the treatment of chronic airway inflammation was an oral prednisone, a corticosteroid that leaves the patient almost paralyzed with exhaustion. After the treatment, Marco felt drained, cramped, confused.

Mamma and Mr. Metamere arrived just in time to hear the doctor's news.

Dai figlio mio, said Mamma. Everybody out of woods now!

Marco was confused. I think I'm a tomato, he said. All goopy inside.

The old man in the next bed pointed a finger at me. I pointed back at him. I took a deep breath, stood on one foot by my brother's side and sang soft and sweet:

Io ti amo, Io ti amo
com'un promodoro . . .

What is she singing? Mr. Metamere whispered to my stunned mother.

Mouth dropped open and shaking, Mamma said: My

daughter, she singing, I love you like—*I love you like a tomato*—and she cried like Nonna's babies must have cried when they were starving to death on dirt. I love you like a tomato.

I, ChiChi Leticcia Maggiordino, knew and I didn't know. Sometimes the story of our Pappa was so near I could enter it as a person enters a dark room that is suddenly filled with light. And then it was gone, sprung back into Mamma's gears, sullen and sealed.

The nurse gives the mamma the boy's release form, instructions for his continued care, a prescription and a sack of bedside things, a pitcher, a pair of paper slippers, a soap dish. Mamma speaks to the nurse in Italian. She is not in Minneapolis.

November, a season for Mamma's steaming bowls of meat ball *zuppa,* and bowls of hot *piselli* laced with Romano cheese. The smells of baked bread, stewed rabbit, and Vicks VapoRub, a time of preparing for winter and for grabbing at breath like an expensive trinket poor people couldn't afford.

I made more promises to God. Whatever it took, God, please, let me pay for the sins that brought this pain on us. I'd be funny. I'd distort my face in a hundred ways. I'd be so funny the world would fall down laughing at the mention of my name.

If I had only one leg, I'd be a ballerina. Are you listening, Marco? I'd dance with a balloon stomach and an umbrella.

(Yes, I am positively serious.) Believe me on this. I'd squawk like a gull. Learn to juggle. And I'd make people laugh.

One day remembering these years in Tar Town, I would think not only of the smell of eucalyptus, the endless pricks of needles, the medicines, or the leaking valves of deficient veins and a lung sent in error, but the dread of the absence of laughter. The memory of these things is what will remain—there, just there, before my face rising up unexpectedly in the middle of a performance when I forget my lines, and I fall down under its weight. I'm spread-eagled on the stage while the orchestra repeats my cue, I'll be remembering sickness and my brother.

Mamma sits at the kitchen table with Mr. Metamere. A platter of *pizzelle* hot from the iron waits untouched at the center of the table. They drink wine the color of chicken livers. Mamma's voice is thick, dark. I won't allow it. No, not in that place, she says.

But he would receive such good care, Giuseppina . . .

My son he stay here, at home. The priest he come. Like before.

(What could she mean? Priest?)

I rush to the bathroom mirror with my makeup kit. I paint my mouth up in a huge red lobster smile, circle my face in egg yolk yellow and my eyes in strings of green cornsilk. My mouth is turned up. I am grinning. I am perpetually grinning. I chant the names of clowns, saints, and angels. I wear my new happy clown face and sit by Marco's bed waiting for his eyes to open. Don't laugh, Marco, just smile.

Mamma sees me coming toward her, she drops her wineglass. She yanks at her apron.

What. Mamma? What'd I do?

She stumbles backward against the sink, and smooth as slicing a plum, falls to the floor.

A name, *la stregona*. What do you mean, Mamma? What witch?

Cripessake, Giuseppina, the kid's just trying to cheer us up. Mr. Metamere smoothes Mamma's hair, pats her arm. He puts his mouth next to Mama's head.

Che stregona, Mamma says again, crosses herself.

Mamma, no! I'm not a witch!

Mr. Metamere scratches his ear. I didn't catch that. Say again?

It dawns on me then. My brother wasn't going to get well. And I couldn't make Mamma happy.

Late that night Mr. Metamere tiptoed into our room and sat on the edge of my bed. He had small feet, like a woman's. Light from the hallway fell like sleet. I watched Mr. Metamere's profile, his wide flat nose, the small eyes.

ChiChi, your mother doesn't mean to be so hard on you. It's just that she's nervous and worried now. Your mother is what one might say at sixes and sevens at the moment.

Oh. Okay. Sixes and sevens.

You're a natural at performing, Sweetheart. Really. You should be on TV. I'm serious.

I scratched my eyebrow. He smoothed his pajama leg. I had rubbed off the makeup using half a roll of toilet paper after Mamma sent me to my room. My face itched.

Your mamma doesn't mean what she says, you know that.

Know? Did he say *know?* I knew the journey that air struggles to get itself through to the lungs, past obstructions, contusions, lesions, and how it got lost along the way. How it dissipated and needed another gulp to heave it forward. Then another and another until there was only pathetic gagging and wheezing left.

I knew the eighteen needle pricks itching and swelling on Marco's forearms when we sat in the posy pink waiting room of the Ear Nose and Throat clinic. I knew about the disfunctioning nebulizer, the enemy pollen grains and mold spores that flowed by the thousand down the trachea. I knew about mucus production, smooth muscle contraction, air flow reduction. I knew that dust kills. And I knew Marco was dying.

Mr. Metamere fidgeted with his hands in his lap. Outside the sound of boxcars rumbled along the tracks, the squeal of steel against steel.

He reached for my hand. His fingers felt spongy on my wrist.

See, your mamma isn't good at putting into words how much she appreciates things, how much she cares for you.

I pulled my hand away, wrapped my arms around my knees. Mamma says if a person is nice to you it means bad luck, I said.

His breath smelled of garlic and polenta.

He placed his hand on my foot. You're a good girl, ChiChi, he said. Don't let your mamma upset you too much. She's a wonderful woman . . . She's just not demonstrative like other Italians.

Other Italians?

Well, yes. What I'm saying is, most Italian mothers are more—well, more family-orientated, aren't they? I mean, outwardly affectionate toward their children, aren't they? Well, I don't see your mother as a typical Italian.

I could tell him about Nonna, about the silkiness of her throat when she held Marco and me on her lap, about the drops of sweat that gathered on the back of her neck and along the hollow of her jaw. Her dark eyes like spoons taking in the world.

I could I tell him about Nonna's fuzzy hair, how it tickled your nose, how it lit up a pillow. How her sugary voice could mesmerize us with her stories. Maybe *she* was a typical Italian.

He took my silence to mean I was offended. He said he wasn't being discriminatory here, really, it's just that he always thought Italian people were so expressive, so outgoing, so carefree . . .

Nonna could say she loved us all day long. Nonna could Put Things Into Words. *Ti amo, carina, ti amo, nipotina bella.* *I love you too, Nonna.*

I chewed the ridge of my lower lip. Stared at him, dopey.

He was quiet, then gave a garlic sigh.

Anyhoo, he said, and left the room.

Mamma didn't want Marco to have an operation. He'd get well at home, she said. But Mamma believed lies. Her lies clanged like the trains in the train yard across the street, like the sounds of the bedsprings in her room at night. Her lies were like the burnt-out porch lights, the shadows under the stairwell, the smell of ether.

The doctor spoke to Mamma like she was hard of hearing. Now, Mrs. Maggiordino! You-must-understand-the-gravity-of-the-situation!

She couldn't decipher the English words, the medical terminology. Words like ventilatory activity. Expressions like geomagnetic disturbances correlating with adverse influences in the cardiovascular system. Histamine, Franol, prednisone, epinephrine, pathology. She held my shoulder.

ChiChi, you read in the books these things. Explain me, she said.

Mamma had her own ideas of medicine. If she could get Marco up to the crater of Mount Etna to inhale the healing fumes of the sulfur! That's what her boy need. A whiff of the Etna. She believed in licorice, apple water, mullein. She believed in altitude and hot baths and candles.

A new word came to Mamma, a word we all had to decipher, unravel, decode. We would have to sort, sound out, examine, speculate on the meaning of three consonants and two vowels. *Tumor.*

I read in the Gideon Bible on his bedstand, *Let not your heart be troubled; you believe in God, believe also in me, John 14:1.* God said that? Was he paying attention? Trouble was all there was in the world.

The size of a golf ball, the doctor said. (What did we know about golf balls?) Like a pomegranate? A bocci ball? Mamma sighed in disgust. Why this doctor man no speak plain?

Mr. Metamere made gestures of encouragement to Mamma, murmured words meant to be comforting.

Now now, he said.

Hold on.

There there.

We couldn't imagine surgery, the process of it, the mystery. I told myself one day I would learn about it. When I would be old enough to drive a car and Marco would graduate from high school with honors.

We would talk about it one day, how Marco was anesthetized. And how the doctor with no face wearing the green puckered scrub suit, green booties over his shoes, surgery cap on his head, white mask over his mouth and nose, bent over his patient with the half dozen other green-gowned figures. How Marco's mouth was pulled back for plastic tubes to run into his throat, no longer Marco, but a patient. In such a condition he would no longer be identified by pronouns. He was only object. Arms, lungs, chest cavity. He was Patient swabbed in Betadine, splayed a shiny yellow-brown under the fire-white lights of the operating room.

Two cuts made in his chest, then the probe with two fingers between Marco's ribs. But Marco would not be Marco, he would be a thorax.

The doctor discovers the coral alveoli of lungs slowly beating, a glistening membrane, a landscape of pink, thin, branching ruddy veins, trembling in the green fluid of pus. Adhesions of his suffering are observed, small, adhering strings of tissue, scar tissue attached to the lung's lobe. They dig in for the tumor, probe, find it by touch. A golf ball could not be that hard to find in such a small space. Or was it a grape? A plum? A marble?

A longer incision is made. Around the side of the chest, from sternum to scapula. The cut flesh then pulled back to better view the rubbery interior, the metal brackets inserted to hold the incision open, then spread apart the ribs to make a hole four inches square for the surgeon with his headlight like a miner's helmet on his head to peer into.

Peer into. Marco's lung deflating and inflating, under the lobe, precision cutting, stapling, tying off. If they went deep enough, would they have found his soul? Where in his body was his soul's home?

The doctor said the size of a golf ball; maybe it was a pea, a lima bean, a garbanzo, a tomato. No, it was a golf ball. Whatever that was.

I walk until I cross the border of Tar Town. I walk past everything familiar, past the gaping lots where houses have been erased for I-35W, past Beltrami Park, and past the corner of Broadway and Johnson where Tar Town ends. I know what to expect. Tawdry storefronts and buildings, warehouses and empty lots, a small sign in the window of a private club, *No Italians*, a sky like a closed door giving way to small houses in rows, houses in the colors of baked bread and fronted with trimmed grass. The people who live in these houses subscribe to magazines; they eat meat during the week and watch Imogene Coca on television. Their faucets and toilets don't leak, they eat something called Jell-O and never polish their shoes with lard.

LaMont leans on a bicycle. His jeans cuffed and his cap on sideways. My stocking falls around my shoe and catches under my heel.

LaMont squints at me. He's not alone. Two Yellow Shirts look at me as though seeing an apparition, their faces stupid. I expect red felt tongues to fall out over their chins like the kind sewn on the heads of stuffed bears. LaMont drops his bicycle to the ground and something falls from his pocket. It rolls toward me on the sidewalk and stops at the toe of my shoe.

He yells in a voice like an egg frying. Hey! Give it here! That's my golf ball!

(You remember and you try to remember it right. A golf ball. Not a garbanzo or a cantaloupe, not a bocci ball, a basketball, or baseball. A *golf* ball.)

Did I throw the first punch? Did the guy with the red face and flaking skin throw the first punch? Did a boy toss a stone at me, knocking me off balance? When did I fall to the pavement? Was the blood on my leg mine or from the arm I bit into?

A girl appears. She wears a pink sweater and she has brown straight hair the color of old snow. Someone's sister.

Get off her! the girl yells. I'm *telling!*

I kick someone in their privates. Someone's teeth clink like broken cups, and I punch again. I'm on the ground, a foot on my neck.

Get off her! yells the girl.

I kick again.

The golf ball rolls into the gutter. Who are you? the girl says. What are you doing here? Don't you belong in Tar Town?

I want to think I jammed my fist into her raggedy face. Her pretty pink sweater has a bloodstain. I want her ruined and permanently soiled, this sister of an all-American healthy boy. The sister of a boy who can play football and beat up little kids from outside the neighborhood. A boy whose golf ball he carries in a pocket, not on his lung.

Mamma didn't turn to notice me when I walked through the door, didn't see my torn jacket or that I had lost a shoe or that there was blood hanging from my nose.

Mr. Metamere said. Good gravy, what's this now?

I had fought the good fight. Proven myself. I stood at the edge of my bed and lowered myself to my knees. I crossed myself, began my prayer of thanksgiving. Tried to remember the one Sister Ursula had taught us on Mother's Day: Holy Mother, Divine and Magnificent, Queen of Mothering, I give you thanks . . . *Mamma mia!* I was a girl who could beat up boys.

Marco possessed scars, a ribboned chest to prove himself. He was a hero. And I had the golf ball in my pocket. Now LaMont and the Yellow Shirts would fear US.

Be brave and do hard things, Amore . . .

The sky outside our window was painted with a million smiling stars.

Leticcia, dear, you are such a conscientious student. Sister Ursula spoke in her handkerchief, blew her nose. Her face appeared ravelly, like an old sweater. She looked uneven, loose-ended, frayed.

There's been no homework from you in two weeks, Leticcia. Why do you refuse to do your homework? Don't you want to graduate, go on to Junior High?

Sì.

English please.

Sì.

I'm afraid I must send you to see Father Tuttifucci.

Father Tuttifucci's office was a small grey room with a heavy grey metal desk taking up most of the space. Its one window was stippled the way windows in public toilets are, so you couldn't see in or out. You could hear the traffic outside on Broadway. I made triangles and rectangles and quadrangles in the air between my lap and the crucifix on the wall.

How is your brother? How is Marco?

I couldn't answer.

He looked in a file folder, flipped papers with his thumb and forefinger. Every day, three times a day, prayers are lifted up for Marco, he said. He is remembered at every Mass.

Yes, Father.

He is dearly loved. We all love Marco. We all pray for his recovery.

Yes, Father.

Your mother says you do your homework every night. Why do you not hand it in? Might you explain it to me?

Let not your heart be troubled, I answered.

Two fifth-grade girls passed by the door whispering, clapping their hands together. I began to count the hands I had touched in my life. Marco's hands were shaped like hearts. Sometimes my hand became his hand. I bit a cuticle. The girls frowned at me, one stuck out her tongue. I stuck out my tongue and brushed my thumb against my chin back at her.

Well! snapped Father Tuttifucci, coming to attention. I am very disappointed in you, Leticcia. But I see where we stand.

He wrote on a pink piece of paper. I bit the inside of my mouth, pulled on my sock. It had a hole just above the shoe.

I gave Father Tuttifucci a look of confidence. Marco is all right, I tell him. He's fine now.

Mrs. Rosalia, the settlement house secretary, a short woman with a slight limp, signaled at the door. She entered and said something in Father's ear. He closed his eyes and removed his glasses. He turned his chair to the smeared window. Pressed a finger to his forehead. You better go home, Leticcia, he said.

Am I in trouble?

There's someone here for you.

Mr. Metamere stood outside the door. His great face was wet. He rolled his hat between his fingers. When he saw me he let out a sob. ChiChi, Sweetheart, oh ChiChi.

You ou wonder what people think. You look at a man like Melvin Metamere who was turning thirty-six years old in another month and how he'd changed since his semester at the Dunwoody Institute, where he took Auto Mechanics and dropped out, how different he was since his foray into selling home mortgage insurance, and the stint at Honeywell, where he tried assembling parts while standing on his feet all day but quit and went on disability. Yes, of course, the dead logs of yesterday were tossed aside, all of them. Is that how he felt? It was a new life he dreamed might be possible.

Now this.

Sometimes he thought about leaving and returning to his own home, but at night lying in bed with Giuseppina at his side, he felt downright needed, appreciated, and those two kids, well, who else did they have in this world? No, here was where he'd stay. As long as he could. As long as she'd have him.

ChiChi, Sweetheart, he'd tell the girl, it would be so nice if you and your mother got along. Maybe you could try a little harder. Be a little nicer to her?

What would the girl say? Okay. Fine. Sure. She'd look at him with those startling green eyes. Such a little thing she was. And he'd be embarrassed.

He was happy in their little apartment in Tar Town, wasn't

he? He had his place at the table, a hook for his coat, a pillow for his head, a woman to take care of him. The two kids like mice sneaking around in their odd mysteries, and never asking for a thing. Happy, wasn't he happy?

What did Mr. Metamere tell himself that afternoon when he picked the girl up from the settlement house to go to the hospital? Did he notice she didn't hop in her usual peculiar way? She didn't count or chant; she was quiet, took quick, nervous steps, and when she looked up at him, those eyes so pathetic, so terrified, did something inside him come unflapped?

She had hair like her mother's, hair so thick her face seemed choked in it, a girl no bigger than an eight year-old, uncombed, silent, walking with her small jerky steps. Did he think the girl was peculiar in the head, did he believe Giuseppina, who said the child was a witch?

What did Melvin Metamere think when he saw me staring up at him, wishing he'd be the pappa, wishing with all my might he'd be the pappa?

Mr. Metamere wasn't thinking of being anybody's pappa, he was agonizing over how on God's green earth we would survive this day.

*T*ell me if dying hurts, Marco.
    (Living hurts worse, he might have said.)
His absence like a torn eyelid.
I rub my face on his sheets, on the stains, the little bouquets left behind.
WHAT ARE YOU DOING? yells the nurse.
I can feel his ear, cold like a piece of lettuce.
I'm having a vision, I tell the nurse.
I'm seeing with *Il Mal Occhio.*
BREATHE, MARCO! BREATHE, MY BROTHER!

We fly to thy Patronage, O Holy Mother of God;
despise not our prayers in our necessities,
but deliver us from all dangers . . .

Glory be to the Father, and to the Son, and to the Holy Spirit . . .
    (And to *Il Mal Occhio*)
He breathed.

He came home.

*C*ame home. Came home. Came home.

I went to the train yard to work out a dance of praise and I found a stray cat. Its body fit in the circle of my fingers. Well, what would Our Lord do? I tucked the poor thing in the folded ends of my T-shirt inside my jacket and took it home to give it something to eat.

Marco had been home from the hospital two weeks and when I walked in, the apartment was too quiet. Like when I found Nonna lying in her splashed polenta. I went into the kitchen and poured some milk in a saucer. I turned on the radio and sat on the floor watching the cat. The weather report indicated snow, heavy winds. Doublemint gum doubled our pressure. The Beatles told us it was a long day's night.

Zat you, ChiChi?

Marco! Don't spring up on me like that.

He showed me what he was working on: a colored pencil drawing in four parts. Two babies in one corner, two little kids in another, then two adults, and two old people. In the middle was a gold cross of clouds. MARCO E CHICHI PER SEMPRE was scrawled at the bottom in black crayon. Marco and ChiChi forever.

Hey, is that a cat?

Cat!

I hardly knew what hit. Suddenly Mamma was in the

kitchen screaming *Cat!* She pulled the broom from the corner by the sink.

A cat in my house!

(Her house.)

It's only a kitten, Mamma, I said, Don't hurt it!

The broom came down on my head, then my legs. I rolled on the floor and the broom struck again and again, head, face, arms, chest.

I gave her nothing but grief, she yelled. Why was I the healthy one and Marco, such a saint, the sick one?

ChiChi, the witch, bring cat in house to torture Marco who has allergic to cats. I was an ugly sore in her life.

Something went crak! in my nose.

Marco walked to school without me the next day. His dark face with the veins outlined on his temples and his funny brown hair sticking up, Marco, allergic to cats, went to school. I stayed in bed and licked the skin on my arms.

I wondered how much grief the walls of our apartment could take, first Nonna's polenta, then the cat, thrown against it until its eyes popped out. No one is born for happiness. If you're lucky you'll get kissed on the lips by a good person once in your life; if you're not lucky, you'll get the whip of winter inside your mouth and it'll stretch and yank at your face until you look like a witch and you scare people.

Mamma came into my room. I couldn't breathe through my nose. *Non mi fai quella faccia!* Her voice came out scratchy and old.

I'm not making a face at you, I said. My face felt like it was packed in an egg carton.

You'd think with Marco still alive and getting fatter every

day we'd be a happy family, but the miracle turned on us, became like an insect bite behind the knee.

Mah, ChiChi, what you make me do? What you make me do? *Madonna Santissima,* what am I going to happen?

She rocked her head in her arms. *Gesù, Maria!* You brother, he have allergic to cats, to everything! Why you hurt you mamma? Why you no love you mamma?

She left the room and I heard her running down the stairs, heard the porch door slam.

Marco came home from school, examined my face, said I looked awful. You got a broken nose for sure, he said.

So? What do I care.

I'd never be cute. I wasn't Annette Funicello.

Marco gave a snort. Get up, he said, and I caught a hardness in his voice, not like the brother who was the good part of me, the one back from the clutch of death, and in an instant his face turned saffron and I knew the Marco helping me out of bed was another Marco.

Get dressed. I'm taking you, he said, to the doctor, NOW.

*A*t home Mamma paced the apartment, drew her hands through her hair, mumbled in Italian and English. Mr. Metamere had been gone for two days. She gave me a whack on the shoulder. Why you no want you mamma she be happy? Her eyes had turned red, like radishes.

Always you think only of youself! *Signorina Leticcia.*

I put my hands over my face.

Mah! You think you Miss Smarty-Smarty! Tell lies about you mamma, lies to my man!

Who?

Melvin, who you think.

Mr. Metamere?

Marco, who had been breathing in his machine, called out in a loud voice, unlike him: LEAVE HER ALONE.

Che?

He startled us both.

She looked at me as though waking up from a dream, then at Marco.

You two, YOU TWO. Always you TWO, she cried.

When she had gone into her room, slamming the door behind her, Marco said, Let's run away, ChiChi.

Run away.

We can have our own place, you and me, he said. A place

where you can practice your clown art and I can practice art.

Sure, Marco, I said. Someday.

I sat on the edge of the school yard picking a scab on my leg and a new girl named Dorella Pavalucci came up to me, said, Does it hurt? Your nose?

Dr. Spano had set my nose and said one day I'd be a real femme fatale, even asked me if I had a boyfriend.

Dorella wore boy's pants under her school uniform and dangling cross earrings which she said she received for her First Communion, and she had a real opal birthstone ring which she was only allowed to wear for good.

I have jewelry, too, I said. Diamonds, gold, pearls, you name it.

Me, too, said Dorella.

We sat in the dust of the playground, arms around our coarse grey knees, staring at our old shoes. Yup, we got it all, I said.

Dorella's father worked for the Northern Pacific Railroad. How about *your* father? Dorella wanted to know. Where does your pappa work?

My pappa? Hunh? Oh. He's in the U.S. Army, I said. He'll be home one of these days.

Marco gave out a groan. You told her we have a dad?

So?

You got polenta for a brain? in a voice like Mamma's. Did that broken nose wreck your brain?

If his tone weren't heated with authority, I would have laughed.

Our Lady of Mount Carmel Benevolent Society sponsored a Life Story Essay Contest for the 5th and 6th graders. We were supposed to write something interesting about our lives. Dorella wrote a five-page essay about her trip to Bemidgi to visit her grandparents for the Italian holiday of Bafana. When her essay was returned, there was a big VERY GOOD on the corner.

My essay started like this:

> Once there was a lady named Grenadine Fletcher whose real name was Gallina and she even looked like a chicken. It came to pass that she became a boarder in the apartment of a mother and her two children. This is the story of what befell Grenadine Fletcher and her lover, Franco Pazzoli, stepgrandparent to one wretched, ugly girl named Natalie . . .

I received a red check mark on my paper and a big SEE ME in the corner.

Sister Ursula tipped her head back and looked at me from the bottoms of her glasses. Why did I ask to see you, Leticcia?

I don't know, Sister.

Your paper, dear. The essay.

I kept my eyes down. Looking at her desk. Grey metal with scratches on the edges. Four ballpoint pens poked up from a Minnesota Gophers glass, a breeze blew through the window against my calves.

Leticcia, dear, the assignment was to write about a *real* experience. What you've written, dear, is what we call *fiction*. Do you remember in class we discussed the difference between fantasy and reality? How will you ever get along in public school? I want you to write about a *real* experience. Can you do that?

The breeze blowing in from the window was now a freezing wind. My teeth chattered.

Leticcia, there are lots of stories in your every day life . . .

I was really cold. My nose thumped with a heartbeat.

Don't sneer, Leticcia. I'm talking to you.

We would rather go hungry than eat fish on Friday, I said. She brightened. Very good! You see? Now that's reality. What I want you to do is to write about ree-al-i-ty.

My nose was really starting to hurt. The pain flew up from my nostril to my eyebrow. I jerked my head, blinked hard.

Leticcia, stop making those faces!

Reality

by Leticcia Maggiordino

If you want to know where the most beautiful place is in the world I will tell you. It's the most beautiful place in the world and nobody else knows about it. My brother and I saw a light in the sky there one night. A big light. It was a light as big as your hand and it came roaring out of the night right at us. I think it was God speaking and granting us a wish. I immediately made my wish and commanded the star to fall on LaMont, an evil white boy from across the park. I commanded the star to kill that terrible boy. Then on that fateful moon-dim night the star fell on us! Our secret place blew up in a million shards. Now we don't have a most beautiful place in the world any more because the most beautiful place in the world was in our heads.

The End.

Sister Ursula marked another SEE ME on the corner of the page.

Marco read art books and examined the works of Ghiberti, Leonardo daVinci, Michelangelo, Raphael, Giotto, Botticelli, and he drew pictures. He copied the pictures in the book of Minnesota artists Mr. Metamere bought him. He painted on cardboard with the acrylic paints Mr. Metamere bought until the tubes were strangled of color like dead insects. He said he understood Rembrandt.

I posed for him until I couldn't sit still. He drew me standing, sitting, sleeping, eating. He was always drawing. He filled notebooks with his sketches of everything he saw. Cars, trucks, children, old people, chairs, pitchers, books, the world to him was something to draw or paint.

And I committed the unforgivable. I showed Dorella some of his drawings that he'd copied from a book of Modigliani paintings.

She was shocked.

Your brother draws naked ladies!

In Dorella's house a statue of a weeping Jesus stood in the living room that her grandmother had brought wrapped in blankets from Abruzzo. It survived the trip across the ocean without a single scratch, but one night in the new country when her father got up to take a leak, he knocked into the statue, and sent it tumbling to the floor where part of its head lopped off. Her mother glued the head back on and the whole family thought the glue looked like real tears.

I think it's spooky how the Lord speaks to us, Dorella said.

Speaks to us?

You know, like through these tears and all.

Glue tears?

It's from the Bible, you know. *Jesus Wept.*

Why? Why, what for?

For our sins, didn't you know that? For the sins of the world.

When Marco found out I had gone into his private things and showed them to someone else, his face turned to wood.

How come you did that?

I'm sorry.

Sorry? That's what I call *betrayal,* ChiChi.

(In all my life I would never hear a word more terrible.)

I waited to hear his revenge.

Now hear this, he said. Dad's coming to school tomorrow.

What?

Your school chums think our pappa is alive and in the army, right? Tomorrow they're in for a little surprise.

Marco won the essay contest. Of course. He was not only a great artist, he was a great writer. Even though I wrote in my notebook every single day and loved words like clowns, Marco was the great writer. Mamma baked him a special torte with whipped cream and raspberries.

My father's wooden leg was the one true secret fact of my life. So private and intimate was this secret relationship that even Marco didn't know how much love was invested in that leg in the closet. But now, I worried, maybe Marco knew more than I imagined.

The next day Marco arrived at school a few minutes late. He carried something rolled up in our bathroom rug.

So Marco would get revenge. *Vendetta.* Ice grew in my scalp. The schoolroom turned bitter, like infection.

We stood at our desks and said our prayers and the Pledge of Allegiance and then my brother, winner of Our Lady of Mount Carmel Junior Essay Contest walked to the front of the room to read his essay.

Sister Ursula announced that Marco Maggiordino had brought something which would be of interest to us all.

Marco held the rolled up log of rug. Marco was right to do revenge, I knew that. I must hold my own and allow him to hold his.

Boys and girls, how many of you had relatives or family who fought in the Second World War? said Sister Ursula.

Hands went up.

Marco will read his essay on the Second World War in which his father lost his life.

Dorella shot me a horrified look. Your dad's DEAD? she shouted.

Jesus wept.

Marco will be awarded a check for twenty-five dollars, said Sister Ursula, in the Sunday service at Our Lady of Mount Carmel. You'll all receive the announcements to take home to your parents.

The windows collapsed, the walls fell away. I was alone.

Joey Minichilli's head was in the way so I couldn't see the rolled wooden leg on the table. Marco read in a high clear voice, pronouncing each word with careful precision.

—*When Hitler came to Mussolini's rescue, he dispatched twenty-five divisions . . . Rome was attacked in September 1943,* etc. etc. etc. . . .

He stood straight and confident like the pictures we cut out of magazines of U.S. soldiers. He spoke trying to affect a silvery Minnesota accent. Very American.

—*When the beachhead at Salerno had been secured, the drive for Napoli began . . . etc. etc. etc.—How conscious is mankind of its identity? We see ourselves in the mirror of war, in man's violent and aggressive instincts. My father lies dead in his grave having left a wife and family to grieve because he was a victim of war and happened to be a cog in its ugly wheel. Was it for freedom he died?*

If I weren't so nervous I might have heard what he was saying.

—*My father was shot and killed following the partial loss of a leg* . . . etc. etc. etc.—*The unconditional surrender took place in April 1945*—

blah blah blah.

He picked up the heavy tube of rug. His voice was low, threatening.

—*And now I would like to show you something important to me.*

He laid the bundle across Sister Ursula's desk and slowly unwrapped.

THIS *is an M1 rifle*, he said. *The type my father carried in the invasion of Maiori when he stopped a German bullet.*

He held the gun, hoisted it to his shoulder, squinted an eye, and smiling, aimed directly at me.

*W*here'd you GET it?
(Laughing, falling on top of each other.)

I bought it off Minichilli's uncle for five dollars. It's useless. Trigger's gone.

He stood the rifle up next to his bed under a new Dracula poster.

In church service on Sunday, Father Tuttifucci awarded him with a certificate and a check. Mamma twittered with pride as the old women congratulated her. *Che bel giovenotto!* Such a beautiful boy!

A face *come un angelo,* like an angel, your boy. *Cosi intelligente,* and so smart! You must be proud of your boy.

A place in my chest felt warm, like I'd just swallowed a cup of soup. He *was* smart.

Mamma didn't remain around the women for long, and when I looked for her, I saw her outside on the sidewalk in a deep conversation with a complete stranger. We didn't get many strangers at our church, unless they were somebody's relative or a lost tourist. This was a tall man in a suit that didn't look quite at home on him, and with him was a boy about Marco's age. A scowling, unhappy kid who looked like he had just had his stomach pumped.

I left the scene of glory and went for a walk in the neighborhood by myself. I walked through the alley, kicking stones, scuffing the toes of my shoes. I stopped by an old house of a tarnished emerald color, looked up at its tar paper roof, counted the bricks along the drain spouts. I was proud of Marco, too. I ached with pride. But how dare they call him *her* boy? I wanted to be quiet, walk on tiptoe, listen for the mistakes in silence.

How was a girl like ChiChi Maggiordino ever to get along in the real world? Sister Ursula wanted to know. ChiChi with such an imagination.

When I got home Mamma was sitting in her chair by the window in the dark. The dust held its breath.

Too quiet. I could hear my fingernails growing.

All is lost, she said.

Had she talked to Sister Ursula?

Melvin, he's leave me forever, she said.

Leave? Mr. Metamere is gone?

I went to our room and sat on the edge of my bed.

ChiChi is the reason Mr. Metamere left us. ChiChi does everything wrong. *Pazza.* ChiChi is crazy, and that's why he left. It could have been the broken nose, the dirty socks. ChiChi should have combed her hair more often. *You got flies in your hair,* he said once. The Annette Funicello haircut had grown out in a long tangle of twigs. ChiChi should not be who she is.

I pinched my arms and legs. This is what you must do when you're bad. You must do penance. Father O'Toole said in Mass we must despise the flesh.

The spirit warreth against the flesh, he said as he leaned over the lectern, the sleeves of his chasuble flared and dangerous.

We must put to death the sins of the flesh! he warned, and his eyes bore directly into mine.

Mr. Metamere's razor stood in a cup with a nail file and comb in the medicine cabinet. I found it by accident when

I was looking for Mamma's jar of Pond's. I held the razor in my hand and examined my face in the mirror. The girl in the mirror couldn't hold things together. Why couldn't the girl in the mirror hold things together? Why wasn't she like LaMont's sister with the straight hair and pink sweater? LaMont's sister wore shoes with buckles, she was the good girl, not me. Good girls don't have to do penance, don't have to work so hard for God's attention.

I ran the razor across my cheek. It left a faint pink line. I tried again and pushed through the skin. Pink spots formed on the rim of the sink. I pulled the blade around the ears, into the hairline. I'd cut off my face. Nip at the edges and pop out its center.

Afterwards I went to bed.

Mamma on the telephone. *Aiuto! Aiuto!* Help! ChiChi, she cut her throat!

Mr. Metamere appeared at the side of my bed. My eyes pressed shut, eyelashes sticky. I could smell him, wearing the aftershave Mamma bought him, his breath like wet mushrooms.

He came back!

Mamma angry, confused, whining, crying.

Mr. Metamere yelling. Speak English, Giuseppina! Tell me what happened!

Then I'm lifted up in his arms, we're in a taxi, his breath hot, angry. Is he angry?

I promise I'll be good. I promise.

Who did this to her?

Mr. Metamere says he's not sure.

Someone poking me, lifting my arm, turning my leg. Look at this! These bruises on her arms and legs.

Madonn'a! Gesù, Maria! (Mamma? Is that you?)

Social workers, the psychologist. ChiChi, did your brother do this to you?

My brovver?

Then Mr. Metamere's voice: ChiChi, Sweetheart. Don't you worry. You're going to get stitched up and we'll all go home together.

It had worked. My penance paid off.

Marco with his mouth next to my ear. They say you're sick in the head, ChiChi. They're saying you need help.

(I'm the girl who works miracles, Silly. I got Mr. Metamere to come back!)

This is serious, ChiChi. They're calling you crazy.

I wanted to laugh. I sank into the sheets.

More voices: Mrs. Maggiordino, please understand. We're not accusing you. She confessed she did it to herself. But your daughter could have cut an artery. She came close to slitting her throat. What we're saying is, your daughter has deep psychological—

ChiChi, why you do sucha thing? Mamma's face above mine. Tell you mamma why you do sucha thing.

The room was like an Italian newsreel, a shape sprayed with pepper.

I didn't do noffing.

Her presence in the room made me feel giddy, like getting caught scratching private parts of the body. I could have blushed. I itch, I said.

They think I bad mamma and you sick in the head. Selfish ChiChi. Shame on you if you sick in the head! *Mah!*

But she was so big sitting there close to me like that. Her face broad, shining, the pale mouth wide, teeth like fingers. I didn't know her face this close up, a younger and fairer Nonna. Hadn't I noticed the soft roses of her gums before?

Nonna's teeth were small as eraser tips, and crooked, and she let me touch her teeth and count them. *Uno duo tre quattro . . .*

ChiChi, why you want to make trouble for you mamma? Look on me! Her eyes so close I saw four of them.

You better no be crazy, ChiChi. I break you head like *melanzane.*

The stitches came out in eight days. Mr. Metamere took me to the doctor for their removal.

Couldn't we have done this ourselves?

ChiChi, it's going to be okay.

Fathers talked like that. In the doctor's office my face was swabbed at with an orange smelly cotton pad. My face looked like it had been basted on. Loose pieces of thread hung around my ears and eyes. They stung as they were pulled out.

Hold on, Sweetheart. When this is over we'll go for ice cream. How's that sound?

He'd never leave us now.

The stitches out. I felt clean, renewed, like after confession. It hurt to smile.

Are you and Mamma getting married?

He ordered two strawberry malteds. I played with a slice of strawberry and waited for him to tell me how much he loved Mamma and that the date was set. I squashed the strawberry on the counter with my pinkie. I turned to look at him and he flinched. Lowered his head.

So what's with Marco and that broken rifle? I can't feature the little pipsqueak playing army or pretending he's a soldier.

He's my brother! I said. He's no pipsqueak!

That shut him up for about two minutes.

Look, you're a good kid, ChiChi, and I worry about you. Such a delicate thing. Like you're made of glass. You got more hair than you got you!

I let a strawberry mush against my upper lip.

I don't have any daughters of my own . . . I've always wanted a little girl, a daughter . . . What do you say about coming to live with me?

I let loose with a cough.

Just hear me out, okay?

I knelt on the stool, speared a strawberry with my straw. My side hurt.

His mouth worked in and out with no words coming out. He pushed a spoon into his malted, swallowed a glob.

Oh, I got it. I said, You have a wife, don't you?

. . . Yes. I'm sorry.

You're already married.

Yes.

(Think of other things. The Northern Pacific boxcars creaking on the tracks—)

Children? You have children?

. . . Yes. Boys. I have two boys.

(Maple branches layered with ice like spit . . .)

Does Mamma know?

No, no, she doesn't know. I was separated from my wife when I met your mother. I was going to get a divorce—but now my wife and I've decided to try and make it work— for the boys—for the family.

Family.

(Careful there, don't grimace. Don't pull the skin, burst the scabs, split the scars. All the pain will gush out, drip down your sweater, spill onto the floor, crawl up the walls.)

When are you moving out? I said.

He sucked on the straw. I've already moved out.

We walked through Beltrami Park. The cars passing us in the slush of the street sounded like toilets flushing.

You won't be here for my graduation?

I don't think so.

The cold air burned my teeth.

I'd like to adopt you, he said.

The park was speckled with black patches of dirt in the snow. The swings were removed from the steel frames and the benches covered with melting ice and dirty snow.

I always wanted a daughter, Sweetheart . . .

I couldn't think of what to say except to tell him I'd be going to junior high next year. The thought made my fingers shake.

You could go to junior high where I live, he said.

But you live here with us.

No, ChiChi not anymore.

Guess what, I said. Sister Ursula says I have a good imagination.

Yes, of course you do, Sweetheart. You're extremely bright and you've got a lot of talent. You deserve a chance.

He patted my wool cap and then bent down and gave me a kiss on the forehead. Think about it, please? he said, I'll convince your mother you'd be better off living with me.

I felt my forehead. Sure. Okay.

The angel who brought this answered prayer must have gotten tangled in traffic. I asked for a pappa for *three* of us!

The lady from the county gave Mamma an ultimatum. An ultimatum is when you do what you're told or else. She had to see a counselor once a week and if she missed she'd be in big trouble. Also, what about the man who was living with her?

That night he came into the bedroom when I was almost asleep. ChiChi, I just want to remind you to think about— you know.

I gave a grunt, a sound halfway between a shove and a snore.

He whispered good night, sleep tight, don't let the bed bugs bite from the doorway. It was quiet except for the wind blowing against the window, the scratching of a tree branch on the wood siding of the house.

Marco shifted the blanket on his bed. A rustle of sheets and legs and he padded over to my bed.

So what are you going to do? he said.

I'm not going anywhere.

No?

No.

He's probably got a nice house, all that. You'd have a dad.

I got a dad.

Ya? A lousy wooden leg?

I practiced breathing through my nose.

He pulled at my blanket. Move over. My feet are cold.

I moved over and he climbed into the bed.

Does it still hurt? Your face?

If it didn't hurt it wouldn't count, I said.

A melting icicle clattered from the roof to the snow bank below. He pushed his feet against mine. He gave you quite an offer, he said.

Call that an offer? It's nothing, Marco. Ask me why.

Why?

He's married. He's got sons.

His body stiffened. Shit. Sonofabitch.

We lay with our heads together on my pillow staring at the ceiling.

ChiChi? His voice emphatic. We need a plan.

I settled my head in the crease of his neck. Shit, sonofabitch, we said in unison, and it sounded like prayer.

*T*he way it is in life you're supposed to think of the implications. You've got to be smart, consider every angle, be aware. The way it is in life you've got to keep control. One day you've got a solid flooring to stretch your ten toes on and next day you're flat on your *culo*. You've got to pay attention, be sharp, watch for snags, you can't trust someone else to pull you through the loops and curves and blank spaces; no, never someone else. You've got to be expert. Read books, be correct, put on weight, remember your rituals. Pray.

Use your imagination.

Don't doze off with both eyes closed.

Hang on hang on hang on.

The way it is in life is you hang on.

Dorella wasn't permitted to play with me. When I showed up on her front porch her mother rushed out of the kitchen swinging a towel at me.

Oh, okay. They thought I was dangerous. Thought I carried a razor.

Mamma took the bus on Mondays to her counseling appointments, forcing herself to sit still and listen to talk about unresolved guilt, denied rage, self-esteem, taking control. She sat in the counseling office twisting her fingers in her lap, her black church dress and shawl layered around her, hair askew from its pins. Surrounding her were modern furnishings she distrusted, unidentifiable plants hanging from macramé'd ropes, dusky lighting.

But then an Italian-American woman whose parents were from Napoli was assigned to Mamma's case. They talked about the suffering and sorrow of Italian women and Mamma started paying attention.

On the eve of my twelfth birthday a terrible thing happened in the person of one Ed Looz. A flaky tit of a boy, a scraggled pleat, sickly erosion, a face like contaminated milk, scab-eyed, mud-toothed, hateful creature on sight, Ed Looz.

And Marco's friend.

Ed Looz was the kid I saw outside the church with the strange man the day Marco received the award for his essay. Okay. I got it. Mamma arranged a friend for Marco, a *boy* for him to play with, to go to the art classes with on Saturday mornings at the settlement house. The volunteer teacher from the Minneapolis Institute of Art would have them drawing pictures, painting on plastic, molding papier mâché, twisting wires, chiseling wood, and Ed, the *caccone,* would take my place.

Ed Looz lived with his father, who, Marco informed me, was a bookie. Does he read them or sell them? I asked. And Marco snorted back, Ya, real funny. Ed wore a black leather jacket like he was some big, tough kid. I figured he slept in the thing.

My face healed, the bruises healed, another birthday limped by, and I spent the next spring and summer kicking stones in the train yard dreaming about life in the circus. Mr. Metamere forgot to take us to a real live circus, but I watched circus acts on Ed Sullivan on TV. I walked alongside the railroad tracks practicing acrobatics, the cartwheel, splits, walk-overs, flips. I walked to the Central Avenue Library and read books about clowns, dancing, and gymnastics. I learned about clown makeup and costumes. I learned about ballet dancing, and how a dancer must be disciplined. I learned that clowns who walk on stilts must practice a long time. Being funny took a lot of work.

I found an empty diary in a garbage can on Spring Street one afternoon. No writing in it at all except on the inside cover:

Dearest Nancy: Protect Your Memories . . .

Love, J.

Dearest Nancy hadn't written a single word in the diary that *Love J.* gave her. She'd thrown it out! The idea! I wiped it off on my T-shirt and brought it home so I could protect my memories. I made lists of things to protect. What things taste like, and how many sounds occur in our apartment at certain times of day. Smells without names. I named the diary "J" even though there is no *J* in the Italian alphabet.

Mamma talking on the telephone.

Her voice a whisper.

No, Manny, please understand what I say. I make a plan. I not stupid!

When she finished the conversation, she sat in front of the telephone moaning and rocking herself as though in pain.

Mamma! Who were you talking to?

She wiped her eye with the dish towel in her hand.

Eddie's father, she said. Manny Looz.

What did he say to make you cry? Did Ed do something terrible? Which I wouldn't put it past him.

Don't say nothing bad about Eddie.

He's a creep, Mamma!

She cried with fresh vigor. Her shoulders rattled, there were tears in her hair. I went to the bathroom, unraveled a handful of toilet paper, helped her blow her nose.

Eddie Looz no is bad, ChiChi. And she fell into a convulsion of sobs so loud I thought maybe I should close the windows.

Sometimes, *Figlia,* she said when she had gathered herself together, Sometimes life play cruel trick on you. Such cruel trick. You open door, walk through, and is only dark pit on other side. But sometime you open door and find garden. Which one you choose? Eh? You think you know. But life, when you stupid, will show you no mercy. It make you pay for be stupid. You pay plenty. You never stop paying. *Cara,* ChiChi, never forget that.

Later that day she pulled the clothes from her closet and threw them into a pile in the middle of the floor of her bedroom. She emptied the drawers of her dresser onto the floor as well.

I'm buy new clothes! What you think? she said.

Dai, Mamma, Mamma—

I have secret! She said.

She was formed in secrets. Secret was her middle name.

I go to work! Earn money!

She said she'd buy new clothes, she'd wear blouses and slacks; she'd throw out the chenille bathrobe with the worn sleeves, the smock and apron with permanent stains. No longer would she wear floppy slippers with her stockings rolled down at the ankles. No more toilet paper stuffed in her cuffs for to blow her nose.

That's right, ChiChi, for a truth.

One short week, seven days later, Mamma sat in her chair by the window, with one leg crossed over the other, wearing a new dress, one with color and a belt at the waist. She tapped a pointy shoe on the carpet. She had an announcement to make to her children.

We sat on the sofa, Marco and I, staring at the woman in the new dress. A gold clip rested in the blur of her hair. Her fingernails were painted a color of purplish red. The same color was on her lips.

Your mamma has job! I'm sing Italian songs at Lorenzo's Ristorante! *Molto elegante!* You like my dress? You think you Mamma she look okay, eh!

Sing. She was going to *sing*. God in heaven and all the saints.

No more I afraid, she said. I make a plan in my brain and good things happen for you mamma. This is America, no? I join twenty century.

And her voice, thanks God, was better than ever, stronger, *voce d'oro*, golden voice, more lyrical the quality.

She told us how she took herself to the restaurant, sang a song like she was back in Italy singing for love, and what do you know, the owner hired her on the spot. He said it was just what Lorenzo's Fine Italian Ristorante needed, a singer, music. She would sing songs she had almost forgotten, but some things, children, you never forget, and that's as true as mozzarella.

She would sing the old favorites, so called. "Oi Mari," "Autunno," "Mare Chiara," "Fenesta Che Luciva," "Turna Surriento," she could remember the words, which she is not surprised; after all, music was in her blood, her bones, what you think, like *vino rosso*.

She had thrown the black mourning dresses into the garbage, her black shawls, too, *madonna*, for too long she not sing, she not live! She, a poor woman with *bambini* in a country full of Normans.

Mamma, why have you never sung to us?

She took a breath. All right. You want I sing now?

Now?

She started. A deep, undulating voice: *Oi Marie, Oi Marie* . . . ChiChi, promise you Mamma you no cut offa you face no more.

(But Mamma, I *had* to make you happy.) Okay. Sure, but I didn't look in her eyes when I said I promise.

On she sang: *Quanto sonno io perdo per te* . . .

Mr. Metamere was not mentioned again and we never told her about his being married with two kids. I graduated from the Margaret Brown Settlement House school and we had cookies and lemonade outside in the school yard afterward. Mamma bought me a new dress, navy blue and white with a red bow at the neck. *Molto* American! she said, delighted with herself. Graduation from the settlement house school felt like being ejected from a country. Sister Ursula and Father Tuttifucci were an entire nation and I felt like I was heading for another Ellis Island. Only this time I spoke English and couldn't remember the country where I was born. What do you know. I was an American.

Part Two

*M*amma's career as a *cantante* took off. How many years had she sat at the window staring down at the railroad tracks planning this? She made her debut at Lorenzo's Ristorante Fine Italian Dining in spite of her terror and inability to hold herself erect. The morning of her first day on the job her legs went stiff and her neck, she said, was broken like a cow. That night she stood at the piano in the corner of the restaurant, barely holding herself up, but after two choruses of *Sorrento*, she began to do something she hadn't experienced in years—enjoy herself. Marco and I watched in flat-out wonder from the kitchen. By the end of the evening you'd have thought she was Giulietta Masina or Kathryn Grayson.

The management took out advertisements in the newspapers: *Lorenzo's Ristorante, Fine Italian Dining, featuring the enticing cantante, Pina Dino.*

Guiseppina Maggiordino. Who can say such a mouthful? said Mr. Rodman, the boss. Her name was now Pina Dino.

Reviews appeared in the food columns of local papers, including the *Minneapolis Star* and *Tribune*; Mamma was mentioned along with Lorenzo's fettucini and the mouth watering *vongole.*

Pina Dino—Fetching, Enticing.

Miss Dino sparkles . . .

Twin Cities public figures and radio and television luminaries ate Lorenzo's pasta and the tortellini and Mamma sang to each of them, moved around their tables, gave them "O Sole Mio" during the antipasto, "Oi Marie" through the piatti, and "Fenesta Che Lucive" with their cheese.

The mayor came, the union men came with their families, newsmen and women, lawyers, doctors and their nurses, professors and their students, they all ate at Lorenzo's. And Mamma, in her new dresses and gold hair clips, sang to them all as though each song was a personal gift to the world.

Dayton's Department Store invited her to sing at their fashion shows in the Sky Room. WCCO televised her. Our mother, a person called Pina Dino, sang live on the radio. She wore earrings and bracelets. She wore clothes that had to be dry cleaned.

You could hear her bracelets jangling through the wall as she dressed for work, the rings on her fingers were like sparks you could light a cigar with. Pina Dino bought shoes with open toes. She painted her eyelids with green shadow. She smelled like lilacs.

She took me to the Promenade School of Beauty for a haircut. The woman cut it short, above my ears, thinned and flattened it out. I cried and said I looked like a seal. Mamma figured if my hair was cut short I wouldn't have to get it done so often, Seal, she didn't know, what is seal?

It's a fish.

She smacked me on the ear. Then be a salmon, she said. Is expensive. Good with Samorillo sauce.

Junior High, a place where a girl could lose her balance, where Marco didn't wait for me at the end of the day. The teachers wore regular clothes, and nobody prayed out loud. No pictures of popes on the walls, no black wind of priests or nuns, and the boys and girls with pink cheeks and bleached eyes wore clothes purchased at stores I never heard of.

I ate lunch, mortadella with a small hard roll from home, in a lunchroom noisier than a flock of squawking seagulls.

Worse, I discovered in horror that my body was engaged in shameful acts of rebellion. The other girls brought to school their tiny waists, their new perky breasts, their rounded hips, their glad and reckless rhythms; they laughed and swung their secrets through the halls and into the girls' gym, and I fell back in shame, cowered in the toilet stalls, stiff and scrawny, with a body like a boy's.

But then a hostile event took place in my body. Mamma said it was something you fold a rag up in your panties to soak up. *Santa Maria*. What next would happen to me? Mamma said I had become a woman and I said, *Gesù* and all the saints, Mamma, I'm bleeding like a stigmata. She said you wear the rags folded up thick and you wash them out at night. *Punto e basta*. No more. She had other things to think about.

After Mass on Sundays we ate dinner at Lorenzo's Ristorante. Marco and I wore the new clothes Mamma bought us at Montgomery Ward's basement sale and we sat at a table with a tablecloth weighted with more silverware than we owned altogether. (Me sitting on a crumpled dish towel in my pants.) Mamma reigned over the meal, a Napolitano queen, ordering our food for us, joking with the waiters, laughing, chatting, introducing us to grown-ups who looked like cigarette ads in magazines. That's Mr. Mitchell Rodman. Be nice to him. Sit up straight. Fix you collar.

ChiChi, why you sit so funny?

Mr. Mitchell Rodman was the owner of Lorenzo's Ristorante, Fine Italian Dining. Mamma smiled at him, showing all her teeth, a practiced smile. I saw her working at it in the mirror at home, teeth together, mouth spread wide, saying *Why thaaaank you* to herself. Marco and I sat like ducks wondering how to manipulate the silverware.

Why you not eat you proscuitto? she hissed through the smile. Eat you proscuitto. *State buon,* be good. You want I break you legs?

Mitchell Rodman, a small, nervous man, brown and hairy, with a shiny face and scrappy mustache, watched Mamma with eyes like hooks. He smoked cigars which floated atop ashtrays in the kitchen and kept a steady path back and forth to the cash register checking receipts.

I endured the discomfort of these meals by worrying about my bad haircut and counting the people sitting at the other tables. I also worried about dying without a drop of blood left in my veins.

I folded my napkin under my chin once, twice, three times, and I tapped my foot one hundred times under the table. This I did to assure Pina Dino would stay happy and keep singing.

The minute we arrived back home Marco was on the phone with Ed Looz talking over art plans. Art art art art, life is art. Art is life. To live is art. God created the world as art and all therein as art, Marco's truth. Marco and Ed Looz had a handle on truth. They owned truth. They had art.

One Sunday afternoon while we were finishing our cacciatore at the restaurant, I looked up to see a family of four enter and take a booth behind the dessert table. A father and a mother with two teenage boys. I dropped my dinner fork. I had been blinking so my eyes were watery and at first I thought I was seeing a ghost. But there was no mistaking the sway of the father's big head, the thick fleshy hand on the shoulder of his son, the gentle, sad eyes, the pink jowls, the collar that met his chin. Mr. Metamere.

A woman hung onto his arm and two boys bumbled into the booth. I heard the woman say, Keep It Down, You Two. They were out of Mamma's sight, in a booth on the other side of the restaurant. I gulped the water, gagged. How could I keep Mamma's attention diverted so she wouldn't turn around and see him? I imagined the room sliding to its center like a sheet held by its four corners. I could hear my heartbeat above the voices and clattering of dishes. Marco caught sight of them at the same time as I had.

Mamma!

She nodded, waited.

Mamma!

She raised her eyebrows.

Mamma!

She cocked her head to the side, narrowed her eyes. I pushed back my chair, reached across the table and took her hand.

Mamma, Marco and I have a surprise for you.

She waited.

Don't we, Marco? Big surprise.

She looked suspicious.

We are so proud of you, Mamma, that we want to give you a—

Give a *what?* said Marco.

Not here. No, not here. Come, follow me.

I led them into the kitchen. Mamma, I said, Marco and I want to demonstrate our happiness for the big success you've made.

What means this, demonstrate?

I guided her to the kitchen's back wall behind the dishwasher where we couldn't be seen or heard.

Sit down, Mamma.

Marco whispered against my cheek. What the hell are *they* doing here? Mamma will blow like *Stromboli* if she sees them!

Cosa? said Mamma, Where is volcano?

I struck a pose like one of Mamma's, hand to the shoulder, wrist limp, head skyward, eyes closed, and I tried to sing. My voice came out like plates scraping. Mamma shivered and laughed. I kept trying to imitate her movements, her gestures, flirting with imaginary customers, ruffling Marco's hair. She seemed delighted! Clapped her hands, laughed out loud. I began another song imitating her movements like a clown. I shook my imaginary hair, I twirled, spun, slunk, pranced, slithered, I made faces, pulled at my mouth, sunk to my knees like Caruso. Finally I planted myself on my knees in front of her and sang in a whispery vibrato "Santa Lucia," her favorite.

One of the waiters had been watching the charade and wagged his head. Mamma called to him, *Guarda,* Sunny! See how my *figli* demonstrate their mamma! The waiter, whose beard looked drawn on his chin with crayon, said *Bravi.* He winked, pursed his lips, and blew us a kiss.

She wiped tears from the corners of her eyes and Marco checked out the restaurant. *Stronzo!* he whispered to me. Metamere had just ordered tiramisù.

I remembered him at our kitchen table lapping up Mamma's tiramisù with a serving ladle like a goat, then patting her behind and whistling with pleasure, vanilla cream dripping from his chin. *You're the best, my love, the best.* Mamma's tiramisù was his favorite dessert, even above Bridgeman's peppermint bonbon ice cream.

Mamma, Marco will now deliver a speech, I said.

Marco slumped before us with the stage presence of an old tire. All right, he said, Mamma, to demonstrate my deep feelings, I just want to say—

He recited his World War II essay from memory.

Mamma blew her nose, reached for her son, and held him to her chest. While she hugged him I went to the door to check on things.

Still there. Slurping up the damn tiramisù.

ChiChi, how about an encore? Marco said.

We were sinking fast. The waiter named Sunny said, *Bravo,* an encore!

I started "Sentimental Journey" and Marco joined in.

I don't like that song, said Mamma.

Marco whispered, They'll NEVER leave. Doesn't he recognize Mamma's picture out front?

Che? said Mamma. Why you not speak so I hear you?

Sing "Home on the Range," said Marco with a smirk.

Who me? I said. Sorry, I'm F.O.B. and I don't know the words.

Hahaha.

What F.O.B. is? Asked Mamma.

Marco's sick, I said, startling myself. Just look at him! We better take him home, quick!

Che cosa!

Ya. He said quickly. Sick.

Mamma's smile stuck to her teeth.

He's got diarrhea! I said.

Diarrhea! said Marco.

He's got to go home. You've got to take him home.

Take me home, Mamma.

Use *gabinetto* here, what you think?

No, he couldn't. Not the public one. Couldn't possibly,

no, no. He had to go home. Home, Mamma, home, before it was too late. Had to have his medicine.

What medicine?

He threw himself against the cupboard, writhing.

Madonna, said Sunny. I'll help you take the kid home, Pina.

We left through the back door of the restaurant, Marco holding his stomach, Mamma pulling him along by the shoulder of his sweater.

Sunny's truck smelled of stale cigarette smoke and pine air freshener. Hanging from the mirror on a gold string was a miniature pink satin brassiere with cotton breasts bulging from it like bocci balls. We climbed in, Marco and Mamma in the middle and me pressed against the door without a handle.

What you think, Sunny? You hear my children? They make good show, eh! Like on television, like on Sid Caesar, no? Then, stroking Marco: Did you eat the provolone? Eh? The provolone bad. I tell Mitchell no serve the green provolone.

At home Mamma stood outside the bathroom door shouting at Marco.

You better have a diarrhea, *figlio,* you better be plenty sick, make plenty ka-ka!

Or I'm kill you. She paced back and forth while Sunny and I sat in the kitchen staring at each other.

You doing diarrhea, *figlio?* Eh! Eh? She held a bottle of castor oil in one hand, baking soda and water in the other. If Marco wasn't sick before, he would be now.

Sunny stayed for a drink of *grappa* and Marco and I went to our room.

I had to swallow the stuff! Castor oil! He shuddered, coughed, swabbed at his tongue with the edge of the blanket.

Did you get a good look at the boys?

Ya, I said.

Didn't you recognize them? No? You got a short memory, ChiChi. They're LaMont's buddies. They were the ones who ambushed us that time I cut myself with their father's knife.

Santa Maria. Boys who would kill us daily.

Mamma and Sunny talked long into the night. She was saying how she cry in her life enough tears for two oceans, so many tears. How she bring her children to America where *moscas* come all year and suck our blood, which is what she was against. She come to America to be rejoined with her husband and all she got was a wooden leg. *Dio mio.* And her mamma, a saint, who accompany her for love of *gli bambini,* die right here in this house, a terrible thing.

Ah, poor, poor Pina . . .

Sì, poor Pina, which is Giuseppina cut in half.

Ah, beautiful name. *Bella. Bella.*

Imagine poor Giuseppina spurned by her sisters and village, ridiculed and called bad names, now all alone in strange country with two children—the daughter, she *pazza* in the head, but *grazie a Dio,* her boy not die, did Sunny know what was tumor? Tumor size of *melanzane,* such the suffering this mother endure. Oh, how this mother suffer. The very words we heard her tell Mr. Metamere a year ago.

The voices hushed. I imagined her hand moving across Sunny's sleeve, her eyes lighted, a sly smile lifting the corners of her mouth. Next she would tell him how lonely she was with no man to love and care for. Sunny's mouth would turn to flames, his skin ignite. His chest would sprout wings.

Allora, Caro . . . Mamma said, her voice feathery. Too much I talk about me—

The murmuring of an autumn wind. Sounds that changed

colors like a kaleidoscope, that sang and reverberated like muffled church bells.

Next time, ChiChi, *you* be the one with diarrhea, Marco groaned.

*W*e moved from Tar Town.

On a snowy day in late November, Sunny's truck with its bed bound together in wooden slats arrived at the curb in front of our apartment on Taylor Street in Tar Town. We were used to Sunny by now, the waiter whose real name was Pasquale, the one who blew kisses to Mamma while we chewed on our scallopini or osso bucco on Sunday afternoons at Lorenzo's. With him was his brother, Tomasio, a short, dark man with a gold tooth whose English was limited to yes, no, and sanka you.

Sunny jumped from his truck, the door cracking shut behind him like bones breaking, and Mamma rushed downstairs to meet him with kisses on both cheeks. She called him an *angelo* and he kissed her on the mouth. Snow fell on their heads and shoulders. Sunny chewed gum and Mamma flushed, the two of them sighing in the November morning of wind and snow under the sad gaze of the Fiores downstairs.

The young people are leaving Tar Town, cried Signora Fiore. One day there won't be an Italian neighborhood in Minneapolis. We'll be a handful of old people sitting outside our houses playing *briscola*. The church will have empty pews, no services during the week, no *Bafana*, no feast day parades, nobody to remember what we suffer to come here, stay here. New people will move into these houses, Polish,

Norwegian, Irish, but they don't come from Ellis Island, no they will be *Americani*. Italian families are spreading out, they're moving to Golden Valley, Saint Anthony, better neighborhoods in the Twin Cities. Soon there won't be a Tar Town.

And good riddance, said Mamma. Is time we let go old ways for new. I left Italy nine years ago but only now I leave Italy for sure. *Now* I come to America. *Now* I join twenty century.

May God's angels watch over and protect you, said Signora Fiore, and she kissed her on both cheeks and gave her a raisin cake. *Per buona fortuna*—and for the children.

Tomasio and Sunny carried our sofa and chairs, bed frames and mattresses, down the stairs to the truck. They carried Mamma's rolled carpet outside where the temperature was dropping fast. The November snowfall had picked up speed. Sunny wore a black T-shirt and pants stuffed inside high boots, he strutted and grunted in front of Mamma. His back was a fan of black. He puffed white air. Marco was forbidden to lift anything, so it was up to me to sneak out our rock collection and other found treasures.

I walked to Mr. Rizzo's house. We're moving, I told Mrs. Rizzo. I came to say good-bye to Mr. Rizzo.

He's sleeping.

Don't disturb him on my account.

I won't.

Please tell him good-bye for us?

Ya, I'll tell him. Say then, will you be keeping your membership at Our Lady of Mount Carmel?

Mamma says no, too far away.

Your mamma! So how's she doing?

Mamma again. Everyone in the neighborhood observed

the change in her. I saw the men's eyes go gummy at the sight of her, the women's spines congeal in her presence, the long rainy silences.

I walked to the convent after evening matins in the chapel to find Sister Ursula. She stretched her arms wide. *Figlia Leticcia!*

She told me she would remember me in prayer.

And Mamma and Marco, too, Sister?

Yes, yes, of course. May the blessing of the Lord be with you all, yes, yes. She gave me a new rosary.

Good-bye is not always a blessing.

On the last night in Tar Town I climbed in bed with Marco.

We'll have our own rooms in the new place, I said.

Good deal, he said.

It'll be weird.

No, it won't.

Well, lonesome maybe. Maybe lonesome.

We lay with our heads on his pillow, our feet together, staring at the familiar ceiling with its spots like map shapes of countries. He talked about what he wanted to sneak with us. He had accumulated a mountain of art. Mamma said no rocks, no junk. But we didn't own anything else except what she called junk. We realized with a quiet burr of two noses that we had never owned toys.

You ever wish you had a doll? Marco asked.

I never thought of it, I said.

While Sunny, Tomasio, and I loaded the truck, Mamma washed the apartment walls, floors, windows, sinks with a fury. Nobody would ever say of her that she was not a clean woman. Giuseppina Sapponata Maggiordino, a.k.a. Pina Dino, kept a clean house.

We hopped down the stairs for the last time. Marco said we'd never come back here and I said sure we would, it was where we lived, we would always live here. What I meant was, Tar Town would always live in us. It was inevitable. It couldn't be any different.

We crowded into the front seat of the truck, and with our worldly belongings rattling behind us unprotected in the falling snow, headed out of Tar Town. Between my legs wrapped in the blanket from my bed was Pappa's wooden leg.

I strained to see into the steamy windows where pasta water boiled and sauces bubbled on stoves. Fences and crooked walkways appeared like religious icons in the falling snow, though I knew in a short time the snow couldn't remain completely white, but would turn a sort of greasy brown like old bread. We drove along the streets of familiar two-story frame houses, the small squares of front yards, the alleys of small wood garages and sheds, past D'Amico's Grocery, past Our Lady of Mount Carmel, past the settlement house, the railroad bridge, down Broadway to Central, away from Tar Town. We watched the river below us as we crossed the bridge, a raging icy river sprayed with snarls of tree branches, and then the dimmed lights in the windows of drooping houses and ragged metal trailers where families with children and grandparents lived. This slow rollicking drive in Sunny's truck in late November, our fingers sticky in our mittens, our breath fogging the windshield, and me thinking of the box of river rocks sinking the rear tires in back, the homemade skooter, the stereo speakers, and the bicycle we never built.

Ed Looz waited for Marco at the door of our new home. He had taken a cab from his place four blocks away.

If you can't help us lift stuff, Looz, make your damn self scarce, I told him.

ChiChi, no talk like that to Eddie! Mamma snapped.

Sanka you, said Tomasio, and he shook Ed's hand.

Our new apartment took up the bottom floor of a three-story house, sandwiched between the Rainbow Ice Cream Company and Ole's Body Shop on University Avenue in southeast Minneapolis. We were a block from the public library and four blocks from Ed Looz and his father.

Each room of the apartment had retained a texture of its own, a feeling of motion. Everywhere I looked, movement. Even in the stillness, the absence of humans and furnishings, there was the swirl of low tones, a slow rhythm, a rocking back and forth. I could imagine in the basement below us the scratching of rodents scraping the walls for crumbs of plaster. The upstairs rooms were rented out to employees of the ice cream factory on the corner and the telephone company.

I could almost hear the voices of other families who had lived in the apartment, mothers and fathers eating dinner at six o'clock, children writing numbers in wide-lined school tablets. The rooms smelled of sour dough and old clothes. Muddy finger smudges trussed the light switches, edges of cupboards, door frames, and window ledges. There was linoleum in every room. Now Mamma's presence in this place, her sounds, her florid, impassioned steps, the way she touched things, lifted a curtain, swabbed at the wall with the scrub brush. Maybe this could really be home.

Nonna came to me in my sleep. She spoke in a strange watery voice, *Cara mia* . . . She kissed the pink scars around my jaw, the raised white lines that healed like barbed wire along my hairline. We were in our house in Praiano, the house built of stone, dirt, and stalk with no linoleum for the floor, no radiators for heat, no gas stove or electric refrigerator. I climbed the sleeping loft above the kitchen, felt the straw beneath my legs. Stood in the room by the bed where Marco was born, breathed the air beneath the chestnut tree by the door. I heard the gulls over the water below. Nonna offered me hot coffee and milk. *Remember,* she said. *Remember.* Spoken as a gentle command. In the morning when I awoke, the snow had stopped falling and my new bedroom on University Avenue was filled with sunlight. I hadn't forgotten Praiano! I remembered! Nonna wanted me to remember and I did! I would write it down.

Without realizing I was being observed from the door, I knelt at the side of my bed to pray the rosary Nonna had given me. I didn't hear the tweaky rub of a leather jacket or the scratching of a stomach, didn't hear the soft toothy whistle. If I had, I would have screamed so loud Ed Looz would be deaf for a year.

*S*aints in heaven, *grazie* to loving Jesus, Junior High wasn't so bad after all. I was transferred to Saint Lawrence, a Catholic school in southeast Minneapolis. At last a crucifix on the wall, a nun or two. Mass.

Make it last.

Don't blow this.

Say a hundred Hail Marys and Lord's Prayers.

Do regular novenas.

Give up milk.

Don't step on cracks.

Eat dirt.

Virgin, most pure, glorious Mary, full of grace, Mother of
God,
Queen of Angels, I humbly honor you . . .

What you got there in your mouth, ChiChi?

Noffing.

Gesù Cristo! Pina, your kid's eating dirt!

Sunny had no knowledge of the penitent's grateful heart. A man with no spiritual fiber.

Here's ChiChi Maggiordino with girlfriends who don't call me names, who like me. These girls treat me like I'm a regular person, like one of *them*. A girl named Jennifer is my friend and she's not Italian. She's an American, born in Minnesota. I'll have you know girls come up to me in the hall and in the cafeteria and ask my name, invite me to sit with them, be on their volleyball team, go ice skating after school. They laugh when I act like a clown, when I make faces and tell stories. Girls with plump, strident faces and combed hair of autumnal colors, girls who wear their birthstones on chains around their necks, girls who eat egg salad sandwiches and packaged white bread at noon and say, Cool Man, when speaking to another girl.

I begged Mamma for skirts of plaid design like the girls at school wore. Penny loafers like the ones Jennifer wore, pullovers, Kickereenos for the snow, a stylish hat instead of my weedy wool cap, a winter coat in a color. Mamma said if I wanted to be a movie star, I should move to Hollywood.

Sunny treated Marco and me like small grown-ups, offered us cigarettes, beer, sticks of gum; used words like *goddamma Fascista* and *goddamma Capitalista*. Always talking about politics, life back in Italy, this corruption, that corruption, everyone was a bad guy, no one could be trusted, all forms of government were nests of oppression.

He talked with a combination of nostalgia and bitterness about his village in the mountains of southern Italy. His talk left us confused and bored, and the only thing that seemed to cheer him up was Mamma's singing. When Mamma sang at the restaurant, he held a glass high to the Napolitano drinking songs, he danced and banged a cup on the table top to the *tarantella,* even though he was a waiter and should be minding his customers.

He moved in with us.

At night when he came home late with Mamma, we'd hear the phonograph music of Carlo Buti, Claudio Villa, and Domenico Modugno trickling through the walls of Mamma's bedroom.

Every day a new rant. We Italians are a people neither mighty nor smart! he raved. Look at us! We outlived the fall of the Roman Empire, we survived the many Barbarian invasions, the raids by Saracens, Normans, and Turks; we've come through wars, communal strife, pestilences, disease, famines, volcano eruptions, floods, earthquakes—and look at us now! Waiting on tables.

I am singer, said Mamma, and that lifted her social status by several notches.

Singers, jesters, waiters, all the same in global opinion. Like insects. Sing? What good is to sing? Does singing end starvation, hunger, oppression? Do we sing "Bella Bimba" while Rome burns?

His tirades were theatrical productions. Tell me, Pina, he fumed while strutting the kitchen, who can liberate Italy? Who can unite us, help our country rebuild itself? WHO can end the corruption and greed and high places?

Sunny, *per l'ammor d'dio.*

Ha! The Greeks, Romans, Saracens, Visigoths, Normans, Franks, all of them trample, invade, conquer us, and still we go on! For what? To SING!

The happy heart sings, said a weary Mamma.

Stupid heart, you mean. The bloodthirsty Turks, the papist inquisitors, Spanish Bourbons, and that snake, Napoleon, invade our country. Napoleon, who thought he'd turn us all into Frenchmen! Think of the gunboats, warplanes, bombings, the Germans, invasions in our own lifetime! The occupation by the S.S. Eight thousand innocent, hardworking Italian Jews killed for no reason—we lose what we have of land, of beaches, our tiny holdings of animals, our vines and our fruit trees—and we go on singing.

Sì, we must sing.

Eh! While the Jews are murdered and the devourers devour.

Yes. We outlast the murderers and the devourers. We sing.

Their arguments were never private. All of University Avenue could hear them. Sunny shouted his rage against the bureaucrats, the bankers, the corrupt politicians, and then he got personal, started in on Mitchell Rodman, their boss, owner of Lorenzo's Ristorante, Fine Italian Dining.

Pina, why you are nice to Mitchell Rodman? That pig!

He not pig. He nice man, said Mamma.

Tell him to drop dead. Quit that job.

The clatter to the table of a dish, a slammed door, more shouting, the hiss of a beer bottle opening. Then one night at the restaurant, Sunny got drunk and started a fight with a railroad lobbyist who complained about too much garlic in the pesto. Sunny called him a goddamn *fascista,* screamed what did he know about the workers and their suffering, a man whose mouth curled in disdain at the ambrosia of garlic.

Mr. Rodman fired Sunny.

Now we had Sunny hanging around the house during the day, sleeping, listening to Carlo Buti records, reading Italian newspapers, popping caps off beer bottles. He took up cooking. Called the kitchen *his* kitchen.

Sunny chopped, fried, baked, and ranted. Who you think make good this country of America? Eh! Cristoforo Colombo! Amerigo Vespucci! *Paesani! Viva L'Italia! E lo sanno tutti.*

Viva, said Mamma with indifference. Far more interesting to her was the pattern on a skirt, the cut of a blouse, the latest evening wear and hair fashion. She wore new dresses and jewelry, the jewelry a particular bother to Sunny.

How much you pay for that?

Basta. Is no your concern.

Is that *stronzo* Rodman buying you presents?

Marco ignored them. After school he and Ed Looz made art in his room, clay and papier-mâché models of airplanes, spaceships, moon habitations. On her days off, Mamma polished her nails, ironed Sunny's shirts, and read women's magazines. She listened to English-in-Thirty-Days records, labored through the workbook, asked a river of questions—What this is? What she say? What this word is?—until Sunny would get nervous and burn the onions.

Sunny sat in Mamma's chair at night and smoked cigarettes, which he rolled himself. Mamma came home in the grey hours of the morning and ordered Sunny not to smoke in the house because of Marco's lung affliction, but he paid no attention to her.

The air in the house became clouded with a grey film of smoke. The sheets, towels, curtains, furniture took on a rusty, stale smell. Even the toothpaste smelled like a match had been taken to it.

Sunny watched with a suspicious eye as I worked on my homework. He snapped his gum and grunted, then ambled back to his simmering tomato sauce or a soup of cow's tongue. Always hanging from the side of his lip was a lit cigarette, the long ashes dripping onto his clothes.

Mamma says you can't smoke in the house, I told him.

What she want me I do? Eh? She want I stand outside and freeze my *culo*? Is like Arctic Ocean out there.

Marco, he said, would just have to learn to be a man.

I had to come up with a plan, call on the Evil Eye. Act fast.

Marco and I wore two sweaters under our jackets and extra socks in our rubber galoshes when we were outside, but the cold gathered in our bones, a living thing with hands that left bruises. Me I didn't worry about, runny nose, toes that burned, stiff fingers, sore throat I could handle by my rituals, like swallowing a hundred times, saying more Hail Marys. But Marco. Marco could break. He could, at any time, break.

More of Sunny's tirades. On and on. Where goes the money De Gasperi established for the South? Eh? The *Cassa per il Mezzogiorno*? The Marshall Plan give to the South! The money go in the pockets of the rich! Money go to North.

Mamma said, Money go to Naples, to Bari-Brindisi-Taranto triangle, and to Syracuse-Augusta. I know. I read about.

Propaganda! said Sunny. The poor backward, hungry south! More than eighty percent of help go to only few regions—Roma north. And for to finance big business, I know these things. I am informed!

He closed the refrigerator with the back of his foot.

He spit in his hand. And lit a cigarette. No question about it. I had to get rid of Sunny.

*M*y calling: Get rid of Sunny.

Rise and shine, pour the water in the pans for coffee and polenta while Marco breathes in his machine. Pull on the wool skirt, the undershirt and cardigan, the long wool tights. Don't make noise. Spread the blanket back over the bed nice, smooth it down, get Marco's medicine ready, the hot milk. Eat the polenta, drink just one cup of coffee. Walk on the sides of your feet, careful, careful, to Mamma's bedroom; sneak her purse, the rolls of bills. Pull off some bills, slip out of the room. Hide the money in a cardboard box in the basement. Be skillful at this. Be imaginative.

Mamma: ChiChi, where was Sunny when you come home from school?

ChiChi: At the movies I think.

Mamma: While I work like a cow!

Sunny responded in a spitting fury. To accuse him of stealing money from her purse! Better it would be to cut from his arms his hands, make sausage of his calluses!

Mamma began to find wads of chewed gum stuck on the underside of the coffee table in front of the new TV, which she bought with her hard work and sweat. Cigarette burns on her sofa, which she paid for with her hard work and sweat.

And where was he getting money to go to the movies?

What? shouted Sunny. The last movie he saw was *Love Is*

She Many Splendored Cosa, and this he saw with her at the State Theatre downtown. When did he have time to waste about at movies when the world was going to the devil?

Meals were eaten in frosty silence as Mamma played with the boiled potatoes and beans on her plate. It seemed all wrong that she wasn't the one bent over the stove cursing the oven. At night Mamma hid her purse under the TV.

The next day she'd find wads of hardened gum on the linoleum in the living room, gum stuck like dirty glue between the cushions of the sofa.

If Sunny hadn't crowded the air Marco breathed with smoke I wouldn't have done the things I did, but I had to hold things together, keep things from unravelling, stay the arm of doom.

Pina, quit that job! he yelled.

Never I quit!

Pina, I love you! Why you do this to me?

Sunny got himself hired as a bartender at the Mile High Bar and Grill on East Hennepin, an American bar and restaurant where the only pasta served was macaroni and Velveeta. On December 22nd, he moved out.

Mamma remained in her bedroom with the door closed for two days, missing two nights of work. When she decided to join us, she announced that with Sunny gone, she was going to work longer hours at Lorenzo's Fine Italian Dining. She would learn modern songs, make more tips. She'd sing "That's Amore," and "Moon Reefer."

Without Sunny's smoke, Marco's hyperresponsive irritable airways could relax, yes, yes. There would be no decline in his lung function. Pollution was not only an outdoor phenomenon, it had lived inside with us, and it called itself Sunny. The enemy was gone, ho ho. It was going to be a good Christmas.

*C*hristmas time the investigators started coming around. What did Mamma know about her husband? Did she have any information about his business? Who were her husband's friends and associates? What did she know about his parents?

They want my children they starve! Mamma ranted. They want to take away my money! His family, puh! I give them the evil eye, evil, Evil Eye! I not speak of husband. Husband, puh! Never do I speak of him!

Before Sunny moved out I had asked him about the investigators. He told me ah, I shouldn't worry. These Americans, he had said, they think all Italians got crime zinging through our veins. They think we got gnocchi for brains. They don't know how *furba*, clever, is your mamma.

I remember Sunny's dark eyes, and watching his jaw twitch while snapping his gum. How much was my pappa like that man? Had my father's arms been short and thick like Sunny's boiled potato muscles? Had he walked with the same anticipation in each step as though expecting a brilliant something, say a thought or a person or a miracle, to pop out of the earth and shake hands with him? Was my pappa *furbo* like Mamma? Sure, sure, he was clever, Sunny had said. He was in Army Intelligence. Forget about him.

On Christmas Eve Mamma, Marco, and I took a taxi to Midnight Mass with Ed Looz and his father. We sat in a freezing draft behind a pillar and sang "Silent Night" to our folded hands. I thought about Army Intelligence and a leg left in a wastebasket in Maiori. Sleep in heavenly peace, sleep in heavenly peace, we sang. Why, oh why, were Catholic churches so cold?

Christmas Day, the coldest day of the year, colder than an act of blackmail, we ate Christmas dinner in the Lorenzo's empty restaurant, Closed For The Holiday. Mamma was without Sunny. She sat on the chair nearest the dishwasher and drank Sunny's kind of beer, Schlitz. She was expecting him to turn up or call, wish her a *Buon Natale*.

Mah, let him suffer, he make his porridge, let him sleep in it, she said.

We ate our dinner in the kitchen, staying warm by the oven. Our dinner was antipasto food. Olives, peppers, and arugula soaked in olive oil and balsamic vinegar, anchovies, cheese, salami, *pane*. Mamma found some rum cake which we forked in with delight and washed down with Pepsi Cola. We burped happily at what we thought was a pretty darn good Christmas dinner. I folded my napkin under my chin once, twice, three times, I tapped my foot one hundred times under the table. This is what I did to assure Mamma wouldn't explode like Vesuvius and sob her head off.

She barely looked at the potholders I sewed for her in Home Ec class, or the necklace of hammered and twisted beer bottle caps Marco created for her. It took him two months of collecting bottle caps to come up with what he thought was the perfect design, the perfect tinny rustling sound, the perfect mess of color.

Mamma opened her presents slowly, as though something inside the box could be injured. She kissed us and thanked us without looking at us. Her way of kissing was to never quite touch her lips to our skin, like blowing out candles on our faces.

I kept my eye on the kitchen door, expecting an inspector to burst in, ruin our Christmas and *Befana*. And then there came a scratching of the lock of the kitchen door.

Mamma smoothed her hair, crossed a leg. The door opened and Mitchell Rodman stood with the snow at his back, wearing frozen blue of the sky on his head. Earmuffs and a coat with a fur collar. A cold wind blew across the floor.

Mitchell Rodman stomped the snow from his shoes.

Buon Natale, Merry Christmas, he said.

He sat down at the table without taking off his coat.

Merry Christmas, said Mamma. Her smile nervous, coy.

Mr. Rodman said, So you dumped the stud, eh?

She winced. Crossed the other leg.

You like the stud types, eh, Pina?

She fumbled with a fold of her skirt. He continued, moving his chair closer to hers with his feet, and lacing his fingers behind his head.

Muscle brains is what I call his type, full of piss, he said. Studs are good for one thing only and when they're done, *pah!* They pack up and go on to the next bird. You get what I'm saying, Pina? You're too good for that punk. He's a fuckup, going to get himself into big trouble one day.

Marco and I slurped air through our straws. Mamma cleared her throat.

Ah, but *you*, Pina . . . YOU got class. You could go places if you played your cards right. Get what I'm saying?

Mamma giggled, a strange sucking sound. Her mouth was pink, trembly.

I'm not want to talk about Sunny, she said.

Terrific. That's what I want to hear, he said with a smacky grin. Let's have a little Christmas cheer, hunh? Champagne?

He unlocked the refrigerator with the good stuff.

Champagne for our *cantante!* The toast of Minneapolis!

You're not the Schlitz type, Pina, you're Mumm's all the way.

They toasted to the birth of Christ and a bright tomorrow. Mamma poured champagne for us, too. We toasted to a prosperous year, *C'in C'in.*

He took Mamma's elbow, guided her through the kitchen door into the restaurant like she was a blind person. We followed, not knowing what else to do. He was telling her his plans for expansion, adding more tables, a bigger bar area. We didn't know if we should sit down or stand up. I counted the lights in the ceiling. He still had not taken off his coat. He chewed on a toothpick. He held Mamma's hand and led her behind the bar.

You kids go wait in the kitchen for your mother.

Mamma looked flustered, confused. He spit out the toothpick.

Go, he said to us. Scramola.

We backed into the kitchen.

What seemed like hours later, she returned to us. Mr. Rodman followed a minute later. He reached into his pocket and tossed Marco and me each a five-dollar bill. Here's from Santa Claus, he said. Then he gave Mamma a nod and a half-smile, Be sure you lock up, turn off the lights, and he left through the kitchen door.

Marco and I stuffed the money in our shoes. Mama poured the last of the champagne into her glass and took a long sip. She spoke in a voice like something patted down and tucked under.

ChiChi, she said, sing to me. Sing "I Love You Like a Tomato"—sing.

So I sang to her. I sang like I meant it.

*C*ame 1957, the year the United States built a new B-52 long-range bomber. The year the first intercontinental ballistic missile was tested by Soviets and the year the North Vietnamese guerrilla activity began against South Vietnamese government; and for me it was the year Pat Boone sang "Love Letters in the Sand," and when Mamma discovered Velcro.

That winter shaking off the residue of Sunny's smoke and Sunny's tirades gave way to another new Mamma, and the winter turned bigger than us, bigger than her new perfumes and late nights, bigger than snowdrift canyons and news of the world, but not bigger than Mitchell Rodman.

He became a phantom presence in the apartment. We could sense him nearby, pressing into our lives.

Snowbanks reached above the top of our porch that winter. Snow didn't fall gentle like you see on Christmas cards and calendars, those nice pictures of snowflakes big as Kleenex—no, our snow bashed us senseless. The wind rattled the mirror in the bathroom and the bowls in the refrigerator, it sent thundery drifts under the front door into the hall. By spring we all staggered with exhaustion. Winter almost devoured us whole, but the surprising thing was, at the first chirping bird and pinprick of melted snow we forgot about being cold. Mamma said we were now Minnesotans.

In Junior High school my new friends taught me how to massage conditioner into my mania of hair, which had grown below my ears and surged out in frenzied torrents on each side of my head. I learned how to smooth it down with a large toothed metal pick, how to layer on hair spray, make the mass stay put. Jennifer said she envied my naturally curly hair. I bit my mouth at that one, held my lower lip with a bicuspid.

Geez Leweez, you sure can't take a compliment! she said.

I learned about shaving my legs and rubbing Nair on my grassy arms. I learned how to read notes in music class and I learned about twirling the baton from Miss Dixie, who gave free lessons after school in a garage on 3rd Street. I practiced with a dust mop.

Mamma, I must twirl the baton, I must! *É il mio destino!* It's my destiny!

Destiny is like door, a weakened Mamma replied. One leads to garden. Other leads to deep pit.

But Mamma, Miss Dixie says I'm doing really good. I could be a Twinkle Star Petite Majorette, Miss Dixie SAID so.

On a Saturday morning as I rolled my hair in rubber rollers, a beautiful new baton arrived at the front door, Special Delivery.

Who would send me a baton?

Mr. Looz, Marco said.

Who?

My dad, said Ed, who happened to be slouched on the sofa making check marks in the *TV Guide*.

His *dad*? I took my new baton to my room, closed the door, and threw it on the bed. Ed Looz's crummy dad.

Ed was at our house every day. He and Marco built space

ships, talked guns, weapons, Spider-Man, Captain Marvel. They collected comic books, abandoned copying paintings by masters, and began cartooning.

Don't call me Marco anymore, Marco announced one night.

Call him *Blade*.

We were becoming two people, distinct, separate, and miles apart. We stopped looking alike, or at least it was around this time I became aware that my skin was darker than his, that my eyes were pale, his the color of night. We had not lived around mirrors in Tar Town. We assumed as pure fact that we were the same, we were one. Brother and sister. Now we looked in the mirror and said who are you?

So why would Ed's dad send me a baton?

He's a nice guy, I guess, said Blade.

Mamma came home weekdays to change dresses, take a nap.

At night I felt my body and wondered how it got there, who put it together in such a way. Other girls were lucky, girls with breasts and legs thick enough to hold up knee socks. Me, I had nothing but hair on my body and now, horrors! My ass mushroomed out behind me with such alarming suddenness, I was stupefied when boys whistled and called me Bubbles. I couldn't be held responsible for such a body.

So how come your brother doesn't have a girlfriend? Jennifer, my new best friend, said. She was chewing on a Daddy Caramel.

Girlfriend? Marco? Hunh?

Well, he's *soo* CUTE.

Marco? But he's not thirteen yet.

So?

He appeared in the doorway of the kitchen. Shoulders sloped, stockinged feet like two wrapped candies. He pulled back the curtain between the living room and kitchen and asked where I put the can opener. Jennifer giggled like an idiot.

I got a flash picture of him the night he pushed Record and broadcasted Grenadine Fletcher's sorry love-life to the world. I also thought of him lying on a gurney gagging for breath.

I should have risen to my feet, thrown my arms around him, and kissed his nose. Instead I said, The can opener is in the drawer, *Mister Bones.*

My voice caught in my throat. His sweet face peeled away and he gave me a look so startling I lost my breath. I got the message.

Jennifer giggled again. I'll help you find the can opener, Marco, she said.

Okay, he told her. And to me he said, Take a hike, *Madame Queen.*

A memory. Shadowy. Marco asleep in his cradle. Mamma crying. A man is looking at Marco. He wants to hold him. I'm afraid the man might try to take him from me. I scream, No! No! He's mine! Nonna tells me to hush . . .

Memory has erratic visiting hours.

We hardly saw Mamma. No more Sunday dinners at the restaurant. Too busy, she said. Too everything. We knew she was up to something bad and if we asked questions, she snapped back, Food is on table, no? Roof over you heads, no? Clothes on you backs! Why you don't thank me for how hard I work for you? Why you ask so many questions, make me crazy? I work hard, I'm make a plan with my brain.

We could do nothing but hold our breaths and wait for disaster.

I auditioned for the school play, *Pippi Longstockings*. I wasn't sure what a play was. Like a movie only live, Jennifer said.

Geez Leweez, ChiChi, where you been all your life?

I thought about it. A play. On the stage. I hadn't told Jennifer about my goal to become a Great Clown like Bongo Bob or Emmett Kelly.

But I remembered another kind of clown. I remembered a fog of noise, music, heat. Me sitting on a man's shoulders. A steamy hot piazza in Positano, was it Positano? Men and women pressed together straining to see the performers. Elbows and bellies, sweaty skirts and pants. *Pantelone, il Dottore, Arlecchino, gli zanni* . . . Costumes with stripes, and hats! Pointed hats, feathered hats, ballooning hats, spiky hats, wood and leather masks. The feet of the performers kicking up dust, so much dust. Music, drums rat-rat-tatting, the funny performers in masks chasing each other, squealing, falling down, getting up. Laughter, lots of laughter. *Commedia dell'arte!*

A slap of my palm the forehead. So that's it!

What's it, ChiChi?

The genesis of my desire! *Commedia dell'arte!*

Jennifer's arms crossed over her angora sweater. Big pout. You talk so funny, ChiChi.

I wrote it down.

Marco got his revenge for the name I called him in front of another person. I found a note on my bed:

Dear *Madame Queen*:
Mr. Looz is taking Ed and me to the circus tomorrow.
Too bad you can't join us.

Signed *Mister Bones*

He let me suffer for an entire day before he told me Mamma and I were invited, too. Mamma said no, too busy, but I, ChiChi Maggiordino, was transmuted in the Minneapolis Auditorium when the lights went down and a spotlight came up on the ringmaster in the sequined tuxedo, LADIES AND GENTLEMEN, CHILDREN OF ALL AGES! (Every syllable stretched to three.) WELCOME TO RINGLING BROTHERS AND BARNUM & BAILEY—

$\mathcal{T}$ he thrill of experiencing the circus for the first time would never leave me, of course. The awe and shock. More color than existed on any planet of the galaxy. Most of all, I was struck by the overpowering awareness that this was *real*, not magic, not illusion, but *real*. I believed every sensation the circus exploded before us. I saw and I believed.

I planned my own circus.

I was cast in the role of Pippi in *Pippi Longstockings*: Me, ChiChi Maggiordino, playing the leading role in a play!

Pippi Longstockings played for two performances in our school gymnasium. The first performance was for the student body and the second on the next evening for the public, for other people's mothers and fathers and aunts and uncles and cousins. I didn't think Mamma would be able to make it, but she showed up and sat in the fifth row with Marco and Ed and Manny Looz. I thought I heard her gasp each time I fell over backwards, or walked into things like I'd seen the clowns at the circus do.

I was helpless to the sound of laughter. So many mouths turned up! My brain became powder and my body fired away at every opportunity for a laugh. I stopped following the script and the actions I learned in rehearsal. The more audience response I received, the more exaggerated my gestures. The other cast members became mere objects whose only purpose was to deliver my cues and fade into the background.

The role of Pippi Longstockings gave me two bruised ribs but it made me a popular person. I was LIKED for acting the fool and making people laugh.

Teachers I didn't know recognized me, smiled when they saw me in the halls, said, Hello, dear, and, How are we today, Pippi?

Marco's good looks, his art talent, and his toughness distinguished him from the other boys. He didn't have to sprain something to get attention. He carried Mr. Metamere's knife on a chain attached to his belt loop which he fingered often. He said things to older boys like, Hey, can it, pal, and, Dig it. Don't mess with the Blade.

Mamma came home, Mamma didn't come home. What went on at home suddenly became inconsequential. Implications didn't interest us. What did we care? We were something. Something, Mamma.

We were something.

*M*amma gained weight. Her cheeks plumped up and squeezed her eyelids. Her mouth vanished in the folds of skin. Her fingers blossomed into sausages and she couldn't wear her rings. Her waistline met her hips. Her ankles thickened, her toes swelled. She bought shoes a size bigger, wore dresses with long flowing jackets. Mitchell Rodman brought her home late every night, long after Marco and I were asleep. We'd awaken to the hum of their voices in her room, the disjointed strains of the radio on her nightstand and the squeak of bedsprings. When the sun came up he was gone.

I watched Marco playing with the knife from Mr. Metamere. Holding the tip on his finger, throwing it so it would hit the floor and stick. Trying it again and again, throwing the knife, flipping it, hitting, flipping, throwing, sticking. This is what boys did, they flipped their knives until the blade hit hard and stuck.

Mitchell Rodman gave us gifts of key chains, playing cards, dice, the kind of cheap stuff you find in Cracker Jack boxes. He held out his offerings, making us walk to where he parked himself on the sofa, and we'd open our hands so he could drop into our palms a small rubber ball, a plastic Superman ring, an eraser shaped like a cowboy boot.

Mamma nervous and frowning: What do you say, ChiChi?

Say?

Mamma, speaking through her teeth: *Digli grazie!*

Oh. Thanks.

Mitchell Rodman wore shiny, pointed shoes, fancy suits, painted ties. He looked like a party ornament. Unlike Sunny, he was nutty about neatness. He picked lint from objects where there was none, he straightened the edges of sofa pillows, pinching their corners up like mouse ears. He ran his fingers across the coffee table in the living room, inspecting for dust. A smudge of marinara sauce on the counter or a heel mark on linoleum was cause for alarm. He called to Mamma, Pina! Will you look at this mess! And Mamma would come running to remove the unclean culprit.

He couldn't bear Marco's coughing fits and if in a room with Marco, he inched to the other side of it, or to the window where he faced the glass with his hand over his mouth. Marco loved that. He coughed with his cheeks ballooning and then he let loose, sneering, coughing, gagging, turning blue, spitting, convulsing in spasms, showering spit everywhere.

Rodman's eyes fogged, and I swear his skin turned fuchsia.

Marco, why you do sucha thing? I'm break you legs you do such a thing again, *capito?*

It must have been several lifetimes ago when Mamma worried over Marco's health and his every breath, when she watched over him like a priest protecting the sacraments.

I wanted to be funny for Marco. But we no longer laughed together. We didn't jump on our beds and throw our pillows at each other. I couldn't make faces and dance for him the way I used to. But I had to be silly, dear Jesus. Had to make someone laugh. Make someone laugh their heads off. The circle of the world would be measured in laughter. As an adult I would have a recurring nightmare of an audience walking out in the middle of my act because I wasn't funny. An empty theater and me with no laughs. The nightmare would draw me sobbing from a tangle of sweat and bedsheets to yell in the dark, Come back! Give me one more chance!

I'd never be able to identify how the nightmare began or where it came from, but always it spelled Marco.

Mamma believed Mitchell Rodman loved her, believed without her he'd be a sad, empty man. When she moved through the rooms of our apartment now, she and her chubbiness made music. She hummed, she bristled, murmured, swished, she made me think of some big city orchestra playing Beethoven from a rowboat. The wind blowing and the violins weeping, a storm brewing in the sea grass beyond, Mamma was every instrument. I know she had ideas of one day marrying Rodman, even though she was well aware of his wife and family in Burnsville.

Mamma was pregnant.

Hey there, ChiChi. *Come stai?*

Mitchell Rodman. At our door while Mamma was visiting the doctor.

I'm fine.

Where's you mamma?

I thought she was with you.

In that case, I'll come in and wait for her. That all right with you? Can I come in?

Sure, why not. He sat on the sofa with his slippery grin, fat hands with rings on the fingers, a box of licorice under his arm.

Come here, he said.

What for?

I got something for you.

I don't eat candy. Makes pimples.

Come here.

No. (Candy was the ruin of many a majorette.)

Then his hands, his dead fish breath.

(Gotcha.)

Marco's door was closed. He was probably lying on his bed scribbling his latest Blade Man cartoon series. I imagined him twirling his pen, frowning, tapping his toe on the rung of his chair.

MARCO.

Mitchell Rodman worked fast, pulled me down onto his lap, jammed my head against his belt buckle.

I tried pulling myself up. That hurts. Cut it out!

Come now, ChiChi, be nice.

He pulled at my shoulders.

I yelled for Marco again, louder.

No Marco.

ChiChi, be nice—be good, be good, hmm?

He pulled my body across his lap and I punched at his legs. He held my head by my hair, yanked hard. Son of a dog! Marco would hear that.

Maarco.

Rodman's breath. Dirty water stopped in a drain.

His hand was between my legs.

I bit his other hand and he released my hair. In that second, I whirled around and jumped to my feet. I stood before him shaking. I flicked my fingers under my teeth, held my fist in front of his face, and pointed two fingers at him.

I curse you! My voice high like an old woman. I curse you with *Il Mal Occhio!* The Evil Eye! The way Nonna taught me.

His look of surprise was about to give way to laughter and I gathered my breath and blew out a wad of spit, spattering his cheek and chin.

That night my brother and I sat at the kitchen table eating leftover ravioli. I watched the neon Hamm's beer sign in the window of the corner grocery and in the steam of night, the multicolored halo around it. The refrigerator made a sound like burping when it kicked on and I caught Marco staring at me, his fork held steady over his plate, his face closed like a door.

What'd he do to you?

A lot you care.

I went on chewing, swallowing.

I could have killed him, he said.

Sure. I noticed.

He set his fork down. But the bastard ran out too fast.

Marco, I gave him the Evil Eye. He took off because he was scared.

Scared? Of you? You spit on him is all, and he saw *me* at the door—with the rifle on my shoulder—

Hunh?

—Aimed right between his ears. How would he know it didn't work? ChiChi, one day I'm going to kill him.

This last sentence my brother said in a voice to stop a clock. Which is what I think happened to him that day. His life clock stopped, or some wire was sprung to create a sudden crush of malfunctioning. I know and I don't know. I think and I don't think, but Marco changed after that day, changed somewhere inside where his convictions were kept, and the softness in his eyes left. He began affecting strange mannerisms like curling his mouth when he spoke and walking with a swagger, his pants low on his hips. He began collecting dead things, birds, moths, bugs. His room took on a sour smell. He stopped cleaning his fingernails, he ironed his hair with brilliantine.

Mitchell Rodman's already a dead man, I said, following him to his room. I laid a curse on him, Marco, *Il Mal Occhio.*

That's stupid.

A pictorial book on World War II lay open on his bed. On the wall above the bed next to the Dracula poster was a skull and crossbones.

Mamma didn't come home until the following Sunday evening. Bubbly and pleased with herself. Rodman, she said, owned a vacation home on Lake Pillacotche and that is where Mamma spent the weekend, in a house surrounded by trees and facing the water.

Two bathrooms. Imagine. Can you imagine?

I stayed in my room. Sat on the floor holding Pappa's wooden leg. Mamma coupling with Rodman! The thought of it. Mamma's face turning watery and fat. Mamma with Rodman's baby growing in her belly.

I could hear a crumbling, a loud falling away, like rats in the basement eating at the foundation of the house.

A knock.
It's me.

Marco closed the door behind him. ChiChi, he'll try again. He's not done with you.

Rodman?

I'm going to kill him. Plain and simple. Another thing. Stop treating that wooden leg like it was a real person.

I held the leg tighter.

ChiChi, pay attention. You gotta be smart. *Furba.* You gotta be careful. Walk with your eyes on the back of your head. Know what's what, who's where. It's the naive, stupid people who get hurt. You gotta be smart, I'm telling you. The Evil Eye doesn't mean shit.

He unclipped the pocket knife on his belt and handed it to me.

Take this.

Metamere's knife? Oh great.

Take it.

I don't want a knife.

Put it in your pocket. Carry it everywhere. And use it if you have to.

You mean cut someone?

What do you think?

Marco, do you really think Rodman will try something again?

I don't think, I know.

*J*ennifer's mother sat at the table kitchen giving herself a permanent wave. I blurted out to her what Rodman did to me. She blinked at the mirror, spilled permanent solution on her blouse.

ChiChi, what did you do to provoke him?

Provoke?

These things happen to us, you know. She covered the curlers on her head with a plastic bag. Us women. Who'd you say this man is again?

My mother's boyfriend.

Ya? said Jennifer's mother. What'd you do? Did you flirt with him? Were you competing for his affection maybe?

Jam stains permanently engraved on the checkered oil-cloth. Blueberry—no, blackberry.

And have you told your mother yet?

The thought hadn't occurred to me. Here I was sharing a private nightmare experience with someone else's mother. No, I said. I haven't told my mother.

She wouldn't believe you anyhow, interrupted Jennifer's older sister, Muriel.

Honey, said Jennifer's mother, ignoring Muriel, we women are the weaker sex and don't men know it.

I had hoped she'd tell me what to do, comfort me, the way I imagined mothers did when their daughters were frightened or hurt. She asked me to set the timer on the stove to remind her when to neutralize.

You said attack, dear? *Attack* is a strong word, don't you think? Really, you are dramatic. You got a pretty good imagination, don't you just.

I could sleep over if I wanted, she said.

However I should examine my behavior. Go to Confession. When's the last time I went to Confession?

That night Muriel poked me until I woke up.

Did you kick him in the balls?

What?

Balls, you know. Nuts.

I sat up. Who?

Him. The *guy!*

Rodman? No. I gave him the Evil Eye is what I did.

—Evil Eye!

Muriel was a senior at Marshall High and rarely even acknowledged my presence. Now she was all ears. Tell her, tell her, come on! Tell!

Your mother didn't believe me, I said.

My mother is deaf, dumb, and blind.

I told Muriel the Evil Eye was dangerous. It was the most horrible curse of the ancients. Yes, yes, she understood. Sure, sure, fine, fine. If I shared its secret, she would go to Mass every day. She would give to the poor—

Never mind the poor. The poor we will always have with us. My voice was low, dramatic. The voice I used when I told Marco my plans to run Sunny out of the house.

I truly did have the power of the evil eye, didn't I? Look at the evidence. Did my rituals not pay off? Was not my brother still alive? Was it not he who was all but pronounced dead? Did I not star as Pippi Longstockings and could I not twirl a baton better than anyone in Miss Dixie's Twinkle Star Petite Majorettes baton twirling class? Did I not eliminate Sunny? Did I not save myself from Rodman's grimy paws and his leaky, quivering penis? Did all this not prove I had Nonna's magic?

Just show us the curse, Maggiordino, cut the crap.

I demonstrated how to look a person in the eye, point the fingers like horns, and deliver the curse.

Muriel could hardly breathe she was so agitated: I can do this, I can do this, she kept repeating. Don't quack! I said. Relax. Focus!

In the morning I kept an eye on their father, a ruddy-faced man with thick arms and dangling, loose hands. He paced around the house in a foul mood. I didn't stay for breakfast.

Mamma and Rodman were sitting together in the kitchen. He smoked a cigarette with a gold holder. An ash hung on its end ready to drop on the tablecloth.

Put that thing out, I said to him on the way to my room.

ChiChi! Mamma's voice coffee-stained.

Where's Marco? I asked her.

Rodman snorted. Where do you think? Out with that pissant buddy of his.

I passed through the kitchen to my room, closed the door.

Their voices rose and fell like a river flooding, dogs drowning, houses floating. Mamma whining. What I am going to do?

Rodman's voice, angry. The sound of water. Mamma rinsing cups in the sink.

Rodman shoved my door open. Get your coat, ChiChi. We're going for a ride.

You're supposed to knock before you enter a room, I said.

I pay for this place, I'll enter any room I want any time I want. I know what you are, little girl. Where were you all night? How many boys you been with?

He pulled my arm, jerked my hand back.

Stop it! I yelled for Mamma. Help me!

The water continued running into the sink, a clink of saucers in soap suds. The Mississippi River swallowing the shacks along its banks.

Mamma!

Did all mothers wash dishes or give themselves permanent waves while their daughters screamed for help?

Your mamma can't get you out of this one, little girl. Think I'm not on to you? Huh? I see how you wiggle that keester around here. How you lean over, dance around, tease.

The man was out of his mind.

My hair itched.

I swung my head back and pulled my fingers under my top teeth. I narrowed my eyes and shouted the curse of *IL MAL OCCHIO*.

The water in the kitchen stopped flowing. I cursed his head and the heads of his children and his children's children.

On I went, shouting and swinging my body around, my hand going to my pocket. I curse you with the curse of a thousand pigs! *Vecchio disgraziato!*

He stumbled back, holding his stomach. Die, you pig. Die with your money and your unholy, miserable restaurant. Die with your family in Burnsville and your house at the lake and your horny ass. Die, Mitchell Rodman. And I pulled Marco's knife out of his stomach.

Mamma at the door of my room.

Mamma screaming.

Screaming *Mitchie!*

Why girls didn't rise up like men and fight I'd never know. Maybe we kick and scratch and scream for mercy, but then we sink like stones, our bodies worth nothing. (Do it, dammit, do whatever you want with me and get it over with.) Is it true we can't save ourselves? Do we need Captain Marvel or Superman or lightning to save us? When do we learn to fight back?

What we need is the Evil Eye.

And a knife from a brother.

It surprised me how easily the blade slid through the shirt, the vest, and into his stomach, like slicing an apple. I stabbed him one smooth even stroke.

Mamma wanted to call an ambulance but Rodman huffed No, he didn't want any trouble; no, no, it was all right, he'd go home. It's just a graze. His face was drained of color, his eyes clouded. He stumbled past Mamma, knocked over a kitchen chair.

Mitchie, *per l'amore d' Dio,* Mamma pleaded. You're hurt! Blood stained his hands, his shirt, his pants.

Let go of me, Pina—

He had doctor connections, he'd be stitched up in no time. No reports. He didn't want reports.

He staggered out the door, his arms around himself, coat trailing.

Mamma sank to her knees. *Dio mio, Dio mio.*

Mamma, he's a bad man—The knife trembled in my hand. He tried to hurt me—he tried—he—

But he say he just want he talk to you, *figlia.* She pressed her face between her wrists.

Did I kill him?

I don't care, she moaned.

Her face went limp and spilled into her hands like cake batter. I not pregnant anymore, she said.

The room smelled of dead things. I felt blood seeping up through the floorboards, blood filling our nostrils, soaking the skin of our ears and necks. There was blood under my fingernails, blood in my hair.

He made me get rid of it, she said. I was three months. I took care of things.

(Took care of things?)

(See, Pappa? This is what we do. We take care of things.)

Mamma punched the table with her fist like a sleepwalker lulled awake and then shocked back to sleep again.

*M*amma in bed. Calling for water, *aspirina*. I moved the coverlet and saw the blood. She was lying in a lake of red.

Mamma, you're sick. Something's wrong.

Her mouth twisted in an *S*. Her body arched in a hard cramp.

Mamma, I'm calling the doctor. What's the name of the doctor you went to?

Doctor?

The doctor who did this!

Not doctor. Woman. In her kitchen.

Mamma, surgical procedures aren't done in women's kitchens.

On kitchen table. She use long wire. Like coat hanger. Push way up inside me, push, push. She tell me not all that's inside come out at once, I should go home and everything will come out in toilet. Mitch, he send me to this woman. To take care of things.

She doubled again in pain. Blood, more blood, jellied masses of it.

Ed Looz brought her a her cup of hot tea.

She babbled and wept.

She's worse. Delirious.

The bathroom floor was black with blood, her bed a red gluey swamp.

Marco, we need a doctor! Someone who won't report this! Mamma's name was already on file in the county office.

I had no choice. I had to call Rodman.

His voice like a dog fart. You got a hell of a nerve calling me at home! If you call me again I'll take care of you and that pissant brother of yours.

He said he hardly knew Mamma. Said she was an EX-employee and if she got knocked up it sure as hell wasn't his problem.

Ed Looz called his dad. Ten minutes later a taxi was at the door and Marco, Ed, and I carried Mamma out the door and into the taxi. We took her to Emergency. Marco and I holding her in our arms, wiping her face with the palms of our hands, stroking her hair.

We waited three hours before a doctor finally saw her.

I'm afraid the infection has gone through her body and the antibiotics might not be effective, he said.

They were taking her into surgery.

A kitchen table and a coat hanger. Rodman and the legal system. A toilet floating down a river of Mamma's blood. Is this what love did to us?

My rituals. A hundred Hail Marys.

ChiChi, knock it OFF. Marco's fingers pinched my cheek.

What? I'm praying.

Your nutty dumb-ass rituals again? STOP.

Mamma's silk dresses with their tails of chiffon and flowing skirts were packed in a hall closet smelling of mothballs and pine. Bearing the stains of sweat and Evening in Paris, the dresses behind the closet door were like relatives you don't want anyone to know are yours. I stared inside the closet as though it were another country. A country of bones and skeletons. A place to bury a dead fetus. Tulle and cheap beads, faded taffeta, crushed satin roses lynched by their neck straps. The closet smelled of murder and disease. The kind you know incarcerated people died of. I felt no sadness by this cemetery of a closet, I was intrigued, I was seized with loss.

I'd stand on one foot until dawn. I'd eat parking lot dirt. I'd—

Marco had both of my cheeks between his fingers. Listen HERE, ChiChi. They got MEDICINE to make Mamma well. Stop with the EVIL EYE.

Mamma was wheeled to a bed in the maternity ward. She lay weak and dazed with an IV dripping into her veins as the women in the next beds suckled their newborns like contented cats. Marco and I pulled the curtain around the bed, stood at her side, watched her sleep. A cheery bouquet of flowers on the bedstand caught our attention.

Who sent those?

She had a visitor, said the nurse at the desk.

What visitor?

I assume it was her husband, said the nurse.

She doesn't have a husband, we said.

Big mistake. Mamma had registered as *Mrs.* Maggiordino.

I had baton practice for the parade that was coming up in a week with Miss Dixie's Petite Majorettes. I promised nothing would interfere with my healing rituals for Mamma. I'd practice my baton for eight hours straight. I'd lie naked in the noon heat and broil like a fish, I'd go without food or drink for thirty days like Jesus in the wilderness . . . It was up to me.

Jennifer and I sat on the school steps, me seeing double and shivering. What's with you, ChiChi?

I'm fasting.

What for? Is it a holy day?

Two boys sat down with us, Charles Svengaard and Hank Johnson. I took one look at Charles and stopped shivering. Hank, right tackle for the football team, sat next to Jennifer and her voice rose an octave.

ChiChi is positively starving, said Jennifer. She thinks it's Lent.

Charles wore a polyester jacket, close enough to me to climb inside. Green, the color of chives and arugula. I could almost taste it.

You cold in this weather? he said. The jacket became the gentlest of arms and eased around me, hands spread open on my back. I was a girl who had few memories of being held, and now arms were pulling me into green polyester.

My voice came out feeble, like a squeak. My mother is sick, I said.

That's too bad, said Charles. I hope she gets better. A broad, smooth face like a large butterscotch candy. I could have licked his chin and been satisfied.

You were really good as Pippi Longstocking, he said. A real professional.

Was he serious?

The hairs on my arm rose up to meet the polyester of his jacket.

I told him about the parade coming up.

She happens to be a member of Miss Dixie's Twinkle Star Petite Majorettes! Jennifer crowed.

I could tell he was impressed.

Later Charles walked me home and at our front door he gave me another hug, the kind uncles give nieces, or nuns give first graders. My head felt like notes of music, like talcum, like rain, I was a velvet alien from Venus. ChiChi Maggiordino, the hugged.

It was a good sign. It meant Mamma would get well, her blood would stop pouring out of her like the Mississippi.

But she went back to surgery. More antibiotics. Cauterization. If she recovered, she'd be sterile.

*R*emember girls, said Miss Dixie, you are taking part in a piece of history today. Twirl with your hearts.

I met Miss Dixie and the other Twinkle Star Petite Majorettes at the parade grounds and warmed up in the new boots which had mysteriously arrived in the mail two days ago.

The asphalt shone like mirrors on Nicollet Avenue. From a great height the parade must have looked like an illuminated worm—crepe-paper-decorated floats, convertibles bearing beauty queens and town officials, men in uniforms proudly carrying the American flag, horseback riders, shriners in their cone tasseled hats and banners across their chests, high school bands, flag twirlers, clowns, and shiny chrome and silver motorcycles—all of us slithering through the city with batons in our hearts. Down close we were frantic butterflies.

Mamma, I'm twirling for you.

She was better, she was rallying, she was eating toast and bouillon, she was yelling at the nurses.

I was third twirler in the second row of sixteen Miss Dixie's Twinkle Star Petite Majorettes. I marched lifting my knees high, my new boots like small flames in the sun. I didn't miss one throw of the baton. I thought about Charles watching me. I was a real professional. Charles was everyone that day, he was all of Minneapolis.

Ahead of us and behind the University of Minnesota homecoming queen's float were the clowns. I tried not to think about them, but to concentrate on my baton routine, although during the struts, I watched their little polka-dotted cars turning circles. Clowns squirting water at the audience, throwing paper flowers and candy, performing tricks with accordions, fake pianos, stuffed animals, and a tiny fire truck with a siren. I felt a peculiar longing or itch, like I'd been snagged by giant fleas. I twirled with heart.

At the end of the parade route I ignored the blisters on my feet and set out to look for the clowns. Through the crowds of beauty queens, shriners, high school marching bands, children, vendors, I found who I was looking for.

They sat on the step of their trailer drinking bottles of Dr Pepper. She wore an orange wig, her face painted white and blue with crystal tears painted under her eyes. His wig was blue, his face painted with a huge smiling mouth.

I walked right up to them. I want to be a clown, I said. I'm a real professional. I've been told that.

Dear God, said the man.

The woman was called Onna. Her husband's name was Omo. They were dwarfs. Little people. The best clowns in the parade. They had the kids cheering, screaming their names. Onna! Omo!

Let me show you what I can do! I said.

I turned a cartwheel, threw my baton in the air, caught it behind my back and knelt on one knee, hands in the air, *tah-dah*.

A yawn. They went inside their trailer and closed the door behind them.

Parade people around me packed up their gear, gathered costumes, equipment, and band instruments. Children and adults clamored, called out to one another, joyous, tired from

all the fun. Vendors hawked their T-shirts and U of M pen-
dants, snow cones, sausages, hot dogs, sun visors. Horse manure scattered on the ground and armies of flies swirled
around ankles and feet, the air thick with smells of hot grease
and manure.

I struck a pose. I want to be a clown! Watch this!

I saw the dwarfs looking at me from their window and
began dancing like someone drunk. I flailed my arms, did a
few pratfalls, hit myself on the head with my baton, and
then I began singing "Carnevale" while dancing with an
imaginary partner. I cartwheeled, somersaulted, fell into the
splits three times, pulled myself up without using my hands.
I thought I heard laughter. I was Pippi Longstocking at sea,
I was ChiChi Maggiordino begging approval.

I ended the number by hurling myself on the ground
spread-eagled. A ripple of applause came from four shriners
watching me.

The door of the trailer opened. Fool, said Onna. Come
on in before you hurt yourself.

Inside the trailer, the size of a small pantry, a closet of
living space. Every inch neatly packed with piles of folded
clothes, costumes, boxes of canned food, toilet paper, motor
oil, empty Dr Pepper bottles, and jars of medicines and vita-
mins. Onna and Omo had taken off their wigs and sat on a
pile of what looked like winter coats. An opened loaf of Tas-
tee wheat bread and a jar of Welch's grape jelly between them.

I want to be a clown, I said, all of me conviction.

Omo spread a wad of jelly on a slice of bread with the
back of a spoon. Look, girlie, it's been a long day for us and
tomorrow we have another gig in Mankato. You want some
of this?

No, thank you. Can you help me in the biz? You know,
get started?

Omo's face softened. His eyes, tired but gentle. Onna and me worked for Ringling for twenty-five years, he said. We've seen them all. He looked me over, he was coming to a conclusion.

You a runaway?

Onna smacked her lips, her mouth full of bread. You got a miserable home life and you're cutting out? Ah, we've see it all. But why tell us your problems? We're not shrinks. We're just a couple of semi-retired circus performers who work weekends during the spring and summer. That's it and that's it. By the way, where'd you learn to sing in Italian?

Wasn't it obvious? I AM Italian, I said.

A light went on. Onna clapped a hand to her chin. Italian! Born here?—No? Born in Italy? Ah! She knew it all along! *Paesana!* A wink, a wiggle of a finger.

And you want to be a clown, *Piccolina?* In the commedia del l'arte tradition, we assume? You want to be *artista!*

Yes, oh yes!

We shall see. We shall see, *paesana.* Such a sweet girl.

Omo looked me over. Let's don't rush things. Look at those skinny legs, she's a kid! Too young. No tits.

How long had I been in the States, they wanted to know. Frankly, they had come in through the Canadian border twenty-seven years ago with the circus. Had to sneak across. Hid in the cook wagon. No physical deformities allowed in, you know. Where'd I come in?

I could hardly make myself speak. Ellis Island, I said at last. Onna gave me a hearty pat on the hand. And here, she said, we are! Lucky in the Land Of Opportunity.

She was born, she said, in a small village in Puglia where only old people were left now. All the young people emigrated or moved up north. When the old ones die off, *punto, non piu,* that'll be the end of the village.

Like Tar Town, I thought.

Onna told me to show up the following Saturday at the YWCA in downtown Minneapolis and ask for her at the front desk.

Don't be late. We'll do a sort of preliminary private clown workout with you. See if you've got the stuff.

More pats on the hand, a squeeze of the wrist. They liked me. This day would be the start of a brilliant career, I could feel it in the blisters on my feet.

Marco was waiting for me when I arrived home.

I saw you in the parade, he said. You were good.

Thanks.

Looked for you afterward. Where'd you go?

I started to tell him. He interrupted.

We gotta go see Rodman. Now.

Rodman!

We're gonna make him pay for what he did to Mamma.

*W*e entered the restaurant through the kitchen. The chef, who was showing a kitchen assistant how to de-bone a chicken, had his back turned to us. We opened the door to the dining room. Mitchell Rodman was sitting in a corner booth counting receipts with an adding machine.

How easy it would be to kill him, said Marco. We could walk out the front door and nobody would know.

We moved like one body toward his booth.

Hello, Rodman! Marco said in a loud, deep voice I hadn't heard before.

Rodman was so startled he knocked his drink over and cracked his knee on the table.

Don't move, Rodman! said Marco. Stay where you are. We're going to have us a little talk . . .

And Marco, age thirteen, did all the talking. Rodman sat stupefied, like he was watching a cobra crawl up his leg.

Mamma came home. Bed rest, vitamin B shots, plenty of liver, no straining or hot baths. We hardly spoke. Finally, she said, Tell me what happen when you go to see Mitch.

(How did she know?)

Tell me, she said.

For starters, Mamma, Marco demanded he pay your medical bills.

Ah.

And then Marco told him if he ever came near us again, we'd have him put away. We'd have his ass in a sling, we'd ruin him, and wouldn't his wife and kids just love to hear how he sexually attacked a young girl and wouldn't they also just love to know about his relationship with a certain lady singer . . .

Gesù, Maria.

And he had exactly ten seconds to agree to a settlement.

Settlement?

He went a little nuts, called us names, threatened. But Marco didn't even flinch. You should have seen him. I jumped in and said, Rodman, you got eight seconds and then we bust your *coglioni*.

Madonn'a.

He paid. And you're also in his will.

Sì, sì. I make demands, too.

(We didn't know Mamma had her own ideas of revenge.)

ChiChi, don't get too cozy, Marco warned. Rodman has friends. And he's going to realize we're just two kids. Hang on to the knife.

Mamma's sorrow soaked the walls of the apartment and I slept with Metamere's knife under my pillow.

When she began attending Mass every morning Mamma's attitude began to change. She said to me one day, If I have found forgiveness in God's eyes, can you not forgive me, too?

She didn't understand how our lives twirled around hers. Marco and I would die for her. I told her about Onna and Omo, the dwarfs. Told her they were Italian, from *Mezzogiorno*.

She brightened. Is good! she said. *Hai una buona opportunità per te.*

Yes. A good opportunity for me.

Onna and Omo accepted me as their student, even though they figured I was unreliable and would probably quit after a couple of sessions. The first thing they told me was I needed ballet lessons. They said I was clumsy, awkward, I lacked control.

Takes more than guts to be in show business, kiddo. The *biz,* that is.

I couldn't ask Mamma for money to pay for ballet lessons when she was in such a devastated state. There was only one thing to do.

Time for ChiChi to find a job.

Bridgeman's Ice Cream shop on the corner of 14th Street and 4th Avenue was hiring counter girls. The manager was a man named Ole, a round-shaped man with bad skin. He spoke with a lisp and called me TeeTee. I lied, said my age was sixteen, and I impressed Ole by digging into the ice cream and producing a nithe round thkoop.

Mamma said, Okay, Miss Smarty Smart, no come to me no more for money.

She was becoming her old self again.

The first time I climbed the stairs to Madame Tomanova's School of Ballet Arts I was breathless with anticipation, but nothing could have prepared me for the sight of Madame Tomanova in the center of the huge studio leading a class of dancers. She wore a bright blue turban and leotard with floating silk scarves and skirt and she moved with the grandeur of someone who should be perched on pillows and carried by camels.

My ballet lessons were ecstatic efforts to please Madame Tomanova. I loved my ballet lessons. Ballet, so like religion. So demanding and all-consuming a love.

Manny Looz, Ed's father, bought a huge custom-made drawing board for Marco and Ed and had it set up in Marco's bedroom. They drew pictures by the hour for a new comic book series, *Blade Man*.

Ed Looz practically lived at our house now. His clothes were everywhere, his shoes and socks on the bathroom floor, his drawings and papers strewn around the living room. I caught him watching me more than once, sneaking into my room, staring at me when he thought I was asleep.

He knew about Marco's allergies and chronic lung disease, and since he wasn't so tip-top in the respiratory department himself, he figured he and Marco had more in common. I found out Ed was born with a collapsed lung.

A collapsed lung!

Mamma, Ed Looz is a sick creep. Why don't you tell him to go home?

He is Marco's friend. He not a bad boy.

He's disgusting! He's always watching me. I don't trust him. Brrrr!

Mamma said Eddie was a good boy and I was being dramatic again. Marco told me to relax, cool it. I was always safe with The Blade on the scene.

After work scooping ice cream at Bridgeman's at night I walked the fourteen blocks up 4th Avenue to our house on University Avenue. You had to walk fast at night, making as little sound as possible because you never knew who might be lurking behind a bush or a parked car. The streetlight didn't reach the sidewalks under the giant oak and elm trees, nor did they shed any light on the fraternity and sorority houses along the street or the hulking once-were mansions now rooming houses in disrepair. I raced along the sidewalk on my toes, still wearing my Bridgeman's pink uniform, when I heard a moist, friendly, Hiii therre.

The man in front of me had grease spot eyes, his mouth vibrating like the thing he held in his hands. He seemed so happy! Smiling away.

Did Rodman send you? I said. Did he?

Nowhere to run but through the shrubbery, across the street, and back the way I came—where everything would be closed. I hiked up the skirt of my waitress uniform and plunged into the bushes, scratching my calves and snagging my sock.

The man called to me in a merry, powdery voice, as though he were just the nicest guy in the world. Hey, I've got someth-iing for you—then, like his feelings were hurt, he whined, Hey, where you go-iing?

I ran through backyards and an alley, jumped a fence, burrowed through some shrubs, scaled a wall, and finally stopped to catch my breath in front of a huge three-story house with lilac bushes on each side of the enclosed porch. I dropped my book bag down on a step leading up the walkway to the house and searched in my pocket for something to blow my nose on.

I smelled the smoke of a cigarette and realized I wasn't alone.

I fumbled for Metamere's knife in my book bag. Flipped it open, whirled around.

Hey, Maggiordino, what the hell!

Sitting in the shadows on the porch step was Ed Looz.

I knew you were crazy, girl, but shoot! he said.

I made my way up the walk and stood on the stair near

his foot. The smell of the smoke was sour, like sludge weeds burning.

Want a toke? he asked, handing the cigarette to me.

No, get away.

Pure Mexican gold, he said.

The suggestion was startling. Looz, is that marijuana?

Bingo.

YOU'VE ONLY GOT ONE GOOD LUNG, WHAT KIND OF NUT JOB ARE YOU? Marijuana. Something I had only heard about. I thought it was for the dope addicts in New Jersey or Shanghai, people who had nothing better to do than lie around on smelly mattresses and mumble to each other in code.

Put that thing out! I said. Put it out NOW.

Ed chuckled. I only smell it, he said, and he snuffed the glowing end on the step. I saw you from the window upstairs. I said to myself, that's Marco's sister running her arse off out there in the midnight moon. Cool.

It so happens, for your information, Ed Looz, I was attacked by a flasher!

And you let him get away? Too bad. Oh well, there are lots more around. You'll get another opportunity.

I wanted to be home asleep. I had a Civics test first hour tomorrow and I hadn't studied for it.

So this is where you live, Ed? Here?

Me and my pop.

(Three floors to the place, maybe more.)

Liar. Walk me home.

No can do. Too strenuous.

For an instant his face looked like Marco's, the eyes warm, sorrowful, but then he was Ed Looz again, kicking the step with his heel and grimacing so his bad teeth showed.

You got a phone? I'll call my brother. I said.

He gave a sarcastic laugh. Ya, call your brother, the Jock.

I followed him inside to an elevator that took us to the second floor. We entered a living room that had probably been a bedroom at one time, small, with a swampy-looking sofa along one wall and a bookshelf filled with newspapers. A telephone sat on the window ledge.

Make it quick, said Ed. My dad's doing business, needs that line.

I heard a telephone ring in another room. How many phones you got?

Lots. It's baseball season.

I dialed and after about ten rings, Marco answered. His voice was gritty. As though he'd been inhaling fish scales.

Wake up, Blade. Come on, wake up. I need you.

He muttered as though talking in his sleep, something like, You too, Babe, and hung up.

Ed hooted with laughter and left the room leaving me to stand there in my pink waitress uniform wiping sweat off my arms. When he returned he had his dad with him.

Hello, Mr. Looz, I said.

Leticcia, he said.

He peeled a five-dollar bill from a roll of bills in his pocket and handed it to me. Here, take a cab, he said. Eddie, call her a cab.

Sure. She's a cab, hahaha!

I'll pay you back. I said. I was just walking home from work. I work till eleven—

You work at Bridgeman's? He looked at me like I had done something bad.

Yes—

You're how old?

I got the implication.

Didn't your mother ever tell you not to walk alone at night?

The room smelled of newsprint and cough drops. I wanted to thank him for the baton.

You gonna report this thing to the police?

No, I don't think so, I said.

Did you get a good look at the man?

Not his face.

When Ed laughed saliva stuck to the edges of his mouth.

I told him I thought maybe this guy named Rodman was after me.

It's okay now, he said. You're okay.

I didn't feel okay.

The telephone rang in the other room.

May I ask you a question? I said to his back.

He turned. Shoot, he said.

Are you the one who brought Mamma flowers in the hospital?

Ya. Is that all right with you?

One more question: Did you send me the majorette boots?

Guilty on both charges, he said.

That night my bed felt like cold ashes. I tried to think of other things besides Mr. Looz and Ed and the flasher. I tried to picture Madame Tomanova. Onna and Omo. The dazzling colors of the three-ring circus. Mr. Looz had given me a card with a telephone number on it, said if ever needed a ride, I should call the number on the card. Memorize it, he said. He didn't care if I happened to be in Halifax or Albuquerque, he'd send a cab for me.

He went back to his telephones before I could say anything.

Ed told me I shouldn't look so shocked, he himself took
tons of cabs. Mr. Looz owned the ding-donged taxi company.

*M*amma was hired as a waitress at a small Italian café called Rocco's, a U of M hangout. On the chef's days off she took charge in the kitchen. She made Italian specialties like *zeppoli*, and Rocco told the customers nowhere else in the Twin Cities would they find a restaurant that served the delicious syrupy walnut-coated *zeppoli* like Mamma made.

Let it be said this was a big deal.

Marco drew little cards to put on the tables telling of Mamma's specialties. (Tiramisu every Saturday.) She sang her songs while cooking and carrying trays of food to the tables, which the students thought was kicky. Instead of evening gowns, satin heels, and sparkling hair ornaments, she wore white oxfords, a hair net, and a cotton apron over a waitress uniform. Rocco's business improved. Families and locals showed up, ate the *zeppoli*, the full dinners.

It surprised Marco and me how cheerful she was at work, taking orders, humming, joking with the men, flattering the women, drumming up conversation with the students. On a Saturday after my clown lesson with Onna and Omo I sat in a booth by the kitchen making weak attempts to complete an English assignment. I was on my third *aranciata*, orange soda. Two old Italians played cards in the next booth, friends of Rocco. They were arguing about who was more beautiful, Gina Lollobrigida or Sophia Loren.

Whose eyes were most beautiful? Who moved with the most grace? Sophia Loren hands down. No no. You have bad taste. Blah blah.

I turned, stuck my head above the seat, How about Anna Magnani? You forgot to mention Anna Magnani.

They came to attention.

Certo! Now there's a beautiful woman! And they turned to watch Mamma deliver a plate of calamari to table four.

Who should walk through the door but Charles The Hug Svengaard. He and a buddy hunkered over to a booth, sprawled down, tapped on the menus, fiddled with the salt and pepper shakers, scrunched up some napkins, cackled to each other—and then Charles saw me.

A smile big as Fort Snelling.

I waved my pencil at him.

What'you doing?

English.

Here?

Ya. I love the food.

They ordered a sausage pizza, Cokes.

That's my mom, I said, and their faces turned doughy, blank.

Buon giorno! gushed Mamma. And on she went about how Rocco's pizza was the best in town.

No skimp on the sauce. All fresh ingredament, she said.

They had been to the movies. Saw *The Day the Earth Caught Fire*. Mamma disapproved. Puh, sucha thing. I'm tell you good movie. You want good movie? See *Il Bell'Antonio,* ah, THERE is good movie.

Is about man who is big with ladies but when he gets married he no can *fffffttt,* and she curled her forefinger down. Ha! Ha!

Charles and his friend didn't laugh. Mouths puckered in

x's. The men in the next booth roared like lions.

I stared at the table. Was this the same woman the neighbors in Tar Town called *boriso,* stuck-up? Had tragedy and singing at Lorenzo's Fine Italian Dining made a ribald comedienne of her?

Hey, ChiChi, said Charles. Did you see the paper today? The article about the Judge Wright Talent Contest?

Charles wore a red V-neck sweater. Sleeves to the knuckles. Beautiful knuckles. Such white fingers, four maybe five blond hairs on each one.

With your talent, he said, you ought to enter this talent contest.

I prayed thank you to the Madonna.

His friend left and Charles walked me home. So you were born in Italy? he said, uneasy. Ya, well, he really liked Eyetalian food, especially pizza. He never met a real Eyetalian, like from Over There.

At my door, he pulled me into the wool of his sweater. A mouth moved across my face, then finding mine, kissed me. A mouth full of teeth and a tongue against my lips. I sailed into the cosmos, I conquered compound sentences, the apostrophe, and the comma. I aced the finals, I flew past verbs. ChiChi, he muttered in my neck, you've got the most incredible skin . . .

I auditioned for the Judge Wright Talent Contest sponsored by the Junior Chamber of Commerce, Grand Prize $500.00, as ChiChi Maggiordino, Clown Extra Ordinaire.

I didn't eat chocolate because Madame Tomanova said it was poison for the ballet dancer. There were many indulgences the serious ballet dancer could absolutely not allow to invade the body, like Coca-Cola and most things that tasted good. Did I ever have anything in common with the girls who drank Cokes with Jennifer after school? The girls who tweezed their eyebrows and ate foods that were french fried? They painted their toenails, wore cologne, knew all the songs on the radio, they chewed on candy bars. When I looked in the mirror in the school bathroom, the girl I saw was a thin person in a pleated skirt whose eyes were unnaturally large for so small a face, and if I looked close, it was a face emblazoned with worry like notes of music, nose misshapen and hair pulled back into a baguette behind the ears. *Madonn'a*, I looked like a Pakistani granny.

Jennifer said I should have my hair straightened, the way Negroes did, and I should buy a padded bra. Jennifer said beauty was not just a woman's prerogative, it was her *duty* and *obligation*. A woman of any race or creed *owed it to the world* to be *beautiful*.

Madame didn't straighten her hair and Madame didn't pad her bra. When I looked in the mirror I wanted to see only one image, Madame Tomanova.

What did Charles see? On Tuesdays and Thursdays after school we met in the alley behind Rocco's. The kisses, the groping, rolling our bodies along the metal of the trash container, Charles and the garbage, Charles whispering how he loved my skin, his hands under my blouse, his hips pushed against my stomach. The smell of Charles's eggy breath and Rocco's exhaust fan of garlic sizzling in olive oil made a singing in my head that filtered down through my body in wobbly high notes. His fingers, the wordless clinging of the buttons and buttonholes of our jackets, his tongue against my teeth—

The mention of Charles in a conversation, the sight of him, the thought of him, and I'd become unpredictable and jumpy. I'd think of his sweater against my cheek, his voice in my ear, I'd feel the odd pain in my chest; there'd be a slimy gathering of tumescent cells in my stomach and I'd be in the throes of death by longing.

But when I saw him in the halls at school, he would nod and pass me by as though I were a stranger.

At a football game with Washburn High School that we were losing 21 to 0, we were cheering our school song— MARSHALL GOES DOWN THE FIELD, FIGHTING FOR FAME—when I saw Charles moving down the stairs of the bleachers with a girl.

WE WILL RAISE OUR BANNERS HIGH . . .

I had not imagined Charles with another girl, hadn't considered another nose pressed against the cottage cheese of his sweater. I was sick with the associations. He had his hand on her shoulder.

WE WILL WIN THIS GA-A-AME!

Charles, look at me.

I asked Marco, Who's the blonde with Charles Svengaard?

What blonde?

The fat one with the ponytail.

That's whatshername, his girlfriend.

I must have done something wrong, left something out, forgotten some important bit of behavior or necessary obeisance. Charles had never liked me in public.

Marco's sneer, his dark eyes, his avalanche of hair. Ever hear the word *prejudice,* my dear sister? *Discrimination?* He's chummy-wummy in private but has he ever asked you out?

Nobody has ever asked me out, Marco.

You had to be vigilant, you had to always balance the balls, play the cards right, be on your guard, stay focused, beware. One little slip and whoosh, you're done for, swallowed up whole, doomed. My brother, not yet fourteen, knew these things.

I began to think about worlds within worlds. I lived in a face with seams at its edges. Inside me, the spinning self.

Back in my room I applied the clown makeup to my face, not like the circles and big nose and smiling mouth I had made in Tar Town when I first discovered clowns. Now my makeup was like Onna and Omo had taught me, each line had to have meaning. Stripes and curls like the commedia del l'arte, like Venezia's *Carnevale,* eyes painted thick and heavy with lashes thick as lava, lips a tiny heart . . . My very own face.

And I was beautiful.

Came the night of the talent show.

I showed up at the auditorium two hours early to dress, apply my makeup, and wait. I could hear the audience entering the civic hall like a surf rising and falling. Rain. The battering of rams. I looked out through the stage curtain to see if I could see Marco. There he was, with Mamma beside him right up in front. She looked uncomfortable and confused. Jennifer came down the aisle with her sister, Muriel. They chatted and ate candies from a Fanny Farmer bag. Omo and Onna sat in the front row dressed in their best clothes bearing the proud expressions of new parents.

I looked for Charles. I thought just maybe.

The music started. Someone was talking in a microphone.

First on the program was a girl from Robbinsdale who played the "Fleur de Lis" on the piano. A tap dancer from Wayzata was followed by a trio from Golden Valley who sang gospel songs. Then a twin sister act with matching drum sets, and a black girl of about seven who sang "The Man Who Got Away." A boy came out on roller skates and juggled heads of lettuce and I thought for sure he'd win. I chewed my nails and paced back and forth.

The music I chose as my accompaniment was Donizetti's "Elizir di Amore." I could hear it buzzing from my inside my overworked muscles, mine was a body humming with tremblings. The Donizetti louder.

Maggiordino, you're ON.

I'm on.

After my final walk-over and finale in the splits, the rolling over, falling backward, I pulled out Omo's tiny red silk umbrella and ended on one toe, leg extended as though saved by the little umbrella. The audience began to applaud as the music started again and I feigned tripping over the umbrella and fell on my face.

I heard the applause and saw my brother on his feet applauding. Other people stood up, too. I saw Manny Looz, with his fingers in his mouth whistling. I took my bow, did another pratfall and bowed again, this time cartwheeling off the stage with one hand. Then I ran back, mugging, for my little umbrella. I knew I overdid the bow but something happened to me when I heard the applause. I became crazy for love, eager to hurt myself for it.

The other acts stood around with placid, polite smiles.

I had won the contest.

Manny Looz invited us out to a restaurant called Jax not far from Tar Town to celebrate my victory. We piled in taxis, Mamma, Onna, Omo, Ed Looz, Jennifer, her sister Muriel, me.

Hey, ChiChi, I practiced your Evil Eye and it doesn't work, Muriel told me in the taxi.

Sure it does. Of course it works. You're doing something wrong.

I'm doing everything you told me, exact.

Forget it then. The Evil Eye, as I know it, is a calling, you might say. It's a gift, you might say. Something you're born with, you might say.

So how'd *you* get it?

We sat at a large round table, the minors drinking ginger ale, the grown-ups pink drinks in stemmed glasses. Mamma, Onna, and Omo became immediate friends. Omo explained to Mamma the classical tradition of my Clown Extra Ordinaire and the influence of commedia del l'arte, but oh how I needed much more training, though I was a good learner, and I had what was the most important ingredient: *imagination.*

In my pocket was a check for $500, which would pay for my ballet lessons until I graduated high school. Manny Looz proposed toasts left and right. He asked for a word from me, and everyone clapped, including Mamma. All those eyes on me, a rush of heat. If joy had a color it was a bright viridian green, the color of the carpet I crashed onto when I jumped to my feet. I heard their laughter, my fall mistaken for a comic pratfall. I climbed back onto my chair, miming the actions of a stumble-bum clown.

Later, getting the into taxi to go home, I whispered in Marco's ear, Tell the driver to drop me off at General. I broke my friggin hand.

Applause had caught me like a needle in the nose, I was helpless to it. I would have leapt across the room, cart-wheeled over the tables, and done a pratfall in the kitchen sink if they had kept clapping.

I missed ballet classes because of my broken finger. The doctor who set it told me my hand had to be kept in a raised position and he taped it so it stayed upright. Mamma slapped me on my good hand. Why you break you bones? It cost money you break you bones!

She calmed down somewhat when she saw my picture in the *Minneapolis Tribune* with the caption, YOUNG COMIC BAL-LERINA WINS JAYCEE TALENT SHOW. The picture showed me in a silly bent-knee arabesque holding Omo's little red um-brella over my head.

I sat on the sofa reading Agnes DeMille's *Dance to the Piper* with my taped hand in the air when Madame Tomanova telephoned, demanded to see me immediately.

Barely breathing. A chuckle with each inhale. This was it, I was going to get a solo in the next ballet production. Some-thing major important. The Dying Swan, perhaps. Me, ChiChi Maggiordino, so unworthy, but so grateful. Yes-yesyes.

Madame. Her woolly voice: Leticcia, well, well.

I could have groaned for joy. I'd be dancing at the Lake Harriet Bandshell in the summer production of *Swan Lake*. I'd be a real ballerina.

She spoke. So my Leticcia is a clown? You prefer to break bones for laughs?

She expelled me from ballet school.

Hennepin Avenue outside her window heavy with traffic, cars, trucks, voices. A radio somewhere, a song playing loud, *Erase me, my sweet erasable you . . .*

I walked up 7th Street to Nicollet Avenue keeping my hand up in the air in front of me. I walked to Loring Park, where I stood near the water and watched ducks swim in circles like bored preschoolers.

First day of spring. *Erase me . . .* Chunks of ice still floated on the lake. Omo said comedy was born the day the first tears were shed.

Something profoundly funny should get born here today. An act of beauty so funny your gut frips up through your nose and your eyes roll around like tongues; so funny you fall right down on the wet grass and laugh so jerky and wild, you gag on the hilarious rush of it all.

*T*he broken finger healed wrong and the knuckle poked out like the end of a child's crayon, the joint a swollen round knot and the tip of the finger turned up in a moon. When I tried to bend it right, it creaked. The doctor, who was not a real doctor, but an intern, said it might never be quite right, and I should be glad I didn't play the harp.

Onna and Omo invited us for dinner to see their circus memorabilia and to remind their ChiChi that nothing in the world is as calamitous as self-pity. They lived in a three-room apartment on Harmon Place in what was like a fun-house museum, every inch occupied by their many collections: tin windup cars and trucks, storybook dolls, snow globes, airplanes, movie star photos, music boxes, spoons, commedia masks, miniature Sicilian painted carts, puppets. All of the furniture in the apartment was small, tailored for them.

See this costume? said Onna. Pretty, eh? I wore it in a film, can't remember the name—the one I did with José Ferrer.

You worked with José Ferrer? Marco said.

Sure, in Rome.

You never told us you did movies in Rome.

Read the scrapbooks. It's all there.

I sat on the low sofa and almost knocked over a beautiful glass clown figurine on the coffee table.

Careful, Love. Judy Garland gave that to us.

You worked with Judy Garland?

An absolute darling. Don't you go to the movies? Didn't you see *Wizard of Oz*?

Marco and I exchanged a look. Movies? We had seen about four while growing up, westerns or Italian, the only ones Mamma approved. Onna poured wine in cut crystal glasses and set them on the coffee table next to the Judy Garland figurine.

Famous celebrity give you these crystal? Mamma wanted to know.

Bought at a flea market in Miami, Onna said and laughed. The guy we bought them from was a circus fan, gave them to us for a song. Literally. And she began singing, *I've got a lover-ly bunch of coconuts* . . . Mamma lit up with laughter.

You're the best, Marco said. Kisses on two cheeks.

I sat sulking and morose, a Ballet School Expellee.

So about your act, said Omo suddenly. I'd say you're a natural if there ever was one. Fact, I got a feeling ChiChi Clown Extra Ordinaire is going to be hugely famous one day. I said the same thing about Frankie Saluto and Lou Jacobs, and look what happened. Now you, you'll be bigger than Jacobs. You'll be, well, Sweetums, you're going to be *legend*. Because I'll tell you why. You are going to transcend the circus. Know what I'm saying? You'll take clowning beyond the ring. Hey, watch out for that vase. It was a wedding present from Anthony Quinn. Did a movie with him in Rome. Actually, a little outside of Rome. *Milano*.

Ha ha.

Mamma slapped her thigh. Big guffaw.

When was that? I said.

Before your time, Darling, said Onna.

Omo tripped on the edge of the rug when he took a seat in the small stuffed chair next to the table. I held my breath and refrained from trying to help him. He winced, shook his head, and plunged on with what he had been saying:

Now about that flaming baton, ChiChi. If a prop is funny, use it. But it has to have *meaning*. Follow me? Clowns are serious while being funny. Keep 'em laughing while breaking their hearts, that's the ticket. What does the baton *mean?*

I wondered if he was trying to make me feel better about the expelling.

Don't give me that look, girlie, he snapped. I don't hand out predictions and compliments so free.

Mamma reciprocated the dinner invitation and Omo and Onna became our first bona fide dinner guests in our apartment on University Avenue. She made *zeppoli*. After our rehearsal at the Y, Omo and Onna came home with me in a taxi paid by Manny Looz, and they came for dinner every week after that.

Mamma was becoming cheery, chatty at home. I smelled something familiar. She was cooking meals in our kitchen again. She wasn't yelling at us. We came home from school to the pasta water boiling, the bread baking, the onions frying. She cooked, cleaned, asked how we are doing, where we're going, where we've been—she was up to something. I smelled a new man in the very near distance.

Okay, Mamma. Out with it. What's his name?

His name? Who?

She said we'd meet him next Saturday.

His name was Arturo, a Napolitano she met when the Italian American Club held a luncheon for fifteen at Rocco's last month. Marco and I placed bets how long it would be before he moved in.

What's he do for a living, Mamma?

Why you not ask about his family? His mamma?

Does he have a *wife?*

She gave me a slap on the head. Then a quick, *Dio mio,*
I sorry. He no have wife. What you think? She was sorry
again. Put her hands behind her back, she hadn't hit me that
hard since her probation.

Omo and Onna liked him right off. No easy task. But
Arturo had seen the Ringling Circus under the Big Top in
Napoli with his brother and that made him more than okay.
He remembered the midgets.

We aren't midgets, said Omo. Dwarfs aren't midgets. And
he excused the error.

Arturo came around every day. He sat in the kitchen eating Mamma's *pizzelli* and *zeppoli* and drinking coffee. He
seemed somehow skewed, as though half of him was made
at a different time than the other. One shoulder was higher,
one side of his mouth more full than the other. He had dark
hair and eyes and a nose that you could hang your coat on.
He spoke in a voice somewhere between a whisper and a
groan, every sound making a gritty mumbly noise that you
had to lean forward to hear. He was a kind man, though,
and gentle with Mamma. It was obvious he adored her and
ate her food with one eye flickering up at her, his lopsided
mouth rocking back and forth in admiration and gratitude.

Arturo spoke to us only when he thought we might answer him.

Yeah, sure, Arturo, we'll have a sip o' that.

He encouraged Mamma to take evening classes to improve her English. They huddled together over the books,
laughing and trying to make sense of the language so infi-
nitely inferior to Italian.

Mamma wore her new cotton sundresses, straps over bare
shoulders. Her skin looked oiled and pulpy. Hair combed
back and held in place at the nape of her neck with a gold
hair clip. White high heeled shoes and nylon stockings with

seams. She sang as she dressed, happy, girlish. I watched her apply her cologne to her shoulders.

Mamma, the cologne is supposed to go on the wrists, I said, cologne goes behind the ears.

No, *Cara mia*, she corrected. Is called, White *Shoulders*, not White Ears or White Wrists, and she burst out laughing at my naivete.

Marco got himself a girlfriend named Suzette, a brainless human being who came lathered in stupid talk and wearing a hearing aid. He could have had any girl in the school, yet he chose Suzette. I didn't trust her. After school the two of them hung out in a booth at Rocco's, where Mamma fed them focaccia, *caprese*, salami, olives, her pizza.

Suzette loved all things Italian. The food, the language, the music. She behaved like Marco Polo at the first taste of basil. By golly, she had discovered *"O Sole Mio"* and tomato paste. *Come stai!* she called out to me when she saw me. I answered, I'm quite well, thank you. When she gave a cheery *Arrivederci* or *Ciao!* I responded as British as I could, How do you do, I'm sure.

Omo was relentless in pushing me to work harder at commedia. I started taking mime classes and something called Physical Theatre with Andre Andre who had studied with Marcel Marceau in Paris. When Omo and Onna watched me practice, it was with such tenderness I wondered if that was what being someone's little girl was like, and if Omo and Onna were like a real honest-to-goodness mom and pop.

That's it, Chichilina, technique! Technique and Refinement. The body is a narrator. With the body you tell stories. Remember that. Now smile.

The senior prom was coming up and all the girls had dates but me. A boy named Paulo sat next to me in Algebra (he gave me the answers) and in a desperate move I asked him to the prom. Paulo was smart in math and everyone admires people who are smart in math. A sign of intelligence. Straight A's in algebra, physics, geometry, calculus, statistics, and chemistry and you could be president.

Paulo had dark hair and sallow skin, looked Italian, but was really what they call Mixed Blood, with a body like a basketball, his pants pinched the backs of his legs and rode up his behind. My brother called him Porkchop. Paulo said he'd let me know about the prom and had I done pages 212 through 215 yet?

Charles was going steady with the blonde, a Sophomore whose name was Cookie, and the feeling of defeat was complete.

Let's hate her, said Jennifer.

Paulo said he'd go to the prom with me, okay, but only if I paid. It cost me $75, my savings from scooping ice cream at Bridgeman's.

Dancing with his stomach against me, his wet, tapioca chin resting above my head, his hot, slippery hand in mine, I felt Madame's smug harumph. This was purgatory—one fat slobbering prom date dripping Cheez Whiz on my arms and sweating bad-smelling rivers through his shirt. The answers to Chapter Eleven in the Algebra book and a semester grade of B+ for this.

To think Mamma took a picture of us with Marco's Brownie Hawkeye. My broken finger started to hurt again.

The Prom. "Misty." Righteous Brothers songs, "Unchained Melody," "You've Lost That Lovin' Feeling."

I saw Charles with his Sophomore Cookie person. He stood by the punch table chewing on a pretzel.

ChiChi, I saw your show.

What show, Charles?

The one you, you know, the talent show you won. You were incredible.

You were there? In the audience? You?

My cousin was the one who twirled the lariat and sang "The Rose of San Antone."

I couldn't remember.

Someday we'll be seeing you on the *Ed Sullivan Show*!

I must have been breathing hard and heavy and pulling the orchid hair off my wrist corsage. I must have drooled punch on my new shoes, must have talked with spit between my teeth because his smile turning wavy. I wanted only to feel his nearness and look at him up close as though with binoculars. I wanted him to do to me what he did behind Rocco's Pizzeria. The pinches, the kisses, the cupping of my *culu* in his hands.

The sophomore Cookie person was at his elbow, smiling the way jealous wives do when their husbands flirt with waitresses.

Jennifer was voted runner-up Prom Queen, which meant she and her date, the runner-up Prom King, got a free dinner at Sheik's Café downtown, and she also got her picture taken by a photographer from the *Minneapolis Tribune*. I clung to Paulo, pressed into him, sang along to "The Wah-Watusi" and "Johnny Angel." Thinking of Charles.

We took a taxi home, compliments of Manny Looz. I told Paulo I had to get up early. Mime class with Andre Andre.

What exactly is that? Mime?

It's art you do with your body. You act out life, human drama, without words.

He laughed. Ya. HA HO HA!

At the door, he took my hand and pumped it like politicians do when they meet each other at airports.

ChiChi . . . Pumping away.

Paulo, thanks and good night now.

Pumping.

I wanted to go inside, take a bath to get his sweat off my body.

Still pumping.

Paulo, I said, and then in spite of myself, out of desperation or a sudden lapse of consciousness, I reached over, shoved his hand against what may have been my breast and kissed him hard on the mouth.

Andre Andre asked me to wait after class.

Oh, okay, here it comes. Don't go into show business, he's going to say. Give it up. Learn touch typing.

ChiChi, he said, the University of Minnesota Theater Department runs a special program for high school seniors. I'd like to recommend you apply for it Acting, Movement, History of the Theater, Makeup, Backstage, and a Full Stage Production.

I applied

Here she is, folks. ChiChi Maggiordino, high school senior, attending the *University of Minnesota*. A walk through the campus was a trip around the blessed, magical WORLD. Sophisticated ChiChi Maggiordino walking around the University of Minnesota campus with people in their *twenties*, people with *cars*, their own *apartments*. People who ate lunch at Rocco's, drank coffee at the Brain. I stopped tying my savage outbursts of hair into globby ponytails and allowed it to convulse around my face, an unashamed blizzard of fur. I was liberated. I was a *college* person.

The first day in acting class we read *The Glass Menagerie* and discussed character dislocations, which is what Dr. Bullette said all playwrights have in mind when they sit down to write. The actor's job is to bring motivation to life and dislocate the character.

Dislocation? Hell, I was an expert. Tennessee Williams was like an old uncle. Here was another person warped by a virulent, mutinous world.

We performed a play called *The Admirable Crichton* by James Barrie and I played Tweeny, the cockney maid. I had my lines memorized before the first rehearsal.

Mamma was confused when I told her my funny talk was a cockney accent.

Italian girl speak monkey talk. Is this what they teach you at University?

The actor playing Crichton was a beautiful young man named Tyrone. He had the face and grace of a girl and he was graduating from the University with his bachelor's degree in theatre.

Then I'm heading for the Big Apple, he said. Nothing for me in this hick town.

I hadn't thought of Minneapolis exactly as a hick town. But what about all the theaters here? You could work here, Tyrone.

Small potatoes, he said. He was going for the big time. Broadway. New York. He was a petite man, skin like gold, the prettiest man I had ever seen. He called me Dahling and got me a false I.D. so we could go to bars.

CHLOE MCPHEE was the name on the phony driver's license. Who were we kidding? No one with 20/20 vision could mistake ChiChi Maggiordino for a twenty-one-year-old person named McPhee. But it worked and we got away with drinking tap beer in the Gopher Bar, a campus hangout, where Tyrone listened to me expound on modern drama, theory and practice, the connections between Euripides, Sophocles, and Eugene O'Neill and let us not forget Chekhov and Ibsen's contribution to realism.

Tyrone seemed to consider my insights important. You *are* theater, Dahling, he said, and cracked open a peanut for me.

The great thing about acting, Tyrone said, is all the unhappiness and sorrow, all the suffering you experience becomes useful. You let it out, examine it, use it! That's what art is all about.

Tyrone listened when I talked, and because he heard me, I found him fascinating. He said I'd always have a place to stay, Dahling, in New York.

Leave Minneapolis, Tyrone? Me? *Fie!* Marco had fooled the doctors, lived past his date with death. And Mamma. Look at her. A new woman. Prayers, rituals, *Il Mal Occhio,* me. Without me, ah! I shuddered at the tragedy of such a thought and spilled my beer.

The Admirable Crichton played three nights and the University newspaper reviewed it. I was referred to as *hilarious, delightful.* Mamma worried these were insults. A woman she is *bella donna,* not hilarious.

Mamma's new boyfriend, Arturo, moved in with us. He never seemed to stop eating and Mamma didn't stop cooking for him. He waited for her at the restaurant nibbling the Specials Of The Day, and at home a marathon of meals took place around the clock. I woke up sometimes in the wee hours and could hear Mamma and Arturo in the kitchen, Mamma frying onions and peppers, boiling coffee, dishes clinking, radio playing, and their voices loud with laughter, jabbering. Working on her English lessons.

And arguments. Arguments about money. Mamma's checks. Mamma's bank account.

High school graduation, a necessary rite. Mamma exasperated.

I'm have so much to worry, she said. It was too much, this graduation of ChiChi.

Like an annoying sore on your ring finger, Mamma?

In a few years our school would be gutted and transformed into an office building and there'd be no trace of us or these years. Marshall High, the students, teachers, clubs—it would all vanish. Gone, poof. The way ice cream melts and leaves a wet spot like an abstract masterpiece by Rothko.

And we thought we'd live forever.

I missed Nonna, I was restless for a place that was safe with belonging—a *thereness*.

I had to make plans. Omo told me the finish was the most important part of the act. Don't leave any fuselage behind. Make it big. You gotta pull out all stops for the finish. I had to make plans, big plans. Right, Omo? Isn't that right? I had to think big.

anny Looz invited me to dinner at Jax, just the two of us, which struck me as peculiar. The way it happened was, he pulled up in a taxi with Ed to pick up Marco for a trip to the Walker Museum.

What's with the face? Ed Looz said to me. No flashers lately?

Very funny.

Leave her alone, said Marco.

Manny Looz said he had a brainstorm. He peeled some bills from a wad in his pocket and handed them to Ed. You guys go on, take a taxi, I don't understand the art at the Walker anyhow. I'm taking ChiChi to dinner.

Next thing I know I'm sitting in a taxi with an old man who hated art.

Who sez I don't like art? I happen to like art. Eddie's an artist, isn't he? And Marco? Another thing, never call an old person old.

Well then.

He ordered the Chateaubriand, baked potatoes with the works, and champagne. I ate the steak, ate the potato, the sour cream, the chives, the bacon bits, the butter, and the dessert, something in flames. A zillion calories.

I was once a bit of an artist meself, he told me. Before I went into the service. I had ambitions. But things happen. I gave it up. That's why I like to help Eddie out, and Marco, too. A couple of kids with promise. Like you. You got talent and ambition. I like that.

I wanted to tell him he was wrong about ambition. I was just trying to hold up the world was all.

Most adults, when they got you alone, talked boring stuff about themselves and what they've learned in life. They tell you what they think you need to know to improve yourself, as if you didn't have a brain to add two and six.

Okay, Mr. Looz, you got me here for a reason. What's up?

I just wanted the privilege of being your first date where the guy pays, he said.

I swallowed a crouton off the salad. So he knew about the prom deal.

I got tons of dates, I said.

His smile was—well, genuine.

Why do you do so much for us, Mr. Looz?

Eddie needs a family. Call me Manny.

He lifted his champagne glass in a toast.

Here's to that clown thing you do. (sip, gulp.) First off, let's get this straight. You got one helluva talent. You got guts, real guts. And I'll tell you something else.

The champagne sent a chirp up my nose.

The night you showed up at our place after a flasher jumped you, I said to myself, here's a kid worth watching out for. A girl all by herself in the world, no dad, a mother who works long hours. So you can take cabs in this city till the cows come home, got that? You and your mamma and your brother and whoever else I feel like handing the privilege. Check the miles, sign the chit, that's it.

He said it was a ding-dong inspiration how dedicated I was taking all those lessons, working with the dwarves on an act. Yessir, gotta hand it to me. I was something, all right.

I thought to myself, here's a real person. Not at all like that sleezeball son of his.

Eddie? Aw, he's okay, said Manny. When his mother died on us, he sort of lost his balls, excuse the expression. He just sort of, well, didn't care no more. You know he's got that lung respiratory thing, right?

Yuppers.

Hey, he'll outlive us all, babe, you watch.

I had the feeling Manny Looz had a lot of lady friends. I gave him a vampish smile, showing my teeth, like Mamma.

ChiChi, is it true you carry a knife?

Who wants to know? Did smelly Ed tell you that?

I'm being serious.

Ed's got a big blabbery mouth! I said.

I know about Rodman, Manny said. You can bring him to court, you know.

Marco and I took care of him, I said. (I gave him the oooeee Evil Eye!)

What? Speak up, girl.

I got him in the gut, I said.

Uh hunh. And your mamma wants to get him her own way.

You're not listening, Mr. Looz. I *said*, we took care of him.

He dropped the subject. Licked a heaping fork of baked potato and sour cream into his mouth.

I wanted to know how he knew Mamma. Where had they met.

Sometime I'll tell you about it, he said. Anyhow, it was a long time ago I knew your Mamma, then bingo, here she is, living in the same town as me with two kids.

I dropped my napkin. Wait a second. You must have known Mamma in Italy.

Yeah.

But how could you know her? You're an American. Were you in the army in Italy?

He turned in his chair, crossed his leg.

Yeah.

A piece of steak clotted in my throat.

My father. Did you maybe know him? My father?

I knew him.

You knew him! *You knew him!*

His name was Bruno.

And when I think of Bruno—Manny said, while I choked on the steak—I think of a guy who—how to put it—I think of a guy who looks after Number One. That says it all.

Maiori? I managed to ask. Were you at the battle at Maiori where he lost his leg?

I was there, he said.

I waited for him to say more, but he was quiet. Mamma would never speak to us about our pappa. If we asked her about him, she told us he was handsome and that was it.

Your mother believes there are things best unspoken, Manny said, wiping his mouth with the corner of his napkin. Someday you'll know more, ChiChi. Give her time. Don't ask me any more because I can't tell you any more now.

He poured the last of the champagne and ordered himself a bourbon. My stomach turned to rubber.

Look, ChiChi. I brought you here tonight so I could tell you if you ever need anything, you can call on me, got that? You and Marco and your mamma are good for Eddie. I know you and Eddie lock horns on occasion, but that don't give me no bother. He needs a family and I appreciate how he's found hisself one.

I was shaking. The Chateaubriand crystallized in the

rubber walls of my stomach. I asked if he would mind if we took a drive by Lake Harriet.

A swim? Now?

No. I want to see the bandshell.

I hiccoughed all the way to Lake Harriet. Manny had the taxi wait for us at the lake's edge near the bandshell. The lake shimmered like a desert.

I imagined Madame Tomanova in her purple turban and flowing serape reaching to give me a hug before I made my stage entrance. I imagined clinging to her like a kid clings to a parent at the dentist. You're a ballerina, *cherie,* I imagined her whisper. Dance!

My music begins. I take center stage. I'm the Dying Swan. The sky is bright with stars and the entire state of Minnesota is in the audience. Marco, Mamma, Onna and Omo, Charles. I dance with heart, with passion. Then I remember ChiChi, Clown Extra Ordinaire. My legs go goofy. I'm dying, living, dying, perky, silly, dying, kapoot. Manny sits on the grass and he's laughing out loud. Madame smiles from the wings. *Perfect,* I hear her sigh. Her Leticcia is perfect. I behold a familiar aroma. Madame is wearing White Shoulders and it covers me like the laughter of an audience of happy people.

At my finish I bowed, flinging onto my knees, arms thrust practically out of their sockets, head thrown back, and then I sank in a heap of white feathery dead swan-ness. Manny let go with whistles and applause. I jumped down from the stage breathless, exhilarated. Bouquets of roses in my arms.

SCREW MADAME GJORSKA DANILOVA TOMA-NOVA, I shouted.

Manny swatted a mosquito, clapped, and shouted, YEAH, CHICHI! I threw him a rose.

I worried about big thighs. Oh sure, God had created me smaller than every girl in the continental U.S., yet I worried about being, well, big. Madame Tomanova had warned us about the evils of poundage. Hadn't I had arrived early for my ballet classes and stayed after class, always practicing, practicing? Wasn't I was preoccupied with the arabesque, the plié, the *rond de jambe*, a decent fifth position?

I discovered plastic food wrap. Before you put your ballet tights on, you wrap your thighs in layers of plastic wrap. That way your legs heat up like muffins while you're working out. They sweat, and sweat is what makes you worthy. I didn't mind the lumpy look of plastic-wrapped legs if that was what it took to have thighs worthy of a dying swan. Each step I took sounded like stones tumbling around in water. I wore the plastic wrap to my university classes under my clothes. Rubber baby pants was another trick I learned in Madame's ballet school. You pull these on under your tights so your *culu* sweat like a fountain while you worked out. The more the big bubble *culu* sweats, the better.

Wake up at 5:00 in the mornings, practice your barre exercises. Stretch and pull and tug and force your muscles to accomplish great acts of beauty, which is what Madame said we were called unto, and beauty was the meaning of life.

Acts of beauty!

I got something for you, Babe.

Manny Looz at the door with a taxi running at the curb.

He was unshaven and I knew he'd been up all night. A bookie's work is never done. He followed me to the kitchen.

A friend of my acquaintance happens to be an casting agent, he said.

Do me a favor, Manny. Nobody calls me Babe. Do you mind?

Whatever you say, Babe. So okay. Anyhow, it so happens, this agent is looking for talented performers such as yourself, you got any coffee? It so happens I put myself out on a limb and arranged an audition for you.

But I'm not ready to audition for an agent. I haven't got my finish yet.

His name is Nate Theilberg, big agent. Books everything from here to Saskatchewan. The name familiar?

Never heard of him. I'm not ready! You want sugar?

Nix on the sugar. This is an open door for you, little lady. Don't say I never done anything for you. I'll have me a couple of those biscotti.

Mr. Looz, my act needs a ton of work. I'm not ready.

Hey, I'm out on a limb for you here. You going to put mud on my face?

I could come up with a hundred excuses not to audition for an agent. My busted finger hurt. I had recurring head-aches. I needed to translate Boccaccio for the blind.

I poured him an espresso. Watched him pick at a biscotti crumb with his pinkie.

You can practice your act at my place, he said.

His place?

You can have my whole cotton-picking third floor. It's

got mirrors and everything. I think it was used once as a ballroom.

I could have kissed him.

What about Ed? I suddenly remembered. Will he be around? That is, if he's not thrown in jail—

Mr. Looz looked at me, puzzled. Don't worry about Eddie, he said. And what are you talking about, jail?

You don't know what happened?

What.

I told him how last night Ed came looking for Marco at Rocco's. For some reason which I cannot fathom, Mamma *liked* Ed. I'd *never* figure that one out. So anyhow, Mamma gave Ed an order of garlic toast and a Coke. A few minutes later Marco and Suzette walked in. Ed started talking to Suzette, probably saying something dirty or nasty because she's such a priss, but Suzette couldn't hear him because he was talking in her bad ear. When she ignored him, didn't even give him a nod of the head, Ed pounded his fist on the table to get her attention.

You got any more coffee? Manny said.

Your son is stinking jealous of Marco's relationship with Suzette. Manny dipped his cookie in the espresso, didn't look at me. And you, ChiChi, you don't know nothing about jealous, do you?

Suzette and Ed think they *own* my brother, I said.

I poured him the rest of the espresso. You want to hear this or what?

Ya. Sure.

I sat down and continued: So anyhow, Marco told Ed to knock it off. Ed was raving on about Marco not having any time for his buddy, and there sat Suzette with her hearing aid off, wearing her nice little sundress with her hair in ribbons, all fresh and springlike. And—

Where were you in all this?

I happened to be in the kitchen filling out an application for a waitress job. My ice cream scooping days are over with this broken finger.

So you're better off.

Am not.

Rocco will never hire me now, thanks to Ed.

What did he do? Let's have it.

All right. So there's Ed yelling holy hell. Marco should know best pals don't grow out of nowhere, etc., etc., when all at once, Suzette jumps up and calls Ed a jealous weasel. I heard her way in the back of the restaurant. The place was filling up. The movie at the Varsity had just let out. Suzette threw the bowl of Parmesan cheese at Ed. Crash! It broke all over the floor and there was Parmesan everywhere. Mamma came hurrying over, tried to calm things down, but Ed was so mad he leaped across the table and Suzette went flying out of the booth. She wouldn't have gotten hurt if she hadn't tripped on the broken Parmesan bowl glass and cut herself up so they had to call an ambulance and haul her off to General.

Manny stood up, bored. Tell them to send me the bill, he said. Gotta run, a cab's waiting outside. He handed me a key from his pocket.

This is to the side door of the house, he said. Stairway is right there. Elevator to your left.

I followed him to the door. I'm not finished telling you! There's more! Rocco fired Mamma! (I this said to his back.) And besides, Suzette's parents are pressing charges! Assault and battery!

He gave a wave of his hand without turning around and called, Big deal. Your audition is in two weeks, Babe, don't blow it.

Omo and Onna and I worked on my act every day in Manny's third-floor ballroom (and that's what it was, a room big enough for a friggin' dance hall). Omo sat on a box in the middle of the room, getting up only when I helped him. The knees, he said. The knees are the second to go.

Oh? What's first?

The spine, of course. You think I walk crooked cuz I like it? But then he turned his attention to the act, to me.

You need a lot of props, Omo said. When a performer isn't brilliant, give them props, I always say.

Omo taught me that to the artist everything had purpose and value. I wanted my life like that, I wanted to live on purpose, like Omo and Onna did. My movements were still clumsy, too exaggerated, false; so Onna made me wear masks when we rehearsed. That way, she said, you can tell if your body is telling the truth or not. Don't be all show, ChiChi. Be subtle. Be honest. Love the truth as much as you love the art. That's the difference between a great performance and a hyped-up side show.

The Sunday before my audition started out peaceful enough. I had just finished pressing my costume when Mamma shouted from the kitchen.

A terrible thing! Terrible! ChiChi!

She was frantic. Omo! Something's wrong with Omo! *É malato!*

Sick? What's happened? What?

Onna was on the telephone. She wasn't sure what was wrong, a stroke, or seizure or something with the heart. Omo woke up thrashing and quivering. Now he was talking slurred and losing his balance.

Tell her to call for an ambulance. We'll meet them at General.

We arrived at the hospital minutes later.

He's worse, said Onna. He can't talk at all.

Omo needed specialists. He didn't respond to the same treatment as average-sized persons. He'd had a stroke and there was some brain damage, it was unsure how severe. They'd like to transport him down to Rochester. Onna could accompany him in the ambulance.

Mamma and I took a taxi.

God was God and He had His ways and His reasons for doing things, Mamma said, repeating what a nurse in another hospital told her once.

I thought the problem was his knees!

Time for my rituals. The Evil Eye. I had to get God's attention. I'd make a personal sacrifice. Something to really impress God. Did I love Omo enough?

Omo lay in Intensive Care with electrodes pressed into his chest, tube in the mouth, nasal mask ventilator over his nose, tubes running in his arms. Rivers of medicine. His large barrel chest was exposed and I pulled the papery sheet under his chin to cover him.

This is what you do in hospitals. I knew about Hospital Behavior. You pull a sheet up to the patient's chin, you pour a Dixie cup of water and you adjust the straw in the cup in case the patient wakes up and says he's thirsty, you smooth the pillow, the sheet. These are the blessings the sick and dying give to us. Sometimes we are fortunate to prop them up in their chairs, wheel them down the hall, walk them with their IV and walker to the door and back, rub their backs, massage their feet, comb their hair, because we want to do *something*.

We must do *something*.

He grunted. A falling-down sound. Some yellow stuff

dribbled from his lip. Omo, I whispered in his ear, *Chi dorme non piglia pesche*. He who sleeps doesn't catch fish! I knew he'd appreciate that. I could hear his smile.

The nurse came in, her feet like balloons on the tile floor. She fiddled with some dials, she adjusted a tube. I watched. That's what the loved ones do, watch.

Watch as nurses puff up blood pressure bulbs.

Watch as they examine thermometers, check the catheters.

We say thank you. Oh thank you.

At least it's something.

In the morning Omo was still alive. Not conscious. Severe damage to the left side of his brain. The brain stem and spinal cord compressed. Symptoms of hydrocephalus developing. A shunt to relieve the pressure: surgery. A tall, bony neurosurgeon with hands like fins gave us the devastating prognosis.

I asked for another opinion. A specialist in achondroplasia dwarfism. Get us neurologists and neurosurgeons from Johns Hopkins.

Omo and Onna were achondroplastic dwarfs who suffered with back and leg pain, pinched nerves and vertebrae, aching feet, but rarely complained. Knees, Omo said, it was the knees. In rehearsal I noticed when either of them sat in a squatting position, they grimaced in pain. The spine was the first to go, he said, but they didn't complain.

When the truth settled in on us that the first doctor had been right and Omo would never be himself again, we fell into a languor, a stupor of not knowing what to think or what to do, what to say. Something about God's will?

Did you know Omo wanted to be a doctor? Onna said. He wanted to finish college, be a doctor. He wanted to go into genetic research. But no medical school would accept him. What medical institution would hire a dwarf?

We came from Italian peasant families, she said. When the war came and our families were practically starving, I was always sick. My legs grew bowed and I didn't walk until late. I had ear infections, breathing problems. It's a wonder I lived. No antibiotics in those days, of course. Even if good medical care existed, we were peasants. What did we know? I had a big head, short limbs, and I didn't grow. My mother had five other children, all average sized, normal, and then me, last born. The result of spontaneous gene mutation. Sick all the time.

Mamma took Onna's hand in hers, rocked her little body as she talked on. I hadn't seen Mamma so affectionate since Nonna died. Onna said her parents had earned a few *lire* hiring her out to a traveling theatrical company, commedia dell'arte. The typical stock characters and routines. Finally, at fourteen, she was hired out permanently.

To a freak show. She traveled through Puglia, then up north. She danced, learned the skits. She didn't have a serious bow and the spinal curve wasn't too bad then. She made money with her double jointedness. For a few coins Onna twisted her fingers and wrists around. People *paid* to see that. When she needed dental work, there was always a local village woman, like a witch, who'd pull out the teeth.

Onna had not talked about the hardship of their dwarfism so openly. When you think of a Little Person, which we prefer to be called, she said, you don't think of a physician or a scientist, do you? You probably think of circuses and freak shows. We've been in show business ever since the Ptolemies and Imperial Rome. We've been wizards, jesters, fools, magicians, comics, freaks. Omo could have been a doctor!

She gave a long sigh, then took my hand. Now listen, ChiChi, honey, you go back home and get ready for your audition. It's what Omo would want.

But I can't leave. We've family! *Siamo famiglia!*

Yes, darling, I know. And you must know Omo loves you like a daughter. So do I. Now you go and make it a good audition—for us.

Mamma gave me a furious look and pulled me into the bathroom.

Famiglia? she said.

Yes, Mamma.

I recognized the streak above her nose, up from her eyebrows to her hairline, that blue line. It surprised me to still be afraid of her.

We stay together, *la famiglia,* she said, because we like bad fruit. I'm explain you why. Because nobody want us!

Scusi? Was she serious? What did she mean? No matter what we did in this life we would never be like other people, is that what she was saying? I could become a great clown one day, even become famous, but I'd always be an outsider? Is that how it was?

Oh, Mamma, what ever happened to you? What ever did they do to you?

I took a walk on the hospital grounds with Metamere's knife in my hand, like a good luck charm. I sat down. I felt the grass beneath me. I felt the cool grass. I opened the knife.

I threw the knife. *Frip.* It wouldn't stick. I stayed there throwing the knife, *frip-frip,* like Marco. When the grass felt too wet to sit on any longer, I started to get up when I tripped. I fell forward and fell on my hand with the knife. It wouldn't have been anything at all if the edge of the knife hadn't caught my eye. In an instant the world turned red.

I always thought if I were ever in a terrible accident where the pain was unspeakable, I would scream out the agony, I'd howl with the pain. But now, falling, I simply sighed a quiet breath of resignation.

I returned to Minneapolis on the train. Half-asleep and through wet lashes, I watched the flat farmland passing by outside the window, the land that gave up its wheat, its barley, and its alfalfa to feed the world. I tried to imagine the farmers who tended the fields. Imagine them sitting at dinner tables or reading books at night in chairs by lighted lamps. I imagined them playing I-See-Something-Blue with their children.

La famiglia.

My mind closed up and I slept.

Marco: What in hell happened to your *eye?* What's that *patch* for?

ChiChi: Nothing. It's nothing.

Marco: Sonofabitch!

ChiChi: I tripped and stuck myself with Metamere's knife is all.

Marco: You've been messing with IL MAL OCCHIO! You did this on PURPOSE to yourself. YOU WERE TRYING TO GET GOD'S ATTENTION! I know you. You were doing the homily from last week in church. *If our right eye offends you, pluck it out,* verses from the Bible, weren't you? YOU THOUGHT YOU COULD SAVE OMO!

Mamma believed I did it on purpose, too. Twenty-two tiny stitches, no damage to the retina, the possibility of scarring to the lid, antibiotics and drops, danger of losing muscle control. And a prescription for Thorazine, an antipsychotic medication.

Omo died of apnea.

The oxygen he received didn't reach his lungs, and a tracheostomy wasn't possible in his condition.

The funeral was attended by circus people and show business friends who came from all parts of the country to honor Omo.

Sideshow people came, fat ladies, a lady with hair growing from her cheeks and chin, a couple of people tattooed all over their bodies, giants, little people, men and women with various parts of themselves irregular: hunchbacked, no arms, twelve-fingered, duck-footed, flippered legs, spines twisted, stomachs protruded, and all nationalities. An obituary in the *Minneapolis Star* appeared with his photograph. Flowers arrived from everywhere. The Little People of America Association honored Omo's memory with a plaque in their Hall of Fame. We all wept unashamed and loud throughout the service. He was buried at Hillside Cemetery and when his little casket was poised over the grave, Mamma wailed and Onna sat stiff and sullen, like something emptied out and finished.

The Thorazine clouded my brain. I felt anesthetized and wobbly. My audition was in two days. My eye hurt clear to my *culo*.

I took a taxi to Manny Looz's house early in the evening and opened the door to the ballroom, my rehearsal room. How could I work without Omo? The place was dark, it had a clammy feel, like an old work boot.

The phonograph was gone. I looked around the room for it. Ed must have been here, that weasel. Why would he take my cheap little phonograph when he could have a dozen good ones of his own if he wanted? Why did he hang out at our pathetic little apartment when he had a huge mansion all his own to rumble around in like a friggin prince all day?

Oh yes, *family*.

Music. Coming from overhead. I hurried out the door and up the hall, looking for a staircase to another floor. I pushed open a door that lead to some narrow steps that ended at a door to the roof. I shoved with my back at the metal flap above my head.

Stars. A cobalt sky. Out on the edge of a flat ledge sat Ed Looz with my phonograph on his lap. He was playing my *South Pacific* album and wearing down the batteries.

I saw three of him. My legs buckled under me. I couldn't feel my arms.

He turned to look at me. All right, big deal. So you found me. Hey, what's wrong with your face?

I sank to my knees. The sky and the ground became one long thin line of cobalt.

The three of him said, Afraid of heights, ChiChi?

I tried to feel something with my hands, something tangible, something I could identify. Stone, leaf, loam, hair, skin . . .

Ed scratched his way toward me across the shingles. ChiChi? Cripes, ChiChi, what are you on?

I couldn't get my head positioned upright. Nauseous. My stomach in my ears. Are we moving? Is this thing moving?

ChiChi, give me your arm. Give me your arm!

Did somebody turn out the lights? Listen, Ed, I think the Thorazine kicked in . . .

Ezio Pinza sang "Some Enchanted Evening."

Ed, I think I'm blind!

The next day I woke up in my bed with a burning head, my mouth a desert, my stomach scraped by heavy machinery.

I heard a man's loud sob.

Who is it? Who's there? Marco? Mamma?

I walked on the outsides of my feet to the kitchen.

Don't turn on the light, said a voice.

Arturo?

A groan.

Arturo? What are you doing in the dark?

Sitting. I'm sitting.

I pulled the string to the fluorescent light over the sink.

He squinted at me.

Where's Mamma? I said.

She and Marco gone to Suzette's house, he said. To talk the mamma and pappa out of suing. They suing everybody. Rocco's, Manny Looz, everybody.

What? Are you crying?

With my one good eye he seemed younger than his thirty years, almost like a teenager.

No, I'm not crying. What you think?

Are you upset about Omo? We all are. It's terrible. It's—what *is* it? Is it me?

Yourmotherdoesn'tloveme.

Speak up, Arturo. I don't understand you.

Your Mamma, she doesn't love me!

I leaned my forehead against the cupboard. *Sheez.* What day is this?

The 15th. I think is the 15th.

My audition's tomorrow! Arturo, I have an audition!

I'm hungry! *Ho fame,* he said.

What time is it? I can't see!

He recognized the patch on my eye, my misshapen face. *Che cos' è quello?* What happened to you?

You think you have troubles, Arturo.

He took a plate of chicken cacciatore from the refrigerator.

I'm on MEDICATION, Arturo. Omo is dead!

I know. I was there at the funeral.

Oh. Right.

I heat 'em up, the cacciatore, he said. I no like cold.

He made us soggy sandwiches, the kind you have to eat with a spoon. He poured himself a glass of red wine.

You hear anything about Ed Looz? I asked. Did he jump?

Who jump? Where? What?

Ed Looz? Did he jump off the roof?

ChiChi, eat you chicken. Nobody jump offa roof. You

crazy. *Pazza.* He let loose with a honk of the nose in his handkerchief. She won't marry me, he cried.

Who?

You mamma! And all because of money. *Phuh!*

Arturo. Calm down. Mamma loves you. She's in mourning now. Someone dear to us has died, you can understand that. Omo is dead! Say, do you know how I got home? What happened to me on the roof?

Pazza, Arturo muttered again. Gulped the wine down in two swallows.

I wanted to take a bath, rest an ice pack on my temples, go back to bed.

She won't marry me! he cried.

Arturo, I said, if you don't mind a little friendly advice. Get a trade. Carpentry maybe. Shoe repair. Barbering. Tailoring. Earn a nice paycheck.

ChiChi, it's not *lack* of money makes for problems. She have plenty! You mamma, she rich lady.

How much of that wine have you had?

It's all because of alimony money! Alimony! If she marry me and she lose the alimony.

Arturo, I've got a terrific headache here. But let me explain it to you. Alimony is something divorced people work out between themselves and it's paid, usually to the wife, after the divorce. Alimony is paid after a *divorce.* So you must be talking about Mamma's little pension. She has received a small pension from the army all these years. I don't know for how much, but it sure hasn't made her rich.

No, not pension, ChiChi. Alimony. After the divorce you pappa he pay her alimony—

Divorce? What divorce? Our pappa is dead.

—And she put all the money in bank for you and your brother. She save it for you and Marco! She think you deserve the money. To start you life, maybe you go to college, go into business. She not want to lose that.

Arturo could get things so mixed up. For a nice guy, he was far too dense in the head.

Arturo, I explained to him, Mamma gets a small pension from the army, not much, like she always complains, but enough to support—

No! *Alimony*. Not pension. Bruno, he pays *alimony* every month and she has been saving it for you and your brother. If she marry me, she lose the alimony. Oh, what I am going to do?

Bruno! What Bruno?

You know! Bruno, your pappa!

Am I hearing you right? My pappa, he's—he's ALIVE?

Certo. Of course. What you think.

The murmur of the refrigerator. The drip of the faucet.

You're lying, I said. *Non é vero.*

He's alive and he's a *stronzo*. A lousy shit.

I hate you, Arturo.

I hate the garlic smell of you, I hate the shattered glass sound of your voice. I hate the kitchen. I hate the tomato stained dishes, this house, and I hate love.

Where you going, ChiChi? Don't go—what's wrong? Stay!

The telephone on the other end rang eight times before Tyrone's sluggish hello.

I'm sorry to wake you up, Tyrone. May I come over?

My voice like crushed bread dough.

Now? Who is this?

It's me, ChiChi. From the University acting class? You gave me the name Chloe McPhee? Remember, the false I.D.?

A pause.

Tyrone, do you remember me?

Gosh, it's late, Chloe. My parents are in bed.

Arturo yelled from the kitchen, What's a matter? Did I say something bad? Your pappa, Bruno, you no like him? Ah, *mal creato,* that one.

Me, into the phone: Tyrone? You live with your parents, Tyrone? I thought you had your own apartment.

I'm saving my money for New York.

Arturo again: ChiChi! Hey! Don't take it so hard. I'll stay.

I promise I won't go away. Okay? Don't you worry! I love your mamma!

What do you want? Tyrone said. Is something wrong?

Everything is wrong. May I—come over?

Here? You? Well, okay, I guess . . . Don't ring the bell. I'll wait outside for you.

Tyrone lived in a two-story house surrounded by pine trees a block from Lake Nakomis.

You didn't tell me you were rich, I said when he met me at the curb.

We're not and do you take taxis everywhere?

I handed him my phonograph case and baton. I carried my clown costume over my arm.

It's a lifestyle, I said.

What's this stuff? A baton?

I got an audition tomorrow. I have to be funny.

With that eye patch? What's with your eye?

Little accident is all. Don't ask.

How are you going to be funny looking like that, Dahling?

He led me up a long staircase to his room. On the wall were family photos, 8x10 baby photos, grade school class pictures, teenagers in graduation caps. We walked along deep green shag carpeting.

Nice, I murmured, running my hand along the wainscoting.

Once in his room, he closed the door and turned on a lamp by his bed. I swear, my mother will slay me, lay me out cold if she finds out I've got a girl in my room. I'll pay bloody hell, he said.

He suddenly seemed younger, less heroic. Tyrone, my life is in pieces, I said. Tyrone, I need a friend.

We sat on the bed and he put his arm around me. I'm your friend, he whispered.

My gosh, Tyrone. Your bed! The foot of your bed faces the door. That's bad luck!

What bad luck?

Well, we believe if you sleep with your feet facing the door, you'll be carried out feet first.

Guffaw. Snort. Oh, that's right. You're Italian, he said.

He reached for the lamp, flicked it off. Now we can't see which way we face. Heehee.

Omo's dead! I cried out.

Ah, that's too bad.

I tried to catch my breath. And Tyrone, I just found out our pappa is alive.

You don't say, he said, and pulled me down onto my back on the bed facing the door.

Never would I speak of that sloppy night above a parents' room in a bed with dirty sheets that smelled of sleep, and never would I say it was his first time, too, and the suddenness of our bodies so close together terrified us into sucking on each others' necks all night, his penis pressed against my thigh, and even when he was on top of me I wasn't sure if we were doing it or not. I'd never tell a soul about it because what I wanted to be was a girl who could be funny, keep the world aloft, keep the living alive.

Still, what was ChiChi to do? Spinning off on the Thorazine like that, grieving the terrible loss of my beloved Omo, and Ed Looz up on the roof like a damn crow, my poor eye, and now *this*. Flopping on a bed with some guy like we're learning to swim. *Gesù, Maria.* And then there was Bruno.

The audition for the agent, Mr. Theilberg, was to take place at a studio in the MacPhail School of Music downtown.

Without sleep or coffee the next morning, I sat dazed in my clown costume in the taxi watching out the window, the haze of heat rising over Lake Nakomis and the long sprawling lawns of Tyrone's fancy neighborhood. A part of the city I didn't know, like a fairyland. My eye itched under the patch.

Tyrone's kisses were still on my face and my neck. I felt a burning in my stomach, a revulsion so fiery my whole head could have blown off. He yanked me out of bed and rushed me out the back door before his mother woke up.

The taxi driver could be Bruno, anyone could be Bruno. The taxi driver could be one of Mitchell Rodman's henchman, could be *Bruno*. I looked over the seat to count his legs.

Omo, what should I do? I rolled down the window and stuck my head out. A Fourth Baptist Family Camp school bus was alongside us. Kids' tinny voices were singing:

I got a river of life flowing out through me—

Singing boys and girls, their easy smiles. They all looked like Marco on his way to Whispering Valley Camp.

I couldn't remember one moment of my audition routine.

My eye winked under the patch. The Fourth Baptist Camp kids sang on about how a River of Life made the blind to see.

Name please?

ChiChi Maggiordino—*Clown Extra Ordinaire.*

Have a seat, you're number seven.

A row of chairs along the wall were occupied by women in what looked like their prom dresses. They held sheet music on their laps. They stared at me, stunned and dopey, like my entrance was a stick-up.

What's with you gals? Never seen a clown?

I plunked my phonograph down on the floor. I could hear a piano and a soprano singing "This Is My Beloved." I adjusted my clown collar and began my ballet stretches.

A glamorous model-beauty-queen–type person in the next chair watched me with dim amusement. So what do you do, kid? she said. She wore a tight-fitting black dress with sparkly things all over it. Rhinestone necklace at her throat. She smoked Parliament cigarettes and was probably about twenty-five.

What's it look like? I'm a classical musician. I'm Maria Callas.

She bristled, puffed her cigarette. How do you do, I'm Van Cliburn.

I almost smiled, but the door opened and a girl wearing an ensemble a person would get married in hurried out of the audition room. She looked stricken.

Like Jesus had taken a swing at her.

That's show biz, said the glamour queen next to me. When they don't let you finish the song, that's the worst.

Rejected? Geez oh gosh golly whiz.

Number six was called and a girl my age wearing a push-out brassiere under a satiny dress rose from her chair and wiggled into the audition room. Glamour Queen introduced herself. Elainey, she said, and here to audition for the Aqua Follies; she passed the dancing audition, now for the singing. She did mostly nightclubs. Did I want a smoke?

I despise and detest smoke with an intense feverish passion, I said, and told her my name.

Ya, ChiChi, I grew up with a mother with asthma, you learn to hate everything that dirties up the air. But I don't smoke around her. Say, you got some hickey on your neck there, honey, she snickered.

Hickey?

And the eye patch. Very original. Every think of wearing one in different colors? Something with a pattern?

At the sound of Number Seven I went brainless, hoisted the phonograph in my arms and took tiny *bourrée* steps into the room. I mimed a greeting with a huge bow, removed my hat, and flipped on the knob of the phonograph. I turned to the four people sitting at a table and with no routine whatsoever in my head, jellied my legs and fell flat on my face. The four people laughed. The music began and I began dancing. By the time I got to the Dying Swan they were laughing so I could barely hear the music. Then the finish, big like Omo taught me, a walk-over, the hooked fish, and my pose with the umbrella.

Silence.

Their forms took shape. Three men and a woman.

The man with the cigar said there was no place for an act like mine in the Follies and then he leaned back in his chair, examined me with the same expression as Nonna when she bartered the price of figs.

So! he said.

So, I said.

Where was my resume? he wanted to know.

Resume?

No resume? Never mind. He asked who had booked me, had I ever been on the road, ever worked clubs? Would I do chorus? I answered in yesses, nos, shrugs. Sure. Of course. Natch.

A short man with short legs, his suit a bath of wrinkles, shoes shined.

What's under that frabjous costume?

I'm under it, I said.

Show me.

(Why, you old so-and-so.) I took off the costume, stood there in my leotard.

The woman put my music on. I began the routine again, except this time my movements were spontaneous, unrehearsed. When I came to the Dying Swan, their faces hollowed out. I was exposed, like the hooked fish in the routine; you cut a fish open, splash its guts on the floor, and what have you got? Certainly not a cartwheel and the splits. You've got fish guts. Seventeen years old, a pearl done spent, dropped in the wet stained sheets of a boy leaving town, a girl whose eye God rejected, who couldn't fit in the Follies, *Bruno's* girl.

Music ending, I moved in for the finish like swimming downstream, I turned, posed, and allowed the umbrella to slowly drop at my side. I held the pose. I understood now what Omo had been trying to teach me about truth and lying.

Frabjous, said the fat man with the cigar.

Then: The kid's got something. I don't know what it is, but she's got something.

The others murmured. Right. She's got it. She's got something.

What'll I do with her?

More murmuring.

Gotta admit, she's an original. Keep the eye patch, honey. It's sexy as all hell.

He stood up and pointed his cigar at me. Let me think on it. I'll come up with something for you. Leave it to me. Call my office tomorrow. Do you tap dance?

Sure. Of course. Natch.

I bowed with my hand over the hickey, backed out of the room, and they called Number Eight.

Marco was waiting downstairs at the entrance of the building. Pacing, head bowed.

Mascara in my good eye.

You didn't come home last night! he said.

I knew what he was doing here. He had heard about Bruno, too.

How's Suzette? I said.

Suing everybody, Manny and Ed Looz, the trattoria—where *were* you all night?

How Marco held his head, moved his shoulders, how he looked at you with all that concern!

ChiChi, I called everywhere! Jennifer's, Looz's, Onna's—where *were* you?

At a friend's from the university.

What friend? A guy?

None of your beeswax. We all got our secrets.

He took me by the arm. I remembered the hickey, shuddered.

ChiChi, listen. Arturo's full of crap. What he said? A crock! He's a dumb wop.

Like us, Marco?

He pulled me to him. No, not like us. We're different. What the hell is that on your neck?

The smell of Marco. Coffee mixed with chocolate, like stones dug from the sweet earth. Like ripe watermelon and Nonna's tomatoes.

So you know about Bruno, Marco? Arturo told you, too?

Yeah. When we got home, he was acting nuts. Raving, you might say. He was afraid he had said something wrong to you. He started in about alimony and wanting to marry Mamma. Then he went on about our pappa, Bruno, still

being alive. He told me you ran out of the house hysterical.
ChiChi, you really had me scared.

Marco, tell me the truth. Did you already know about
Bruno?

No. Swear to God. I absolutely swear to God.

Swear on your father's grave?

Bad joke. I bit the inside of my mouth, tried to think of
a song, a lyric, some kind magic to brace me.

*I'll be down to getcha in a taxi, honey, better be ready 'bout
half past eight—*

STOP IT, ChiChi! *Basta!* Come on. I've got Suzette's
dad's car outside. I'm supposed to be at their lawyer's. I hate
it when you start that muttering thing. And take off that
stupid eye patch.

Can't. My eye is all runny and ugly.

Are you going whacko on me, Cheech? Is that it? You
going ding-dong on me? What am I supposed to do when
they take you away and lock you up? Do you think about
that, ChiChi? Do you think about what happens to me if
they take you away from me?

Santissimo, Marco.

Why do you do such awful things to yourself? I find you
on Looz's roof O.D.'d on Thorazine, and how about that
time you tried to cut your face off? Now look at you. Your
eye. Your eye!

(Didn't he know it was an accident? Who would poke
themselves in the eye with a knife on purpose?)

ChiChi . . . *per l'amor d'Dio.* For the goddamn LOVE OF
GOD!

When had he become taller than me? When had his arms
grown this long?

Since when are you driving a car? I said. You're not sixteen for another month.

He wiped his eyes with the back of his hand. Since Suzette got a permit. Come on. Mamma's waiting.

Mamma who?

In the car. She's got some explaining to do.

It's better to get angry than go crazy, he said.

Sitting in the front seat staring out the window, her jaw poked out like a foot, body stiff, eyes narrowed and filled with heat, Mamma.

I forgot my baton.

Marco followed me back in the building.

Geez, don't let Mamma see that thing. He was looking at my neck.

ChiChi, we've got to stick together on this—my God, that thing on your neck is *huge*. Who did that to you?

The audition waiting area was still crowded with females of all ages and sizes, each looking like they polished their faces in custard.

Name please?

I already auditioned. I left my baton in there.

The glamorous Elainey came out of the audition room. Heads lifted to gaze at confidence incarnate and the smirk of a Mona Lisa.

How'd it go? I asked her, as if I didn't know.

I'm hired, she said. They said I was frabjous—is that a word?

Marco put his mouth in my hair and whispered. Mamma has lied all these years! It's up to *both* of us to get the *truth* out of her. Then we can figure things out together, like we always do!

The baton was lying by the door and I grabbed it as the next girl entered with a gooey smile as if this was something she was happy about doing. Elainey walked out with us.

You really ought to get sheet music, she told me. Carrying

around a phonograph to auditions isn't exactly professional. What is it you *do* anyhow?

My sister is a dancer and clown, said Marco, a little too eager. You watch her perform and she rips your heart out. You laugh and cry at the same time.

Elainey looked mildly interested. I could tell she was caught by the expression on Marco's face, how the light reflected on his forehead, how dampness had gathered around his ears. In Marco's presence female voices grew softer and higher, their stomachs pulled in, their toes went under. If they looked directly into his eyes, they became lumpish and stuttery, no matter what age.

She wanted to know would we like to have a Coke or coffee somewhere, could she hitch a ride with us if it wouldn't be too much trouble?

Can't do, I said. We got a sick woman in the car. I took her card and told her to break a leg, sweetheart, in the Follies.

Marco shook her hand and we left her standing on the sidewalk wearing the smile of someone who knew how to audition.

Marco sat with his hands on the wheel, the heat in the car as unbearable as the silence. I need a minute, he said. I'm feeling kind of funny.

Mamma glared at him. Me, I'm burn up in so much the hot weather. What you think!

We happen to be in a state of SHOCK, Mamma, I said to the back of her head. Who the hell is Bruno?

Mamma turned, angry. I knew it! All right! Why you no thank you Mamma for what I do for you!

Thank you, Mamma? For what? *Per che?* said Marco, coughing.

Mamma twisted around in her seat, pointed a finger at me. I do all for *you!* My *children!* So you don't be outcasts forever. So you have money for life, for future! I'm think is better he dead than alive and my children never know what happen.

Her voice broke and tears slid along the ridges of her nose. She hit the dashboard with her fist.

So it was true. Our pappa wasn't dead.

I wished Marco were sitting next to me so I could touch him, hear him breathe.

He began to wheeze. There's no air in here, he said.

I reached over the back of the seat to touch his shoulder. Marco's breath. My preoccupation, like other people collect butterflies, porcelain teacups, hats, antique farm tools. Mamma's hands remained clenched in her lap, her shoulders rigid.

Manny knows Bruno's alive, doesn't he? I said.

Of course. What you think.

He wouldn't tell me.

No. He have respect for me.

I knew what she'd tell us before she opened her mouth. She'd order us to listen to her, what she do for us, how she do all for us, not for herself. She was good woman, she work hard, she make good home, put plenty good food on the table, her children not go hungry. Always she try to protect her children from pain, the pain she suffer, and what thanks is her reward for such the sacrifice? *Puh!*

Marco coughed into a used tissue he pulled out of the door's side pocket. Marco really was mine. Mamma had handed him to me minutes after he was born. *Lui è mio,* I proclaimed when I was just two years old. The two selves I was formed of were Marco and ChiChi. He wheezed. He gasped. *Sacre Madre!*

He was choking on life.

Marco, stand up. Get out of the car and stand up! I said.

Just give me a minute. He gagged into the wet tissue.

I pushed myself out of the car, pulled opened the front door. Out, get out. You're going into an episode. He doubled over gasping.

Breathe out! I shouted. Relax! Inhalator! Where's his inhalator?

I felt in his pockets for the inhalator, searched the front seat of the car, the glove compartment.

A woman's voice from behind us: Lie down on the sidewalk, stretch out your arms! She ordered.

Elainey.

She helped Marco lie facedown on the sidewalk, then hiked her skirt up to her hips and straddled his body.

That won't help, I said, exasperated.

It works on my mom, she said, and she began to push and lift on his upper body. She lowered her head to his, rolled him over, then her mouth on his. In a few minutes the spasms stopped, his body relaxed.

There now, she said, I think we aborted the attack. Easy does it. She was positioned on top of him with her rump stuck up in the air like a flag atop the Foshay Tower. Mamma knelt by his head wringing her hands. *Figlio—*

He was shaken, pale, his skin the color of a bland fruit drink. Elainey helped him to a sitting position. He had stained his pants. His mouth was smeared a bright crimson with Elainey's lipstick.

Get off him, I ordered. He's going to General.

Not a single hair had been misplaced on her head, as though her permanent wave had been carved in wood.

Is this your car? she asked.

Elainey, licensed driver, drove us to the hospital. Marco stretched out in the front passenger seat, Mamma glowering next to me in backseat. Elainey talked merrily about how she had been trained in CPR when she toured with the USO and how her own mother had suffered with chronic lung disease and she knew all about episodes and treatment and such things, not to worry, everything will settle down and be back as normal, zipiitty doo-dah-day. What Marco needed was swimming lessons. Swimming, don't you know, to develop the lung capacity. (And goodness gracious, while we were at the hospital, maybe ChiChi could have that eye checked.)

I fingered the hickey on my neck. Mamma scowled out the window and tapped her knuckles on the armrest. Her lips moved in prayer. Then she fired the story at us about her husband who came home from Germany after serving in Army Intelligence, how they gave him a new leg of poly-urethane, and how, by mistake, they sent the old wooden one to her address on the Mississippi Flats. She couldn't read English when the telegram came, she thought he was dead, and then found out he, the *diavolo,* wanted a divorce so he could marry an American woman, a registered nurse from Spring Lake Park.

She clutched the back of the seat in front of her. She signed the papers, she said, insisted on alimony, and he married the American woman, just like the opera, *Madama Butterfly.* Did we not think she suffered? Eh? But did she throw herself upon the sword like Madama Butterfly? No! She lived for her children! *Per gli bambini!* Bruno's parents dismissed Mamma's marriage to Bruno like so much crumbs under the table. She was abandoned with two children, a poor immigrant woman who couldn't speak English, *puh!* But he kept his promise to pay alimony, which she saved for her children when they grew up. She had SAVED the money, SAVED it, in First National Bank for her CHILDREN, and were they grateful? NO.

All this she shouted in the presence of a complete stranger.

Trembling, she lifted her chin, jerked her head to the window. She was finished. *Punto.*

*M*arco painted pictures of one-legged ghosts in blue, then he'd paint over the pictures in Franz Kline slashes of white and black. He dripped and threw paint like Jackson Pollock using only the color red. He flogged at the canvases like de Kooning. He created macabre Dalí-esque dioramas of dead rodents and broken clocks.

We walked around dull, quivery, wondering who we were. We had a million questions about Bruno. Where he lived, what kind of person he was, what he looked like, what did he do for a living, why didn't he ever try to contact his children?

Mamma went to church and sat in the back twisting the beads, click! Click! She wept, she developed lines around her mouth, lines fragile as cobwebs.

And she cooked.

On the hottest days when the apartment walls turned oily with sweat, she cooked. She baked. Onna now stayed with us at least three nights a week. Her legs and spine gave her bad pain, she was finding it harder to walk, but she didn't complain. Mamma cooked diet food for her, beans without salt, soup without chicken fat.

ChiChi, honey, Onna said in her Advice Giving Voice, you need to forgive your mother. She's a woman locked inside herself. She loves you, in her way.

Sure. Of course. Natch. (Onna, *you're* my mother.)

I thought of Mr. Metamere telling me how Mamma loved me after she beat me up and broke my nose.

Onna went on in her high nasally voice: It had taken her a long time to forgive her own mother, she said, for selling her to that traveling theater company in Puglia. But she realized her mother did it out of love. Did I know how many major surgeries Onna's had? Thirty-four, not counting the braces, the orthodontia, the ear infections, the bouts with pneumonia, oh, on and on. She could never have survived life in the village. See? ChiChi had to forgive her mother.

Okay. I'll go to Confession.

That's my girl.

Onna could no longer drive because of trouble with her back and the brace which no longer fit right, so she sold her car and trailer. She spent her days sorting through their possessions, cleaning, throwing out, donating.

I went to Mass every morning to plead with God not to let me be pregnant. People have sex, they get babies. Holy Minerva, is that what I had? Sex?

Marco's romance with Suzette lost its steam and we were all relieved when her parents figured it wasn't worth it to press charges for the incident at Rocco's. What did I care? I could be *with child*. I wanted to confide my fears to Onna, but she had turned her attention to Ed. Such a sensitive, boy, so misunderstood, dear thing. (Had they all gone nutso?) Eddie didn't need a police record, Onna said, the poor boy.

I didn't tell my dread to Marco either. He still blubbered on about Elainey. He hadn't forgotten what she did for him. Her body on top of him on the sidewalk like that. Every once in a while he said to me: That was pretty spectacular what your friend did, don't you think?

She's *not* my friend, Marco.

I started taking modern dance classes five times a week.

To take my mind off the horrors of impending motherhood. Onna said my technique was improving. She said I had transcended the slapstick. I was becoming an artiste.

I came home from my dance class after staying late to practice and I found Sunny sitting on our front step.

You rob a bank or something? he said. Taking a cab?

He smoked a hand-rolled cigarette.

Ya. Sure. What do you want?

I got something to show you, he said. He handed me a folded newspaper clipping from his shirt pocket. An obituary and a photo of Mitchell Rodman 1890–1961. Restaurateur . . . Heart attack . . . Survived by . . .

You seen this yet?

. . . No.

I reached for the paper as though it had jaws.

You want to hear how it happened, ChiChi?

Did somebody kill him? I hope?

You decide, he said.

I waited, staring at the photograph of a man in a suit and tie looking like a man who could run for office.

Sunny began the story not in the newspaper about how Rodman was in Fiji with some young chick and he had a heart attack in the hotel bed.

Good, I said.

Wait. Listen to this! The chick he was with panicked and flew back to the States without so much as calling the front desk for a doctor. She ran out of that hotel as fast as she could. The maid found his body stinking up the place two days later, on account of the Do Not Disturb sign on the door. What you think! said Sunny laughing. If that chick had called a doctor, the bastard might still be alive.

I won't be lighting a candle for him, I said. And how do you know all this is true?

The chick confessed, and I got connections, said Sunny.

I invited him inside to wait with this news for Mamma to come home but he said he had an appointment with a client. He was selling life insurance.

Give your mamma a kiss from me. He handed me the obituary.

Dead. Rodman was dead. Why didn't I feel vindicated? Or at least relieved? Nothing like a lovely scandal to smear a guy's headstone. The thought of Rodman brought his stink back. I could feel his hands, his sour breath. I threw up.

Arturo wanted Sunday at our apartment to be a feast day. He reminded Mamma that back home in Italy his whole village ate together on Sundays. In the summer after church they put up the tables outside on the street and ate all day long!

Men eat. The women cook, said Onna.

Manny, Ed, and Elainey sat at the table with us. Mamma prepared *cappuccio imbottito,* her special stuffed cabbage with lamb and pine nuts, a vegetable minestrone, and her home-made *maltagliati,* noodles that she had rolled out, cut, and hung to dry on the backs of the kitchen chairs early that the morning before Mass.

It was festive, like a holiday. Manny sat at the table, glum and pristine, his usual self. If he said anything, he directed it to Onna or Ed. Mamma was fluttery, expansive. She told jokes about donkeys in hats. She sang "Volare" and wanted everyone to join in. She dismissed the matter of Bruno and was pleased about Rodman's death. She was, after all, in the will.

The table was crowded with dishes, fresh arugula, basil, and cilantro, Parmesan and Romano cheeses, Mamma's fried *pane.* Washed down with red and white wine and sparkling water, everyone sighed, bloated and contented. Then the

dessert, a cold ricotta pudding, which Onna could not touch
due to her diet.

Onna remembered in her village how they ate *maltagliati*
from a wood trough. All afternoon. Imagine. Ten, twenty
people bent over a trough outside under the trees, their bellies swelling with joy!

Were you ever in Italy, Manny? Arturo wanted to know.

Manny's face hardened.

Yeah. In the war.

The fan whirring on top of the refrigerator. The room
hot.

Arturo negotiated a spoon into the pudding.

I waited. It felt like a few months passed before Elainey
cleared her throat, asked for the cream for her coffee.

I said I had an announcement to make. About Bruno.

Now? Here? ChiChi, be cool, said Marco.

Here's what I have decided, I said. I don't want one penny
of the money Mamma squirreled away in the First National
Bank for us. To me it's unclean money born of a lie and I
don't want one single penny. Marco, you can have it all.

The refrigerator kicked on. A stray cat scratched at the
screen. Mamma slid a peach slice onto her fork, raised it to
her lips.

Then I don't want the money either, Marco said. It's supposed to be both ours. Our *legacy*, so-called.

Manny asked for another glass of wine, the red.

I'll work and earn my money *honestly*, I said.

Mamma's fork fell with a clink.

Me, too! said Marco.

Manny picked at a tooth with the nail of his little finger.

Mr. Theilberg offered me a booking, I said, in Wisconsin.
Eau Claire.

Arturo's face brightened. You're leaving home?

For two weeks.

What? What's this? said Marco.

It's a nightclub, actually. I'll be dancing in the chorus. $150 a week.

Nightclub! gasped Onna. But you're still a baby! You're not eighteen yet.

You're sixteen, said Mamma.

Seventeen, I reminded her. You've never known when it was my birthday, Mamma.

Nightclub! My daughter dance in nightclub! She sank back into the chair, slapped her forehead with the palm of her hand.

I signed the contract, Mamma. Mr. Theilberg says this booking will be sort of a stepping stone to bigger things for me.

Good going, smirked Elainey. There's money in club work. Even though I don't quite picture ChiChi as the club type.

Mamma turned to Marco with a look that said he was the man of the family, he should do something.

I'll check this out, he said. What's the name of the club?

What's to check? I signed the contract!

Elainey asked if I'd be doing my clown act.

Not exactly. But this was an opportunity, a *start*, $150 a week wasn't exactly pigeon droppings—

Not doing the clown act? What then?

Tap dancing.

I had never had a tap lesson in my life. I didn't know a shuffle from a hop.

The stitches were removed from my eye and surrounding area leaving the eyelid drooped. I looked like a half-awake basset hound with a lot of hair. Mr. Theilberg said I should get rid of the patch, I was doing chorus now, people wanted to see a face. But when he looked closer he changed his mind. An eye patch on a female is sexy as all hell, he said.

Bernice, the director of Tops in Taps, and the choreographer of our nightclub show, said the routines were easy enough to learn, she herself having been one of the top tappers in the Aqua Follies as well as the St. Paul Winter Carnival. And besides, I had a cute little figure. That's what counted. I would do just fine as the newest member of the Spitfire Girls.

I wanted to know why Mr. Theilberg hadn't hired me for the Aqua Jesters, the Aquatennial Parade clowns.

You're no *normal* clown, he woofed. Normal clowns don't wear toe shoes, they aren't baton twirling Marcel Marceaus. Normal clowns act like *clowns*, they throw confetti and do tricks. They do bits! Where's your three-foot cigar, your dog and baby buggy? Where's your sledgehammer and peanut routine?

I'm not that kind of clown, I said.

He grunted. Look. If you want to get work as a clown, prop a ladder up against a horse, sweep him off with a broom. That's funny! Hang your laundry on the tight rope walker's line, now that's funny! See what I mean? What you do is, well, concert stuff—and you got to be a *name* to do concert. I told him I had been taught by the best and I was an original.

He laughed. Original. Original is for paint jobs on cars.

Ever hear of Omo and Onna? I asked him.

The midgets?

No. The achondroplastic dwarfs.

Ya. I booked 'em. They were about the only midgets around in the midwest. Damn funny, too. I heard Omo died. Too bad.

Said like he had just dripped bacon fat on his collar.

Too bad.

Part Three

The Spitfire Girls drove to Eau Claire in a Chevy van driven by Bernice's boyfriend, Max. Five young dancers with big show business aspirations sitting like children staring out the windows of the van, two of the girls still sporting retainers on their teeth. We looked of the age to be still wearing pajamas with feet.

I had packed my things in the suitcase we brought with us from Ellis Island.

Marco laughed when he saw it. I thought that thing died, he said.

It did, I said.

I concentrated on all the money I'd be making so I wouldn't be so nervous. I'd save every penny so Marco and I could get our own place and get away from *her*. If I was pregnant, Oh God, Oh Saint Cecilia, Oh Dearest Jesus— Marco would understand. Yes, he'd understand. Marco would help me.

I sat in the backseat of the van by the window, watching the towns pass by us like so many candles on a flat grassy cake. Houses and fields passed us on as though they were on their way someplace, lawns and flower beds, clipped hedges, dogs barking around the muscled trunks of trees, a boy straddling a bicycle riding backwards—and the sky, more sky than I'd ever seen at one time.

So this was where they kept the sky, here at the Minnesota-Wisconsin border at Hudson.

Bruno. Why hadn't he ever tried to see us? Did he know I owned a part of him in the closet at home?

The Annual Italian Pepper Festival was in full swing in North Hudson, but nobody wanted to stop. Silent faces stared out the window. A light rain began as we passed the towns of River Falls and Menomonie, the tires on the pavement making slick sounds like cracking china dishes.

The Dragon Lady Club in Eau Claire was a dark room with low ceilings, rock walls, black leather chairs, and eerie blue lighting. It was not an establishment you'd bring children to. The stage was smaller than we had rehearsed. I was the end girl and had to squeeze myself into the line, sometimes hitting the beaded curtain with my kicks.

The band of four musicians was situated below the stage and the drummer, a man with eyes like eggplants, looked up our skirts and ogled our fannies. I could barely define an audience. Two or three couples at tables and a bar lined with men smoking cigarettes and drinking beer.

I couldn't get the hang of tap dancing. Even after a week of rehearsal with no pay, the simplest steps confused me. The shoes felt clubby on my feet and even the high kicks, which I could do with ease, became awkward jerky heaves of the leg. My alignment was off. I need not have worried. It wasn't the dancing that got me the job. The first night we were ushered out to the bar and told to have a good time, told to mix. Get them ordering mixed drinks, order a drink called C'est Vous, which was a champagne cocktail, only without the champagne. Ginger ale and bitters in a champagne glass.

Mix? What on earth? How was I, a girl who hadn't even dated to *mix*? I looked at the bar, grown men, men with creased necks, men with receding hairlines, hairy knuckles, wedding rings. Now I understood what Bernice meant when she said not to worry about my tap dancing skills. You got what counts, she had said. A cute little figure.

You girls got it good, she told us. You keep your clothes on, you got good choreography, nothing raunchy, we don't even have a stripper on the bill.

The other Spitfire Girls didn't seem to have any trouble mixing. They slid onto bar stools, chatted gaily, ordered C'est Vous, tossed their heads hee-heeing like they were at a party with rich relatives. I reached into my purse for a package of gum.

Buy you a drink, honey? said a man with a gold tooth.

I wore one of three dresses I owned, the light green seersucker cotton with the Peter Pan collar and full skirt. I teetered on a pair of high heels borrowed from Elainey.

Ya, okay, I said. I'll have what you're having.

The bartender grimaced and brought me a bottle of Pabst. Bound to the stake with Ed Looz would be better than this. I had forgotten we weren't supposed to order beer.

The music began again and a short, fat comedian told dirty jokes for thirty minutes. The sound and sight of him made me nauseous, dizzy. How could I do another show in this place? Four shows a night with a man who, if he was bleeped, would be verbless. He reminded me of Mitchell Rodman. I would remember to carry Metamere's knife in my dress pocket.

The Pabst man asked me if I'd care for a smoke.

No, I hate smoke.

Oh? And what do you love, hmm, huh?

The lights dimmed, the drummer swung at the drums. The bass and piano swung into "Dancing in the Dark." Couples moved out onto the dance floor. The Pabst man moved in closer, his cigarette stuck to his lower lip like a thumb. Wanna dance?

At the end of the first week I was shell-shocked, dazed. I spent the afternoons taking long walks in downtown Eau Claire, I bought magazines I didn't open or read, I bought food I threw away. Most of the time I stayed in the room I shared with two other Spitfire Girls, who treated me like I was invisible. If I was taking a bath or a shower, they filed right into the bathroom and used the toilet.

I didn't know how to flirt with men. I didn't know how to talk to them. What did men talk about? What was in their heads besides sex and dirty jokes? Football? What did I know about football? Cars? I had hardly even ridden in one.

Did these grown men still dream of being astronauts or dog mushers? What had they settled for?

Mister, I don't want another drink, and touch me again and I'll rip your friggin hand off.

The club owner wanted to see me in his office.

This your first club job?

No. I've worked lots of clubs.

He leaned across his small metal desk, his cufflinks big as your great toe. See here, he said. You can't wear those little girl things here. Buy some decent clothes.

Sure.

And do something with that hair. No ponytails! How old are you?

Twenty-one.

And I'm Genghis Khan. Let's see your I.D.

I opened my purse, took out my wallet.

What's this? He said. Your name ain't Chloe McPhee.

That's what it says, isn't it?

Hey, I know a fake I.D. when I see one.

He thought for a minute, scowled. The name stinks. From

now on you're Cleo. Cleo Patra. Good name for you with that face.

I shopped for dresses with my first paycheck. I bought two—shiny, tight things with low necklines, the kind Elainey would love. I made an appointment at a hair salon, had my hair swept up in a French twist. It took all day.

I bought sunglasses, sling-back high heels like Grenadine Fletcher wore, lavender perfume. I examined my body in the mirror for a bulging of the stomach. Every day I imagined it to spread out like a giant potato and my life to be consigned to diapers and another fatherless person.

My room didn't have a telephone so I had to call Mamma from a cigar store two blocks away. How was Marco doing in the heat? Was he getting his shots, avoiding milk? On one call Mamma gave me the news that Arturo's cousin, Leonardo, who they called Nardo, was here from Sicily, and he was staying in my room now that I was gone.

Mamma, I'll only be gone two weeks.

Selfish ChiChi.

But it's my room. What about me?

Always ChiChi think only about ChiChi, said Mamma.

Marco said he and Elainey were swimming every week in an indoor pool. They planned to drive over to see me. I thought of his reaction if he saw the place I worked in with the neon sign outside, and among the girls' photos, mine in living color wearing a sequined bikini and the name CLEO PATRA beneath it.

LIVE! ON OUR STAGE
BEAUTIFOL SPITFIRE GIRLS
HOT 2-NITE! SIZZLING 4-U SEEING IS BELEIVING

One of my roommates was a thin, paste-face girl named Gladys Chechnik.

Where you from? she asked in an attempt to be somewhat friendly.

Minneapolis, I said. Northeast Minneapolis. Tar Town.

Oh. Me, Duluth. 4th Street.

She told me this was her first job in a nightclub, too. She was really a ballet dancer and would I like to go to ballet class with her sometime?

Sure, I said. Absolutely, yes. Definitely.

The Spitfire Girls were housed in a hotel two blocks from the Dragon Lady Club on a narrow side street of bars and all-night diners. Our room was on the first floor near the ice machine.

Gladys chewed on chunks of ice and told me her mother was one-half Cherokee so that made her one-fourth, right? She asked it like she wasn't sure of the math. She had an odd way of talking. Normal one minute, then a lapse into baby talk the next. On our first night at the club she wore jeans and moccasins to work, a ballet bag with her dress and shoes slung over her shoulder.

She was called into the office.

She bore a dopey expression, as though everything in life was beyond her, and what did it matter.

That is, until nighttime. At once she became a little girl playing dress-up. We sat at the bar with two insurance sales-men from Madison and she flirted and hustled drinks like a machine. She laughed, giggled, jabbered, danced, gyrated— and kept drinks coming across the bar in a blizzard of glasses and ice cubes. She ran up a tab that outdid any girl in the place. She was a genius at this.

In the nights to come Gladys began wearing false eye-lashes, shiny lip gloss, nylons with seams. On the dance floor

she wiggled and twirled her body, and I thought it looked
like she was actually having fun. Men loved it when she
talked baby talk in their necks.

When she saw Metamere's knife in my purse she said, Her
is just a cwazy widdow wommann.

One morning while the Spitfire Girls slept, I looked out
the window and there was Gladys, hurrying up the street,
her thin, watery hair tied back in a rubber band, wearing
jeans and tennis shoes and lugging the ballet bag over her
shoulder.

I raced out to join her.

And I was in for another shock. When Gladys slipped into
her toe shoes and strode onto the ballet floor, a magical thing
transpired and she was at once a perfect combination of muscle, technique, and arrogance. She moved like a nymph,
fiercely serious. Her body stretched and reached with control
and grace and to watch her execute a particularly difficult
combination was like seeing feathers wafting weightless
through the air. Her turns were sharp and clean, her leaps
high and easy, every movement precise, energetic, and natural. When she raised a leg in extension, the limb seemed
to remove itself from her body, higher and higher, until it
held fast above her head, the knee straight as a rod, her back
strong, her neck and head steady and elongated. Then suddenly she was posed *en pointe* for the turns, down to fourth
position, and in a spinning blur she completed six turns in
place.

She said she planned to audition for the Joffrey Ballet the
following spring and there was no doubt in my mind that
they'd accept her. She took this job as a Spitfire Girl to earn
some money, same as me. Right?

We went shopping together and she bought strapless, tight

dresses and high spike heels. She had her hair curled and dyed red. At night sitting with a customer you'd see her in her sexy dresses laughing and flipping her red hair and ordering drinks left and right. I bought dresses, too, dresses cut low in the back, short and sassy. I bought spike heels like hers. I bought false breasts and false eyelashes. I felt like Grenadine Fletcher must have felt in her big, clumsy, buttery body.

Cleo, those eyelashes do wonders for that weird eye of yours, she said. Were you born with that eye?

I thought maybe the new clothes would make me less inhibited, but I couldn't get the hang of dressing up and playing nice to strangers.

During the day in ballet class, the other Gladys surfaced: serious and dedicated to dance.

Cleo, you're a great dancer, she told me after class one day.

Me? I was thinking you're the great dancer.

Yes, I'm good. But what you have is imagination and spirit.

Her dopey expression was gone.

Cleo, your technique is interesting, but what is beautiful is your interpretation. Your dancing is, well, mesmerizing.

She sounded intelligent!

And that night at the club she told me again, Her is just a cwazy widdow wommann.

In her red hair and falsies, she talked baby talk, giggled, flirted, and held court like she'd been doing this all her life.

Hey, Cleo? You in there?

We were in the ladies room at the club; she at the sink, me in the stall.

It must have been two A.M.

Uh huh, I'm here.

Cleo, do me a favor. Don't call me Gladys anymore, she said. Call me Flame. Okay?

Call you Flame?

Yeah. Flame Desire.

Well, ring the bells, Flame Desire! I shouted out. Her words hadn't registered because I, Cleo Patra, a.k.a. ChiChi Maggiordino, was not—(*grazie a Dio, Sacre Madre, Gesù, tutti*)—pregnant.

Payday didn't bring the money I had figured I'd be raking in, what with the deductions, costume rental, room rent, agent's fee, and mandatory tips to the bartenders and musicians, plus our food. I hadn't accounted for living expenses either, things like the hairdresser, soap, Kotex, makeup.

After the last show one night a trucker from Sioux Falls bought me my third glass of ginger ale and laid his arm around me like we were somehow involved. I braced myself for the come-on when he stared at my hands in astonishment. Well, looka here at those fingers, wouldja!

You chew your nails like a kid! he said.

At once I was called to the office again.

We don't want no trouble here, Cleo. You better be ready to show your I.D. Do something about those hands. Grownups don't chew their nails.

Bernice arrived to choreograph new routines and bring new costumes. I was wearing Godiva false fingernails and couldn't work the zipper on the costume.

So how's things, Cleo? Here, turn around.

Just dandy, I said.

You'll get the hang of things, don't worry. Where else could a girl like you with that eye and your looks earn $150 a week for such nice, easy work?

The Spitfire Girls were held over for another two weeks at the Dragon Lady. Okay, it meant more money. I'd save up, I'd show Mamma. Maybe I'd buy Marco and me a car, and maybe I'd learn how to swim, too.

The other girls had dates which they referred to as Johns. The girls wore glittery jewelry and had a special deal going with the bartenders who pointed out men at the bar they called Live Ones. These girls avoided me like an unnamed virus.

By the middle of the third week, tap dancing started to come easier for me. I knew the steps now, and when Bernice gave us two new routines I learned the combinations faster.

Bernice, in her short shorts and spangled halter and heavy legs, had the body of a true tap dancer, the thick ankles, the flippy arms, the white toothsome grin. (Why did tap dancers always grin like that? We were like those contestants in beauty pageants who smile their heads off with the message, I'm Incredibly Dumb And You Can Have Me.)

Dancers have a way of behaving toward each other. It's a pecking order thing. Dancers judge the whole world by their own abilities. Alicia Markova, Baryshnikov, and Gwen Verdon were great and worthwhile human beings. A person who couldn't do a decent time step? Well!

The following week, Bernice enthused, Cleo, just look at you! I can see the Dragon Lady has made a real woman out of you.

Must be the French twist. The scowl.

And I found a new hair spray. It could caulk tile.

Say, why don't you think about doing a solo act, Cleo? You've got the *body*. Those nice legs. You could make two, maybe three hundred a week, and if you headline, even more. Plus, you earn tips.

Tips? Now I was paying tips out of my salary.

No, dear, the customers, they tip you.

For what?

She laughed.

Oh. I got it. Bernice, I am a clown. NOT a stripper.

That evening as we dressed for the show, half my Godiva nails fallen off, I told Flame about Bernice's suggestion. Her hand stopped in midair. Her eyes widened. I could see the wheels of her mind chugging.

I know what you're thinking, Gladys Chechnik. But you're a serious ballet dancer. You're headed for the Joffrey Ballet.

Ya but, she nodded, staring at herself in the mirror—but a solo act, that would be *frabjous*.

The sixth week we got another raise, $165 a week.

I wrote letters. I wrote to Marco, Manny Looz, Onna, Jennifer, and finally I even wrote to Tyrone. Only Marco wrote back.

Some of the men actually asked for me by name when they came in to the Dragon Lady. Where's that little pistol, Cleo? Tell her I want to buy her a drink!

I had earned a reputation. When fingers slipped under my skirt, or an eager body on the dance floor pressed in too close for a feel, I gave a quick chop of the hand intended to hurt. At first it surprised me that some men liked that.

One night before the show I sprawled across my bed, picking at a hangnail and reading the latest *Theatre Arts Maga-*

zine when Flame Desire emerged from the shower and positioned herself in a seductive pose, mouth puckered sideways, chin trembly.

I was thinking, she said. There's probably people who have shined their shoes on our bedspreads. Blown their noses on the sheets. Let's move out of here.

I gave a sigh and returned to my cuticles. Yanked at a hangnail.

She poked her foot at the carpet. Her shouldn't bite her nails. Her could get germs.

Brilliant minds bite their nails, I said.

She fell into riotous laughter, falling backwards on the bed, slapping her thighs.

Us is soul mates, she burbled in her annoying baby talk. Me and yousie. I looked at her, the little girl profile, five months out of high school like me. We took this job for the money. Okay. That made us practically blood relatives.

Gladys/Flame wanted to do everything with me, including share her dates. Her is such a prude, she sulked, and continued to pester me with pleas to double-date her johns. What could be worse, I wondered, than spending one extra minute with those disgusting men and Flame's baby talk.

At each of my refusals Gladys became more indignant. Then she was angry, downright angry.

Do you know what the other girls call you, Cleo?

Do tell.

Here's what, and don't take it personal. They call you a PROUD ASS DAGO!

Where do they get off calling me proud?

You think you're better than us poor working girls. And you think I'm stupid. You treat me like I don't have a brain in my noggin. Well, it just so happens that I am a high school graduate, for your information.

Her voice was high, shaking.

So that hardly qualifies me for stupid. I happen to think YOU'RE stupid because YOU don't grab hold of a business opportunity when it stares you in the snoot.

Maybe she was right. Maybe this was the only work I was cut out to do. Maybe this was as good as it gets.

Flame became pals with a dancer named Sizzle. I saw them touching each other, teasing, flirting. Well, so be it.

You ain't nothing but a cold fish, Sizzle said to me, her first and last words to me.

The engagement at the Dragon Lady Club lasted for thirteen weeks, until October when the weather started getting cold. Men began staying home or working late in the colder weather. Business tapered off. The eager-to-spend customers who clustered at the bar each night thinned out. I imagined them, these men and their wallets, out from under our blue lights watching TV at home eating chips and dip with wives. I thought of them shopping for fishing tackle, buying school clothes for the kids, having the in-laws over for dinner, singing in church. And the Spitfire Girls moved on.

I arrived back home to a Minneapolis exhausted by summer, the streets steaming with weariness, the buildings forlorn in the remaining thrusts of heat. I could smell November waiting in the wings, like a bath and clean clothes. I would always love autumn in Minneapolis, when the days shrunk into themselves, and the nights were cool and damp so every maple and oak leaf could be smelled clear to Nicollet Avenue, where they were tearing down old hotels to make way for a mall. Every lilac bush around doorways on the lakes spread their aroma as far as Washington Avenue and the soup kitchens. Minneapolis wore new shoes in autumn, it dressed up and perfumed itself. It washed its socks and danced at night to the sounds of crickets retreating to their pockets of mud, to fires crackling in bonfires along the lakes, to high school football teams stirring up cheers, and the new school semester beginning.

Everything in autumn seemed to be going back to school in the Twin Cities. You could hear the sound of new books opening on desks, you could hear leaves falling on window-panes of classrooms, you could feel the anxiety of making the grade, always that. And autumn in Minneapolis was also about what you didn't think about and what wasn't clear to the eye yet. Oh, you sniffed at it in the night when the temperature dropped and you had to put on another sweater, or you allowed it a fleeting consideration when you rode on

a bus and had to ask the person in the seat ahead to please
close their window. You got out your wool-lined gloves and
your jacket with the alpaca hood. You talked about the
weather.

I arrived home on an October evening in 1961 wearing
my snug-fitting tight black sheath, rhinestones at my neck,
high heels, my hair lacquered up and back in a French twist.
Perched on my nose were my new horn-rimmed dark
glasses, which I bought at the Rexall in Eau Claire.

ChiChi?

None other. (Big lipsticky grin.)

I slid the Ellis Island suitcase across the kitchen floor, settled it against the wall.

Mamma, Arturo, and Marco sat at the kitchen table. Their
faces stopped like a camera had polarized them in place.

It was one of the longest moments in the history of our
kitchen.

Finally I said, Thanks for meeting me at the station.

ChiChi, *figlia,* is that *you*? Mamma's voice tinny and small.

Marco rose to give me a hug. I wanted to inhale him,
keep him close to me until the jangling inside my body
stopped.

A kiss in the air near my two cheeks from Mamma, same
from Arturo.

Well!

Mamma removed a bowl from the cupboard, brought it
to the table.

Will you eat *zuppa,* ChiChi?

There it was, my name. Thanks, Mamma, I said.

Marco set a chair in place for me. The air was nervous,
strange.

Guess what, ChiChi. You mamma, she now is head chef
at Cucina Garibaldi. Pretty good, eh?

Auguri! Congratulations, Mamma. But you already told me that on the phone.

Why were they so nervous?

Arturo, I said. How's your cousin from Napoli?

Fine, oh he's fine. *Bene.* We all work at Cucina Garibaldi.

Except me, said Marco. I got a job at S&L selling shoes. But then you already know that, too.

So everybody has jobs. *Va bene,* I said. But why are you telling all this again?

They were quiet. Marco patted the back of my hand. We missed you, he said.

Liar. How's Elainey?

Great. She's great.

Quiet again.

Maybe it was the way I looked. Sophisticated.

Mamma said, You can have you room, ChiChi. Nardo, he can sleep on couch.

I'll have some of that wine, I said.

I ate the soup and went outside to sit on the back steps. October could be a comfort, a friend you ran into occasionally, yet never asked more of it than it could give you.

Today was my birthday. I was eighteen.

*M*amma's espresso and a plate of polenta in the first slanted rays of morning, was I really home? I stood on the back porch feeling like a diseased person on a new antibiotic.

On the nightstand by my bed was a package wrapped in paper painted with hundreds of stars and the name ChiChi. A birthday present from Marco.

Think I'd forget? said the card.

Inside was a silver charm bracelet with a charm engraved with *Gotta Dance.*

I was alone. Everyone had left early that morning for school and work. The empty apartment smelled like men's shoes. I thought about calling Tyrone.

Mamma was now working as chef at an Italian restaurant with tablecloths on the tables. Marco, a high school senior. I still hadn't met Nardo, the man whose hairs I found in my sheets, and whose shirts hung on hangers from my bedroom door, whose shoes stank up my room.

Mamma liked the silk robe I brought her, but the cheese I brought her from Wisconsin she'd give to the Polish girls who lived upstairs. She preferred her cheese imported from Italy. She distrusted the cows from Wisconsin. She said in Italy the priests, they bless the cows. In Italy the cows so blessed they have their own Mass! Arturo screeched with laughter at that one.

Marco's paintings lined the walls of the living room, new abstracts after Dubuffet and Larry Rivers. Brazen strokes of color and texture smothering rendered details. A portrait of Mamma wearing a dress I'd never seen before, her hands folded on her lap and her hair arranged in tight rivulets around her face. The skin was a metallic grey, the mouth bunched up in a fist. It unsettled me to think that their lives had pushed on ahead without me. That Mamma showed up on canvas like a pissed-off Pompeian doyenne.

I dialed Onna's number. I thought I'd take a taxi over to her place, bring her the pretty satin quilt I bought her. No answer.

Marco's room had changed. In place of Dracula and skull and bones were Castelli Gallery posters of Rauschenberg's collages and Roy Lichtenstein prints. Photos and drawings of Elainey were taped around the edges of his mirror, which I ignored. I wondered if he still had the broken WWII gun in his closet. Had he gotten rid of the wooden leg?

I felt a haunting fear of Bruno. Who was he? Where was he? Now that we knew about him, I wondered if he'd make his appearance. We still knew nothing about him. Which suited me fine. It was the wooden leg I wanted.

To hold it.

Just for a little minute.

A few seconds would be enough. The cool metallic smell, its coldness, and the hard shank of the misshapen calf, paint peeling at the top of the thigh.

I opened Marco's closet. I shouldn't snoop in his closet. We had boundaries we never crossed, an unspoken respect for each other's things, for our private space. When we shared the same room in Tar Town, we had respect. What I was doing was wrong.

Still.

I moved aside the hanging pants and shirts, the winter jacket, the school sweats, felt along the back wall for the leg.

I'm just looking for Pappa, Marco. Don't be angry.

I put my hands in his shoes, clapped them together. A small pile of his laundry lay in the corner, socks, shorts, undershirts. Pieces, parts, tops and bottoms, smelling like erasure crumbs and chalk.

What need did I have for sunlight or noise? Me, a chorus girl who netted a grand total of $240 for thirteen weeks of hard labor and humiliation. I inched myself farther into the closet—ah, there it was. My hand between Marco's hanging pants, the buckle of the leather strap. Against the wall, oh lovely wall. I pulled at the leg, held it. I was ten years old again and I believed in pictures found in rocks, I believed Saint Anthony would answer my prayers, I had my Nonna and my rituals, and I would keep us all alive and happy. I would not cry, no, Pappa, women always cry. A strong woman sings. My singing came out like Eeeeeeeeeeeeeeeeeeeeeeee . . .

Something or someone moved in the room. I should have heard it, should have been more alert. I sang, or moaned, on, and Nardo, who had come home for a nap between his shifts at the restaurant, heard what he was certain, being from Napoli, was a thief in the house. He picked up a chair, unsheathed the knife at his ankle, and crept into Marco's room. I didn't hear his feet scraping across the floor, or see the shadow. The closet door winged open and I looked up to see a gangly dark-skinned man staring down at me with eyes big as tires.

I gave him a friendly *Buon giorno*.

Buon giorno youself! he said.

I think that was the moment I fell in love with Leonardo Della Vecchia from Napoli.

I crawled out of the closet on my hands and knees and sat on the floor, looking up at his wonderful, wild-eyed face. He wore his hair in a hairnet, which made him look as though his head had been torched. He was the color of oak. I smelled rosemary and lime.

I shivered. I'm ChiChi.

A grunt. I am Leonardo.

Yes. You are.

Marco informed me later Nardo was a man of no skills, a failed farmer who tried his hand at carpentry and couldn't drive a nail straight into a plank of pine to save his soul; came to America where the money was to work on the railroad with a cousin. But when he got to Chicago, he couldn't wield a pickax on the extra gang and the Sioux Line fired him, so he hitched boxcars to Minneapolis to find his cousin, Arturo.

Now he cleared the restaurant tables of dirty dishes, replaced the tablecloths. Even this he had trouble with. Arturo warned him to work faster, why did he have to stop filling his bus pan to scratch his shoulder or smooth his mustache? *Per favore, Nardo!*

And he had attitude. He distrusted me from our first meeting in Marco's closet, but he didn't tell anyone about it. You'd hear him playing a game of *Scopa* at the kitchen table with Arturo, passing judgment on the world, not a good word for any country or world leader, *but* when he tilted his head a certain way and the light hit the clean angle of his jaw and you could see the shine in the fold of his eyelids, the bells rang in Bangkok, birds sang in Leningrad, bagpipes partied in Cork, violins rhapsodized in Rome, and accordions trolled in Fridley.

I tried calling Onna again. Still no answer. Two days passed before I found out why everyone behaved as though

I were something delicate and foreign. Why they smiled for no reason, became suddenly quiet in the middle of conversation, told me things I already knew. I didn't know what to make of it. What was it? Bruno? Was something afoot with Bruno? Mamma said no, nothing, *niente*.

Onna's number again. For the umpteenth time. No answer.

ChiChi . . . Mamma fidgeted. ChiChi, there's something—

Now what.

Ah!—*Non fa niente.*

What do you mean, never mind? What? What is it?

Dai, ChiChi. They hadn't wanted to tell me earlier, she said, because they worried the news might ruin my engagement in Eau Claire, which was so successful, being held over and all.

(Successful!)

ChiChi, sit down. Marco has something to tell you.

ChiChi—Marco began. ChiChi—Onna died the last day of August.

In her sleep.

Mamma was sorry, they all were sorry. They withheld the news out of respect for my work.

My *work.*

A service had been held at Our Lady of Mount Carmel church even though Onna wasn't a member. She was buried next to Omo in Hillside Cemetery.

She left an envelope for me with a color photograph of the three of us posed in front of their circus trailer. I'm doing a side split with my hands in the air. Tah-dah! Onna had scribbled at the bottom of the picture. Our *Carina*, June 2nd.

Also in the envelope was a key with a note. *ChiChi will know what to do,* it said.

The weight of the stone inside my chest was more than I could carry. I was unable to speak. I couldn't get up to walk. My bad eye burned. The thought of never seeing the loving gentle face of my Onna again! The thought of it!

Every tear I had never cried flew out of me. They say you can cry yourself dry. Not so.

I should have known Onna wouldn't wait long before joining Omo. I should have been more alert, aware, so I could stop her, so I could argue her into life. When she packed up and sold their everyday items, I should have known what she was thinking. It was my fault. I should have used the Evil Eye.

No, ChiChi, it wasn't your fault! Marco held my shoulders, wiped my face with a kitchen towel. Onna died of heart failure. Her heart just stopped beating. It was her time!

I'm going over there, I said.

No, you're not, Marco argued. It's late and their apartment is in a bad neighborhood.

Don't stop me, I said. I took the bus downtown to their apartment on Harmon Place. The street was dark and a cluster of men lounged on the corner drinking beer and smoking cigarettes. I had to pass them to get to Onna and Omo's building and they whistled, smacked their lips, and two of them followed me to the middle of the block. I turned around and faced them. YOU GUYS ARE BUGGING ME! I yelled. They stopped short, like LaMont and his gang when Marco whacked at his stomach with Metamere's knife, and then they broke into laughter. Fall-down, slap your leg laughter, and I ducked into the front door of Onna and Oma's building. I could hear them cackling and whistling on the street as I climbed the stairs to their apartment.

The apartment had the feel of purposeful abandonment, like the vanishing of the Incas, or an abandoned pulsar. Omo and Onna had been erased.

They kept receipts. Heaps of them, drawers jammed with them. Hundreds of medical receipts. On Onna's little dressing table was a stack of unpaid bills. A telephone bill for $22.50, a Powers Department Store bill for $180.00, notices of termination for unpaid magazine subscriptions. All totaled, Onna died owing this world $371.38.

Omo and Onna were gone and the world had the audacity to go on functioning. That's how it is with death. A drop of water spills from the cup and the cup remains full. What Nonna taught me: Fear is our greatest enemy. Be brave and do hard things. Our Father which art in heaven . . .

What to do with their little museum? The Judy Garland vase, the gifts from Anthony Quinn, José Ferrer. Onna had left most of their collection for me to figure out. Treasures of famous circus dwarfs, their footstools, their costumes and wigs, pinkie rings, props. *ChiChi will know what to do,* she had written in her note.

I heard a scratching sound in the hallway outside the door. I tiptoed across the floor and listened. What the—? Heavy footsteps. Hard breathing, the scraping of a body shifting its weight.

Who's there?

No answer.

Footsteps.

Hello?

Grief can make you stupid. Careful you don't O.D. on the Thorazine again. I found the light switch in the kitchen, the long plastic rod attached to it. Cold and humid, the room smelled of dead leaves. I'd donate everything to a chapter of the Little People of America. I'd send them the scrapbooks, clippings, circus programs, and photographs later. All I'd take now was the box of memorabilia and the rug for Mamma. In the morning I'd go to the bank, withdraw my savings, and pay Onna's bills.

Footsteps again. I peered out the peephole of the door. The circle of hallway was empty. I fastened the chain lock and positioned Onna's chair back under the knob, like I'd seen in the movies.

Maybe Mamma would like the vase from Judy Garland. What to do with the stuff in the refrigerator and under the kitchen sink? The grape jelly, the almost full box of Oxodol?

More shuffling outside the door. I took one of Onna's kitchen knives from the box by the stove and held it in front of me, and with a careful twist of my other hand, the wrist and fingers, I pulled out the chair and unlocked the door. I opened fast and jumped into a karate pose with the knife in front of me.

Jeans, boots. A man over six feet tall with a wide, pocked face, a scowl like a wolf. Breath like boiled peas.

Heyhey, Girlie, he said, stepping back.

Do me a favor, I snarled. Make a move so I can run this knife through your fat gut.

Sheesh. Put that thing down.

I jabbed the knife at him.

You been sneaking around this apartment all night, haven't you? I said.

Nope.

You're lying.

I don't sneak, he said.

I held the knife three inches from his belt buckle. Go back and join your buddies on the street while you've still got a gut.

Look, he puffed, I just want—

I've used a knife before, Bub, back off!

(Here was a man who just plain smelled bad.)

Hey now, look here: he said, getting excited. I extended the rent for a month considering the circumstances and I need to rent this apartment out. I want you people out of there!

I kept the knife aimed at his belly. What did you say?

I'm the landlord, he said. I own the place.

I nodded, stepped back into Onna and Omo's apartment. Oh. Right. Fine. We'll be out by tomorrow. Thank you, and a very good night to you.

I slept that night in a child-sized bed and in the morning woke up to a couple of sparrows twittering on the windowsill. I opened the window and a breeze flapped into the room like four very large wings which paused for the smallest sigh and I swear, patted me on the back.

You threatened the landlord with a butcher knife, ChiChi? You know what that means? Lawsuit! The man could press charges. Assault with a deadly weapon. Lordie Geesh.

Manny Looz shook his head. Our ChiChi is a case, all right.

What's with you and knives anyhow? he wanted to know.

I don't think what I did was unreasonable, I said. A girl has to protect herself, doesn't she? How did I know who the guy was?

It was a disturbing thought that I could have run the knife through the man, easy as I had stabbed Rodman, but such an act, even if he were as dangerous as I imagined, wouldn't bring Omo and Onna back to me.

A contract came in the mail for Cleo Patra and Mamma watched me open it, her face a question mark. ChiChi, who *this* is? Cleo Patra?

Oh, someone I know, I said.

Marco didn't want me to take the booking. You've been gone thirteen weeks already. It's too much.

I must. I'm broke, I said.

Two weeks at $175 a week with five new girls, new routines.

Mamma bristled at the thought of me being broke. There's money for me, she wailed, in First National Bank! Why was I such a stubborn girl?

Bruno's alimony? I already told you, Mamma, I consider that dirty money.

She blinked at the backs of her hands.

Bruno. I refused to connect the name with a real person. You might as well talk to me about Vespucci.

I brushed my hair in a trinity of piles on top of my head, packed my sparkly dresses for a booking in Omaha.

Marco watched me pack. Don't go, he said.

I'm broke, Marco, and the job is decent money. I hope it's the last chorus job I'll have to take. Marco, I've got a plan. An idea. I've been thinking about a show—my own show. These routines I've learned with Omo and Onna, they're all great, I love performing them, and now I'm thinking about one long piece, something framed on story. I'm thinking of creating my own show, my own story. And, Marco, I've got to show Mamma that I can make my own money.

Is this place in Omaha you're going to also a four-star club, like the last place?

Sure. Sure, I lied.

He kissed me on both cheeks and we clung to each other like we did as frightened children.

The club in Omaha, called the Voila!, was a palace compared to the Dragon Lady. A big stage, a dance floor, grand piano, and a six-person band, tiered tables and banquettes, waiters in jackets, no television sets in the bar, this was a place you'd go for an anniversary or Valentine's Day. The atmosphere was warm and welcoming, and wonder of wonders, the dancers were not required to mix. I was surprised, when between shows, the girls went to the bar anyway.

One girl told me, You meet nice people. Why not?

Our choreographer was a black dancer named Roland who came from New York. He gave us routines that made us look good. He worked with lighting, strobes, sound effects, and beautiful costumes. I knew I could learn a lot from this man and so I took notes at every rehearsal and performance.

The dancers stayed in a motel near the club, each with our own private room with kitchenette. I had never stayed in a motel. Every day the maid came and gave me fresh towels and soap like the flat stones you pick up along a path in a train yard.

This was a happy place. The other dancers were friendly and we all got along. It was going to be a great engagement.

I called Marco and told him I was going to be real happy here and not to worry. I don't know how many stars the place has, four at least for sure.

I worked on my ideas for a full-length performance piece in the afternoons at a local dance school. I had time to work out, take dance classes, and write. This was going to be perfect.

What was especially wonderful about doing our nightly shows (three a night, four on weekends) were the costumes. They were designed for effect and spectacle, so every costume doubled as a prop or a part of a group montage. At one point in the show, we pulled up our skirts cancan style and a gigantic rose bloomed, the skirts being its petals.

Mamma sent me a box of biscotti and on some days that's all I ate. I was determined to save every penny I could.

I went to Boys' Town, which was a regular city. Schools, police station, fire station, churches, farmland, and it had all started with *one person*.

I remembered what Sister Ursula had told us: You take a magnifying glass and you hold it over paper in the sun. Hold it long enough and you'll start a fire. Focus, *figli,* focus.

Alongside Father Flanagan's house was a rose garden, now dormant with winter on the way. This was where he taught boys and girls to love the soil, to love making things grow. I had never planted anything in my life, I had never stretched the palms of my hands on the earth. I leaned down and poked the tip of my finger at the ground. Maybe Father Flanagan was so focused on God he knew God's thoughts, knew what God felt about certain things other than sin. I placed my hands flat on the ground, stayed there. I wanted to feel what was inside that earth to make Father Flanagan's roses grow and change bad kids to good.

Before me was a bronze statue of a boy carrying his brother on his back. I smiled up at the statue. I patted the hollow metal of the foot. Yes, the blessed weight of a brother.

I received a letter from Marco.

> You'll never guess what. Elainey and I are thinking of tying the knot after I graduate. What do you think? Wouldn't that be a kick in the head?
>
> You O.K. there in dull old Nebraska? Ed's dad said it's the flattest state in the union . . .

I chewed my nails and tried to draft a letter back to Marco.

> Dear Marco. Don't do it!
> Dear Marco, Reconsider! You've got your art to think of!
> Dear Marco—
> *Managgia!* TYING THE KNOT?

Elainey was converting to Catholicism, going to classes with Father Tuttifucci, she was getting baptized and she was a finalist for Miss Downtown Saint Paul.

> Everyone sends their love. We don't have your phone number so please send it. Ciao con amore, M.
>
> p.s. I saw your friend Jennifer. She's going out with some a.h. college dude who drives a Thunderbird and thinks he's big S. I gave her your address.

Tying the KNOT! My body turned to plaster.

I called Mamma, begged her to stop Marco from considering such a thing as marriage at his age, but she was not unhappy with the idea. She like Elainey. She hoped they'd move in with her.

I called Marco. DON'T DO IT. And he laughed at me. Told me not to be jealous, nobody could ever take my place, etc., etc. And besides it wouldn't be for a while anyhow.

I called Manny and he told me no-can-do, he wouldn't step in where wise men fear to tread.

I talked to Arturo, who thought I was *pazza*. Nobody, she can stop love. You might as well try to stop the pot from boiling on the stove. *Madonn'a.*

We were held over another two weeks at the Club Voila. In spite of my stomach-twisting worries about Marco, I began to feel comfortable in Omaha. My performance piece, *ChiChi Clown Extra Ordinaire,* was becoming more physical, more difficult as I rehearsed each day. I worked on each movement again and again until it felt as if I had come out of the womb dancing. Never had I worked so hard. Omo and Onna would be proud of me. In just another few weeks it would be ready to be performed on stage. Just a little longer . . .

The snow came and business at the Club Voila continued steady. Roland came in to give us new routines for the show, and he said he'd help me with ideas for my show. He began working with me, giving me advice on lighting and costumes, critiquing my performance, and showing me how to work out some of the trouble spots. I felt I was understanding the art of performance—that it was more than the gift, more than talent, it was the something that managed to cross the boundaries of self and other, and yet take all of everything human into itself. I had so much yet to learn and Roland was the perfect teacher.

I hoped this engagement would last a long, long time. In another week I'd be able to open a savings account. I'd tell Mamma I had money in the bank. I wore my *Gotta Dance* charm from Marco every day, slept with it on my wrist. I went to church, lit candles. I thanked every saint I could name.

Thank you, thank you, thank you. ChiChi Maggiordino Cleo Patra was earning her own money and was (heavens!)— pressing on. Charlie Chaplin couldn't have had it better.

And then the call. Arturo's voice. Teary, upset.

ChiChi, you Mamma she fall.

Che cosa?

She fall and she not good. She bad hurt.

Slow down, Arturo. Tell me what happened.

Marco, he take her to hospital. He tell me to call you.

Three hours later, checked out with suitcases packed, I was on the Great Northern for Minneapolis. My nightclub career was over.

*A*rturo met me at the train station. I managed to get out of him that Mamma had fallen on the ice on the stairs outside the apartment.

How IS she? What HAPPENED?

Marco, Elainey, and Eddie were bringing her home right now. In a taxi.

She's been released from the hospital?

She had broken her foot.

Under the sheath of snow our house appeared like something had snapped its spine. It looked smaller, bent, arthritic.

Mamma came home looking like a child diminished. A cast went from her toe to her knee. After the hugs from Marco and the thank-you's for getting here so fast and the you look greats from Elainey, I threw myself at Mamma's knees.

Mamma! Mamma! Are you in pain?

Chichilina *mia,* she groaned with a dramatic sweep of her hand to the brow, those people in hospital, they no know what is dignity. Treat me like *animale. Comm'u bestia!*

Mamma, no, I told her, *Non siamo animali—*

They try to kill me, *figlia* . . .

Such a world that demanded she shit in a metal doughnut. Her eyes went tragic. Her longing to be treated with dignity. To be appreciated.

Fascisti! she cried out.

(It hasn't been easy, said Marco.)

Arturo heated water for tea.

Mamma, said Ed, I got a joke for you.

(*Mamma?* Since when?)

His joke: When a person goes to the hospital there are three things that are important!

Eh?

Eating, eliminating, and pain medication, that's it. If a person don't eliminate, they're full of shit. Haw! Haw!

Mamma giggled. Oh that hurt.

(Mamma, how can you find anything amusing that little creep says? How can you *like* him?)

The pain medication didn't help her. Instead of producing a calm attitude, it made her angry. She hallucinated. What THEY had done to her, Bruno's parents who rejected her and her children, Bruno who abandoned her, and the family in Italy who condemned her for her sin of love, her dear mother who upped and died on her. *Gesù, Maria,* was there no mercy?

(What about Bruno, Mamma? Who is he? Where is he? What about Bruno?)

Marco kissed my cheeks. You home for good now?

Unh.

That bad eye of yours seems much better. And your face is fuller. What are you eating?

(Eating? What was I eating?)

Where's Nardo? I said.

Mamma came home from the hospital and I volunteered to take care of her during the day. Mamma and I in the apartment together all day, she asleep, me drinking coffee in the living room. Over there the sofa, the mess of blankets and flattened pillows, Marco's paintings on the walls; ah, he's experimenting with a new technique, thicker paint, impasto, more variations on the color red. A table by the plastic-covered window was lit by a fluorescent lamp over pans of dirt. Nardo was growing basil in the living room. The place smelled like wet wool and pork rinds.

In my room Nardo's clothes hung on hangers from the dresser drawer knobs. I ran my hand over the mattress, then leaned down and laid my face against the blanket. I could smell him, Nardo. I could *feel* his smell. I climbed onto the bed and laid my body out on the mattress. I imagined Nardo lying beside me. Here's ChiChi Maggiordino having intimate synthesis with a worn-out mattress.

Cars and trucks ticked past on University Avenue, trucks in tire chains creating the metallic staccato of winter streets, a familiar hymn.

Wait.

The air had an all-wrong feel to it. Like when Nonna had her stroke. Same silence, same dust. The same fermented, curdled feeling in the air when they hid the secret of Onna's death from me. The smell was a bad one. I sniffed, waited. Sniffed again.

Mamma clung to the door frame of her bedroom. Her skin grey, eyes wild. She had crawled out of bed, her leg dragging behind her on the floor.

Strega! She shouted. *Strega!*

Mamma, you're hallucinating. There's no witch.

She pounded her fist at the wall, screamed. *Stregona!*

Mamma, it's me, ChiChi. You're having a reaction to the Percodan.

Her face twisted in rage and terror. I'd never seen her like this.

Mamma, you'll hurt yourself. Let me get you back into the bed.

She wouldn't let me near her. She screamed and cried with such passion I knew she could do something terrible.

I tried talking to her. Mamma, who's a witch? What are you seeing?

Between her raving and babbling I figured out she thought she was in Italy . . . On her wedding day. Someone had put a curse on her. A witch, Mamma?

A witch in a mask.

A mask like mine? Like my painted clown face?

I reached my arms to her and she hit me. She tried to grab my throat. She clawed at me. Spit.

So that was it. All my life I was the fruit of a curse.

There was no use trying to talk through the Percodan in her system. She was beyond my voice. All I could do was repeat again and again. I am not a witch. I am your daughter. You are not cursed.

Finally, when I realized she wasn't going to stop flailing and she might hurt herself in a serious way, I starting yelling back at her with *Il Mal Occhio*. I shouted words I'd heard Father Tuttifucci pray when Tar Town was being attacked by white kids across the tracks. IN THE NAME OF JESUS! I yelled.

I tried remembering Bible verses. LET NOT YOUR HEART BE TROUBLED! JESUS WEPT!

She lifted her head and stared at me. *ChiChi, sei così pazza.* ChiChi is crazy.

I continued: IN JESUS' NAME! I flailed my arms, I commanded the curse to leave her, I used *Il Mal Occhio;* I acted like I was addressing the witch herself; scaring the tormentor.

I jumped up and down, kept repeating JESUS JESUS.

Mamma became calm, her body softened, she sighed, patted my arm. Oh ChiChi, she said, you are crazy for sure. And she threw her head back and laughed. It was a jubilant laugh, the kind of laugh so exuberant and joyous, I could only look at her, amazed and somewhat stupefied. There is no doubt in my mind that she could have killed me that day. I carried her back to her bed and she laughed so hard she got both of us wet.

Three days before Christmas.

Nardo and I decorated the apartment; Nardo's hands holding Nonna's silver bells, draping them across the doorway. Nardo's hand brushing mine as we pulled the strands of tinsel from the box. Nardo placing the small nativity figures in place. The little wooden cow, the wise men. My forefinger touching his Joseph with my Virgin Mary.

The temperature sank to 26 degrees below zero, and this wasn't the worst of the cold. Yet to be upon us was January and February, March, an Arctic explosion. Winter was more famous than Jesus.

Then came the matter of Christmas Eve, *La Festa Della Vigilia Di Natale.* Christmas Eve to Italians is a most important day. It revolved around midnight Mass and the big meal following. I tried cooking something from an Italian cookbook I found at Perine's Bookstore near the University. A special marinated herring, *aringhe marinate,* which sat barely touched in the center of the table.

ChiChi, too much the cinnamon, Mamma complained, how much cinnamon you use?

I don't know, Mamma. A tablespoon.

Dai, too much. Only a touch, use only a touch.

The tortellini were equally unsuccessful. Look at this, will you, she sighed, after our second Chianti toast to her health. The pasta ChiChi buy from supermarket. She no make it herself. The panettone, she buy. What is happen to our children?

The old ways make room for the new, said Manny Looz.

Aiutime o Dio.

(Yes, help her, God.)

The kitchen to me was territory as strange as Burma to me. I could have been in Calcutta or the laboratory of Doctor Frankenstein. My fingers had never been baptized in garlic. I didn't know a tenderloin from a filet, didn't know a pinch of rosemary from a handful of flax.

And now ChiChi will sing for us, Mamma said after finishing a chunk of marzipan I bought at Russo's bakery.

My tongue went thick, I stuttered, fumbled with my hands. I will sing if Nardo sings with me, I said, and began a Christmas song Nonna taught us:

Tu scendi dalle stelle

(Do you know this one, Nardo?)

o re del cielo
e vieni in una grotta
al freddo e al gelo . . .

You have come down from the stars
O King of Heaven
to a cold and freezing cave . . .

Mamma sighed, wiped at her eye with a knuckle.

O bambino mio divino . . .
Dear little divine baby . . .

Nardo looked reverent. Like an altar boy who just smoked a joint in the john.

Sing "Ninna Nanna," said Marco, meaning *lighten up, ChiChi.*

More my style. I began the song with a dramatic vibrato and goofy face. Marco chuckled but Mamma looked stricken. I thought by the horrified expression on her face that she was imagining the face of the *strega* again.

But what she was really thinking was, ChiChi would never be someone's wife. No man would have *pazza* ChiChi.

Arturo took her hand and we all sang "O Come All Ye Faithful" in English, me singing harmony and Mamma joining in on the last verse. The only voice I could hear was Nardo's. Everything about him was golden, was glassy, was symphonic.

Mamma's confinement had a smell to it, like vegetables gone bad, like laundry, old dishwater. I sat in my room and tried to read my *Dance Magazine* and thought about the next time I'd be able to rehearse, work on my show, my C.E.O. *Madonna Sacra,* I was lost. Without Onna and Omo the colors were missing, the dazzle.

Superstitions bloomed up around Mamma. (The new pain medication.) A spoon left on a saucer at a certain angle meant someone was going to die of food poisoning. If you looked at a blind person you could go blind yourself. If you watch a dog urinate, you'd go deaf.

The broom, ChiChi, the broom, no leave the broom near open door! she screamed. (It meant the house would burn down.)

But she never again called me *Strega*.

(ChiChi make evil curse go away because she so crazy funny, she told Nardo. This followed by unrestrained chuckles.)

Arturo moved out of our apartment and moved in with a waiter named Fred at the restaurant. He said Mamma needed to sleep alone and get well. He stopped coming around as much, and by *La Befana*, January 7th, he was eating all his meals at Cucina Garibaldi.

I fantasized daily about Nardo. When he was in the apartment, my nerves went rainy. I became frazzled and damp. I could hear him in the bathroom bathing and perfuming himself.

That one, he love the ladies, Mamma sighed from her throne on the sofa. I say he need *one good woman*, get married, that's what I'm think.

Arturo was falling out of our lives. Like cheap gold, *l'oro fasullo*, Mamma sneered. Cheap gold look so good at night in moonlight but in morning is make a green crumble in you hand.

But he wanted to marry you, Mamma.

At this she gave a wheeze from the gears of her head. Futility wrote its name in her eyes. I reached my hand out to her. My hand wanted to smooth the knotted hair around her face, rub her neck, but I pulled it back, held it with my other hand, and sighed hard, the way she sighed.

Basta, ChiChi, she said.

The obdurate lift of her chin, the pulling back of her shoulders, the fixed mouth, and a loud inhale, like the hiss of lighted matches.

Va'tenne, ChiChi. Go away.

*O*h to be ordinary! To be a college coed, like my high school friend, Jennifer. To go out on dates, to be casual. Casual! To know romance, to love and be loved. Omo always said you can love show business but show business will never love you back. I was dizzy suddenly, my neck grew sweaty, the backs of my knees stung. Flame Desire told me, Sex is serious business, Cleo. Get with it.

Let it be said I was not with it. I thought of Nardo. Beautiful, beautiful Nardo. I pictured the sunflowers along the fence leaning their faces toward him as he passed by. I imagined children and small animals clinging to his pant leg for the privilege of looking up at his cumin skin, his black pepper eyes. I thought again of Flame and her soured career in ballet.

Maybe ChiChi should go to college, Mamma said. Maybe you meet nice man. Like Jennifer.

Oh boy. ChiChi Clown Extra Ordinaire sits in a college classroom like Jennifer, smelling the pages of the books, listening to the hum of the fluorescent tubes overhead, feeling the bones of the lower body bent into the shape of a desk . . .

In Omaha I almost had my performance piece finished. I had Roland to help me, I had a studio, and I was earning money. Now was I to start planning a college venture? Was I to dedicate myself to notebooks and a life of writing down important war dates or psychological classifications?

Oh, but to be ordinary! To appreciate the incandescent voice of a bespectacled professor at the front of the room, to observe his proud straight nose, excited nostrils, greying teeth. To imagine his arms around me, his penis bent sideways and stiff in his pants. Is this how ordinary girls thought? College girls?

When you can't identify an ache, it's like having a blister on your instep and a gnat in your eye at the same time.

Jennifer fixed me up on a blind double date with a History Major from Edina. Chapped lips, rosacea, and crazy for fried food. We downed beers, listened to Jim Reeves and Merle Haggard, watched the Lakers on TV, talked about Marilyn Monroe's supposed suicide, ate peanuts in the shell, and I thought maybe this is the life for me. Maybe I could be a coed, a history major, someone's girlfriend.

The next day he told Jennifer I reminded him of a Mafia Moll.

Exactly what's a Mafia Moll, Jennifer? I wanted to know.

Hells Bells, *you* should know, she said. Those eyelashes! I realize you have that floppy eye and all, but the eyelashes, I mean! And those false fingernails? And that dress? Geez Leweez.

I felt struck in the stomach with a beer bottle.

My rabbit fur jacket I thought was so pretty now sprouted boils. My kelpy hair housed termites. My nice perfume I thought was so sexy bought at Rexall called Gift of Love now seemed like something Grenadine Fletcher would use. I stank of tap dancing. And the dress I thought was elegant with the attractive sequined bodice I now thought of as contaminated with a virus, like what the Calvary gave the Indians.

I reeked Off-Campus.

I forced Mamma out of bed to take a sponge bath in the kitchen with the oven turned on, the only room in the place where she didn't freeze herself to ice, and where she could keep her leg up while I washed her. The oven heat blasted our faces like a nasty hand-grip. My cheeks felt like a baked apple. ChiChi, she said, looking at me as though Mussolini had risen from the dead. Poor ChiChi! she said.

Hold still, I said, and squeezed a trickle of warm water onto her stomach.

Will ChiChi NEVER have a man to love her? She said this as though struck by a realization too awful to put to words in Italian.

It was going to be a long winter. An apartment full of winter, dry nagging heat from the oven and gas heater in the parlor, air scrappy like dead skin, our nights in front of the TV set with Johnny Carson, Ed Sullivan, Rod Serling, and *The Twilight Zone*.

When Marco wasn't in school or selling shoes, he spent his time with Elainey. Ed Looz hung around like someone's traded-in house pet, moping, making art, trying to earn anyone's approval. I dedicated myself to clearing up a pimple on my chin, fantasizing about Nardo, and watching television with Mamma.

The squeak of rubber boots in snow, the clatter of ice falling from the eaves of the roof, the ravenous screech of the wind, and Mamma's tedious grievances, all of it maddening without Onna and Omo, without a hook to hang a plan on.

The peculiar smell in the apartment had its own personality. A litter box smell, stagnant water, sour apples, dead things. The smell grew stronger, it soaked the walls, the carpet. Mamma wept with pain, she raked at her leg under the cast with a coat hanger.

Something was wrong.

Back to Emergency. By now they knew us by name there. The cast was removed and with it the flesh of her leg. Green pus, slime, and blood oozed out. Mamma's eyes rolled back in agony. The deformed infected leg lying across the doctors knees appeared nothing like a leg.

Don't look, Mamma, I said. Don't look.

She knew what a severed leg looked like. She had seen infection, had seen gangrene. No, *Carina,* I not look.

While Mamma lay with antibiotics dripping into her veins and fighting to save her leg, we discovered Arturo was having an affair with a waitress at the restaurant named Cherry. Tomas, the owner, said he was going to fire Arturo and the waitress if they didn't stop horsing around while on the job.

Horsing? *Che è* horsing? Mamma wanted to know.

Mamma, use your imagination.

Lo so. She was not so stupid that she didn't know what *horse* meant. Horse meant *cavallo.* Ah ha! See?

I explained Arturo was having an affair with Cherry, a waitress. He was having s-e-x with her.

She gave a blasé shrug.

I dropped the subject. The infection was crawling up her body. The doctor said she might, yes, might lose the foot, possibly the lower leg. I couldn't permit the thought. I couldn't have two parents with wooden legs.

That was one thing I could not bear in this world.

No, there were two.

Mamma losing her leg and Marco marrying Elainey.

I slept by Mamma's bed. I called on my rituals, on *Mal Occhio*. I prayed, ladies and gentlemen, the best I could.

Marco jabbed me on the back of my knee with his shoe. ChiChi, that's enough.

I had been holding a yoga pose called downward dog for thirty minutes. I had been doing three hundred Hail Marys.

Cut it friggin out, ChiChi.

No, Marco. They operate tomorrow.

The leg looked like an entire human being, skinned, throbbing.

But the antibiotics did their job. The doctors cut and grafted skin, and the leg was saved. She'd walk, she'd be fine with rehab. She's one lucky lady, they said. We can be grateful for modern medicine.

Why is it, I wondered, do we not want to give credit to God, to the Holy Loving Mother, to Jesus, the angels, and all the saints when blessed favor is looked upon us? Why do we chalk miracles up to fate and medicine? Is it so inconvenient to turn up our chins and whisper thanks to God, to *Mal Occhio?*

Manny brought her home in a taxi and Nardo made gnocchi. Nardo's beautiful fingers in the flour, pinching the little ears of gnocchi, then with the wooden spoon between his fingers, stirring the sauce, and popping the cork of Manny's champagne. Such light in Nardo's eyes, he was happier than I'd ever seen him. Giuseppina is going to be fine! he kept repeating.

Mamma nibbled the gnocchi, sipped the champagne, her leg wrapped and warm in another cast.

Arturo? *Dove è Arturo?*

Mamma, you remember. He and the waitress?

Ah. *Sì, sì.* Arturo and waitress. Horse.

She laughed. Shrugged.

But aren't you upset, Mamma? Aren't you angry? He wanted to marry you! I stared at her waiting for the explosion.

I have horse of my own, she chuckled.

No, you don't have a horse, Mamma. Horsing around doesn't imply an actual animal.

She laughed, poked a finger at my chest. Ah, Miss Smarty-Smart!

She pursed her lips, rubbed her arms. I speak of *love.* You know what is love, ChiChi?

Have you been into the Percodan? Mamma, did you find the Percodan?

Such *love* I speak of! Mamma prated. My lover make me feel like million *lire.* He tell me I am his sun and moon. You know him.

What are you talking about? What? Who?

ChiChi, I'm tell you—you mamma, *she in love.*

It had to be Manny. Who else? Manny, around for years like a rich uncle, paying for this, paying for that. Marco told me he shelled out thousands in tips for all the taxis we took. And now Manny was talking about paying for Marco's tuition in art school. Whenever I asked why he did so much for us, the answer was always the same. Eddie needed a family.

All right, Mamma, sock it to me. Who's the new big love of your life?

Nardo! she exclaimed, *Nardo!*

Nardo? My forehead turned icy, my bad eye creaked.

I felt cut.

$\mathcal{T}$he leg and foot healed, though the skin on her leg would be scarred. Mamma began rehab and returned to work as chef at Cucina Garibaldi. Nardo moved into Mamma's bedroom.

Everything in my body hurt. Nose, eye, toes, teeth, liver, esophagus.

Elainey got the brainy idea to spend her modeling money to throw a dinner party at the Ye Olde Wagon Wheel Steak House in Golden Valley for Marco's seventeenth birthday. She invited Ed and Manny, Mamma and me. (Me, did I have a date I'd like to bring, hmm, Sweetie? NO, ELAINEY, I DO NOT. I disliked this woman more every day.) She invited a diver named Olaf from the Aqua Follies who happened to have bad eyes, maybe we'd hit it off, she said. Nardo couldn't come because he was working double shift at the restaurant.

I told her Mamma would prefer cooking dinner at home, a nice pasta.

Pasta pasta pasta, said Elainey. I say we kick up our heels, do something special. I'm sick to here with pasta. It's high time someone did something really special for Marco.

(High time.)

I had to sit next to disgusting Ed Looz at the steak house. He was dressed in a vest and tie, his hair slicked back, shoes shined. He looked like an anorexic Argentinean tango dancer. You want my body, admit it, he sighed in my face, and blew at my ear with his smoky dead-person breath. Elainey and Marco cuddled together at the other side of the table, ignoring us.

Marco so beautiful, if you peeled his skin, you'd release a million sweet charimoya doves. Seventeen years. And they said he wouldn't live to see ten.

Fall on our knees.

Where's Mamma? Eddie wanted to know.

She's *not* your mamma, I snarled.

She told us she'd be a little late, Elainey said, and she introduced Olaf, star diver in the Follies.

Me, I hate water, I said.

Elainey frowned at me, smoothed the perfect part in her hair. Olaf pulled at his tie. His hair was the color of typing paper.

My dad should be here pretty soon, Ed said. He wouldn't miss the chance to tip the cup of merriment in honor of Marco's seventeenth. That's Dad's words exact.

On the walls of Ye Old Wagon Wheel Steak House were steer heads, looped lariats, pictures of the Wild West. Three musicians wearing cowboy hats and boots were busy in the corner of the dance floor, adjusting their sound system.

Ed lifted his hand for the waitress the way his father would, and ordered a double Scotch on the rocks. Dewar's.

I hit him hard on the arm. You're sickening, I snarled. At the Dragon Lady Ed would be a surefire sucker, a Live One, a john who the girls would take for everything, including his watch, belt, and socks.

Elainey turned to me, pleased and secretive. Wait till you see the cake! I ordered it special.

Does it have nuts in it? I said.

What?

Italians need nuts in their cakes, I said.

She stared at me like I was a Halloween character, then took Olaf's arm and said, Let's dance, Olaf.

Marco said, Hey ChiChi, be nice to Olaf.

My god, Marco, the guy's got white eyebrows.

I wanted to dance with my brother.

Marco. How's about we give it a whirl?

We walked to the dance floor as I heard the waitress ask Ed, You want a refill on that there firewater, baby?

In my brother's arms I could smell his skin, the skin that was my skin, too, I could smell me in him, in his neck, his hair. His hand on my back, strong, confident. His long legs, long back, his fingers wrapped around mine, our one body, our one blood, our one set of teeth, eyes, ears. If I am him and he is me, then I am altogether beautiful in him. If this body holding mine and swaying to "Unchained Melody" is formed of the same bone and gut as I, then I can believe I have purpose, am necessary, too. Happy birthday, I said into his chest. We twirled around, our thighs and feet in perfect sync. His face next to mine. Skin's skin. His mouth moving across my cheek, nose, mouth's mouth. Hey ChiChi, he joked, we haven't smooched since we played with Grenadine Fletcher's underwear,

My voice came out plugged. You know something, Marco?

Shut up, please.

I love you like a tomato.

His cheek on mine. Me, too, he said.

Don't marry her, I wanted to say. Get rid of her. Dump her. We'll buy a car. We'll collect rocks. We'll make our own skateboard. But my brother seemed happy at last, joyful, you might say. The tough guy persona was gone. Is it possible that love can do this to a person?

Hey, you guys, Elainey called out. You been practicing? Going pro on us?

There came a commotion at the front entrance. I turned in time to see Mamma leaning on her new cane, shouting at the manager. She wore her red satin dress pulled and puckered at the seams, her hair pinned up with a gold clip, frenzied strands loose around her face. She was flushed and excited, her free hand flying through the air. Manny Looz was at her side, carrying a large cardboard box.

She had come to the restaurant with an almond cake she baked and a large bowl of pasta still warm in the pan.

Is that allowed? Olaf wanted to know.

Of course not, Elainey answered through her nose.

Manny saw Ed's glass and flicked him on the head. What's that you're drinking, boy?

Manny took Ed's Scotch away and saluted Marco. I'm proud of you, Marco, my boy. Let's tip the cup of merriment to our Marco.

Our Marco, said Mamma.

The restaurant charged us a plate fee for bringing our own food, said it was highly irregular under normal circumstances. Manny said Mamma wasn't a normal circumstance. He blew her a kiss.

Mamma took Elainey's seat next to Marco so she could scoop pasta onto each of our plates. Elainey pouted throughout the meal and when she spoke, she addressed Olaf, who ate more pasta than anybody.

Manny asked Mamma to dance. I thought I saw her blush. Blush.

She rose from the chair and took his arm to the dance floor. She moved with clumsy grace, self-conscious, but somehow elegant. Watching her dance with Manny without her cane and smiling up at him, I thought she looked strangely magnificent. On the dance floor in her red ill-fitting party dress, her hair swept up and messed; though not yet forty years old, she seemed young, she seemed *happy*.

Anna Magnani, Elainey said. Doesn't your mother just remind you of that famous Italian movie actress, Anna Magnani? Dancing with Manny, gliding and shaking her hips, Mamma was as mesmerizing as a movie star, yes, like Anna Magnani.

We lit the candles on two cakes and waiters in cowboy hats gathered around to sing happy birthday. Mamma held up her hands, cleared her throat, and then rose to her feet and led us in "Buon Compleanno a Te." When she finished singing, the people at the table next to us applauded. Then Mamma pushed Elainey's cake aside, sliced her almond cake, and served us and the people at the next table.

Good thing I bake a cake, look at what they give you in restaurant—paste, no nuts. Beh!

Manny laughed and kissed her hand. I got up to talk to the guitarist.

A few minutes later he stood at the microphone and broke into a loud, rousing rendition of "Home on the Range."

For you, Marco.

He laughed and clapped his hands. We still didn't know the words.

Elainey gave Marco a stuffed dog with a big red I LUV U heart on its belly. Marco adores dogs, she said with a titter. Were we thinking of the same person? Marco, horribly allergic to animals?

My little love puppy, murmured Elainey, whispery and kissy-face.

Marco actually beamed, he shone, sparkled. My little family was *happy*.

Two more bottles of wine and a dozen country western

dances later the steak house closed. Most of the customers
had gone home when we finally asked for our check. Manny
snatched it up from the table. This is for Marco. Our man.
We're only seventeen once!

Bravo, said Mamma.

I watched Elainey take Marco's arm as they left the restaurant together. I saw her throw a brief glance over her
shoulder at me, and I knew for sure she would one day take
him away from us. Mamma and Manny left the restaurant
together, too, her arm in his. They stepped into the taxi,
Mamma with the leftover pasta and cake in the box, Manny
holding the door for her, the coy thank-you, the skirt lifted,
the hips undulating. I picked up the cane she left leaning
against the table and followed them to the curb. I was
trapped waiting for the next taxi with Ed Looz. I begged
Olaf to ride with us, to sit between us, but he suddenly
remembered another engagement.

Ed and I drove in silence until he lit up a cigarette and I
shouted that he was a pig dog. *Porco Canne!* I yelled. Ever
stop to think how selfish a death wish is?

Screw you, Dago girl.

One day you'll be sucking those things through a hole in
your neck, I said. Why don't I just kill you here and now,
Looz?

He grunted. Threw the cigarette out the window. I don't
actually smoke them, he said, I lit up just to piss you off.

I hit him with Mamma's cane.

The driver said, You kids want to hear the radio?

Me: No!

Looz: Yes!

Suddenly Elvis Presley: "Love Me Tender."

I hit him again. I'm as American as you are!

You're a stupid wop immigrant, *Leticcia.* That's all you'll ever be. That droopy eye of yours hanging down. Your screwy ways. You're plain crazy.

I hit him again. He punched me back.

He got me on the side of the face.

I slugged him where I knew I shouldn't. In the chest.

He doubled like a paper boat.

I warn you, he said, his face going bright pink. Watch out for me. You just better watch out for me.

Did I get you in the lung? I'm sorry. I really am—

I'm not going to forget this, *Leticcia*.

I'm warning you, he gasped, furious, don't you ever get to feeling safe in your skin because I'll tell you why. Because one of these nights you're going to be sleeping in your bed, you're going to be dreaming your whacky little dreams, and there's going to be a noise behind you. An itsy bitsy noise you won't even hear until it's too late. And you're history.

A purple line formed alongside his face and around his eyes.

Ooo-ee. I'm scared, Looz.

His face clouded, the pink turning grey. Don't EVER, he snarled, don't EVER get to feeling comfortable in this life. Because I am going to get you! He socked me in the stomach.

—for my darling I love youuuu,
and I always willl . . .
Love me tender—

I nodded my head, readied.

Then I slapped him so hard on the face my hand felt burned, singed by fire. I slapped him again.

How DARE you threaten Leticcia ChiChi Maggiordino! I've used a knife before and I'll use it again. And next time, you ugly wart, I catch you hanging around my bedroom, I'll break your face!

For my darling
I love you, and I aaaaaalways willll.

In the apartment I sat in the dim light of the parlor lamp and stared at Marco's present from me on the coffee table. Wrapped in silver and gold with curled silver ribbon. A Minolta camera with two lenses and a roll of 135 film, bought with the last of my money.

Marco didn't come home that night. Neither did Mamma. I slept with Metamere's knife under the pillow and my good eye half open.

*E*lainey became a regular model for Young Quinlan Department Store and we'd see her picture in the *Minneapolis Star Tribune* leaning on a Cadillac wearing a fur coat or posed at some local landmark like the Grainbelt Brewery, wearing the latest fashions with price tags that sneered at most people. Marco graduated from high school with honors, applied for and won a scholarship to the Minneapolis School of Art. I started gymnastics classes.

I read about a famous clown and mime around the turn of the century named Bert Williams who was known for a pantomime he performed of a poker game where he played all the players. I developed a mime around the card game of *Scopa*, playing the characters as they dealt, bet, cheated, and peeked at each other's cards. I practiced at home under the watchful gaze of Mamma, and several times I caught her smiling in spite of herself.

Mamma, am I funny?

I didn't wait for her to answer.

How it would be: Me, ChiChi Clown Extra Ordinaire, famous performance artiste, starring on Broadway, touring the world, making films. Me, renowned, admired, sought-after.

Mamma sighed. Yes, that is how it will be. And what man will want you?

One afternoon I came home to find Manny Looz sitting

on the sofa with Mamma. Well well, what have we here?

Manny cleared his throat. Sit down, he said. We want to talk to you. I sat. Waited. They looked at each other. Back to me. Fiddled with fingers. Sighed.

What? A piece of advice? Now? Is it about Bruno?

Mamma sucked in her breath. I make coffee, she said, and left the room.

There's this woman I know, Manny said, quick and nervous, her name is Dodee Priscarp and she's good people. A real estate agent and entrepreneur. She produces variety shows. You oughter audition for her with your clown act.

Dodee Priscarp? She one of your gambling clients?

So what if she is? Think I'd tell you?

What's this all about? Level with me. You're acting peculiar.

Na na, Babe, this Dodee's legitimate. Her show is called the *Star Spangled Revue,* how's that for patriotic? Did I mention she pays fifty bucks a show?

Fifty?

You want me to set something up for you or not? It's no skin off my arse if you say no.

Sure. Why not.

Dodee Priscarp was a jolly blond lady who told knock-knock jokes and prattled on about her Maltese dog named Midnight (though the precious thing was white as snow, ha ha) and how *très merveilleux* it was to have the best talent in the Twin Cities under her wing. She'd try me out in her *Star Spangled Revue* in the fall, just in time to play Rochester; the hospital, that is. Dodee's Best Talent in the Twin Cities played hospitals, prisons, and retirement homes, supermarket openings, benefits—you name it.

Sometime during the summer Ed Looz carted his crappy self off to a Billy Graham Crusade at the Minnesota fairgrounds and got himself something called Saved. He tossed out for good what he considered Every Evil Influence in his life, he stopped cursing, he took baths and read the Bible. Manny said it was like living with Bishop Sheen.

I didn't believe it about Ed. It's a *fregatura*, a ruse, I told Mamma. I imagined the creep holding a cross over my head before kicking me in the shins. A prayer before murder in the cathedral.

While Marco was working selling shoes or out with Elainey, Ed attended Bible Study classes, his new church (Pentecostal), and his Everlasting Love Helping Others Mission. I didn't like the smell of this new wind, not one bit.

I worked on my handstands.

By Marco's graduation day Mamma had finished an English course she had been taking in night school and was ready to go to Level Three. Nardo watched on, cleaning his fingernails, kissing her neck, scribbling in the margins of her papers. Arturo was ancient history.

Marco graduating high school, Marco living another year.

Elainey landed a screen test in Hollywood. (How? How did she do that? I demanded to know.)

Marco shrugged, acted as if getting a Hollywood screen test when you'd never stepped foot out of Minnesota was a common occurrence.

Someone from Paramount, a talent scout, he guessed, saw Elainey perform.

Perform where?

At the Edgewater Inn, with that musical deal she was in.

The Gershwin show?

Ya. They invited her to Hollywood, all expenses paid. For a screen test. It's legitimate, all on the up-and-up.

I didn't care what Elainey did. She could hire a camel and cross the Sahara in a Gucci stocking, what did I care. Marco mattered. And I'd die if he left me for Elainey.

Don't sweat it, ChiChi, we'll be back.

We? WE?

Marco did leave me. Elainey paid his way to LAX on Northwest Orient Airlines, and Mamma and I watched them walk down the long runway to their plane at the Minneapolis airport without so much as one tear on their faces. Marco turned and waved. I was shot asunder with fear of being separated from my brother for good; then came the sudden absence of blood in my legs, the spinning of the boarding area, the moan of the courtesy cart, something shockingly cold in my nostrils, ceiling lights like small bombs falling. The roar of silence, the cocoon of it, alone and wrapped in the fine sticky hairs of something unborn. I had never fainted before in my life, not when I nearly cut off my face, not when Mamma beat me with the broom, not even when I failed at the out-plucking of the eye.

Oh my brother, did you have to marry her?

It was quick, the wedding. The ceremony happened at Our Lady of Mount Carmel Church in Tar Town. I was Maid of Honor in a tangerine tulle dress a school crossing guard would wear to work and Ed was Best Man. He leered at me during the whole service. (I did NOT leer, I SMILED, he insisted.) Over a hundred people came to the little church on Buchanan and Spring Street for the nuptials. The basement of the church had been newly renovated with money donated by Rose Totino, and the reception was held there complete with a champagne fountain, tables decorated with miniature lemon trees, mountains of food, and an accordion playing tarantellas. Elainey did all the work herself, including the decorations, with her girlfriends from the Gershwin revue.

The bride wore a wedding dress from Young Quinlan and looked every bit the movie star she wanted to become. Marco was giddy with pride, talkative, silly. He said Hiya to the wedding guests, and to male friends, a sporty Hey Guy!

The church was crawling with Elainey's show business friends decked out in their finest, models so gorgeous I shrivelled like fried okra at the sight of them.

Ed Looz was a new person. Shaven, hair cut short with an actual color to it, calm. What happened to you? I stuck my glove in my mouth.

Made some changes, he said, in my life is all. First off, I got accepted at the Minneapolis Art Institute.

Rub it in. Marco gave up his scholarship.

And for another thing, I stopped getting high, he said. Cold turkeyed.

So you'll prolong your life. May it be long and miserable.

Tut tut, my dear. No way to treat family.

I bit my glove. *Family*.

Want to hear more about me? he said.

Spare me.

God reached down and touched me with his love and mercy. God has made me whole, given me a new chance at life.

How nice of her, I said.

He cleared his throat. And you? he said, What will Big Sister do now without Little Brother?

The thought crossed my mind to jump on his foot. I cuffed my chin at him.

Oh, come on. Out with it, he said. Marco's running off to sunny California with his new wifey. What's going to happen to poor little Leticcia?

Cleaned up, combed, and Saved, Ed Looz was still a nut job.

Where's your Dad? I said.

He's around here some place. Celebrating the momentous occasion. But hey, don't be depressed about Marco's tying the knot. You'll find a man of your own one day, ChiChi. Soon as you get well in the head and that eye of yours goes back to normal.

My eye is fine, Looz! It's distinct! And I'm perfectly normal!

Hey hey, Sis, don't go getting all worked up. He laughed and I saw the skin of his throat was no longer scaly and flaked and with the weight gain, he looked almost like your standard average human being.

I started down the steps. Whirled back at him. Looz! Don't *ever* call me Sis!

He took my shoulders and held on. I was too stunned to move. God Bless you, he said in my hair.

Manny Looz was smoking a cigarette on the sidewalk at the side of the church. Hey, kid. You don't look so good.

I just talked to Ed is all.

Ah, he nodded. Since he cleaned up his act and got religion, he's a ding-donged pain in the arse. Goes to some church downtown called Souls Harbor.

He squeezed my hand, I leaned in to him. He put his arm around me like an old uncle. I worried his tobacco smell would stain my skin, stick to my orange bodice and the doughy heap of my hair.

Jennifer pulled up in front of the church with her latest beau and her sisters. I watched them tumble out of an MG like grapes from the vine. Hugs all around and how have we been? Lawsie, how we've missed one another, and then they piloted themselves into the church. I didn't see them for the rest of the afternoon. They vanished at the reception somewhere between a tarantella and the distributing of the Jordan almonds. Jennifer didn't even stop to tell me how dreadful I looked in the orange old lady dress.

It's the Big Day for our boy, said Manny. One of the biggest in his life. You're born, you get married, you die. Them's the berries.

How could I witness my brother pledge his troth in the church we sat in as children and swore we'd never ever leave each other?

I tried to imagine Marco sunning himself on his patio in Hollywood and walking along streets with names like El Camino Real, Sepulveda, and Paseo Rodeo. Marco eating fondue in outdoor restaurants, Marco drinking tall drinks in poster colors. Marco driving a white convertible down a coast highway by a beach with sand shining like the back of a beetle, his arm around Elainey, singing along to show tunes. Sandstone cliffs, palm trees, bougainvillea, and flowering cacti; oranges dripping from trees and Marco waking up mornings to the wonder of tropical sunlight. Marco with a *tan*. Marco by a twinkling swimming pool thinking out loud. I hear him. Yes, I can hear my brother's thoughts from Los Angeles.

He thinks he's happier than he's ever been in his life and he'll never leave the paradise he's found, never. He thinks he loves his wife, his beautiful Elainey, his Paramount starlet wife, and he's sighing right now, ohhhhhh. Like Blanche DuBois. So suddenly there is God.

Our old Tar Town neighbors came dressed in their finest clothes for Marco's wedding. Mamma invited them all so she could show off how well she had done since leaving the neighborhood. Mount Carmel Church hadn't changed a bit. I recognized the back of a woman's head in the fourth pew. Though her hair was now a navy tint of silver, I'd know her anywhere. Mrs. Ricci, by herself, shoulders squared, staring straight ahead.

My stomach gave a shudder.

Once you clothe a person with indignation the coat won't ever change its color. I remembered Mr. Ricci's work shed, the speakers we rigged up to the tape recorder, and Grenadine Fletcher's fateful farewell performance; I remembered his story about the cousin getting mutilated in the machine at his factory. And I remembered him telling us how Northerners don't understand the Sicilians, and visa versa. Never forget who you are, he said.

There sat Mrs. Ricci alive with her blue hair, dabbing at her eyes with a hankie, ready to give us the news that Joe Ricci was dead.

So many familiar faces. Mrs. Lucca who lived next door; the Fiores; and Nonna's friends, Signora Luppo, Signora Ciccione, Signora Musetti and her nieces, at the reception all sitting on chairs by the wall, plates of food on their laps. Signora Fiore pinched my cheeks, kissed me. *Dai.* Leticcia, growing up hasn't been so good to you, eh! But not you worry. Beauty is in *here*, she pounded her breast—in the *soul*.

Signora Fuetti complained how so many young folks had left Tar Town. It's just the old ones left now. The church, she practically empty on Sunday. No more daily Mass. We no more need full-time priest. Young people going to church in Saint Anthony. And who makes wine at home today? *Mah!* Gardening, keeping chickens, our stories from the old days, *le feste,* our festas, *beh!* When our bones are lowered into the ground, our traditions will be lost forever.

I hardly recognized Luigi D'Amico. His hair had turned white, his face dark with age. Leticcia, he said, your nonna was wonderful woman. She bring Italy here, she light up everything.

I know.

A swelling of the nostrils, a burning of the eyes.

Do you remember the time on Feast Day of Our Lady of Mount Carmel, July 16th, how she insisted Father Tuttifucci explain why Our Lady was not known as Our Lady of Mount *Carmine* or Our Lady of Mount *Carmelo*, being she was supposed to be Italian? He laughed, waved his hands in front of his face as though wiping away cobwebs.

Signora Ciccione joined in. Ah, I remember when the statue of Our Lady was carried through the streets and your Nonna was singing and clapping her hands right up in front with the men! And always, who was hanging on her skirts, who was clinging to her like a flea in her ear? *You,* Leticcia, her little ChiChi!

Marco and Elainey left for Hollywood, California, the day after the wedding. That would be a Sunday. It was on a Sunday that my brother left me.

I want to put the world on rewind. Where is the girl who slept on a straw mattress and played with a goat who ate the laundry? I want to hear the sounds of the village in Italy, I want to say their Italian names. Saying their names I will belong to them again.

I remember being very small and holding a man's hand in the market, walking on the sides of my feet through the stalls. . . . I remember leaning against his knee and his hand on my head. I eat chocolate cream from a paper cup. The man licks the chocolate from my fingers. He has two legs. The white walls are cold with sweat, the small shuttered window too high for me to look out from.

Mamma is laughing. We all laugh. We laugh and laugh.

Our sins are absolved.

Mamma gives me permission to dance our story in words on paper.

A Thursday night in feverish, hot August. The windows were open and we could hear June bugs thudding against the screens. A floor fan was beside the TV. Nardo sat on the sofa, his feet up on the coffee table.

Nardo, I said. Do you really love my mamma?

More than anything. Why you ask?

Because you better not be just playing around, understand?

I found the love of my life. Okay?

Okay.

Okay.

Okay.

The ten o'clock news was just starting, and it was too hot to get up and go to my room. Mamma came in, sat down next to Nardo. These are the details I remember now. I remember the June bugs, Mamma's slippers patting the linoleum, Nardo's frown at my questioning his intentions, the yellow cast of the lamplight against the Italian newspaper on the chair—

Then the news. A video clip on the screen. A river—weeds—bright sunshiny day—police car—policemen—yellow police tape—a black plastic bag—a body.

Dave Moore, the newscaster reads: A young woman's body was found this afternoon washed up on a bank of the Saint Croix River, apparently the victim of a brutal murder. The victim has been identified as nineteen-year-old Gladys Chechnik of Duluth, Minnesota. Homicide investigators are saying the woman was beaten, stabbed, and raped. It has not been determined if the victim died by drowning or by the wounds inflicted upon her body—

I jumped up from the chair.

Shh, we can't hear, said Nardo.

It's Gladys! I cried. GLADYS!

Dave Moore was saying Gladys Chechnik, also known as Flame Desire, was an exotic dancer in Wisconsin nightclubs . . . Then a film clip of a tawdry nightclub, her picture out front. IN PERSON—FLAME DESIRE . . . Any information about this case, please call police at the following . . .

Play with fire, die by fire, Mamma said in Italian.

I didn't sleep that night.

Or the next.

I would see Flame's face in every place, her dopey, lovely, tragic face.

I pushed myself to more lessons, classes, practice. I wanted the narcotic of exhaustion.

Gladys/Flame Desire murdered. The reporter on the scene interviewed some of the other dancers. They all looked like Bernice.

Mamma enrolled herself at the Minneapolis College of Business. She needed a typewriter to practice.

Practice for what?

She was learning typing and bookkeeping in the school.

Ah, oh. I got it. Okay. You're planning to open your own trattoria, aren't you, Mamma?

One day, *Figlia,* she said, lips puffed out, eyes blooming fluorescent. One day you will see you mamma no is stupid woman. One day you will eat dinner at Pina's Trattoria on Lake Pillacotche!

Electric, the typewriter had to be electric.

Guardi, ChiChi, look you mamma she read the English, eh! I'm like you, eh? She tapped her skull. Ah! One of these days you going to see you mamma she know a few things, too, Miss Smarty Smarty.

Nardo was promoted to waiter at Cucina Garibaldi.

Oh the change in Nardo! He cut his hair, removed the mustache, he used deodorant, smelled of lime. He wore shirts with pressed collars, pants held up by belts. He no longer wore white socks and worn sandals. Let it be said, Nardo looked respectable. He talked with a low, even voice, thinking out the words he used. Isn't it a splendid soup? he said once at dinner. And then he said, I believe the loon will prevail in Minnesota, for it is the State Bird.

I came home one afternoon to find Mamma searching and tearing through things in a frenzy. The apartment was littered with emptied drawers, cupboards, closets. She was a whirlwind of sorting out and looking through.

Papers! She shouted. The papers!

In your closet, I said, calm as I could. In the box on the shelf in the closet. Everything's there. Our passports, citizenship papers, all that.

Not those papers! she shouted. Papers!

Ah. The divorce papers? I said.

She gave a timid nod. Nardo, he want proof, she said. In Italy divorce is impossible, he want to see American divorce, how is possible.

The apartment was in chaos. Clothes, boxes, furniture turned over, things thrown, piled in heaps. Calm down, Mamma, I said. Your divorce papers are in an envelope taped to the underside of the sofa right where you hid them.

I didn't tell her I only just made the discovery last week when I was feeling around under the sofa for a lemon sour ball that had fallen out of the wrapper. A corner of the tape had peeled and I pulled at it.

You really ought to get yourself a safety deposit box, I told her.

I have one, she said.

She spent the rest of the day sorting out and cleaning. A stack of things she didn't want was heaped by the back door. Onna and Omo's oriental rug was rolled up in the pile.

You're throwing this away?

I picked it up and carried it to my room. And what about this?

I picked up the ceramic tiger Mr. Metamere liked to stroke. You throwing this out?

ChiChi, you always want what nobody else want, eh? she said, frustrated. All you life since you *bambina,* always you looking for something nobody else want! What you look for? *Dimme,* tell me, what you look for in garbage? You and your brother going through trash, bring home garbage, bring home what nobody want. *Rifiuti! Mah.* Why you want that old thing? Is trash.

It's not trash, Mamma. This rug, for instance, is a gift from Onna.

The gift is in the *heart,* she said, thumping her chest. You not understand what is in the heart. You not understand what is gift.

That night with Mamma and Nardo at work, I ate dinner standing on one foot at the kitchen drainboard. One orange, one banana, one stalk of celery, prosciutto. What else had Mamma hidden from us? What did she need a safety deposit box for?

I got to thinking about Gladys again. I couldn't get the picture out of my head of the body bag with Gladys dead inside. A teenage ballerina who left home to make a little money before heading for New York and the Joffrey Ballet.

I played Blossom Dearie records on the record player. I put on my bathrobe and stretched out on the sofa with a can of Fresca. *Oh, your eyes are lighted windows, there's a party going on insiiiide . . .*

Sad. Sounds of the street, sad. My body, sad. The air, sad. *So I'll lead a lush life in some small diiiiiiive . . .* I stretched out on the kitchen floor and thought of the cool linoleum as comforting hands. *Mah.* An idea for the act! ChiChi Clown ExtraOrdinary, Clown C.E.O. will now perform the complete Swan Lake Ballet while lying on the floor.

I called Manny Looz.

What's up, ChiChi? I'm right in the middle of things. I'm working. His voice crackly like standing on newspapers.

I called to say good-bye.

Terrific. Hello, good-bye. Anything else?

Mister Looz.

Mizz Maggiordino?

—Nothing.

A clearing of the throat. A rattly, phlegmy smoker's sound. Nothing? You called to say nothing? What? I'm busy, what?

You may never see me again, that's all. You will never have to look at my face again!

I hung up, but the receiver fell off the hook, hung by its cord over the edge of the table. I didn't bother setting it right.

Silence fell on me like light. This is how it would be. I'd live out my life thinking in terms of strange metaphors and difficult body moves. I'd go on dancing; I'd give my clown the job of making sense of things. My act, my one-person show, my rituals were what I needed. I imagined myself in my makeup, my chalk face and tragic eyes, my scarlet heart mouth, blue triangle nose, bright carroty cheeks—a famous commedia clown.

Button up your overcoat, la la la lala, take good care of yourself, you belong to me—

I danced around the living room. Omo taught me you've got to embrace the bad times like a lover, you've got to concentrate and find grace and beauty in pain. I danced until my arms got ropey and imaginary audiences of happy strangers laughed and clapped their hands and shouted *more more.* I can do this, I can do this.

Oh God, poor Gladys.

Without turning on the light in the bathroom, I ran hot water into the tub, watched it turn black and fill. When I stepped into it, I was ChiChi C.E.O. enjoying a baptism on the banks of the Jordan.

I slipped into the tub, stunned at the sensation of water between my legs. Maybe I should write a birth act. Coming up through the waters. Or maybe a drowning act! Down, down, into the blackness, down until the black becomes white . . .

Tired. Take your bath and go to sleep, ChiChi. The water rushed into the tub like a full orchestra behind a Louis Armstrong record playing in the other room. *And I said to myself, what a wonderful woooooorld . . .*

Nobody could have expected a knock at the front door, nor could the same nobody have heard the door open and a man enter the apartment. I could not have known I wasn't alone.

I kicked the water, squirmed, rolled on my belly. That was when the bathroom door swung open and a shadow of a hand reached in for the light switch.

A crash of light.

I lifted my head slow, like a marionette with wooden joints. The light stinging, I stretched my neck and peered up into the wild eyes of an unshaven man in a denim jacket buttoned wrong.

—Manny?

What the hell! he screamed.

He stared at me with his mouth open and panting like a runner.

Wha—ChiChi! What's going on?

The steam soaked the walls, the sink, faucets, toilet seat cover. It felt sloppy. The room turned syrupy. I was suddenly cold. I covered my chest with my arms, doubled over. I squeaked out, Holy Cow, Manny!

He handed me a towel, his face the color of bread mould.

You've flooded the damn place, ChiChi. His voice high, like a woman's. What the hell is going on?

Tell me what's GOING ON! His face had grown multi-colored, a bad bruise.

I'm taking a bath! What does it look like?

He stepped to the other side of the door and stammered at it. You call me to say good-bye! I get to thinking that's kinda funny. You tell me I'll never see you again. Sounds to me like a threat. So I dial your number. Busy. I dial again. Busy. I call a dozen times. The operator tells me the line's off the hook. So I get in the car and drive over here, and there's no lights. Not a light in a single window! No lights and the phone's off the hook. That don't sound good to me. No, that's not a good sign, ChiChi! I'm thinking what the hell is it this time? So I come up to the door. There's thumping. I hear weird sounds. Maybe it's crying. Maybe you've done something!

I wrapped the towel around me in a storm of folds and knots. Stop shouting, Manny. You'll rile the neighbors upstairs.

I swear to almighty God, ChiChi!

He threw open the door and brought his arms around me, his hands on my bare back. I breathed in his smell, garlic, cigarettes, Old Spice.

You're crushing my face, I said to the denim jacket.

He released me and I lifted my face to look at him. He was so close I saw four eyes. Then I saw the tears. The panic.

Tell me something, I said. Are you—are you Bruno? Are you my father?

His fingers tightened on my bare skin. His breath on my neck, like warm dots. My mouth was so close to his I could smell his teeth. It was a hug filled with need. His mouth moved to my forehead where he gave me a kiss, swift and gentle as a watercolor brushstroke.

I'm not Bruno, he said. He pulled back, reached for my robe hanging on the back of the door.

Get decent. I want to talk to you, he said.

We chose Mamma's room, the only room in the apartment with an air conditioner. We sat on her bed. I wanted to laugh, Mamma's bed. Manny turned on the light of her lamp, stared at the wall for a long minute.

WHAT? I said.

It's something your mamma ought to be telling you, not me.

All right so you're not Bruno, I said. Oh, I get it. You and Mamma are lovers. You two must be *something*. Maybe you're just in love with her? Unrequited love?

He got up to fiddle with the knobs of the air conditioner in the window. It's like an oven in here, he said. And you, ChiChi, are teched in the head.

Manny, the free taxis all these years, helping Marco and me the way you have, being part of our lives, always there, always watching over us . . . You and Mamma have something between you. A *thing*, right?

Eddie needed a family. I told you that.

I found Mamma's divorce papers, I said. Pretty upsetting. All her friggin secrets.

ChiChi, you've got to understand, your mother has tried to protect you kids, tried to do the best for you.

Mamma is an ocean of secrets, I said. She has secrets pumping in her veins. Marco and I, our blood runs the same, we share the same veins. Everything we know about this world we learned from each other. You could call us the same person. I'm asking you, don't you keep secrets from me. From us. It's not fair.

It's an unfair world, ChiChi. You're born, you die. Anything in between is bad luck.

My hair hung to my shoulders wet and scandalous. It had a damp biscuit smell.

Your mother means well, she really does.

Tell me about Bruno.

We were Army buddies, he said. You already know that.

Go on.

He talked slow, looking at his fingers. We were in the battalion that landed at Maiori. I told you that.

Yes. You did.

That was September 1943. At Maiori I took a bullet in the shoulder . . . The place was your worst nightmare, guys bleeding, dying left and right. It was like standing before a firing squad. That's what it felt like. I thought it was all over. I was shot, went to a hospital, or so they called it. It was a field hospital. An old church.

And Mamma was a volunteer nurse?

That's how we met.

I closed my eyes. I could pretend I was flying. Riding steel girders over the city.

Bruno was in pretty bad shape. His leg was shot up so bad they had to cut it off. That hospital! A makeshift deal in an old church. Half the guys were dying and dead and they piled the corpses up outside the door where my bed was. In another room carpenters hammered and sawed making coffins for the dead! Well, Bruno makes it, he pulls through. Your mother took a liking to him and when they transferred him to the army hospital in Naples, your mother used to visit him. And over the course of time, one thing led to another—and she gets pregnant. With you.

The air conditioner fizzed, headlights of a car pulling into the parking lot of the ice cream factory cast two cruel lights across the bed.

I want a cigarette, said Manny, his neck slippery with sweat.

Matches make me nervous, I said. The thought of smoke makes me want to hit something, I said.

Okay okay okay, he said. So your grandmother throws a big wedding for your mother and Bruno. She didn't care much for Bruno, but he was the father of her grandchild, and no daughter of hers was going to be disgraced, even if it was Giuseppina who didn't have much sense, those are her words exact. Yours truly was the best man.

Why do you do smoke? You have a kid with respiratory problems.

(He ignored my outburst, continued:) And there was this fortune-teller who predicted disaster and misery with that marriage and your mother really took it hard. Her sisters tormented her with it.

Did she wear a mask?

Who?

La strega? The witch!

Come to think of it, I don't exactly know. But yeah, I think so. Anyhow. Want me to go on? Yes or no.

Yes.

Next thing you know, Bruno is transferred to Army Intelligence in Heidelberg. He has this wooden leg and he's doing pretty good with it. Giuseppina stayed in Praiano because frankly, she didn't want to leave her mother, and she had you. She asked me to your baptism to sort of stand in for Bruno. Leticcia she named you. Beautiful name. So anyhow, she and I start seeing each other . . . As friends, you know. Nothing more.

The man on the beach, the man whose shoulders I sat on in the piazza watching the commedia dell'arte performers.

I swallowed. Tried to speak. Finally: What—about the wooden leg?

What about it?

The wooden leg. It was sent to Mamma. It was his leg, Pappa—

Oh yeah. All his stuff was shipped to the States, to your address. The only thing that got there safe in the worst flood in years was the wooden leg. He got a new one. Polyurethane.

I shuddered in my robe. I felt like winter.

—Now here's the part that's hard, ChiChi. Don't interrupt me. I'll give it to you straight. Okay. It's 1946. I re-upped and was stationed in Naples. Your mother and I become more than friends.

I knew it.

The smell of his cigarettes, the voice, his chest . . .

See, it was just something that happened, ChiChi. Neither one of us wanted it. And if she hadn't turned up pregnant we probably wouldn't even know each other today—she used to sing to us, did she ever tell you that?

Hold on. Pregnant? Manny, did you say she got pregnant?

Yes. And it became the scandal of the village. Everyone knew her husband was in Germany. Her sisters tormented her, neighbors ostracized her, called her a bad woman. She suffered.

Pregnant?

Yes. She had a baby boy.

Was it June? Did she—in June?

Yes.

Gesù, Maria.

He was a sick little thing, not expected to live. They wouldn't let me see her or the baby . . . By some miracle, the baby survived. He lived.

I grabbed my throat.

YOU are Marco's father.

He looked at his sleeves. He looked at his hands.

Yes, he said.

He said yes.

*W*hen did you find out, Marco?
I held the telephone receiver with both hands.

Manny flew out here day before yesterday. Sat me down, told me the story. He insisted I let *him* be the one to tell you. I told him no. I told him it had to be me to tell you. He should have waited—

So you know the whole thing.

Same as you.

I squinted my bad eye shut. What do I say to Mamma? She'll argue how she tried to protect us!

ChiChi, just remember, it's the wounded who wound.

The wounded who wound.

What doesn't kill us only makes us stronger.

Nonna's words.

Yes yes, that's right. Okay. Handle this. ChiChi will press on. Stronger. Yes. ChiChi will be fine.

I called Dodee Priscarp about her *Star Spangled Revue*. Could I try out right away? At fifty dollars a performance, I could pay for my lessons, plus start another savings. Dodee, licensed real estate agent, was thrilled, she said, to have me aboard the, what she called, Star Maker Express.

Mamma avoided me. When she was home she stayed her distance, spoke only the necessary, like: ChiChi no forget to turn off lights, and ChiChi, wipe you feet. I announced to her I was booked to perform my act in Rochester. At the same hospital where Omo died.

Her face softened. It will be sad for you return to that place, she said.

I know.

I wanted to tell her how it was. Omo lying unconscious and Onna calling to him, begging him to come back, don't leave her . . . the violent act of a knife colliding with an eye in a tranquil garden that had been designed for spiritual contemplation . . .

And you, Mamma. *You.*

I rode to Rochester in Dodee's new Lincoln Continental. In the car with us was a juggling act called Sniff and Snuff, and Dodee's white Maltese dog called Midnight.

Dodee was a woman who wore cheeriness like an out-of-date hat or a comfy sweater. She was cheery ALL the time. And she loved knock-knock jokes.

Knock-knock!

Okay. Who's there?

Oswald!

Oswald who?

Oswald mah gum! Harharheeoh haha!

(And we had a hundred miles to go.)

Dodee introduced me as her new star of the *Star Spangled Revue* and my act, *ChiChi Clown Extra Ordinaire Plays Scopa with the Boys* in a Dynamic Premier Performance. Patients, hospital staff, and visitors at the Mayo show actually cheered for my act. Dodee called me back for an encore.

I returned to the stage and performed the dying swan in my baggy pants and floppy shoes. I walked on my hands, added the acrobatics. I saw a man in a wheelchair laugh so hard he nearly tipped over his IV pole. Later, the stand-up comedian in the show, a black guy from Saint Paul, told me, I don't pass out compliments, girl, but you I gotta say you are hilarious. Did you hear me, girl? Hilarious.

So. You don't have to feel good to be hilarious. I wrote that down.

My premier performance with the *Star Spangled Revue*—an elixir. I called Manny and thanked him for hooking me up with Dodee. You were right about her, Manny, I think she's good people.

Hey, I did something right, he said.

Manny, I said, does Ed know about Marco?

I'll let him know soon enough, he said.

He offered his third-floor ballroom again for me as a re-hearsal hall. Hell, you can bring an eighteen-piece orchestra in, who'd know it?

Thanks! Manny, I mean—!

Yeah, yeah, save it.

I took him up on the offer to work out in his third-floor space. But Monday morning I didn't have the energy to do much more than tap my foot to the music. I couldn't con-centrate. I went downstairs and knocked on his door.

Got a few minutes, Manny?

No.

Good, then I'll come in. I have some questions.

Can you make it quick?

No. What about Bruno?

Why not let sleeping dogs lie, ChiChi? You're better off. Look, I can't talk now. I'm busy. Come back. I'll take you to dinner.

Just tell me one thing, Manny. Didn't he ever want to see us, me?

Yes, Babe. He did. He even tried to finagle that Metamere guy into getting you away from your mamma. No dice. She wouldn't let you go. Your mother has socked all that money away for you kids, you know. I've helped her with her investments. She's got a shitload of money. She's clever, your mother. Taking in boarders, getting alimony out of Bruno, working hard, she's ambitious—like you.

Like me? We don't have a thing in common, my mother and I. Manny. You see things in superficial light.

He frowned. Look, he said, Your mother would have told you all this sooner but she was afraid you'd leave her, she was afraid Bruno would take you away from her.

My eye itched. I felt it clamp shut. I flicked the lid with my finger.

You're going to have to do something about that eye, ChiChi. I'll give you the name of a doctor.

I should have tried Mamma's cure of wrapping the skin of an onion on a wound.

Instead of pratfalls and rib injuries, I turned somersaults and did walkovers in my act. I added more flips, splits, hand stands. I created a four-minute segment where ChiChi, C.E.O., gets dressed and keeps losing things, her shoes, her hat, her pants, and finally goes off twirling a cane à la Charlie Chaplin in her ballooning bloomers. Sniff and Snuff showed me some juggling tricks and I practiced with disks, hats, shoes, until I could manage four objects at once. I was a funny, clumsy, and a sad clown.

A man who had been in the audience that first show in Rochester handed me his card as I was getting into Dodee's Lincoln for the drive home.

I want you to call me, he said. I think I can do something for you.

Do something for me. I'd heard that one before.

I'm an agent, he said.

Surprise, I said, not looking him in the eye.

Do you already have a New York agent?

Sure. Dozens of them.

I'm her agent, said Dodee. Talk to me.

He introduced himself. Martin Fleeborn. Here's his card.

Martin Fleeborn! screamed Dodee.

On the drive home Dodee pounded the steering wheel with her palms. Did you see how he was dressed? That suit? Must have cost over five hundred dollars, just bet you. And that haircut? You can always tell a successful man by his haircut—that and his fingernails. And did you see his shoes? Florsheim, I'll bet.

Who's Martin Fleeborn?

ChiChi, you're kidding, you've got to be kidding. Of course you're kidding. You are such a kidder. Oh, ChiChi!

Sundays brought on a restlessness in me that made my scalp go jumpy. After twelve o'clock Mass I went to Cucina Garibaldi for Mamma's special Buffet Italiano Only $6.95 All You Can Eat: lasagna, meatballs, chicken cacciatore, chicken marsala, shrimp with fava beans, shrimp in cream sauce, shrimp in pesto, and her specialty, Chicken Pina. Mamma's Sunday Buffet Italiano menu packed them in. People love to stuff themselves. Most of the time I had to eat in the kitchen standing up by the back door because of the long line of hungry, eager patrons waiting for tables. I ate the chunks of fruit from Mamma's salads, drank espresso.

Oh, the torpid unraveling of it all. Nothing to look forward to but food. Watermelon and cold *farfale* tossed with olives. It would have been pointless to confront Mamma about Manny. She'd throw up her hands and call me thankless.

I began to wonder if maybe secrets were necessary, like sleep or bread. Maybe there was a loving kindness to secrets I didn't quite grasp. Without secrets could we bear the light of day?

Three months with *Dodee's Star Spangled Revue* and I had saved almost $400, but it was hard work. I almost had to break a bone or lose a tooth before I could haul out a chuckle from some of those hospital and prison audiences.

Dodee suggested I wear something with more sex appeal. The elderly as well as the incarcerated appreciate a little booty.

Martin Fleeborn was on the phone from New York. Wanting to know where I was performing next.

I'm booked at the prison in Stillwater, I said, and then I'm off to a gala opening night at a psychiatric inpatient facility in southern Minnesota.

He laughed. Yeah, all celebrities do charity. It's expected. He said the reason he caught my act was because he was visiting his mother, who was recovering from cancer surgery, and she loved my performance.

And ChiChi, my mother is not an easy audience. You know what she said to me? Two words. *Sign her.*

He wanted me to get to New York ASAP.

(No. No. Heavens, no. Any day now my brother would be calling and *insisting* I come to California. New York? *Dio mio,* out of the question.)

In one month I did eight shows for Dodee as her New and Brightest Star. I deposited more money in the bank, and the incarcerated, the infirm, and the mentally challenged had been entertained. Maybe.

I told Dodee that Martin Fleeborn asked me to come to New York so he could book me.

New York! (As if the idea were as probable as vacationing on Sputnik.) And she burst into the story of the time she herself went to the Big Apple on a package tour and saw James Dean in the flesh at Paddy's Clam House on 34th Street eating raw squid. Now let's get back to next weekend. I've got a retirement home in town on Saturday for you— can you do puppets?

Cucina Garibaldi thrived with business now that Mamma was in full force as head chef. And she now spoke of Nardo in the future tense:

Some day when Nardo and I—

Nardo and I going to do—

Next year Nardo and I—

Nardo, he good man. What you think, Chichilina?

I think—I think—

We were alone at home in the kitchen. I had taken the utensils out of a cupboard drawer and was lining them up end to end between the wooden dividers. The room had became compressed. *Basta,* ChiChi. Why you play with spoons?

Mamma, I have something important I want to talk to you about.

It was her day off.

Dimmelo. Say it.

First of all, I want to say I'm still in a state of shock that you kept Manny's identity a secret all these years. But I know you went through shame and suffering . . .

Vero. Vero. True, so true. You mamma suffer, said Mamma.

I squeezed the small handles of the garlic press, looked at the floor, and then said as calmly as I could that I wanted my money, the child support money she had put in the bank for me, that was mine. She didn't say anything, didn't look at me.

Finally she pulled herself erect, waved a finger at my face. *You want money?*

Yes.

We go to bank now! Her voice was more of a squawk. *Va bene?*

Sure, Mamma. *Va bene.* Very well. Everything was *va bene. Va bene. Va bene. Va bene. Va bene. Va bene.*

She left for the bathroom and closed the door after her. No angry words, no accusations, no reminding me that I had already refused the money, why was I changing my mind now? No loud tirade.

Silence.

I sat at the kitchen table and picked at the newspaper, read the classifieds and chewed my thumbnail. When she came out of the bathroom she was wearing her old black cotton dress which hung almost to her ankles. Heavy black stockings on her legs and tattered black lace-up shoes on her feet. She moved as though she had borrowed the action from a movie, every step a performance. Get my—*thing,* she ordered.

You don't use your cane anymore, I said.

I do now. I have pain.

Mamma, what's this? What's with this getup?

I not so stupid, ChiChi. I dress for to dying.

What are you saying? Nobody's dying.

Shut up you mouth. *Zitta!*

Outside the noise of the street diminished us. Mamma looked small and disposable. Against the street of factories I wanted her to be like a found item of jewelry, I wanted her to sparkle, like at Marco's birthday party when she danced with Manny. But she moved slumped and with effort.

Never was there so much grey on one city block, this grey mess of concrete and gasoline fumes, the whites of our eyes greyed in such traffic noise. In such air our teeth could turn brown like seeds of apples. Our feet could sink and stick in asphalt. Never had a street seemed so hostile.

At the bank Mamma withdrew $10,000 from a savings account and deposited it into a checking account in my name. I made a telephone call from the bank manager's desk. Dodee, I said, pick us up in an hour.

Dodee's voice was sugary, like a Disney ingenue. All rightie then. Two o'clock.

Mamma sat on a bench in the bank's lobby, her back straight and proud, her head high, and I had a sudden urge to run across the floor, fall on my knees—*oh my mother, try to love me.*

Ma, ho fame, mangiamo, I said. I'm hungry, let's go eat.

She frowned her way through lunch. The soup was packaged, she can tell these things. The bread, *beh,* made with old flour. *Her* bread she use the best ingredament, she bake in tile *forno,* spray with water for to give nice crust, *this* bread, *unh!* Full of chemels.

Camels, Mamma? Camels in the bread?

Chemels, she repeated.

I think you mean chemicals.

Give me Coca-Cola, she said. No chemels in Coca-Cola. ChiChi, *figlia,* when do you leave me and go to New York?

Her jaw was pushed forward as though her chin was in a state of spasm.

Two coffees and one apple pie, I told the waitress. My voice splashed like ice water.

Mamma waited. Soon her eyes would flare, she'd throw her napkin on the table, and push back her chair. She'd struggle to her feet, yell at me calling me ungrateful, horrible, a disgrace, and a shame to her. She'd tell me what a bad daughter I was, how I had always been bad, and how she had never wanted me in the first place.

Mamma, how did you know? I stared at my napkin.

No response. Nothing. Smooth quiet movements of the hands. We shared the pie, spearing it crumb by crumb with our forks. We drank the thin American coffee sprinkled with saccharine pellets while Johnny Mathis sang over a scratchy sound system. I paid the check to "Chances Are."

I took her arm. It seemed heavier, softer, like something formed of latex and glue. She stopped, turned to me, looked at me with her face close to mine. I fell into her eyes like a lame person trips on stones.

What you think? You mamma no is *scemo,* stupid—Is like I die now. My girl, she leave her mamma. When, *figlia?* When you leave me?

The way she looked at me. Her eyes, the tragic universe in her eyes.

Let's not talk about it right now, I said. Mamma, I've got a surprise for you. Dodee Priscarp is meeting us in a few minutes, she's a real estate agent.

Her expression changed to one of alarm. *Chi?* Who?

You know, Manny's friend—

She rolled her eyes.

—the lady who books me in her *Star Spangled Revue,* Mamma.

I told her I was going to buy her a house with my money. Puzzlement. Then shock, struck by lightning.

I kept talking. I'm going to put a down payment on a decent house for you, and the mortgage payments won't be any more than the rent you're paying now for that dump we live in. Dodee explained it all to me. I want you to have a nice house, Mamma.

Dodee arrived, all smiles, wearing a suit with a skirt so short her short, fat legs sprouted out from it like macaroni. Mamma greeted her with, You speak Italian?

Afraid not, Dodee chuckled. I have enough trouble speaking English, ha ha.

Mamma was not amused. Dodee went on: About the only thing I can say in Italian is *pizza.* Ha ha. But I knew someone from *Baloney* once. Hoo ha.

Our backs stiffened. (Dodee, please don't tell a knock-knock joke.) When Mamma and I looked at each other and smiled I felt for a brief second or two that we could be friends, that maybe we were related.

Dodee drove us to three houses, two in North Minneapolis and one in Moundsview. Mamma inspected them with one eyebrow raised, her arms folded across her chest, the cane hanging from one hand. She stood at kitchen windows and gazed out at sprawling fenceless backyards. Yards that melted into other yards so you couldn't tell where one property ended and another began. Spindly trees no bigger than twigs scattered here and there without much of a plan. Garage doors that opened by pressing buttons. I saw the neighborhoods with Mamma's eyes, the rows of low houses shaped like cigar boxes, the flimsy sameness they shared, the sparkling cleanness, each house and yard neat and orderly, and tried to imagine Mamma happy here.

We were on our third house when I came upon her in the master bedroom sitting on the owner's bed. I had been downstairs in the basement looking at something called the rumpus room. Her eyes were red and her face was strained and puckered.

She spoke in a low, disjointed voice. Now I know how you pappa he live, she said.

I didn't think I heard her right. *Bruno?*

He live just like this, she said, with a registered nurse lady, and she smoothed the satin bedspread. For *this* and a registered nurse lady he forget about me and my children. For this.

Manny says Bruno is a bad person, Mamma. And Arturo said so, too. Is he really a bad person?

She nodded. Yes, Chichilina, he is. Bad person.

She sighed, scratched her hip. ChiChi, you crazy girl. Why you want buy me house?

Because you need one. Our apartment stinks. You broke your foot on those rickety steps—

But I no need house.

Wouldn't you like a nice house of your own?

But I already own house, she said.

No, Mamma. You're *renting* that dump.

I tell you, I own house.

No, Mamma. Listen to me. Renting is not the same as owning.

ChiChi, you think I'm a *scemo?* I know what is rent and what is own. I own house!

Okay. Fine. What house do you own?

The house Mitchell Rodman leave me at Lake Pillacotche! In his will! What you think! I make him sign papers in lawyer's office. I tell him I want house on Lake Pilla-cotche. I do *vendetta* for my family.

I was a hot air balloon, levitating.

Mah. So dramatic, ChiChi. Stop that. Always so dramatic.

She had the power to kill me with her secrets.

Her face darkened. You think I need you buy me house? I no need you, *Figlia,* I no need you money, I no need nothing from you.

Mamma, why didn't you tell us about the house? Why didn't you ever take us there?

Is bought with *blood.* I will not go there. I tear down that house. Build new place on property.

She let loose with a moan.

Ayyyy. My son, he marry Elainey and move away, he leave his mamma. In Italy the son not leave his mamma. Now you! And you no leave for marry, have babies to give me grandchildren, no! *Mah,* tell me when you leave me, what day I'm die. Is ask too much?

Mr. Fleeborn said I should be there *yesterday.* I've got to prepare, rehearse my show, which is now running ninety to one-hundred-and-twenty minutes, and then I—you mean that? You'd die without me?

She avoided the last question. Did you discuss with you brother how you do to his mamma?

I haven't told him about New York, no.

Because you brother, he tell you *pazza.* Crazy.

Marco's letters had dwindled to one a week. He was accepted at an art school in Pasadena. *I'm doing everything I ever dreamed of doing. My life is charmed. Charmed, ChiChi!* Elainey was under contract at Paramount and up for a part in an Otto Preminger film.

Dearest Sister, Be happy, could you please?

———

At home Mamma decided she needed sleep. I make sleep now, said Mamma. My head, she tired. Tired. She went to her room and I watched the space she left behind her fill up with wall, dresser, window and its crooked shade, chintz curtain shivering, a rug puckered. Mamma, a home owner, taking her rest. Were you ever going to tell me? I asked the wall.

I dialed Marco's number.

She got the house on Pillacotche? he screamed. No kidding! She got the house! What about the money we got for her in the will?

Rodman ignored that. There was no money, Marco.

He promised! He signed our paper!

Big deal.

All right. All right. Don't sweat it, Cheech. Calm down. We've got to be calm about this.

(Marco, beg me to come to California. I'm shaky. I'm losing my balance.) Marco—

I'm glad mamma's got you there with her, ChiChi. At least she's got one of us. Are you still on the Thorazine?

I gave a snort. I've been off the medication for ages.

I don't want you to hurt yourself, is all, don't get mad.

Like stand on one foot? Like cut off my face?

I wasn't going to enumerate your sacrificial acts.

(Those sacrificial acts were created by me for YOU, my brother. Famiglia!)

ChiChi, someone's got to take care of Mamma.

She's got Nardo. And she's got Manny. And she's got the *house*. And don't forget Saint Ed! Your dear half brother.

(Now. Ask me now. Ask me now to come to California.)

I waited.

So Rodman's dead, he said. And Mamma actually got a house out of him!

His voice folded up and went quiet.

She got the friggin house in the friggin will, Marco. You didn't think she'd tell us, did you?

Of course not.

Of course not!

(A brother and sister three thousand miles apart pound their fists on their thighs. They run their fingers over hairlines at the back of their necks. They wait for the other one to say something.)

Marco, I've made a decision.

Pause.—Is it good?

I'm going to New York.

I heard his scratchy intake of breath. NEW YORK? He yelled in a voice released from captivity. No! New York is too rough! New York is not for you! Besides, that agent guy I think has something to do with Bruno.

I imagined him giving his thigh another pound of the fist.

Ask Elainey about the Martin Fleeborn Agency, Marco. She'll recognize that name. (Tell me to come to California!)

It's sounds fishy. I'm telling you, I smell Bruno in this.

Silence. The man of the house, the don of the family, had spoken.

You're telling me NO, Marco? Did you tell Elainey no when she got the Hollywood offer? At least I've got TALENT. I've created an entire performance piece. What does SHE do?

ChiChi, you're not hearing me. Listen up! I don't like it. Not at all. It's a bad idea!

Marco, I want your blessing. Marco, I'm going to New York.

ChiChi, *hear me!* Bruno's in this somewhere!

I hear you. *Grazie mille,* Marco.

Fine. Now put that mother of ours on the phone, he said.

New York City, you say? Well, lotsa luck then—(from a total stranger). The clerk at Woolworth's wishes me luck, a wait-ress at Jax wishes me luck, a taxi driver, a salesperson at Powers, a deaf guy on the street handing out cards printed with the sign language alphabet for a handout. Yuppers, I tell them all, just thought I'd let you know I'm taking the big plunge! I'm heading for the Apple, I'm off to take a bite of the big one, the big terrifying lonesome bite of the big one. They look at me and say, Oh. Lots of luck to you then.

A box came in the mail from Marco. Small, the size of the palm of my hand. The note read, *Do Not Open Until You're On The Train. xxoo, M.*

Manny Looz took me to a play at the Old Log Theater, the last play of the season. A going-away present, he said. When he arrived in the taxi to pick me up, he had Ed with him.

He's going with us? I said.

Do you mind?

(Did I mind.)

Would they please drop me off for a few minutes at a house a few blocks from here? I had to run inside. I'd be right out in a jiffy.

Who lives there? Manny wanted to know.

My best friend in high school named Jennifer grew up there, I said, sounding casual. Her mother still lives in the house. I want to run in and pay my respects.

This smells like a *vendetta,* said Ed.

I am twelve years old again. Jennifer's mother is whispering to her daughters behind the kitchen door: Italians only bathe once a year, she is saying. That's why their skin has that dark, greasy tinge. Jennifer's mother has me use paper cups and plates, considering the germs. They don't call them dirty dagos for nothing, she tells Jennifer when she thinks I can't hear her. She wants to know what I did to provoke Mitchell Rodman. After a sleepover at her house, she boils the sheets I slept on.

Yes, I'd pay my respects and say farewell to Jennifer's mother.

I wouldn't have recognized her if I saw her anywhere but in her own house. Sleeveless blouse buttoned up to the neck, hair dripping onto her neck like a map of Florida, small angry eyes behind glasses. She examined my skin, my face, my languid eye.

New York? But is there a call for your—*type*—in the theater, dear?

I rubbed my hands together.

You know, I hardly ever hear from my girls anymore. Months go by. Did you want to come in? Are your feet clean?

I spit into my palms, took her arms, and rubbed my hands on the bare skin. Spitting again, I baptized her cheeks.

A few dago germs to remember me by, I said. *Ciao. Arrivederci.*

I dedicated my little demonstration to LaMont and his gang, Natalie, Mrs. Ricci, Charles, Mitchell Rodman, the words *wop, dago,* and *gumbah,* the pictures the media produces of Italians: spaghetti-slurping gangsters. Gondolier tenors. People who drink the water their pasta is cooked in.

I saw Jennifer's mother's horrified face through her window, it wove across the overgrown green of the hedge and the heads of the wooden elves grinning on the lawn into the backs of my legs and my neck. I hummed "America the Beautiful" and lifted my hand, two fingers pronged like horns, giving a farewell *Il Mal Occhio* blessing.

Manny and Ed were waiting with the taxi motor running.

Wow, said Ed. Far out.

The play we're seeing is called *Mother Courage,* said Manny. He liked the title.

Ed stared at me from where he sat on the other side of Manny.

What are YOU gawking at? I said.

Have you ever considered, said Ed, the Lord's Prayer? We pray, *Forgive us our trespasses as we forgive those who trespass against us.*

Can it, Ed, I said.

All right, you two, said Manny.

I looked out the window. A whole evening with Ed!

ChiChi, do you remember Marco's birthday dinner party? Manny said. Your mother spent the night at our place.

Oh that.

Well, we did nothing but talk. Believe me. We had things to square away. We were planning how to tell you about Bruno and about me.

Too bad I wasn't there when you told Marco who you are, I said.

Elainey was with him. She's his wife. She has to be the one to share his life now.

The way things happen. You could be in New York and somewhere else at the same time.

You could be standing in line at the subway station to buy your tokens and you look down at the pavement and see a scrap of paper, a candy wrapper, a cigarette butt, and you're suddenly in the train yard in Tar Town, you're collecting rocks with your brother. You hear a baby cry and you breathe the comforting sour aroma of his shirt, his little sweater, your brother's sweater.

You could be at the theater with a man who's been like your father all your life and you could feel so full of love that you're civil to his son named Ed.

You try to focus on the movements of the street, the shapes of movement. You think of breath as the plucking of guitar strings. But that's because you're an artist. You're in search of metaphors, in search of truth.

You are on your way somewhere. You pass a barefoot man with a beard and a backpack who pauses to stare at you. The sky is a lake of ice. A woman stands on the stage as a ray of light slides down to caress the top of her head.

When you breathe, the empty spaces under your skin fill up like pages of a book. You're on another street. You carry Marco's baby girl, Leticcia Nina, in your arms. You rush for an appointment with the producers of your new show. The baby holds your neck with fat perfect fingers. You're famous, you've had a nose job, and you've made your hair blond. What's this? A baby? asks your producer. *Lei è mia,* you say. She is mine, of course, the baby is mine. It can be no other way. You walk on the outsides of your feet to the edge of the stage.

Everything in my life has been preparation for this.

I sat next to Manny in the theater. He leaned in to me, clucked under his breath, and said, You got guts, kid. I got to hand it to you. You've always been a little teched, but going over there and giving that woman the Evil Eye. Shoot.

I did more than that, Manny. I gave her an Italian keepsake.

He smiled at me like a proud pappa.

He wore a cashmere sports jacket and the grey hairs of his chest were matted and flattened under the open collar of his shirt. Shined shoes, thin black socks to the knee. Sitting next to him I couldn't stop looking at him, hair trimmed and slicked back, tall, thin, shaved, smelling his Old Spice, he was young, not old. I reached across the theater program on his lap and stroked the raised veins on the back of his hand, squeezed the fingers.

After the play, Manny said he had someone he wanted me to meet backstage. An apprentice called Mary Jane Udall. She earned her Equity card this summer at the playhouse.

You need friends, Manny said.

Mary Jane had red hair like Gladys Chechnik and no chin. She laughed like something not human. Manny invited her out for coffee with us. Which seemed to please Ed a lot.

Lookie here, he told her when we were settled in our booth at Perkins, I can do an imitation of Boris Karloff!

Oh? She giggled.

AntiPATHto, said Ed, which Mary Jane thought was hilarious.

Manny said, This little lady, ChiChi Maggiordino, is headed for New York and the Big Time.

Mary Jane had big teeth and a fierce overbite. Me, too, she lisped.

I think you two girls got things in common. Take ChiChi here! You should see her perform! Her clown act is spectacular. She's a genius. And that's a fact.

Mary Jane was the friendliest girl west of the Mississippi.

I'm enrolled at the American Theater Wing in New York, she bubbled. School starts in two weeks.

You don't say, said Manny.

She asked me if I would be her roommate in New York. In the taxi on the way home I tried to imitate her giggle.

She's a good little actress, be nice, Manny said.

Everyone's good at acting, Manny. That's all anyone does in this life. Act. Perform. Some are just more aware of it than others.

All right. Enough. I got something I want to say, said Manny. I asked Ed here with us tonight because I want him to know this too. It's about Bruno.

Stop right there, I said. I don't want to hear another word.

What I want you, Manny said, to know, is he is up to something. Word gets to me. I want you to be careful. He's got a *vendetta* for us all. Ed, you keep your eye out, too!

He showed us a color photograph of a small man with dark hair and a mustache. The eyes. The eyes were green.

You see this man hanging around, you call me. I don't care what time of day or night it is. Or where you might be, Saskatchewan, Beijing, or Saint Paul. Call me collect.

I had just looked at a photo of a man who was supposed to be my father. I saw it and I didn't see it. Bruno? Should I have looked closer for things like facial similarities? Should I have cared?

September 16, 1964, Mary Jane Udall and I meet at the Minneapolis train station with our suitcases.

Mamma, Nardo, and Manny and Ed Looz are here to see us off, along with Mary Jane's parents.

Ed pulls me aside. Looks me in the face, serious. God bless you, Sister, he says, his tongue between his teeth.

You look like and sound like a friggin preacher, Looz. That's not a compliment. And don't ever call me *sister* again.

Whatever God has for us, he says, that will He do. I trust the Lord, he says. Then he wraps his arms around me, kisses me on both cheeks, and stuffs a book of daily devotions and a paperback Bible into the pocket of my carry-on.

Cazzo! I cuff my chin at him.

The conductor is doing his All Aboard calling.

Mamma, in a skirt with a matching jacket I never saw before, looks like a customs inspector. When you come home, *Figlia mia,* she says, your mamma will have her own trattoria.

Mamma, I tell her, I know there is nothing in this world impossible for you.

Sì, sì. Is good, no? Nardo, he good man, no? You like him? Hmm?

Sure, Mamma. He's a good man.

You come home for our wedding, no? said Nardo.

Wedding? What's this?

(Ask me to stay. You need me!)

ChiChi, *figlia,* be careful youself, says Mamma, her eyes tearing up.

I look over at Manny with his hands in his pocket, his long thin body tense. His eyes are half closed, his mouth pulled in, deflated.

(Just say the word, Manny. Ask me to stay. Somebody ask me to stay!)

Take it easy now, kid, Manny says. Keep your nose clean, work hard, keep a lookout and keep in touch.

Manny . . .

(Tell me not to leave. Doesn't anyone want me to stay?)

Give my regards to Broadway, he says.

I slip into his arms, hold him, my face rests on cashmere.

Passengers climb the metal steps to the train car. A conductor shouts again to get on board.

Call me collect, Manny says. Don't forget.

(Yes, I'll stay. I'll stay.)

Manny's face is somber. Anytime, babe. Call collect.

I turn to my mother. Good-bye, Mamma.

I reach for her, expecting her feathery kisses near the cheek as usual, maybe a light embrace. Instead, she bursts forth in a terrible tempest of tears, she pounds her chest, sobs, rocks her body like a widow at a wake.

Mamma, what on earth—?

She throws herself against me, clings, rakes her hands down my body, screams, sighs. People stop, watch in wonder at the scene. Manny rushes to Mamma, tries to pull her off me. Nardo holds her by the waist. Giuseppina, calm down. Stop now—

Figlia! Figlia! Sei tutto mia vita! ALL I LIVE IS FOR YOU!

My mother has lost her mind. Mamma, please . . .

Figlia mia! Sobbing, thrashing, raking at her throat with her fingernails.

I tell her, *ti amo,* I love you, Mamma. And she lets loose a jagged, gurgly sob, *Ti amo amore mio! Ti amo, figlia mia! Chichilina!* followed by a rush of fresh hot tears and sobs, loud enough to leave echo prints against the concrete walls of the train station, loud enough to make holes in my hands, stains on my clothes, a dent on the side of my head. I cannot remember her ever telling me she loves me.

I wave at them all from inside the train. I expect Ed to give me the finger, but instead, he makes a prayer gesture with his two hands.

Mamma howls, sobs, thrashes, and throws her arms up to me like a baby screaming to be held, and Manny and Nardo struggle to keep her from hurting herself against the side of the train. Okay, I get it. She is, after all, a good Italian mother saying good-bye to her Italian daughter. It's what we do.

I watch them disappear as the station fades into the dark tunnel of tracks and I lean back in the seat with the little box from Marco on my lap. I know before I open it what's inside. Metamere's knife. *You forgot this,* says his note. He is not for my leaving home, he knows what waits for me. But then beneath the knife, under a thin layer of cotton is something else—a small gold charm in the shape of a perfect tomato.

I love you like—

I STARE out the window as the vanishing city of my heart falls away. I hook Metamere's knife onto my belt. The conductor asks for our tickets.

ABOUT THE AUTHOR

Marie Giordano has authored more than thirty works of nonfiction under the name Marie Chapian. She's won the Gold Medallion Award, two Campus Life awards, a Gold Book Award, and an AAUW Achievement grant, and has published and won awards for poetry and fiction in literary quarterlies. Giordano has an MFA in Creative Writing from Vermont College, and she teaches creative writing at Mira Costa College and at conferences across the United States.

Marie Giordano has been an actress, a therapist, an artist, and a teacher. Her most recent book of poetry is *Slow Dance on Stilts* (La Jolla Poets Press). *I Love You Like a Tomato* is her first novel, the first in a trilogy about the Maggiordano family.